THE RELUCTANT DEFECTOR

John Faudin, Director of Security at the
Ministry of Defence knew there was a high-
powered Soviet agent in the Ministry. A trap
had narrowed the suspects to a few, but Neil
Lavery had been way down the list. When he
failed to arrive home for a dinner party he and
his wife Imogen were holding for important
guests—including a senior American intelligence officer newly arrived in London—it
looked as though he had bolted. But is this
really the case? The truth turns out to be both
more complicated and more sinister as Neil
Lavery becomes the focus of an elaborate game
of bluff and double bluff between the Security
Services of the two nations. His unsuspecting
wife, his family, and his friends have no idea
where his true allegiances lie, and whether or
not he has betrayed his country. Imogen herself
faces a test of loyalties as she embarks on a love
affair with Guy Cantel, the MI5 man sent to
investigate Neil's disappearance. Then one day,
at last, she receives a telephone call from
Moscow . . .

THE RELUCTANT DEFECTOR

PALMA HARCOURT

PARAGON
CHIVERS PRESS

Library of Congress Cataloging-in-Publication Data

Harcourt, Palma.
   The reluctant defector / Palma Harcourt.
      p.   cm.—(Eagle large print)
   ISBN 0–7927–1258–7 (softcover)
   1. Large type books.   I. Title.   II. Series.
[PR6058.A62R45   1992]
823′.914—dc20   91–41206
                                                             CIP

British Library Cataloguing in Publication Data available

This Large Print edition is published by Chivers Press, England, and Curley Publishing, Inc, U.S.A. 1992.

Published in the U.S.A. by arrangement with Murray Pollinger Literary Agent and in the British Commonwealth with HarperCollins Publishers Ltd.

U.K. Softback ISBN 0 7451 3375 4
U.S.A. Softback ISBN 0 7927 1258 7

Photoset, printed and bound in Great Britain by
REDWOOD PRESS LIMITED, Melksham, Wiltshire

CONTENTS

NOTE

In the real world trust between nations depends on reasonable certainty that one knows not only part of the truth about the capabilities and intentions of potential opponents, but the whole truth—or almost the whole truth. That is why, even in this era of *glasnost* and *perestroika*—words that now need no translation—the secret war continues and, if anything, grows in significance. Such developments as satellites and electronic high technology provide information largely limited to capabilities. For reliable information on intentions we must turn to the human agent, beloved of fiction-writers.

And this book *is* fiction. A few famous—or infamous—individuals are mentioned in it. Apart from these, any relationship between the characters in this novel and any person who exists in reality, including persons who may hold or have held official appointments mentioned in it, is purely coincidental.

THE RELUCTANT DEFECTOR

PROLOGUE

Pavel Kaski was a highly respected London dentist, who had been in practice in Harley Street for many years. His patients were mainly wealthy, busy individuals, who appreciated the luxury of his waiting-room and surgery, the convenience and regularity of his appointments system, and above all the competence he offered.

From Mondays to Fridays Kaski worked long hours, only relaxing in the evening with Nina, who doubled as both his dental nurse and his mistress. Weekends he spent in the country with his wife and their two young sons. By now he was a rich man, middle-aged but still attractive. And he had lived dangerously for so long that he rarely thought about it.

This morning was an exception. He realized that he was nervous. There was no reason for such a weakness. It was inexplicable and absurd, he told himself. True, the next half-hour might be difficult and he was far from sure how the man in the waiting-room would receive what he had to be told. But the outcome of the interview was inevitable.

'Shall I show him in?'

'Please, Nina.'

She reached up and kissed him gently on the lips, her naturally blonde hair brushing his cheek. 'He's a sensible man. He won't make a fuss. Don't worry, Pavel,' she whispered.

Pavel Kaski stroked her head. No one but Nina ever called him Pavel now; indeed, no one but Nina knew his real name. Not even his wife was aware

1

that her married name of Mrs Paul Cascon was false—part of a 'legend' devised long ago and built up over decades. He had always been careful and occasionally, he had to admit, lucky. But luck could change.

There was a tap at the door as Kaski slipped out of his dentist's white coat. He went forward, hand outstretched, to greet his visitor.

'Come in! Come in!' he said, over-heartily. 'For once I can offer you a drink. You're my last "patient" of the day.'

'You're not working this afternoon?'

'No. It's my older son's birthday and I shall be driving down to Kent as soon as we've finished here, so it'll have to be a small one for me.' Kaski went to a cabinet and produced a bottle of Glenlivet, two glasses and some bottled water. 'Whisky all right?'

'Yes. Fine! But don't be sparing with mine and don't drown it. I've a feeling I'm going to need a good, strong drink. I assume you haven't summoned me here so urgently to tell me it's time my teeth were cleaned.'

'Unfortunately not.' Kaski found it difficult to continue. At last, back still turned as he poured the drinks, he said, 'We've known each other for some years now and it has been, I believe, a satisfactory relationship—for both of us. So I'm sorry to bring you instruct—' He paused and started again. 'I'm sorry to bring you news I'm sure you won't welcome. It may be no consolation to you, but I regret what I've got to say.'

The other man was staring at him. 'What on earth are you talking about? It's not like you to be so—so abstruse. You mean you're no longer to be my controller? I thought—'

'No! No!' Kaski gestured to a chair which stood by a desk at the side of the surgery and himself sat on the high stool he used while he was at work. Illogically this commonplace position restored his confidence, and he reminded himself that he was indeed in control. 'What was it you thought?' he asked, sipping his whisky.

'That you were going to make another damn-fool request—like the last one that nearly ended in disaster. Moscow may have been delighted with the information I provided, but somehow it got out that there had been a serious leak. Anyway, John Faudin and the Ministry security boys came swarming round the department looking for those who had access. They're still far from happy, and they're a persistent crowd. All I can do is lie low. You understand that, and so must Moscow. I can't take any more risks for the moment.'

'There's no question of such a thing. On the contrary. Quite on the contrary.' Kaski rose and took the empty glass that was being held out to him. 'As you know, our masters invariably look after those who serve them well, and everyone appreciates what you have done.'

He refilled his visitor's glass and handed it back, ignoring the cynical smile with which his remarks had been received. He gritted his teeth. The conversation was not going well. Perhaps he should be blunt.

'You're quite right when you say you can't take any more risks,' he said. 'In fact, you may not be fully aware of it, but the situation—your situation—is hazardous in the extreme.'

The other man gulped at his whisky. 'Hazardous,

3

is it?' he said. 'How can you be so sure of that?'

'Oh, come now. It's true, all right. You must know you're not our only source in London.'

Kaski paused for his visitor to absorb the implications of this statement. Then he said, 'Listen to me!' He tried to quieten his voice which had become harsh and assertive, and continued. 'It has been decided, at the highest level, that in these circumstances—these hazardous circumstances— you should retire to Moscow, where you will be duly rewarded for your excellent service. I realize—'

'Retire to Moscow! You mean go and live there? Permanently? Join the other so-called Western defectors, those of them who haven't drunk themselves to death? No, thanks. I know that things are changing, but I'd rather—'

'Rather what? Spend the next twenty years in gaol in Britain? You could scarcely expect any special treatment, could you? And gaols even here aren't pleasant places. Look, my dear chap, I accept that this has been a shock to you but I assure you it's necessary for you to go. The alternative, which is a very real danger, doesn't bear thinking about, does it?'

There was no answer. Pavel Kaski cast a quick glance at the figure sitting opposite him. He noted the grim set of the mouth and the pale knuckles of the hand grasping the glass; he could sense the strain the other man was suffering.

Kaski said gently, 'You must have realized that this might happen one day—'

'One day, yes, perhaps. In ten, twenty years. It wasn't something I worried about, any more than I worry about old age or death. Less, in fact. It was

4

something that might never happen.' Suddenly he was angry. 'And it bloody well wouldn't have happened now if you hadn't insisted on my taking such a wild risk, and then somehow letting it leak that you knew—'

'I know,' Kaski said. 'Moscow knows, too. A mistake was made. But I can only repeat my assurance that the part you have played—both recently and over many years—is fully appreciated.' He had to make an effort not to look at his watch; time was passing and they were getting nowhere. 'Come, it won't be so bad, surely. All will be arranged for you, and once you are—are—'

For a moment he stuttered. He had been about to say 'home', but Moscow was not the Englishman's home, and never would be. There was a world of difference between an official, like himself, who worked for his country, and a man who betrayed it. The Englishman might receive ostentatious honours in the USSR, but he would always be secretly despised.

Quickly Kaski recovered. 'Once you've settled down in Moscow,' he said, 'you'll have a very good life—there are still privileges, you know, in spite of changing times—a large apartment, perhaps on Aleksei Tolstoi Street, a chauffeured limousine, your own *dacha*, holidays by the Black Sea.'

'And a medal—a Hero of the Soviet Union, say?' the man demanded caustically.

Kaski held his anger in check. 'That can easily be arranged. Would you really prefer twenty years in a top security wing? Because I can assure you that if you refuse this offer—a low-risk operation that we can carry out quietly—it's extremely unlikely that anyone will bother to plan the much more complicated business of springing you from gaol, or organizing an exchange. You'll be left to rot.' He paused, then: 'For heaven's sake be sensible,' he concluded, almost pleadingly.

'I am being sensible. And I don't want to go to Moscow. The situation may be different in these days, but it's unstable and likely to remain so. Who knows what's going to happen?' He sighed. 'And what about my wife and children? Would you bring them out?'

'Yes, if they want to come, but perhaps—'

'Perhaps they won't? Certainly I can't see my wife being too happy to claim her relationship with a traitor.'

'Would it be better for your family if you stood trial here and got a long prison sentence?' Kaski was growing impatient again. 'And that is the probable—more than probable—alternative. You must accept that fact. I only wish it weren't so, but it is—and surely it's not an option you can consider for a moment. Dammit, man, after all you've done you can't pretend to love the UK so much that you're loath to leave it.'

'I don't love the UK, or the things it stands for—its so-called ethics. But I love London as a place—the parks, the streets, the shops. I'd miss strolling through St James's, popping into Fortnum's or Hatchards, going to Harrods. Where would I get my books in Moscow? Where would I get my shirts, my shoes, made there?'

'For heaven's sake, be serious!'

'I am being serious. I'd miss *The Times* crossword, the cricket in summer—football's never interested me—the English theatre. I'd miss weekends in the country, holidays in Italy and the

6

south of France—my whole way of life, I suppose.'

You should have considered all this earlier, Kaski thought, but refrained from voicing it. He felt some sympathy. He knew there were things he himself would miss when he went home. Perhaps he had been in the UK too long.

He tried a joke. 'You sound like a dyed-in-the-wool Tory,' he said.

'A wolf in sheep's clothing, eh? Look, you can tell Moscow that I appreciate their forethought on my behalf, but I don't believe the situation is nearly as dangerous as they imagine. With any luck I shall weather this storm. Tell them, too, that while I hope to serve them in the future as in the past, I propose to do it from London.'

He stood and picked up his briefcase. In his well-cut grey suit and college tie, he could have been the prototype of a senior Civil Servant, honest, responsible, trusted. He held out his hand to Kaski. He, not Kaski, had decided that the interview was at an end.

'Thanks for the whisky. I needed it. You'll stay in touch and let me know the answer?'

'Of course, but—' Useless to say it would be a waste of effort; Moscow was not in the habit of reversing decisions. 'I'll contact you as soon as I get a response,' Kaski said weakly, taken aback by the other man's sudden determination.

'If you would. Thanks again.'

'In the meantime I suggest you reconsider—give your position very serious thought.' Kaski made an effort to reassert himself. 'Get accustomed to the idea that you must go, and make what preparations you think necessary. I don't have to tell you to be careful. You're almost certainly under surveillance—and don't forget phone and mail taps. And, remember, when it happens you won't get any warning.'

'No. Er—suppose I need to talk to you again before you hear from Moscow?'

'Usual procedure. Phone to say you have toothache and I'll fit you in among my patients. Otherwise my nurse will call you and make an appointment. However, I'm sure you agree that too many meetings aren't advisable.'

'Absolutely not. Goodbye then.'

'Goodbye.'

Kaski shut the door of his suite behind his visitor and leant against it. He was sweating. He had feared some kind of scene, though he couldn't have explained why. The Englishman had never in the past shown great emotion.

Nina came into the little hall. 'That was a surprise, Pavel. A blank refusal. And what a message to send to Moscow! The cheek of it.' She had been listening in the adjoining kitchenette. 'What will you do?'

'What can I do? Send a temporizing message. I've an idea he may have second thoughts when he fully realizes the danger he's in. It may be partly my fault; perhaps I should have emphasized how close they were to him. He seems to believe that Moscow's panicked and that if he lies low for a while all will be well. Between you and me, Nina, there's a small chance he could be right, but our information suggests—'

'He's done some splendid work,' she said. 'It seems a pity he should have to stop now. After all, he's only in his forties and he's got every chance of being promoted still further. He could become even

8

more useful.'

'Not if he's in gaol,' Kaski said firmly; he sometimes thought that Nina took too much interest in this English agent.

As if reading his mind, Nina thrust her arm through his and drew him towards the empty waiting-room. 'You go and sit down and relax, Pavel. I've made some sandwiches and I'll bring us coffee. You needn't leave for the country yet.'

'Bring the tape of that meeting, too. We'll play it back while we eat.'

Nina sighed. 'OK. If we must.'

When she returned with the tray she found Kaski staring out of the window at the busy scene below, the hurrying pedestrians, the stream of taxis and private cars. During the day Harley Street was always buzzing with activity. In the distance Nina thought she saw the figure of the man who had left them a few minutes ago, but it was impossible to be certain.

She put down the tray and poured the coffee. Together they started to eat smoked salmon sandwiches and listen to the tape.

At length Nina said, 'Pavel, he sounds very determined. What will happen if he continues to refuse to go?'

Pavel Kaski finished the last of his sandwich and carefully wiped his mouth with a paper napkin before he replied. 'My dear, that won't arise. Moscow would never allow it.'

★　　★　　★

Moscow's reaction was also in the mind of the man who had just left them as he huddled in the corner

9

of his taxi which was crawling slowly down Bond Street. Though it was not a cold day he felt suddenly chilled, and shivered.

Kaski's instructions had come as a shock to him. He had been under a great deal of pressure recently, but had begun to think that the danger of exposure had receded. There were at least a dozen people, apart from himself, who might have been responsible for the treachery, and as far as he knew there had been nothing to suggest that he was the most likely candidate. But of course he could be wrong. Kaski had seemed very certain, and Moscow could easily know more than he did.

Perhaps he had been mad to spurn their offer. Offer? It was hardly that. It was an order that he had bluntly refused to obey. True, he had no wish to live in Moscow. The idea appalled him. He knew the kind of life that strangers in his position still led there, lonely, despised, putting on a brave face but hankering for the good things that were part of England. Because there were many such good things—at any rate for those who weren't short of money.

For the umpteenth time the taxi made a yard and then stopped again. On the crowded pavement, walkers were making more progress. He tapped on the glass panel behind the driver and passed him some coins.

'I'll get out here,' he said.

'Don't blame you, guv'nor.'

Hurrying, not caring if he jostled passers-by, he made much better headway on foot. What he wanted was a pub. He badly needed another drink. He'd already had two whiskies and he knew he was drinking too much, but for once he didn't care.

He wondered how long it would be before he heard from Moscow. Would they give him a second chance or—He leapt for the pavement. A motor-bike, swerving between the traffic, had narrowly missed him as he crossed the road. Perhaps after all he would forgo that third drink. He swore aloud. As his controller had advised, he must give his position serious consideration.

PART ONE

THE AGENT IN PLACE

CHAPTER ONE

Imogen Lavery stood in the doorway and regarded her dining-room table with a critical eye. The candles were upright, the silver gleamed, the sparkling glasses were perfectly aligned, the napkins immaculate and the centrepiece—prepared by her sister, Rosalind, who had a gift for flower arrangement—would certainly bring tributes from the guests. She nodded in satisfaction.

'Nice, isn't it, Mrs Lavery?'

'Lovely, Mrs Price.' She turned to smile at the woman who had been her household help for the last ten years.

'And, if you don't mind my saying so, Mrs Lavery, you're looking lovely yourself this evening.'

'Thank you.'

It wasn't really true, Imogen thought, but she was at least looking her best. Her hair had been done that morning; the highlights in the dark brown were a success, in spite of her initial doubts. She had taken trouble with her make-up, and at thirty-six, after two children, she had kept her figure, which the black velvet skirt and white silk blouse showed to advantage.

Imogen knew she would always envy her sister's classical beauty, though she couldn't hope to compete with it, but she had never resented the fact that Rosalind, the elder by five years, had inherited their mother's blonde hair and violet eyes. Rosalind, in fact, had become not only a beautiful but also a compassionate woman, and the sisters were close, brought closer perhaps by the fact that

15

their children—each had a boy and a girl—were much of an age, though tragically Rosalind's daughter, now ten, had suffered brain damage at birth and had a mental age of four.

Nevertheless, Imogen reflected, it was good for one's morale to receive an occasional compliment. She hoped Neil would be equally approving. Suddenly reminded of her husband, Imogen frowned. Where on earth was Neil? He had promised faithfully that he would be home early because of the party, but it was already after seven and there was no sign of him.

That damned office! Neil had been working much too hard lately. He needed the spring holiday in Italy they were planning, but that was still some weeks away. She sighed and turned to Mrs Price, saying that she had better do something about the wine, because Mr Lavery was obviously going to be late. He would hardly have time to shower and change when he came in, and certainly wouldn't want to waste minutes in the cellar.

It took her several trips from the basement to bring up the required number of bottles, and she swore when she caught her heel in the hem of her skirt and heard it rip. Now she would have to change it for the old brocade one that she had often worn and didn't like much. She cursed Neil—it was too bad of him not to have made a special effort this evening—and then reproached herself for her aggravation.

She ran up the two flights of steep stairs to their bedroom, and arrived out of breath. She loved the tall narrow house in the square off Knightsbridge which her father had given her as a wedding present, but there was no doubt that it was less than

16

ideally convenient. It had been even less so when the children—Matthew, now fifteen, and Verity, twelve—had been small and before they had gone away to school. Hurriedly she changed her skirt and went to look out of the window. There was still no sign of Neil.

The door-bell rang as she went down to the drawing-room, which occupied the whole of the first floor. She hoped it would be Rosalind and her husband, Philip Glenbourne. Philip worked in the same directorate at the Ministry of Defence as Neil, and indeed was his superior. He might know why Neil was so late.

Unfortunately, when she looked out of the window she saw that it was the Sinders' large and luxurious car that was parked directly outside. Kevin Sinder was a colleague of Neil's, and he and his wife lived quite close, in Belgravia. Mrs Price let them in. She offered them the cloakroom and showed them the stairs, at the top of which Imogen waited to greet them. Imogen was fond of Kevin in spite of the minor snobbery he sometimes displayed, but not of his wife, Joyce, who could be trusted to make a point of being sweetly uncharitable. This evening her first remark was characteristic. 'Oh, Imogen, you're wearing that pretty skirt of yours again. I've always admired it.'

Before Imogen could think of an appropriate retort the doorbell rang again and Mrs Price admitted a couple called Cecil and June Green whom Neil had known at Oxford and who were now in publishing, followed by the Glenbournes. There were introductions, and Imogen was able to draw Philip aside.

'Neil's not home yet. Have you any idea where he

could be?'

'Poor old Neil! He must have been collared by the Minister or the Under-Secretary. He'll be here soon, I'm sure.' Philip was sympathetic, and helpful. 'Meanwhile, what can I do? Kevin's started to pour drinks, I see. Shall I take over?'

'Please, Philip.'

Imogen gave him a grateful smile. She thought she heard voices downstairs and, hoping it was Neil with Mrs Price, she slipped out of the drawing-room and looked over the banisters. Behind her she heard Joyce Sinder say, 'No, you've got it wrong. My husband's in the Foreign Office. He's a diplomat. He's merely seconded to the MOD.' And Philip, laughing to take the sting out of the remark, but happy to put Joyce in her place, said, 'Kevin used to be my fag at school, and now I can say he's fagging for me again. *C'est la vie.*'

There was laughter, which Imogen didn't share. She was disappointed. The man standing in the hall below Mrs Price was not Neil, but a total stranger. As a woman came from the cloakroom to join them, she realized that this must be the couple from the American Embassy—she racked her brains but failed to recall their name—whom Neil had particularly wanted to invite; the date had even been changed to suit them. But Neil wasn't here to make the introductions. Where was he? Imogen asked herself yet again, torn between anger and anxiety as she prepared to receive these special guests.

She need not have been embarrassed. A big, heavily built man climbed towards her, breathing somewhat deeply and with hand outstretched. 'Good evening,' he said cheerfully. 'You must be

18

Mrs Lavery—Imogen, I think Neil said. I'm Hank Christiansen, and this is my lady wife, Melinda. I hope we're not late. I've given my driver the evening off, and we thought it best to come by cab because of the parking problem, but then we couldn't find a free one.'

'And the traffic's just awful.' Melinda Christiansen was short and plump, and also slightly breathless.

They were both in their late fifties, outgoing, friendly, pleasant people. As Imogen offered them her hand she wondered if Neil had warned them that they would have to climb the stairs again after dinner. He certainly hadn't told them that the party was informal; Mr Christiansen was wearing his tuxedo, and Mrs Christiansen was in a low-cut, off-the-shoulder gown.

'Come along and meet my other guests,' Imogen said. 'You're not a bit late. In fact it's I who should apologize—for Neil, my husband. He seems to have been held up at his office and hasn't arrived home yet.'

Imogen led the way into the drawing-room and introduced the Christiansens. Philip got them drinks and drew them into the conversation. The party was going well, but time was passing.

Rosalind put a hand on Imogen's arm. 'Where is Neil?' she asked quickly. 'Hasn't he phoned?'

'No, he hasn't. And I've got no idea where he is,' replied Imogen, by now really angry and worried. 'I've never known him to be so late on a party night—or, for that matter, on any night without phoning to warn me.'

'My dear, he really should be here. It's insulting to the Christiansens. After all, they're high-ranking

19

people, used to VIP treatment and—' Rosalind stopped; Imogen was frowning. 'You didn't know? Hank Christiansen's the Head of CIA Station London, though of course that's meant to be a great secret. He's only been here a few weeks.'

'It was certainly kept a secret from me.' Imogen was bitter. 'But he did mention his driver, so I thought he was someone important. Why on earth did Neil ask them?'

'Probably because he met Mr C. in the line of duty and took a liking to him. Neil's not without ambition, but he doesn't go out of his way to fawn on VIPs—unlike some people. Just wait till Joyce finds out what a chance she's missing.'

It was unusual for Rosalind to be bitchy, and Imogen, seeing Joyce Sinder busy talking to Cecil Green and ignoring the Christiansens, laughed. She felt more cheerful. She looked at her watch. It was useless to wait for Neil any longer; he would have to make his excuses when he arrived. They must go and eat or the food would be ruined.

She clapped her hands lightly, 'Ladies and gentlemen, dinner is ready. Would you come down to the dining-room?'

* * *

As she led the way Imogen hurriedly rearranged the seating-plan in her head. She didn't want to remove Neil's place completely; such a drastic change would only cause confusion if he arrived in the middle of the meal, as surely he must. But she couldn't sit facing an empty chair at the head of the table.

She put Philip there and he murmured to her,

20

'OK, I'll buttle, but the next time you come to us I'll make Neil earn his keep.'

Melinda Christiansen laughed doubtfully, failing to understand the simple joke. And Joyce Sinder said, 'If my husband stood me up at one of my own dinner parties I'd never speak to him again.'

There was silence. Everyone was now seated, except for Philip who was pouring wine. The smoked salmon was already in front of them, and Imogen gestured to the plates of brown bread and butter on the table. It would have given her great pleasure to throw one of them at Joyce.

June Green, who had an empty seat kept for Neil beside her, suddenly said, 'It may not be Neil's fault. Perhaps he's had an accident.'

It was a thought that Imogen had been keeping firmly at the back of her mind. She swallowed hard, and was surprised to feel Hank Christiansen, who was sitting on her right, give her knee a friendly pat under the table.

'I'm sure we don't need to worry about young Neil,' he said, suddenly dominating the table and very clearly cutting short any further speculation. 'He's the kind of guy who can look after himself.' He changed the subject with practised ease. 'Tell me—I expect all you good people are ardent theatre-goers. What's on at present that you'd recommend to Melinda and me?'

The dinner continued. The food was excellent and Philip kept the wineglasses full. Imogen, who was having to force herself to eat and take her part in the conversation, realized that she was drinking too much. She was thankful when it was time to leave the men to their port and brandy and take the ladies upstairs. Neil had still not appeared.

21

Leaving the women in the main bedroom, she hurried downstairs again. On the way to the kitchen she seized the opportunity to use the telephone in the ground-floor hall. She tapped out the MOD number. A male operator answered and she gave Neil's extension. There was no reply, she was told after a pause. She hesitated, then said, 'There must be a duty officer.'

'Indeed. A couple of dozen, madam. Which directorate?'

At this point Imogen felt she could desert her guests for no longer. She merely answered, 'Thank you. Leave it.'

More worried than ever, she went along to the kitchen to collect the pot of coffee which Mrs Price would have made; the tray with the cups, cream and sugar would already be in the drawing-room. She carried the coffee upstairs carefully and went into the room, where the women were chatting. As she entered she was momentarily unnoticed and in time to hear Joyce Sinder comment: 'Maybe Neil's run off with his girl-friend.'

'Has he got a girl-friend?' June Green was amused.

'No!' said Rosalind. 'Joyce has just invented her because she thinks it would make a good story.'

'A malicious story—and quite untrue,' said Imogen from the doorway.

Joyce had the grace to blush. 'Imogen, I was only joking. I—'

Imogen ignored her. She put down the coffee pot, then turned and announced, 'As a matter of fact, I've just had a message from a neighbour. It seems our phone has been out of order or something, so Neil couldn't get through.

22

Unfortunately his mother has been taken ill suddenly, and he had to go to her. It's as simple as that. He apologizes profusely.'

There was a general murmur of sympathy. Imogen gave her attention to pouring the coffee and wondering what she would do if Neil suddenly walked in with a quite different excuse. She had lied spontaneously, determined to end conjecture about him, and especially to cap Joyce Sinder's snide remark; now she could only hope that he wouldn't arrive until the party was over.

She yearned for everyone to go, and eventually, except for Rosalind and Philip, they did. Automatically she said goodbye as her guests left, offering her hand, or her cheek for a kiss. She accepted their thanks, apologized once again to the Christiansens for Neil's absence, and gratefully shut the door behind them.

In the kitchen she found Mrs Price putting on her coat, and thanked her for coming in for the evening.

'My pleasure, Mrs Lavery. I'm always glad to earn a little bit extra, as you know.' Mrs Price waved a comprehensive hand around the room. 'Everything's neat and tidy. The silver could do with a polish, but I'll have plenty of time for that in the morning.'

Imogen saw her out. On the doorstep Mrs Price turned. 'I'm sorry Mr Lavery missed the party. His mother was taken ill, I heard one of the gentlemen say. I hope it's not serious.'

'I hope so too,' said Imogen, wishing she had never invented the story about old Nora Lavery. 'Good night, Mrs Price.'

'Good night, Mrs Lavery.'

23

Imogen shut the front door and for a moment leant her forehead against it. Then she straightened herself. Rosalind and Philip would be waiting for her upstairs. They had only a short distance to walk to their own house, and usually stayed after a party for a night-cap. But tonight was not usual. Neil wasn't there. And she couldn't lie to her sister and brother-in-law. Slowly she went up to the drawing-room.

'A brandy?' Philip asked as she came in.

Imogen shook her head. 'My dears, it—it's not true what I told everyone about Neil. There wasn't a message. His mother's not ill. I phoned the Ministry and he's not in his room. Somehow I didn't like to bother the duty officer. I haven't the faintest idea where he is or what's happened to him.'

Her voice broke, and she had to bite her lower lip to check the tears. She heard Philip's sharply indrawn breath. Then Rosalind's arms were around her, hugging her and leading her to a chair.

'Dearest Imogen! What an evening for you! Never mind, there's probably a simple explanation.'

'Yes, of course,' said Philip, aware that in the directorate in which he and Neil laboured, individuals were logged in and out; it would be readily possible to establish when Neil had left, if he had. He added, 'But we've wasted a lot of time. You look after Imogen, Rosalind. I'll get on the phone.'

CHAPTER TWO

It was some time before Philip Glenbourne rejoined his wife and sister-in-law in the drawing-room. The two women looked up anxiously as he came in, and he gave a quick shake of his head to indicate that they shouldn't raise their hopes.

'I'm sorry,' he said. 'Such news as I've managed to get is all negative, though in some ways that's good to know. First I phoned the Ministry. Neil was logged out of the directorate at five-fifteen, and one of the men on duty at the north entrance remembers seeing him leave the building soon after. Then I called Scotland Yard and, with a little string-pulling, got hold of a senior chap whom I know slightly and who's intelligent and was prepared to be helpful. No one answering Neil's description has been taken to hospital as a casualty in the part of London between the Ministry and here in the past twelve hours.'

'I never really thought he could be in hospital,' Imogen said. 'If he were, we'd have heard by now. Neil always carried identification in his wallet.'

'I put that point to my Chief Inspector friend, but he said he should check nevertheless. Apparently, if someone's knocked down by a hit and run driver or has some bizarre accident like being concussed by collapsing scaffolding or a bit of falling masonry—or merely collapses unconscious in the street—it's not unheard-of for some kind passer-by to relieve him of his wallet.'

'That's an abominable idea,' said Rosalind, 'but I'm sure it's true!'

Philip shrugged. 'It's the way of the world, nowadays. Anyway, we're pretty certain that Neil's not in hospital. And he's not in gaol either.'

'What on earth do you mean by that?' Imogen was indignant. 'Why ever should he be in gaol?'

'I mean exactly what I say. He's not in police custody anywhere. My man checked that too. Imogen, it's not as wildly improbable as it sounds. Neil might have met a friend, gone to a pub to have a drink with him and got involved in a brawl or something, or so the Chief Inspector assured me. However, it's not happened to Neil.'

'Wouldn't he have phoned, if it had?'

'Yes, I expect so.' Philip was becoming slightly impatient at this cross-questioning. 'The thing is, the Chief Inspector advises us to wait till morning. He couldn't suggest anything else. He did say that not long ago a man who had been reported missing was found in a small lift where he'd been stuck all night.'

Imogen sighed. 'That's not very likely, is it?'

'No, my dear. I know. I'm sorry. But it does show that there could be some simple explanation for Neil's—Neil's apparent disappearance.' Philip hesitated. 'There was one other possibility my policeman suggested. Loss of memory. He asked me if Neil had ever had concussion or suffered from black-outs. He hasn't, has he, Imogen?'

'No. Of course not. He'd certainly have told me about anything like that. He's always been perfectly healthy and he has regular medical checks, just as you do.'

'That's what I said,' Philip agreed. 'Look, there's one other thing I could do, and that's phone Joy Aubyn. But it's after midnight and she'll probably

26

be asleep so I won't be too popular.'

'Might she know something?' Imogen was surprised. Though Joy Aubyn was Neil's personal assistant she had rarely given her a thought. Now, unbidden and unwanted, there came into her mind Joyce Sinder's remark about Neil's girl-friend.

'Possibly.' Philip was beginning to regret that he had mentioned Joy Aubyn at all. He had recently had an acrimonious argument with her about a mislaid file and he didn't relish the idea of waking her. 'I merely thought that Neil might have said something to her about going to the Foreign Office on his way home, or calling in at another department. The point is, shall I phone her now, regardless of the time, or wait till morning?'

'Now!' Rosalind said when Imogen didn't answer.

'All right.'

But when the phone rang and rang and there was no reply, he was glad. Then, as he was about to replace his receiver, a man's voice said, 'Ya! Who is it?'

Taken by surprise, Philip paused before he answered. Then he said, 'Is a Miss Joy Aubyn there, or have I got the wrong number?'

'Why?' snapped the voice at the other end.

'My name's Glenbourne. I'm from the Ministry of Defence, and I want a word with Miss Aubyn.'

'Wait!'

Philip waited and eventually, after some mutterings in the background, Joy spoke. 'Yes, Philip, what is it? It had better be important. I'm not paid to be on duty twenty-four hours a day, you know.'

'I wouldn't have disturbed you if it weren't

27

important,' Glenbourne said. He tried to speak appeasingly, but he thought what a bitch Joy was. He pictured her, with her red hair and very white skin, lying naked on her bed, but he couldn't visualize the man, who had sounded foreign. He went on bluntly, 'Joy, Neil Lavery has disappeared.'

'What? What do you mean—disappeared?'

'The Laverys had a dinner party at their home. He'd promised to be back early, but he simply never arrived here. We've got no idea where he is, and as you can imagine Imogen's out of her mind with worry.'

'Yes—of course. I assume you've tried the police and the hospitals.' She seemed to be digesting the news slowly. 'But why ask me? He's certainly not here.'

For a moment Philip was irascible. 'I never thought he was,' he said shortly. Then he regained his composure and added, 'I merely hoped he might have said something about where he was going when he left the office.'

'Home!' Joy didn't hesitate before she replied. 'It had started to rain, and he was afraid he'd have trouble finding a taxi. He even said he had to get back as soon as he could because of that party you mentioned.'

'I see. Well, thanks, Joy. I'm very sorry to have disturbed you.'

'That's all right. Poor old Neil! Philip—'

'Yes?'

'You didn't say, but you have—you have contacted John Faudin?'

'No, not yet,' Philip said coldly. 'Time enough in the morning for that, I'd have thought, if Neil still hasn't appeared.'

He said goodbye, thanked Joy again and slowly put the phone down. John Faudin? Brigadier Faudin, Director of Security in the MOD? He had been surprised that Joy had thought of that angle so quickly, though it was true that a case of even temporary unexplained absence or a case of apparent suicide, raised doubts—at any rate when persons employed in sensitive areas were involved.

But still, Philip was not pleased. Joy's intervention had put him in an awkward position. After all, Neil was his brother-in-law and no one could have blamed him for disregarding questions of security, at least overnight. But in a sense Joy Aubyn had forced his hand. There was no way he could ignore her suggestion, much as he resented it. He would have to act.

Philip returned to the drawing-room. He told Imogen and Rosalind what Joy had said and, slightly distorting the truth, added that she had urged him to waste no more time, but tell Brigadier Faudin about the situation at once.

'Faudin, your security man?' Imogen knew that name and reacted indignantly. 'But what's it to him?' she demanded. 'He won't know anything and—and it's not as if you kept large sums of money at the Ministry and Neil might have absconded with an odd million.'

Philip stared at her. Was it conceivable that she was being deliberately obstructive? He banished the thought, and refrained from saying that the MOD contained secrets—some worth millions of pounds, some worth far more in terms of international relations, to the right buyer. He was quite certain that Imogen knew all this perfectly well, and he had no desire to mention a possibility that would only serve to anger her.

Rosalind sensed the confrontation and said, 'Surely there's no need to rouse Faudin at this hour of the night. If Neil's not found by nine or ten tomorrow—' She left the sentence unfinished.

'Today.' Imogen corrected her immediately. 'My dears, it's high time you went home. You've done everything you can for the moment—unless Philip thinks he must call his security chief.'

'No. I agree. Let's forget him,' Philip said quickly. 'Imogen, listen. I suggest that I go home, and Rosalind spends what remains of the night with you. Obviously we can't leave you here by yourself.'

'Why ever not? I'll be perfectly all right.'

They argued for several minutes. Fond as she was of Rosalind, Imogen now wanted to be alone. She had no wish to talk to anyone any more. She wanted to think, to collect her thoughts, her speculations—probably to cry, and to take out her frustration on some inanimate object like a pillow. She'd done this as a child, and she found that her present instincts were similiar. With Rosalind about, she couldn't do it—and there would be no comfort to be offered by anyone till Neil was found, alive and unharmed. She couldn't, wouldn't, believe that he had just walked out on her.

'Please go, both of you,' she said. 'I'll be fine. I'll hope to get some sleep.'

* * *

And at last they went, Philip striding along the street so rapidly that Rosalind protested she couldn't keep up with him.

'I've no alternative but to get hold of John Faudin as soon as I can,' he said.

'But you agreed—'

'I know, Rosalind. That was for Imogen's benefit.'

'I don't understand.'

Philip slowed his pace. 'So what do you think has happened to Neil?'

'I've no idea. We seem to have eliminated all the possibilities.'

'Except one. There's one that's not pleasant, not pleasant at all. We never considered it in conversation, though we skirted round it. Imogen would have refused to believe it; the very suggestion would have incensed her.'

'Philip, what are you talking about? Not—?'

'Yes. We've got to face the fact that it's possible—though most unlikely—that Neil may have defected. On the other hand it's also possible that Brigadier Faudin could have forestalled any such move on his part by arranging with the Security Service to pick him up and take him to a safe house for interrogation of some kind. I just don't know. It's not my line. But I do know that I can't avoid putting Faudin in the picture.'

'Neil? Neil Lavery? Our Neil? You must be out of your mind!' Rosalind had stopped dead in her tracks, and Philip was forced to halt too. 'Philip, do you realize what you're saying? Neil is Imogen's husband, your brother-in-law and mine, your colleague—and you're accusing him of being a—a traitor of some sort!'

'Dear God, do you think I want it to be true? It would affect the whole family.' Philip took Rosalind

31

by the arm and urged her along. 'Come on, Rosalind, and listen to me. A short while ago there was a very serious breach of security in the MOD, and it was traced to the directorate in which Neil works.'

'The same one in which you work!'

'Yes, and a good few other people.' Philip sighed. 'I couldn't expect Imogen to understand, but I thought that you—Rosalind, it's Neil who's disappeared. Surely you see the implication.'

'Of course I do. I'm not a child. But—but none of this makes him guilty. He could easily be lying unconscious in some alley somewhere, and the police haven't found him yet.'

'You mean he's been mugged?'

'Yes. Why not? It happens all the time.'

'Between Whitehall and Knightsbridge in the middle of the rush hour?'

'Don't be so bloody sarcastic! And even if there is anything in what you say, and he's holed up somewhere with this man Faudin, Faudin could have made a mistake, couldn't he? Or Neil could be helping him interrogate someone else.'

'Yes.'

By now they had reached their home, and Philip was not prepared to argue further. He was tired, his head ached and he foresaw a difficult day ahead, both personally and officially. He turned the key in their front door, and secured it behind them.

'I'll pop up and make sure Belle's all right,' Rosalind said. Though Belle had a nurse she always liked to check on her if they had been out late. 'Then would you like some tea?'

'That would be fine,' Philip said absently.

His mind was on the conversation with Brigadier

Faudin that he was about to have. He accepted that it was essential, but he was not looking forward to it with any pleasure. He'd have to keep his wits about him. All he said would be checked and rechecked later, and he had no wish to be accused of complicity with his brother-in-law, or of misleading the authorities in any way. On the other hand, the last thing he wanted to do was to imply that he believed Neil 'guilty'.

There was a fine line to be drawn between the two sentiments—and John Faudin was not a fool.

★   ★   ★

Brigadier Faudin was approaching retirement age, after a long and distinguished military career, largely in the fields of intelligence and security. In some ways the appointment of Director of Security at the MOD was a sinecure, dealing with matters of physical security, supervising the military 'vetters' and so on. Though he would play a role in major investigations, it would be largely as a liaison officer; any enquiry of substance would—in theory—be handled by the Security Service.

This appointment—almost certainly his last— suited Brigadier Faudin very well, for his life had been tragically marred; his wife had been afflicted with Alzheimer's disease. For a long time he had done his best to look after her himself, but as the complaint developed this had become impossible and he had had to find her a place in a home. The Brigadier had sold their house, moved into a small flat close to the MOD, and concentrated on his job, his monthly visits to his wife who no longer knew him, letters to his married daughter in Canada, a few carefully chosen friends, his books and his music.

Recently, however, it was his job which had excluded almost all other interests. What he had suspected for some time had finally been substantiated. Now he knew that there was a high-powered agent in the Ministry. He knew in which directorate this traitor lurked, and a trap had narrowed the field to one of a dozen or so individuals. But that was all. The trap had failed to do more, and the Brigadier was afraid that the quarry was now on his guard. In other words, he had missed his chance. This both worried and angered the Brigadier—particularly so because in his eagerness to save the Ministry from scandal he had tried to handle the case himself, without involving the appropriate authorities.

Faudin was awake when the telephone rang, having read until late and then been unable to sleep. He seized the receiver on its second ring. Either his wife had had another accident—the nursing home couldn't guarantee that she would be watched every moment of the day and night—or it was the Ministry.

Thankful that the call was not about his wife, he listened to what Philip Glenbourne had to say with a mixture of horror, surprise and regret. Neil Lavery had been low on his list of suspects, and he certainly hadn't expected anyone to bolt, not at this point. Clearly he had misinterpreted. In fact, he had made a hell of a mess of it. Now it was too late, and he would have to go cap in hand to his superiors and the Security Service. There would be one devil of a stink.

'...of course I could be bothering you

34

unnecessarily,' Glenbourne was saying. 'Neil could have been mugged and left behind a pile of dustbins somewhere. In that case presumably he'll be found in the morning, but—I just hope to God there's some explanation like that. Only in the circumstances . . .' His words drifted into silence.

'I quite understand,' said Faudin. 'It's a difficult position for you, Philip, but you did the right thing in calling me. Let's hope there is an acceptable explanation. Anyway, leave it to me to make any further inquiries. I'll do my best not to sound a false alarm.'

CHAPTER THREE

John Faudin was not looking forward to his meeting with the officers from MI5. Early that morning he had faced the fact that he now had no alternative but to place the developing case in the hands of the Security Service, and he had phoned Munro Graffon, a senior man with whom he had worked before on several occasions and had found to be understanding and co-operative. Faudin hoped he would be sympathetic now.

In fact, Graffon had wasted no time on recriminations over the delay in informing him of what now looked likely to turn into a major operation, but had agreed to take the necessary immediate action. A conference had been arranged in Faudin's office at nine o'clock.

His secretary had just produced the pile of personnel and vetting files for which he had called when the two visitors arrived. Faudin organized coffee, and gave orders that they were not to be disturbed.

The men from MI5 were very dissimilar types. Graffon—the senior—was an unprepossessing man in appearance. Short, dark, fat and hairy, he was in his middle forties and, of his own choice, a confirmed bachelor, though many women found him attractive.

The other MI5 officer Faudin had not met before. Guy Cantel was tall, with a lean, athletic body, curly fair hair and serious grey eyes. He looked as if he might have become a professional cricketer and indeed had got his Blue at Oxford, but the life had not appealed to him. After his degree and a year spent travelling, he had responded happily to an approach from the Security Service. He was twelve years younger than Graffon; outside the office, they had little in common, but they worked well together.

With a minimum of preliminaries, Graffon said. 'I've done everything I can on the basis of your phone call—ports, airports, small airfields, the usual, though—' he couldn't resist one reference to the delay in being briefed '—there's a lot more we could have done if we'd known of the problem earlier. It may well be that we're too late. If he's our man, the chances are that he's already out of the country. Anyway, we—or Special Branch—are rechecking hospitals and anywhere else we can think of, including the mortuaries, just in case. In fact, we're doing all we can for the moment on that front. After all, he's not been gone twenty-four hours yet. That's the routine, as you know. Now put us fully in the picture.'

This was the moment Faudin had been awaiting

36

with some trepidation. He would have to admit that for some time it had been known that leaks had been taking place from one of the most sensitive directorates in the MOD, culminating in the certain loss of a most important list of data. Worse, without consulting Graffon's Service he had tried to catch the culprit with an elementary ploy—a ploy which had failed.

He told the story as briefly and bluntly as he could, making no excuses for his action. As he expected, in spite of his initial reasonably sympathetic attitude, Graffon couldn't contain himself.

'You claim there were only a dozen people with access? You're sure you can limit it to this lot?' he demanded, looking at the list of names that Faudin had handed to him. 'What about secretaries, messengers and so on?'

'Yes, in this instance, I think I can. Security in this directorate was—supposedly—extremely tight; everyone on that list has an extra full positive vetting, too. At the other end of the scale, of course, there's the Minister, the PM and the Foreign Secretary—but we must take it they're above suspicion.'

It was Graffon's private belief that no one was ever above suspicion, however senior or important he or she might be, but he accepted that the inquiry should start with the more likely candidates.

He grunted, and commented. 'Well, all I can say is that if we'd been brought in earlier we could have had the more probable suspects under surveillance; almost certainly we'd have got warrants for phone taps, even mail taps. But you—you just haven't the resources, the facilities. And as for that trick of yours—probably all it did was warn the agent that it was time to make tracks.' Graffon paused. 'But that's water under the bridge,' he added resignedly. 'Let's get on with it.'

After a lengthy discussion they agreed that, although the odds were strong that Lavery—if he were the agent—had defected, or was in the process of attempting to defect, there was no certainty on this score. They must keep open minds, just in case.

Finally, Graffon rose to his feet and stared out of the window through its net curtain. 'OK,' he said. 'Guy here will be responsible for the work on the ground, getting what resources he needs, and he'll answer to me. I'll organize any necessary high-level briefings through my Director-General. Is that all right with you, John?'

'Fine!' Faudin turned to Cantel. 'Tell me what you need. I've got the relevant files here.'

'Thank you. I'll certainly need those.' It was almost the first time that Guy Cantel had spoken. 'And an interview room in the directorate's area with a direct outside phone line—not one through the Ministry switchboard. I'd like some time with the files, and then I'll start interviewing—Lavery's brother-in-law first, obviously. Incidentally, sir, I notice you've been careful not to mark any favourites on this list. Who would you say were the front-runners—apart from Lavery, of course?'

'I wouldn't say.' Faudin was firm. 'I know these people. Some better than others. Or I think I do. I don't intend to prejudice you in any way.'

Cantel smiled. 'As you wish. Am I right in assuming that they'll all know by now that Lavery has disappeared?'

38

'Most of them, I expect.' Faudin shrugged. 'If not, they soon will. It's hard to keep something like that quiet.'

'Nevertheless, we don't want to spread the glad tidings,' Graffon intervened. 'The longer we can keep the media in ignorance the better. I'm afraid it won't be for very long.'

'How do you judge the chances of finding Lavery?' Faudin asked somewhat hesitantly.

He had looked at Cantel, but it was Graffon who answered.

'A thousand to one.'

'I suppose so. He's had plenty of time to prepare his run,' Faudin said bitterly. 'My fault.'

'True enough,' said Munro Graffon. 'But don't blame yourself, John. Anyone might have done the same in your place. It's water under the bridge, as I say. We must take it from here.'

★　　　★　　　★

Guy Cantel shut the file that had been lying open on the desk in front of him and looked up, smiling. 'Come in, Mr Glenbourne,' he said, pleasantly and unnecessarily; Philip Glenbourne was already in the room and, as Cantel had noted, he hadn't bothered to knock. 'Do sit down. I'm Guy Cantel, and I'm sure you know where I'm from and what this is about.'

'Unfortunately, yes.'

An attractive man, Cantel thought, and in spite of the occasion very sure of himself. 'How did you and your brother-in-law get on?' he asked without further ado, and was pleased to see the blue eyes opposite him momentarily narrow in surprise.

39

Glenbourne recovered himself quickly. 'As a relation, or in the office?' he asked.

'Both.'

'Well, as a colleague to take that first, I couldn't have asked for better. He was—is—brilliant in his field. To some extent I suppose I envy him, though I'm senior to him. He's brighter than I am, but not aggressive, not overly ambitious. I simply can't believe that—'

'And as a relation?' Cantel interrupted. 'How did you feel about him as a brother-in-law?'

'My sister-in-law's husband, to be exact. I'm never sure whether that constitutes a brother-in-law or not.' Philip Glenbourne ran a hand through his hair; he was obviously giving himself time to think. 'We got on well enough together. Our respective wives are very close, and it was essential that we did. But, as you can tell from our files, we come from very different backgrounds and we didn't really have that much in common.'

'Do you think he resented that?'

Glenbourne looked at Cantel doubtfully. 'I'm not quite sure what you mean, but I'd have said not. He seemed to me a forthright, honest man.' Glenbourne shook his head. 'Dear God, I don't know what to think. I feel ashamed of myself for suspecting him even for a moment.'

'Did you suspect him before he disappeared?'

'Definitely not!'

'You knew there had been some serious disclosures of information. Whom did you suspect?'

'Only a limited number of us had access. John Faudin will have given you our names. I'm sorry, but I'd be picking one out of a hat if I mentioned anyone in particular.'

40

Guy Cantel nodded his understanding, and the questions continued. To Glenbourne many of them seemed irrelevant, but he was sure they were not. In fact, Cantel's objective was to gain a preliminary impression of the people involved and their interrelations. He found Glenbourne helpful and kept him longer than he had intended, but finally he asked for Joy Aubyn.

When she appeared he greeted her, explained his presence and then asked, without further preamble, 'What's your opinion of Neil Lavery, Miss Aubyn?'

'He is very intelligent, conscientious, reliable—'

'Miss Aubyn, I'm not thinking of employing him. I'm not asking for a reference. Did you like him?'

'Yes. Yes, I did,' she said defiantly. 'He was always kind and considerate, though he wouldn't stand for sloppy work.'

For a moment Guy Cantel was silent, watching while the girl fidgeted. He wondered why she should be so tense and nervous.

Changing the subject, he said, 'Presumably you never suspected Lavery? Whom did you suspect?'

'Of what?'

'Oh, come, Miss Aubyn. You must have been aware of the leaks of information from this very closed circle.'

'Yes. Yes. Of course I was. But, as for suspecting anyone, I—I don't know.' The question had obviously worried her. 'It could have been any of them. All I can tell you is it wasn't me, and if you try to put it on me, I'll fight.'

Cantel decided to leave it there for the moment. He was sure the girl was hiding something but, whatever it was, it wasn't going to emerge at this

41

first interview. 'OK, Miss Aubyn,' he said dismissively. 'I'd like to talk to Mr Sinder now. Would you be kind enough to ask him to come and see me, please?'

'You mean that's all?' she said, scarcely believing she was getting away so easily. Then she pushed back her chair. 'Right. I'll get him.'

While he waited, Guy Cantel studied Kevin Sinder's file. Sinder had been born with a silver spoon in his mouth, right enough. He had been at Eton with Philip Glenbourne, though he was a little younger than Philip, and had taken an Oxford degree with First Class Honours. He hadn't married until his middle thirties, and his two children were still very young. He had just been promoted to Counsellor in the Foreign and Commonwealth Office, but was at present attached to the Ministry of Defence.

A thump on the door—it couldn't be described as a knock—made Cantel look up quickly. A large man lumbered in and, without being asked, seated himself. Across the desk Cantel smelt the whisky on his breath. All the files contained photographs of their subjects and Cantel knew that this wasn't Sinder, but he asked nevertheless.

'Mr Sinder?'

'No. I'm not Sinder. Kevin seems to be missing, like old Neil.' He leered at Cantel. 'But I dare say you'll find Kevin at the FCO. I can't see him defecting. He likes his creature comforts too much. No, I'm Robert Tyneman, Bob Tyneman. I thought you'd be wanting to see me too.'

'And you were quite right, Mr Tyneman.'

'Not that there's anything I can tell you, except that I'm jolly glad Neil's hopped it. Sorry that it's him, of course, but glad for all the rest of us. It's not been any fun the last few weeks, with a cloud of suspicion hovering over us, and that fellow Faudin looking as if he's ready to swoop at any moment.'

'You think this has solved the problem?'

'Well, it has, hasn't it? You're not suggesting we've been harbouring two spies in our midst, are you?'

'No, Mr Tyneman. One's quite enough to be going on with. Are you surprised it's Neil Lavery who's hopped it, as you so pleasantly put it?'

'I am indeed. I had my money on Bill Plimpton. Or, failing him, Kevin Sinder.'

'Really? Why?'

'Sinder as an outside bet because, in my opinion, of those with access he was the least likely—though, come to think of it, Glenbourne would run him close. But Plimpton was my favourite. He's not been complaining about lack of money so much lately. His wife is said to have got a good job, been promoted—she teaches at LSE—but they're not brilliantly paid there, and he's got three sons at Winchester. The fees must be horrendous, and he's not a betting man so he hasn't won the Pools.'

'I imagine not. Do you have any children, Mr Tyneman?'

'Haven't you read my file? Yes, of course I have—a son and a daughter.' The large, shapeless face became uncertain. 'But at present they're in Canada with their mother, visiting friends.'

Guy Cantel was observant. He had been trained to notice items like Tyneman's expensively tailored suit and his silk shirt, and he had also noticed that the suit was stained, the shirt dirty at the cuffs. It seemed to Cantel that Tyneman was someone who

43

had been used to a woman's care, but no longer received it. Besides, it was term-time; the children should have been at school. He guessed that Tyneman's wife had left him, at least temporarily.

'Anyway, this is all academic now Lavery's bolted, isn't it?' said Tyneman. 'I suppose we'll have to go through a ghastly damage assessment routine but apart from that, as I said, we should be thankful.'

There were a few more questions, and Cantel let him go. Time had crept by. He had managed fewer of these preliminary interviews than he had hoped, but he felt he'd had enough for now. And there was one visit he had promised himself he would make before the morning ended—a call on Neil Lavery's wife.

*   *   *

Guy Cantel collected his car and drove to Knightsbridge. He wasn't looking forward to this meeting with Imogen Lavery. Apart from what he had learnt from Lavery's file he knew nothing about her, but wives of traitors or suspected traitors were never easy to deal with.

He drove slowly around the small square where the Laverys lived, and told himself he shouldn't have brought his car. Then, on the second time around, he saw two men in brown overalls come out of the Laverys' house. They flung what looked like tool bags into the back of a small, unmarked van that was parked some twenty yards along the street, and drove off. Hurriedly Cantel accelerated forward and swung his car into the space they had abandoned. Blessing his luck, he locked the car and

44

went to the house.

A small woman in a large white apron opened the door to him. 'Yes?' she demanded uncompromisingly.

'I'd like to speak to Mrs Lavery, please.'

'Mrs Lavery is not at home.'

'I understand, but I'm afraid I must insist. Would you please tell Mrs Lavery that I need to see her urgently. My name is Guy Cantel, and I'm from the Ministry of Defence.'

'I don't care if you're from Buckingham Palace, Mr Cantel. Mrs Lavery isn't here, as I told you. She's gone to the Shop.'

Cantel gave the woman a long, hard stare. He wasn't sure whether to believe her or not. He had assumed that Imogen Lavery would be at home, sitting by the telephone in the hope of hearing news of her husband. That she should have gone shopping, which is what he had understood, surprised him.

'When do you expect her back?' he asked.

'Any time now, Mr Cantel. Shall I tell her you called?'

'If you would. Thank you.'

Guy Cantel returned to his car and sat, watching the door of the Laverys' home. He had decided he would give Mrs Lavery half an hour to come home with her shopping.

CHAPTER FOUR

Guy Cantel had but a short time to wait. Less than five minutes after he had settled himself in his car a taxi drew up at the Laverys' house and a woman got out. She was tall, slender, dark-haired and wearing a cherry-red suit which, even from where Cantel sat, looked expensive. She was not carrying a shopping-bag or any packages, but when she produced a key and let herself into the front door, Cantel assumed she must be Imogen Lavery.

Inside the house, Imogen went straight to the kitchen, where Mrs Price was busy polishing silver. 'Any calls?' she asked immediately.

Before she left that morning she had felt compelled to take Mrs Price into her confidence and tell her the truth—that Neil had not been summoned unexpectedly to the bedside of a sick mother, but had simply disappeared. Mrs Price had been shocked and sympathetic but, to Imogen's relief, had accepted the situation with a minimum of excitement and few questions. Now she shook her head sadly.

'I'm afraid not, Mrs Lavery, unless you count your sister. Mrs Glenbourne phoned, and I told her you'd gone to the Shop. She said to tell you that she had no news, but if it was all right with you she'd bring Belle around for tea this afternoon.'

'Thank you. I'll call her back.'

It was kind of Rosalind to phone again. By 'no news', Imogen knew, she had meant no news of Neil. After an almost sleepless night Imogen had felt exhausted when she woke from a doze first thing that morning. All she had wanted to do was pull the bedclothes over her head and lie in a semi-comatose state, perhaps slipping into sleep again and ignoring the fact that Neil was not beside her. But she had forced herself to phone Rosalind and Philip, and assure them that she was able to

46

continue her daily life with some semblance of normality. They had agreed that this would be the best course of action for the present. But it had not been easy.

In fact, it was neither the Glenbournes' encouragement nor the imminent arrival of Mrs Price that had forced her to get up. Today was one of her days at the Shop where, as part of her efforts on behalf of Oxfam, she sorted second-hand clothes and unwanted small possessions, or served behind the counter. It wasn't work she enjoyed, but because she despised voluntary helpers who took on jobs and then were half-hearted about their commitment, she hated to make an excuse and stay at home.

This morning had been particularly trying. There had been few browsers and fewer buyers, though the Marylebone High Street was thronged with people, many of whom peered through the window at the objects on show. Time had seemed endless, and she could have kissed the woman who was due to relieve her when she arrived punctually.

'. . . said he was from the Ministry of Defence.'

Imogen returned to the present and tossed back her head. 'I'm sorry, Mrs Price. I'm tired and I must have been half asleep. What did you say?'

'There was a man came to the door who wanted to see you. A Mr Cantel from the Ministry of Defence, or so he said. He could have been from some newspaper.'

'I doubt it. Not so soon. What did he want, Mrs Price?'

'You! I told him you were at the Shop but would be home soon. He thanked me and went away, but I think he'll be back.'

'Yes. I expect he will,' Imogen said slowly.

'And that's all, Mrs Lavery, apart from the Telecom men.'

'What Telecom men?'

'They said our phones had been reported out of order. They showed me a piece of paper and they had your name, so I let them in. Did I do wrong, Mrs Lavery?' Mrs Price asked anxiously, seeing the expression on Imogen's face.

'No. No, of course not, but—As far as I know there was nothing wrong with the phones. What was on that piece of paper? Did they leave it with you?'

Mrs Price shook her head. 'No,' she said. 'Oh dear! What have I done? They seemed pleasant and efficient, as if they knew what they were about, and it never occurred to me they could be anything other than what they claimed—Mrs Lavery, do you think they were thieves? We'd better look and see if anything's missing, and we should call the police.'

'Hold on! Let's look around first, Mrs Price. You take this floor. I'll go upstairs.'

*   *   *

In the bedroom Imogen went at once to the small wall safe hidden behind a portrait of herself by Maggi Hambling. It was apparently untouched. So was the leather box in which she kept her less valuable jewellery and a purse containing a few pounds' worth of emergency change. Everything seemed to be in order, yet for some reason she felt certain that the stranger recently in the room had done more than examine the phone on the table beside Neil's side of their bed. Quickly she opened

48

one or two of the drawers in a dressing-table and gained the distinct impression that they had been searched.

She lifted the receiver of the phone. It was working. She turned and opened another drawer which held some lingerie and regarded a flimsy white nightgown. It was neatly folded, but not exactly as she would have folded it. Mrs Price always left the laundry on the bed and Verity, who might have been poking around if she had been at home, was of course well away at school. Imogen shivered.

Apart from the adjoining bathroom there was a small study on this floor, seldom used except by Neil. Imogen stood in the doorway and inspected the bookshelves, the filing cabinet and the desk. If anything were missing, she thought, she would never know. Or would she? Suddenly she became still.

There were the usual things on the desk-top. The leather-covered blotting pad, the calendar, a few reference books between glass book-ends, a tray of pens and pencils—they were all there. But the photograph had gone—a photograph that had been taken some years ago when Matthew was ten and Verity seven, and they had been on a seaside holiday in the Channel Islands. It had been a good photograph of her and the children, and Neil had been proud of it. He had insisted on putting it in a silver frame, which always sat on his desk in the study.

But it was not there now. And why would anyone have taken that? It had only sentimental value, apart perhaps from the frame and that was worth very little. Imogen could feel her heart thumping.

49

Had Neil taken it with him? Or sent messengers posing as British Telecom men to retrieve it? She wished she could remember when she had last noticed it.

If Neil had got it, she thought, it surely meant that he still loved his family, even if he had left them. Inevitably the questions returned. Where had he gone? And why? Why hadn't he told her he was in some kind of trouble—if he was? She couldn't believe for a moment that he had gone off with some other woman, as that bitch Joyce Sinder had suggested. Nor did she believe that there was any serious question about his integrity or loyalty, whatever the MOD might be prepared to hint.

She wondered about this man Cantel. She had met John Faudin, but the name Cantel meant nothing to her. She was sure Neil had never mentioned it. As her mind played on the problem she was automatically opening and closing the drawers of the desk. Suddenly she came on a bundle of passports.

Hastily she took them out and sorted through them. Neil's current passport, which had been renewed about a year ago, was missing. And there was only one conclusion to be drawn from that, Imogen thought miserably. Coupled with the absence of the family photograph, it must mean that Neil had planned to disappear.

The front door-bell pealed, and she went out on to the landing. Looking down into the hall she saw Mrs Price admit a tall, fair man and show him into the dining-room. She hurried down the stairs.

'Mr Cantel,' said Mrs Price softly, pointing to the door that she had closed after the visitor. 'And there's nothing missing, Mrs Lavery, thank God.

I've had a good look round and we're all as we should be.'

'Good. Thank you.'

★   ★   ★

Imogen squared her shoulders, opened the dining-room door and walked in. 'Good morning,' she said coldly. 'I'm Imogen Lavery. I gather you're from the Ministry of Defence and you want to speak to me.'

'You're quite right, Mrs Lavery. My name's Guy Cantel and I do want to speak to you. But I'm not exactly from the Ministry of Defence.'

'Then where the hell are you from?' she demanded. 'Not from British Telecom again? Show me some identification.'

Having caught a glimpse of Imogen Lavery paying off the taxi and entering the house, somehow Cantel hadn't expected her to be ready to dissolve into tears at the first mention of her husband's place of work. But he hadn't anticipated such aggressive arrogance either. Well, he thought, if that was the way she wanted to play it—

He smiled at her slowly, knowing how irritating such a smile would be in the circumstances, and offered his identity card. 'I'm from the Security Service, Mrs Lavery. Brigadier Faudin has asked my department to enquire into a serious breach of security in a certain MOD directorate—the directorate in which your husband works. If you would care to check with the Brigadier I'd be only too happy.'

'That won't be necessary.' Imogen's voice was stiff as she handed back the identity card. When she

51

had spoken to Rosalind that morning, her sister had said something about 'trouble at the office', but fatigue or stupidity had led her to assume that this was going to be the result of Neil's disappearance rather than the cause of it. Now she was appalled by what this Guy Cantel had implied.

'Incidentally, Mrs Lavery,' he continued when she remained silent, 'what did you mean by asking if I were from British Telecom?'

'The two men who came this morning, weren't they connected with you? They said they were from BT and someone had made a complaint that our phones were out of order. Mrs Price, my cleaning woman, let them in. But I know the phones were perfectly all right when I left the house this morning.'

'So?' said Cantel encouragingly.

'These men were no ordinary thieves. They seem to have searched the place, but they didn't steal anything.'

'How odd!' Cantel made no attempt to hide his surprise. 'If I may use your phone I'd like to check, and then perhaps I could speak to Mrs Price.'

'If you wish. I'll show you.'

$$\star \qquad \star \qquad \star$$

Cantel returned to the dining-room within ten minutes. 'You were right, Mrs Lavery,' he said. 'Those men were not from British Telecom, and neither my department nor Brigadier Faudin knows anything about them. Mrs Price described them, and by chance I myself saw them leave your house shortly before you returned from your shopping.'

'My shopping? What do you mean?'

52

'Well, Mrs Price said—'

'Oh, I see. You misunderstood, Mr Cantel. I work in an Oxfam shop once a week and I didn't want to let them down, so I went today in spite of—in spite of Neil.'

Cantel nodded his comprehension. 'Anyway, I saw these men leave the house and drive off in a plain van. But that really isn't much help. For the moment they remain a mystery. However, I've taken the liberty of sending for a couple of my own people, who will search your house thoroughly and—'

'Why?' Imogen guessed that if Cantel wished he could easily get a search warrant, but she felt she had to protest.

'It's possible they've put listening devices in some of the rooms,' said Cantel. 'Who knows?' He didn't add that the house would have to be searched anyway.

Imogen heard herself laugh. 'What a strange world you live in, Mr Cantel,' she said.

'Yes, Mrs Lavery,' he agreed. 'That's true. And unfortunately for the present it's become your world too.' He regretted the remark as soon as he saw her wince. 'You'll be able to watch my people,' he added hurriedly. 'In fact, I'd like you to do so.'

'Very well!' There was no point in arguing further, Imogen thought.

'Thank you. They'll be here soon. Meanwhile perhaps I might ask you some questions.'

'What—what sort of questions?'

'Fairly personal, I'm afraid. Such as, where did you meet your husband, and what were your relations? Did he talk much about his work? Would he have confided in you if he had any problem of

53

any kind—financial, professional, social? That'll do to start with.'

'And you really think all this will help to find Neil?' Imogen said coldly.

'It might. To some extent the more I can fill out my picture of the shadowy figure I'm looking for—shadowy to me, that is—the more likely I am to find him.'

'Very well,' said Imogen again. She was resigned, but she told herself to keep her wits about her. Inevitably she and Guy Cantel were on opposing sides. 'I'm sure you've already read all the files on Neil, but I'll do my best. First, we've been married for sixteen years and it's been a happy and, I believe, successful marriage. I met Neil at a charity ball. I hadn't wanted to go in the least and he'd only been asked at the last minute to fill in for someone who had been taken ill. He couldn't dance much, but he made an extra man. Anyway, we took one look at each other, and that was that. Three months later we were married.'

'With everyone's blessing?'

'With no one's blessing. Neil had just started in the Civil Service, and his parents, who ran a small store and had made enormous sacrifices for his education, said he was much too young to marry. My own Dad, on the other hand, said Neil was a fortune-hunter after my money, though eventually he relented and gave us this house as a wedding present.'

'Us?'

'Well, me. It's in my name. Dad also gives me an allowance and of course when he dies Rosalind —that's my elder sister who's married to a man called Philip Glenbourne, as I'm sure you must

54

know; he's Neil's immediate boss.'

'I know of Philip Glenbourne, Mrs Lavery.'

'I thought so. Anyway, sooner or later, Rosalind and I will get quite a lot of money. So Neil and I have no financial worries; we're very fortunate in that respect. And we have two healthy, attractive children, unlike the poor Glenbournes—their George is a clever boy but, as you may or may not have learnt, little Belle is mentally retarded. As for the office, no, Neil doesn't discuss his work much, but I know it interests him, and he enjoys it.'

'Thank you. That covers a pretty wide field.' Guy Cantel smiled at her. 'Your husband is an only child, and you have just the one sister, is that right? Rosalind and Imogen—pretty names.'

Imogen found herself returning his smile. 'My mother was a romantic, or so I'm told. I don't really remember her. She was killed in a riding accident when I was five.'

'That still leaves your children with three grandparents, which is lucky for them. Do they get on well together—your children and the grandparents, I mean?'

It sounded an innocent question, but Imogen hesitated. This was a shrewd and subtle man, she thought. He lures you into a state of compliance and then casually asks you something important—or something he considers important.

'My father gets on well with both of them, but especially with Matthew. They're very close. I suppose it's because Dad never had a son of his own. Neil's parents would, I guess, prefer Verity if they had to choose.'

'Why?'

She had tried to answer truthfully, but he had

55

spotted at once that it wasn't the whole truth. 'If you must know it's because my son is a snob.'

'And your daughter isn't?'

'She's devoted to Neil and therefore she's prepared to love his mother and father. God knows how she's going to take his disappearance. Probably she'll blame me—as I'm sure they will.' Imogen concluded her statement with some bitterness.

'You've not told any of them yet?'

'No. Rosalind and Philip know, of course. And Mrs Price.'

'Your guests last night believe your husband was called to a sick mother, and couldn't phone because of a fault on the line, I gather.'

'Yes. I lied to them,' Imogen said defiantly. 'It wasn't their business.'

'Good for you.' Cantel was sympathetic.

'But I suppose they'll learn about it. Kevin Sinder's in the Foreign Office, and his wife...'

She was still talking about Joyce Sinder when the door-bell rang. Cantel's team had arrived.

CHAPTER FIVE

The two searchers came with large briefcases packed with equipment, and started their operations at the top of the house. To Imogen's surprise, one of them was a girl, younger than herself, but apparently as fast and skilful as her colleague. They worked as a team, and seemed to have little need for conversation.

Eventually the man, who had been carefully examining the instruments in one of the briefcases

56

while the girl passed what looked like a small metal detector over the walls and searched every inch of the room, said, 'Nothing on this floor, sir.'

'OK.' Guy Cantel, who had been standing with Imogen, and watching the sweep and search with close attention, accepted the verdict. 'Let's try the next one down.' He gestured to Imogen to lead the way.

These were the rooms she dreaded, the bedroom which for so many years she had shared with Neil, and the study without the silver-framed photograph on the desk. She steeled herself not to show her feelings, and was unaware that Cantel had sensed her increased anxiety. He continued to observe her closely.

They found the wall safe almost immediately. Imogen produced the key without being asked, and the contents were inspected—private papers, some jewellery and about three hundred pounds in various currencies. Cantel was interested to note that Lavery hadn't taken the money with him.

The girl searched through Imogen's clothes, while the man set up his equipment and took the telephone to pieces. Between them, they combed the room both physically and electronically, but discovered nothing. As if by agreement, they had left Neil's half of the closet space until last. The man looked enquiringly at Cantel.

'Mrs Lavery,' said Cantel, 'would you mind looking at your husband's clothes to see if anything is missing?'

'I have looked.'

'But not very carefully.'

'No.' Reluctantly Imogen made the admission. She forced herself to sort through the shelves and

57

the hanging space in more detail. Neil didn't have a great many clothes, but he insisted on the best of whatever he bought. His suits, shirts and slacks were tailored, his shoes hand-made to his own last. Everything seemed to be in order—or almost everything. Imogen was frowning as she came to an end.

'What's wrong?' Cantel asked before she could conceal her doubts.

'It's stupid,' she said. 'One or two things aren't here, but—'

'What things?'

'Well, apart from the suit and things he was wearing to go to the office, a couple of ties. One is a college tie. I can't find that and—'

'Might he have been wearing it?'

'No, I feel certain he wasn't. It has light-blue stripes on a dark background: not his favourite combination at all. The other tie is even more mysterious. It's absolutely hideous—Neil hated it—but Verity gave it to him as a birthday present, so he had to wear it occasionally when she was at home.'

'Anything else?'

'A rather distinctive cashmere sweater, a sports shirt and a pair of walking-shoes that he only wore in the country. It's such an odd collection.'

'Scarcely what you'd expect your pseudo-telephone men to have stolen?'

'And not what Neil would choose to take with him—anywhere!' Imogen answered in a burst of annoyance and disquiet.

Cantel could have made a variety of replies to this comment, but he didn't offer them. The bathroom had yielded nothing, and he suggested they went

58

into the study. He noticed the set expression on her face as she took care to avoid glancing in the direction of the desk.

'Is there something missing from here?' he asked gently.

'No!'

Imogen spoke firmly, but he knew she lied. He nodded to the searchers to go ahead. Nothing was locked and they worked quickly. Imogen leant against the door-jamb, and a less practised observer than Guy Cantel might have thought she had become indifferent to what was happening. He himself drew the contrary conclusion. And when the girl produced the passports he knew that Imogen had already discovered that Neil's was not among them. He didn't bother to question her on the point.

Meanwhile the pair had finished with their sweeping apparatus, and the man had turned his attention to the filing cabinet, which contained old income-tax returns, receipted bills, insurance policies and similar personal papers. He held out one document to Cantel, who glanced at it and turned to Imogen.

'I saw you arrive home by taxi today, but you do run a car in London, Mrs Lavery?'

'Yes, we have a Jaguar, but parking's so difficult it spends a lot of time in the garage—which is in the next street.'

'Perhaps I could see it when we've finished here?'

'Of course.'

The searchers were now at work on the books. Each was pulled from its place, shaken separately and then replaced once the space behind it on the shelf had been inspected. The twentieth book was

59

being shaken when a thick piece of paper fluttered to the carpet.

Cantel picked it up, opened it and glanced through it. 'Do you know anyone called Marta, Mrs Lavery?' he enquired.

'Marta? No, I don't think so. Who is she?'

Cantel looked at her curiously. 'Seemingly a friend of your husband's. Perhaps you'd better read this.'

Imogen took the piece of paper from him. It was a handwritten letter. There was no address, but the seven in the date was crossed in the European style, and at first glance the spiky, angular hand was unEnglish. It began, 'My darling Neil'. As Imogen took in the significance of such a greeting, her eyes involuntarily blurred with tears so that for a moment she could take in no more. Then she braced herself and continued to read:

What is the matter? You have not been to see me for days and days, and you have not telephoned. I have been so worried that I thought of phoning you at home or at your office, but you always impressed on me that I must never do either. Surely, my love, you cannot mind that I should write now.

What is it? What has happened? I cannot believe that you have stopped loving me, not after all that we have been to each other. If you are in trouble I will do everything I can to help. Please, please, my darling, get in touch with your devoted Marta soon.

The stress she had been under, lack of sleep, and now this! Imogen suddenly felt overwhelmed. She shut her eyes to stop the room revolving round her, but it didn't help. The floor was about to come up and hit her. She made an inarticulate sound and pitched forward.

Guy Cantel caught her before she reached the floor. He picked her up, carried her into the bedroom, motioning to the woman searcher to follow him, and laid her on the bed, while the searcher stood inside the door. He was surprised how light Imogen was. He fetched a glass of water from the bathroom and was holding it to her lips as, muttering 'Neil! Neil!', she opened her eyes.

She had never completely lost consciousness. She had been aware of Cantel's arms lifting and carrying her, and momentarily she had felt safe. Now, for no rational reason, she suffered a revulsion against the feeling. She sat up on the bed, nearly knocking the glass of water out of Cantel's hand.

'Thank you,' she said coldly. 'I'm sorry to have been a nuisance. It was stupid of me to faint like that. I'm quite all right now.'

Cantel, who had been sitting on the edge of the bed, stood up abruptly. 'I'm glad you're better,' he said with equal formality. 'Perhaps when you're ready we could rejoin my colleague.'

*   *   *

The search continued, but nothing else was found to be missing, and nothing came to light to incriminate Neil in the slightest. Neither had the house been bugged in any way, so that the reason for the 'Telecom' men's intrusion remained unclear.

'That's that then,' said Cantel as the searchers packed their equipment and prepared to leave.

'Thank you for your cooperation, Mrs Lavery.'

'Not at all. Is there anything else you want?'

'Your garage and the car.'

Imogen suppressed a sigh. Her overwhelming desire now was to be rid of Cantel, so that she could think about Neil—and this unknown woman, Marta. 'Yes, of course. I'd forgotten,' she said. 'I'll tell Mrs Price I'll be out for a few minutes, then I'll show you.'

The garage was only a short distance away, and they walked together in silence. Imogen handed Cantel the key and he opened the door. As he had half-expected, the garage was empty.

Once more Imogen was shocked. 'Do—do you think those men stole the car, too?' she asked. 'Or did Neil—?'

'I've no idea—not at the moment,' replied Cantel. 'When did you last see the car?' he asked as he inspected the bare space.

Imogen tried to think. 'On Sunday night,' she said finally. 'We'd been to the cottage for the weekend and we got back about nine. Neil dropped me with our various bits and pieces and brought it round here.'

'I'll need to come back and get its documents,' said Cantel, slamming the garage door shut. The lock, he noticed, would have been no deterrent to anyone. 'And this cottage of yours? You haven't mentioned it before.'

Imogen stared at him. 'Why should I?' she demanded. Then: 'It's really a small country house that belongs to my father. He rarely goes there, but there's a housekeeper and the family uses it whenever they wish.'

'The family?'

'Neil and I and our children, and the Glenbournes—Rosalind, Philip and their two. But it's only occasionally that we're all there together.'

Cantel nodded his understanding. 'Then it seems I shall have to contact your father if we need to search the property, Mrs Lavery. Perhaps it would be a good idea if you warned him that your husband has disappeared. He's going to have to know soon, and I'm sure you wouldn't want him to learn about it from another source.'

'No.' Imogen thought of her father and Neil's parents and the children. She would have to warn all of them because, as Guy Cantel was hinting, if Neil wasn't found quickly there would be a blare of publicity.

'. . . hope of keeping it out of the media,' Cantel was saying.

'No, of course not,' she agreed, though she hadn't heard what he had said. 'I'll find you the papers about the car,' she added as they reached the house.

'Thank you, Mrs Lavery.'

Cantel waited in the dining-room, and when Imogen returned with the information he required he gave her a card with a telephone number. 'If you should want to get in touch with me at any time,' he said, 'call this number, and I'll return the call just as soon as I can.'

'All right.' Imogen took the card reluctantly. 'I can't imagine why—'

'And this is very important, Mrs Lavery. If you hear from your husband, either directly or through any intermediary, I should be told at once. You understand that?'

Imogen looked at Guy Cantel and nodded her assent, though she could find no words.

* * *

It was late afternoon and Guy Cantel was in Munro Graffon's office, briefing him on the day's events.

'Do you think Mrs Lavery would inform you if Lavery or one of his chums did contact her?' Graffon regarded Cantel with amused scepticism.

'No, I don't. She was badly shaken by the letter from this Marta, but I'm sure she loves her husband.'

'Enough to follow him to Moscow?'

Cantel shrugged. He wasn't prepared to make predictions, certainly not about Imogen Lavery. He had found himself unexpectedly sympathetic towards her, but he had no intention of revealing this to Graffon.

'I asked Philip Glenbourne if he knew anything of a Marta who was associated with his brother-in-law, and he looked blank,' Cantel went on. 'I didn't explain, just said the name had cropped up and let it go at that.'

Graffon sniffed. 'Those mysterious phone men could have planted the letter, I suppose. But why? For that matter, why did they take the ties and things—if they did?'

'Including whatever was missing from the top of the study desk. It was quite obvious Mrs Lavery was worried about something in that area. I don't know why but I had a vague idea at the time that it might have been a photograph. But now we're guessing in the dark, aren't we? We don't even know if those guys were friends or enemies of Lavery's.'

64

'Friends or enemies? My dear Guy, surely you're over-complicating the problem. They must be acting for him, or they wouldn't have been so eclectic in what they took—if they did take it, as you say. No one except Lavery would want those things or, apart from his wife, even be aware of their existence.'

'Maybe not.'

'Anyway, to return to Mrs L. I've put a tail on her, and I've arranged to have her phone tapped. I don't want her suddenly disappearing too. As for Lavery himself, it's unlikely he's still in the country, but we've no actual evidence that he's skipped. There's a slim possibility he might not have left yet, and naturally the port and airport alert for him stands.'

'He's not a fool, Munro. I can't see him turning up at Heathrow and presenting his passport now, twenty-four hours after he's known to be missing.'

'Neither can I, but he may have another passport, and he might try a disguise. I agree it's a remote chance, but if he were bold enough and got away with it, think what colour our faces would be.'

For a while they continued to discuss Neil Lavery and his colleagues in the directorate who had come under suspicion. But there were too many imponderables for them to make any progress and at length Graffon produced a bottle of whisky and two glasses from a filing cabinet. It was a sign that, barring emergencies, work was over for the day.

He had poured the drinks when the telephone rang. He picked up the receiver, snapped 'Graffon,' and listened. The call was brief. He replaced the receiver and gave Cantel a sardonic smile.

'We've lost him, Guy. He's gone—to wherever

good little agents go. Lavery's Jaguar's been found on a parking lot in Dover, and a man answering his description took one of last night's ferries to Calais. Presumably it was Lavery travelling on a false passport.'

CHAPTER SIX

No one was ever quite sure how the news of Neil Lavery's disappearance came to break in the course of that night, but it seemed most likely that (in a convoluted sequence of events that was almost routine in such circumstances) an incautious remark by a senior MOD officer to a colleague at a party was overheard by another guest, who mentioned it to the editor of one of the tabloids, who happened to be present. Back at his office, the editor immediately set one of his 'investigative' reporters on the trail.

Like all such journalists he was neither omniscient nor omnipotent, but he did know how to use a telephone, and had a wide variety of contacts. Initially, there was a good deal of confusion about who had disappeared and why he might have gone and where he might have gone to, and it was not until just before the early edition went to bed that the paper's lawyers felt there was enough back-up material to risk a very short, but suggestive, story on page one. Even then, the editor decided to wait for a later edition to avoid giving his competitors too much time to match his story before daybreak.

When they did get the hint, however, the rest of

the media were not far behind, and by morning the pack was in full cry, and the Laverys' house under a full-scale press siege. Fortunately the original editor's delaying tactic, and a kind of 'reverse tip-off' from the newsroom in question, had given the authorities time to make their own preparations, and the reporters and photographers, followed later by the radio and television crews, found the house guarded by a couple of burly police officers.

Inside, Imogen Lavery, having failed to sleep until the early hours, woke late, disturbed by noises in the street below. She was not to know that she had been protected from the doorbell's ring by the police, and from the telephone's trill by a makeshift call interception system hastily organized by Cantel. Tired to the point of exhaustion, she pulled the duvet over her head and tried to ignore the unwelcome sounds, but they refused to go away.

Eventually she roused herself and reflected on the events of the previous evening. She had discussed the matter with her sister Rosalind during the afternoon, and phoned her father to tell him about Neil. As a result he had come storming round to the house. A battle of wills had inevitably followed. He had been determined that she should return with him to his apartment, so that she could distance herself from Neil and allow her father to cope with Guy Cantel and his like on her behalf. She had been equally determined that her place was at home, in case Neil should make an attempt to get in touch with her.

'Imogen, you're a fool,' her father had said. 'You've always been a fool as far as Neil Lavery's concerned, but now it's time to take stock and see sense. The man's obviously let you down—let us all down. If you won't think of yourself, think of Mat—and Verity. But it'll hit the boy hardest. The girl may shed more tears when she hears the news, but later with luck she'll marry a good chap and change her name. Mat will always be a Lavery, and that fact will haunt his life and any career he chooses.'

There was truth in what her father said, Imogen had agreed, at least some truth. Nevertheless, she had remained adamant. She would shield Matthew and Verity to the best of her ability, but not at Neil's expense. And at last her father had gone, declaring his devotion and support for her.

Alone, she had let misery overwhelm her. She had told no one, not even Rosalind, about the letter from Marta, but later, lying in bed unable to sleep, she found that her faith in Neil was capricious. At one moment she was haunted by this woman who had clearly been her husband's mistress. At other times she took the view that everyone else could condemn Neil, but she would not—not yet, not as long as she could believe in his love for her, which surprisingly enough she still did, she told herself, in spite of that damned letter. Eventually, on this thought, she had slept.

Now, awake again, wondering at the noises outside, she was startled by the trilling of the bedside phone. Automatically she stretched across and lifted the receiver. She heard muttering as if several conversations were taking place simultaneously, backed by the clatter of typewriters. Then a female voice said, 'Mrs Lavery, am I glad to get you! Would you comment for me on your husband's defection to the USSR? We'd like an exclusive, of course, and we'd pay—'

The voice was cut off, almost in mid-word. There was a moment during which the open line sang, and only inertia prevented Imogen from replacing her receiver. Then a different voice said urgently, 'It's me, Mrs Lavery—Guy Cantel. Don't hang up!'

'Mr Cantel?' Imogen was hesitant.

'Yes. Sorry about that last call. I'm coming to see you. I'll be there in five minutes.'

'Why? Has something happened? Have you heard—'

'Look out of your window. The media's on to your husband's disappearance. We're doing what we can, but—'

'Oh, God!'

*   *   *

Imogen paused only to fling on a gown and take a glance at herself in the mirror. Then, very carefully, like a character in a private eye movie, she stood beside her bedroom window and opened the curtains a slit.

An extraordinary sight met her eyes. On the pavement, kept well back by two policemen, was a collection of individuals—men and women—some with cameras or recording equipment, and two or three obvious sightseers who had chanced to pass by and been attracted by the gathering. It was lucky she thought fleetingly, that this was a day on which Mrs Price didn't come.

Then she realized that on the bottom step before the front door was Guy Cantel, standing where he could be recognized by anyone inside the house. As she watched, he was joined by a fair-haired girl, young and pretty, who had just rung the doorbell.

69

For a moment Imogen was horrified by the implications of the scene in the street. She sat on the edge of the bed, suddenly conscious of steps she had failed to take and overwhelmed with guilt. She had been so disturbed by her argument with her father the previous evening that she had done nothing about Mat and Verity—or Neil's parents. Now they would have learnt about Neil's disappearance from radio, television or the press, without prior warning to forearm them. As for Cantel and the cohorts outside, she bitterly resented them all.

But the door-bell and the telephone rang again simultaneously. Leaving the phone, she hurried down to the hall, and cautiously opened the front door. Cantel and the girl slipped in as a questioning chorus arose from the swelling assembly on the pavement and in the road. As soon as he and his companion were in the hall, Cantel said good morning, but Imogen didn't return his greeting. She was conscious of being unwashed and dishevelled, caught at a disadvantage, and this made her unresponsive.

'Mrs Lavery, I've brought Mary Derwent with me,' Cantel went on, 'because I think you're going to need help today, as time goes on and more and more of the media get organized. I'm afraid we'll have them camped in the street soon—watching your every move and awaiting any developments.' Cantel gave Imogen no chance to protest. 'Mary will answer your phone, and pass any personal calls on to you—' he had decided not to tell her of the arrangements already made to intercept all calls '—and deal with the media when it can't be avoided. She'll also answer the front door when I or

70

those who are authorized give a certain ring. In any case, she'll be in contact with them through her personal phone.' The girl produced a small handset from her shoulder-bag.

'Should I think of myself as—as a kind of prisoner then?' Imogen asked coldly.

'Certainly not,' Cantel said cheerfully, 'but you must realize that if you go out the cameras will whirr and click, questions will be fired—shouted—at you, and whatever you say will be reported in such distorted fashion that you probably won't recognize it. Faced with a story that seems likely to develop—or can be made to develop—into a national scandal, the press knows no bounds. Surely you realize that?'

Imogen nodded reluctantly. She knew that Guy Cantel was right. And he was proved so. In the course of the day coverage widened, and by the evening the story *did* show every sign of becoming a full-scale national scandal. Of course, no reporter or commentator ever actually stated that Lavery was a traitor who had fled to Moscow—after all, no one, not even the authorities, had any proof of that—but the implication was clear, and as the hours passed the distinction between fact and supposition grew more and more blurred.

But this was in the immediate future. Earlier, Imogen had had the idea that she must go out. She must see Mat and Verity and, if possible, the Laverys. Fortunately the children's schools were not far apart, but Neil's parents lived in the opposite direction. It was then she remembered that the Jaguar was no longer in its garage. She could borrow Rosalind's car, but—

'Damn!' she said aloud.

71

'What is it?'

'Have you any news of my car?'

'Your car?' Cantel indicated his surprise that she should be concerned about the Jaguar at such a moment. 'Yes,' he said slowly. 'It's been found, Mrs Lavery—at Dover. I'm afraid it won't be available to you for a day or so.'

'I need to visit my son and my daughter.' Imogen's voice was tight; she understood the implication of the car being found at a ferry port.

'I'll arrange for—'

'Sir!' Mary Derwent interrupted. While they had been talking she had gone to answer the phone ringing at the rear of the hall. 'There's a Maurice White on the line for Mrs Lavery. He says he's her son's housemaster.'

'Yes, he is. I'll talk to him.' Imogen was eager.

White had become a personal friend of the family. She liked and trusted him, and Mat admired him and respected his judgement. Imogen knew that, if anyone could help Mat at this time, it would be Maurice White.

'Maurice, you know—' she said, turning her back on Cantel and Mary Derwent so that, though they could hear what she had to say, they couldn't see her changing expressions. 'And Mat—'

'Mat's fine, Imogen. He's here with me in my study and he'll speak to you in a moment. All we know is what was on the radio and what's in today's *Times*, which is probably a garbled version of the truth. But first, are you all right?'

'Yes. I'm sorry I didn't contact you before, but—'

'I understand. This must be hell for you.'

'And for Mat. How did he hear?'

72

'George Glenbourne heard it on the radio and broke the news—and being George he broke it none too tactfully. Mat had the sense to come to me. Imogen, what's really happened? Do you know?'

She told him to the best of her ability and at length, even saying that the car had been found at Dover; the only thing she didn't mention was Marta's letter. In constant expectation that Cantel would stop her, she spoke quickly. She didn't realize that unconsciously she was putting off the moment when she must speak with Mat.

Then Mat's voice came on the line, a voice surprisingly mature for a boy of fifteen. 'Mother, this is a ghastly, sickening business. I can scarcely take it in. Can Dad really have done it? And if he has, why?' Mat was clearly hurt and angry.

'I don't know, darling. Try not to judge him too harshly.'

'I can't help it. He's buggered up all our lives.'

'Mat!'

'Well, it's true, isn't it? Cousin George says Lavery'll become a dirty word like Burgess or Maclean or Philby.'

Imogen heard Maurice White expostulate in the background and said, 'Do you want to come home, Mat?'

'No, thank you. That is, unless you want me to. There are exams coming up and a house cricket match next week.'

A cricket match! Imogen wondered at her son's priorities—and his apparent resilience. She was glad when she could say goodbye to him and Maurice White. But then she had to face the question of Verity, who had been at her present school for less than a year. Prior to that she had been a day girl in

73

London, and she hadn't taken too well to being away from home. This problem, Imogen thought, was the last thing her daughter needed at the moment.

She put through the call at once. Miss Crane, Verity's headmistress, clearly agreed. '... a dreadful thing for the child to have to take on board,' she said somewhat over-heartily, 'but that was no excuse for such an hysterical outburst. She literally flew at the girl who was accusing Mr Lavery of being a—a traitor, not to mince words. Verity knocked her down and tore her hair, and the mistress in charge had difficulty pulling her off.'

'I'm sorry,' Imogen said dully, feeling overcome. 'Is the other girl hurt?'

'Not badly. Shocked more than anything. And, between us, Mrs Lavery, to some extent she deserved it. Nevertheless—'

'What about Verity?'

'She's in the sanitorium, sleeping peacefully. I sent for the school doctor, and he gave her a very mild sedative. Matron's keeping an eye on her. She'll be all right, Mrs Lavery. Don't worry.'

Don't worry! Miss Crane meant well, Imogen thought, as the call ended with her promising to come down to the school as soon as she could. But it was useless advice. How could she help but worry, about Verity, Mat—and Neil.

She turned to Cantel. 'I'll have to speak to the Laverys, Neil's parents,' she said wearily. When he nodded she gave Mary Derwent the number, but there was no reply.

*   *   *

74

An hour later Edgar and Nora Lavery arrived in person.

Guy Cantel, aware that he had spent more time than was warranted with Imogen Lavery, had left to finish his interrogations of Neil's colleagues. Mary Derwent had continued to monitor the telephone and, alerted by a phone call and the police officer's coded ring on the bell, had admitted Rosalind Glenbourne to the house without any delay.

Imogen and Rosalind were in the kitchen drinking coffee and once again mulling over Neil's disappearance. Imogen had washed and dressed and, with her sister—to whom she could talk freely—for company, was feeling less jaded. Even in the kitchen they heard the commotion in the street.

'What on earth's that?' demanded Rosalind.

'The police having difficulty with a persistent reporter, perhaps,' Imogen suggested.

'Probably. Thanks to your Miss Derwent I had no trouble, but I'm sure they could be tough. Incidentally, Philip's not going to be pleased. I couldn't avoid having my photograph taken and he won't like to see Mrs Philip Glenbourne's face plastered over the papers tomorrow. In fact, he wasn't too keen on my coming round here at all, but I told him not to be a—'

Mary Derwent interrupted them. 'There's an elderly couple outside. He says this is his son's house, and he'll come in here whenever he pleases. He's already knocked over a cameraman and hit a policewoman. She's in tears, and the cameraman's threatening to sue. The media are having a wonderful time.'

'Damnation!' exclaimed Imogen. 'That's all we

needed. It must be my in-laws. For heaven's sake, let them in quickly before they cause any more trouble.' She hurried into the hall.

The Laverys came through the front door with a rush. Edgar a short, greying man in his late sixties, was red in the face with anger. He made no attempt to kiss or even greet Imogen. Nora was sobbing desperately. A few years younger than her husband, she still had the dark hair and deep blue eyes that she had bequeathed to Neil. Without thinking, Imogen led them into the kitchen, where Rosalind, ignored by Edgar, helped Nora into a chair.

'Would you like coffee—or some tea?' Imogen asked.

'What? Here in the kitchen?' All Edgar's rage erupted as he rounded on Imogen. 'That's what you think we're fit for, isn't it, young woman—the kitchen, the tradesmen's entrance? You've always despised us, you and your family, every single one of you except little Verity. She loves us. You know, I wouldn't be surprised if your lot weren't responsible for starting these ludicrous rumours about Neil.'

'For heaven's sake, Edgar!' his wife protested. 'You mustn't say such things.'

'Shut up!' He quashed his wife effectively, and turned to point at Mary Derwent. 'Who are you? You stand there, listening to private conversations and—'

Mary Derwent didn't give her name. 'Security,' she snapped. 'But you needn't worry, Mr Lavery. We already have a very complete file on Neil Lavery from his schooldays on.'

There was a moment's complete silence. Edgar Lavery's face went a deeper purple. Nora stopped weeping. Mary Derwent, happily in control of the situation, smiled at Imogen.

'I shall be leaving now, Mrs Lavery,' she announced. 'We've made other arrangements for your telephone. If there's any doubt about the caller, the call will be referred to you first.'

'But—' Imogen didn't know why she was disappointed; she hadn't been pleased when Cantel had originally brought the girl in.

Mary Derwent allowed her no time for further comment. She wasn't going to explain that the hastily organized and makeshift arrangement in the empty house for sale across the street had now been superseded by a fully manned and sophisticated operation, to supervise and record all phone calls, and to observe and photograph all comings and goings at the Laverys'.

'The police officers will keep the press at bay, and deal with any unwelcome visitors,' she continued. 'If they're in doubt you'll be phoned. Just lift your receiver if you want to get in touch with us. And I'm to tell you that Mr Cantel will phone or drop by later in the day. Is that all right, Mrs Lavery?'

'Yes—thank you,' Imogen said weakly, fairly sure that she wasn't to be offered any alternatives.

Mary Derwent departed. Imogen took the Laverys up to the drawing-room, while Rosalind prepared a light lunch for the four of them. Edgar Lavery, by now a little calmer, asked endless questions about Neil and the security people, most of which Imogen couldn't answer.

For her part Nora contributed unhelpful comments about the iniquity of sending children to boarding-schools at tender ages and thus breaking

77

up family life; once that happened, she maintained, you never knew what might follow.

Eventually Neil's parents rose to go. Imogen, who had managed to keep her temper in spite of their obvious belief that, if Neil had defected, the fault was primarily hers, saw them leave with relief. To her amusement Edgar Lavery had not been eager to meet again the police officer and the cameraman he had assaulted on arrival, and she had to assure him that there was no back way out of the house. In the end Rosalind had departed with them, and escorted them to their car, parked some distance along the road.

It was a comfort for Imogen to find herself alone. She cleared up the luncheon and, resisting the temptation to telephone her father, who would be busy at his office, went upstairs to have a rest. She slept almost at once.

*   *   *

When she awoke two hours later she turned on the small television set to listen to the news. It had already begun. The lead item was the unexplained disappearance of Neil Lavery, senior Civil Servant, employed in a sensitive area of the Ministry of Defence. There was a photograph of herself and Neil at their wedding and another of Neil playing cricket, live views of their 'expensive Knightsbridge residence' and finally clear pictures of Edgar Lavery's attack on the policewoman and the cameraman. Imogen turned off the set.

She couldn't know that Verity in her school's sanitorium was also watching the programme, and loudly applauding Edgar Lavery's behaviour.

78

CHAPTER SEVEN

Guy Cantel was watching the same television news, as were hundreds of thousands of other individuals throughout Great Britain. He felt no special sympathy for the senior Laverys, but he blamed himself for the incident, which he thought he could well have foreseen. He was alone in his flat, having returned home after a series of interviews and interrogations which had taken the inquiry little further forward. He had found time to shower and change his shirt to refresh himself for the evening, for his day's work was still unfinished.

He had debated with himself about his next move, and had decided to pay an unexpected call on Joy Aubyn, Neil Lavery's assistant. She intrigued him. Of all the people connected with Lavery whom he had met, she had shown the most tension and anxiety, and it seemed to him that she had been the most reticent—even secretive. But what had prompted him to investigate further so soon was a casual remark thrown into the pot by Kevin Sinder, whom he had seen that afternoon: the suggestion that Joy Aubyn and Neil might have been lovers.

Cantel collected his car from the garage beneath his apartment block, and set off for Hampstead where Joy Aubyn lived in a flat in a converted house. He knew that he was probably wasting his time; Miss Aubyn might easily have gone out for the evening. But it was worth the risk. He wanted to surprise her, to shock her, if possible to shake out of her whatever she was concealing.

He parked the car outside the house in a pleasant,

79

tree-lined street, and studied the bells beside the front door. J. Aubyn appeared to live in Flat 2B. There seemed no option but to ring her bell and speak to her on the entryphone, though that would give her the option of refusing to open the door to him. Chance, however, intervened. An elderly lady carrying a cumbersome parcel emerged from the house. Cantel hastened to hold the heavy door for her, and smiled encouragingly at her thanks. As she went down the narrow path to the pavement he slipped into the building.

His first impression was that the place was well kept. The hall and stairs were thickly carpeted, and there were fresh flowers on a table to one side; even a small flat here would be expensive. Cantel avoided the lift, though it was clearly modern, and walked slowly up the stairs. He found Flat 2B without difficulty and put his thumb on the bell. He had already determined on his approach to Miss Aubyn.

There was no response, so he tried again, this time keeping a finger on the bell. Then he lifted the flap of the letter-box, and bent to peer inside. He could see a light shining through a half-open door, and could hear the murmur of voices. He banged with his fist on the door panel. The murmur ceased. If the noise had come from a radio or television, someone had turned off the set.

He called softly but clearly through the letter-box, 'Miss Aubyn, if you don't answer your bell within ten seconds I'll raise such mayhem that you'll regret it.' He really had no idea what he meant by this threat, but he suspected that Joy Aubyn would not be prepared to risk whatever he might have in mind.

Cantel waited until he saw her coming along the

hall towards him, and then he released the flap. By the time she opened the door she was knotting the sash on her gown, but he knew that underneath she was naked. He was not concerned. It was the apprehension in her face that interested him.

'What do you want?' she demanded. 'I was just going to have a bath.'

It was an obvious lie. There was little doubt that she had been with a lover. He could hear someone moving in the room he assumed to be the bedroom. He pushed Joy aside and made for the door, now shut but with light still shining around the edges. She followed him, expostulating and trying to hold him back, and for one hopeful moment he wondered if Sinder had been right and he was about to discover the missing Neil Lavery.

As Cantel flung open the bedroom door this hope was immediately dashed. The man who turned to swear at him bore no resemblance to Neil Lavery. He was fair-haired and brown-eyed, with classical features and a tall, solid body. He had clearly just struggled into his trousers, and was tucking in his open shirt as he glared at Cantel.

'Who are you? What is it you want? Is this blackmail? The famous honey-trap? Because I do not pay.' His English was good but the man had a definite accent.

'British security,' Cantel snapped. There was no point in dissembling; Joy Aubyn was perfectly well aware of his identity.

'So it *is* a set-up? Girl lures foreign diplomat to her bed. It's an old story, Mr British security. My ambassador will appreciate it.'

'No! No, that's not true, Stefan. He's as much a surprise to me as to you. I love you. I swear it.'

Joy Aubyn was pulling at her lover's arm, hindering him from dressing. Cantel walked across the room to the chest of drawers where Stefan had neatly piled the contents of his pockets, and picked up the passport.

Stefan Cheski was a Cultural Attaché at the Polish Embassy in London, or at least that was his official title. Cantel smiled grimly. Cheski's relationship with Joy Aubyn could be innocent, but his character was far from being a desirable boy-friend for a girl who held a sensitive post in the Ministry of Defence. Cantel replaced the passport.

'OK, Monsieur Cheski,' he said. 'I know where to find you if I need you, but at present my business is with Miss Aubyn. I'll wait in the sitting-room. Five minutes.'

It was nearer ten before Joy Aubyn joined him. He had heard them whispering in the hall and the slam of the front door. Then there was a pause, during which Joy had obviously thrown on some clothes. When she appeared she was wearing slacks and a shocking pink sweater that made a dazzling contrast with her hair. She was still bare-footed, but she was much more composed than she had been at their first meeting in the Ministry. Cantel could only suppose that it was because her secret was a secret no longer.

Joy Aubyn flung herself into an armchair. 'You said your business was with me, Mr Cantel. Well, here I am, under protest. What do you want?'

Guy Cantel regarded her calmly. He would have given much to know more of her thoughts and her feelings. 'What I want are truthful answers to some questions,' he said at last. 'First, how long have you and Cheski been having it off?'

82

Joy's nose wrinkled with distaste at the brutal expression Cantel had deliberately used, but she made no attempt to camouflage the facts. Indeed, Cantel was surprised at her candour.

'We've been lovers for six months,' she said. 'We met at a party after the opening of an exhibition at the Tate Gallery. Stefan asked me for a date and I was delighted. It didn't matter that he was a Pole. He's not interested in politics, but in painting and music and really important subjects. He's a Cultural Attaché, Mr Cantel—not a spy of some kind.'

'I see,' said Cantel, wondering if she really could be as naïve as she appeared. 'And did you ever discuss your work with him?'

'Sometimes, but only in the most general fashion—the fact that I'm a Civil Servant, for instance.' Joy leant forward in her chair, her face tense. 'You don't understand, do you, Mr Cantel? I love Stefan Cheski. I love him enough to go back to Poland with him when his tour of duty here is over.'

'Has he asked you?'

The question startled Joy. 'Not—not perhaps in so many words,' she admitted. 'But he knows I'll go with him. I'd do anything rather than give him up.'

It was Guy Cantel's turn to be startled—at the apparent intensity of her feelings. He had retained only a fleeting impression of his brief meeting with Cheski, but even so had some difficulty in convincing himself that Miss Aubyn's emotions were reciprocated. He decided to change the subject.

'Before you met Stefan Cheski, I assume you had other lovers. Was Neil Lavery one of them?' he enquired.

'Lavery! No, of course not. The idea's ludicrous! When I met Stefan I was leading a celibate life. I'd had a long-term affair with a married man—a television producer, nothing to do with the MOD or anywhere like that. Then his wife got pregnant, and I knew he'd never leave her. So I broke it off.'

'And you found no consolation with Lavery?'

'Dear God, you're persistent, Mr Cantel!' Joy Aubyn shook her head in exasperation. 'The answer's still no. Neil was my boss, and we were on good terms. But that was all. He never once so much as made a pass at me. For what it's worth it's my opinion that he was in love with his wife and devoted to his family.'

Cantel found himself believing her, and accepting her judgement of Lavery. The woman Marta had still to be explained, but he couldn't visualize Lavery as a casual philanderer.

'Have you any idea why Lavery should have gone over—if he has?' he asked.

Joy shrugged. She seemed almost uninterested in the subject. 'It's not always ex-public schoolboys—like Kevin Sinder, for example—who turn that way,' she replied.

'Why mention Sinder?' Cantel probed at once.

'Well, you seem to be so intrigued by my love-life,' she said, amused, 'and I did find some consolation, as you call it, with Kevin before I met Stefan.'

A strange woman, Guy Cantel mused as he ran down the stairs and let himself out of the house. He didn't know whether or not to believe her about Sinder. He wouldn't put it past her to try to muddy the waters out of sheer perversity. He reached his car, and the telephone claimed his attention at once.

84

He listened, his expression grim, until the security officer on watch in the house opposite the Laverys' stopped speaking. 'OK,' he said. 'I'm on my way. Keep in touch.'

Cantel drove fast, glad of the action. Marta had made an unexpected appearance, and now had a surname. She had driven up to the Laverys' house in a taxi, and asked the policeman on duty to tell Mrs Lavery that Miss Marta Stein, an old friend of Neil Lavery, would like to speak to her on an urgent matter. She had been admitted, and had been with Mrs Lavery for some ten or fifteen minutes.

The car-phone was trilling again as Cantel reached the Knightsbridge area. He was stopped at a red light a short distance from the Laverys' house, and was fretting at the delay. 'Yes?' he snapped.

'The lady is just leaving, sir.'

Guy Cantel swore under his breath. 'Which way?'

'East. Towards the top of Sloane Street. I'd guess she was looking for a taxi.'

'Can you describe her?'

'Five foot six approx. A bit plump. Dark-haired. Wearing a bright red coat. Difficult to miss.'

Cantel grunted. In the distance he had spotted a small red figure waving at a taxi which sailed past her. The figure walked on. The lights in front of Cantel changed, and he had to move. He was drawing nearer to his quarry, but he was on the opposite side of the road, and going in the wrong direction. There was no time to get any back-up cars. If she stopped a taxi—

She did. Cantel, praying he would hit nothing, wrenched his wheel around. There was a squeal of brakes behind him, but the road was wide and he made a successful U-turn. The problem now was to follow the taxi that contained Marta Stein through the evening traffic.

Luckily for Cantel the journey was fairly short—round Hyde Park Corner, down Grosvenor Place beside the Palace and along Victoria Street. He was a mere hundred yards behind when the taxi drew up in front of a block of seemingly gloomy mansion flats near Westminster Cathedral. He was out of his car and striding towards the woman in the red coat while the cab driver was still finding change.

'Miss Stein? Miss Marta Stein?' he asked.

'Yes. Who are you?'

She was attractive, he thought, in a simple but agreeable style, and she was well dressed. But there was nothing outstanding about her appearance or her personality, unless it was her composure. She had shown no surprise at being accosted by a strange man who knew her name.

'Guy Cantel. Security.' Again there seemed little point in concealing his mission. He offered her an identity card, but she barely glanced at it.

'Come along in, Mr Cantel,' she answered at once. 'I was expecting you, or someone like you.'

Miss Stein's flat was on the ground floor. The furniture was modern and impersonal, with only two items of interest. One was a grand piano, the other a photograph of Neil Lavery in a leather frame. Without seeking Miss Stein's permission, Cantel walked straight across the room, picked up the photograph and examined it with care.

The print was an enlargement of an excellent Polaroid shot. It was signed, 'For Marta, with much love from Neil'. As far as Cantel could

86

remember, the handwriting looked like Lavery's, but he knew it could be a copy or a trace. And why should this Marta Stein be so eager to claim involvement with Neil Lavery?

'A drink, Mr Cantel?' said Marta Stein, ignoring his interest in the photograph.

'Thank you, no.'

'Why not? After all, you're not a policeman, and I badly need one myself. I've just had a very trying time with Imogen Lavery. I'm sorry for her, of course, but it's not easy for me either, and she could have been more sympathetic.'

'Can you expect the wife to be sympathetic to the—the mistress?' Cantel demanded, not disguising his coldness.

Marta Stein smiled sadly. 'I told her that he loved her—and the children. I told her the truth, that if it ever came to a choice between them and me, he would have given me up. Regretfully, I believe, but without a second thought.'

Cantel put down the photograph and moved over to take the chair to which she had waved him. Marta had gone to what looked like a 1930s cocktail cabinet and he noticed that her hand shook as she sloshed gin into a glass. He said, 'May I change my mind and have a gin and tonic with you?'

'My pleasure.' She brought him the drink and sat opposite him. 'Now for the questions, I suppose. What do I know about Neil?'

'First, tell me about yourself.'

'There's little to tell. I was born in Germany—West Germany—but my mother was English and I've lived in this country for ten years. I am thirty-three years old, unmarried. I work as a secretary, a "temp".' She mentioned the name of a well-known firm that provided temporary staff for businesses. She also, she said, did some freelance typing, which was how she had met Neil Lavery. He had been asked to write a series of articles for a magazine, and didn't think it fair to ask his own secretary to type them.

'That was two years ago, Mr Cantel. We were immediately drawn to each other, and we became lovers. Then a few months ago Neil seemed to become very worried. I asked him why he was so tense, so on edge, but he wouldn't tell me. Perhaps I persisted too much because suddenly he stopped coming to see me. And he didn't phone. Just a blank. I didn't know what to do. Eventually I wrote him a note, but no answer. And now...'

★   ★   ★

Marta Stein produced names, dates, facts which could be checked, and certainly would be checked. But her story was consistent, and there was no immediate cause to doubt it. To Cantel her reason for visiting Imogen Lavery—that she hoped Imogen might know more about Neil's position than had appeared in the media—seemed thin but, if she were really in love with him, as she maintained, it was by no means totally preposterous. Nevertheless, the fact remained that, had she not made herself known to Imogen, the Marta of the letter slipped into one of Neil Lavery's books might never have been traced.

'Another strange character,' Guy Cantel said to himself out loud as he drove home. 'I'm a suspicious bastard, I suppose.' Which was fair enough; being suspicious was an important part of his job. However, it was not within his remit to be prejudiced in anyone's favour, so when he telephoned Imogen Lavery later that evening, he kept the conversation brief and businesslike.

CHAPTER EIGHT

Guy Cantel sat at the breakfast bar in his kitchen drinking coffee and brooding over Imogen and Neil Lavery, a small pile of newspapers at his side.

It was Saturday morning, four days since Lavery had failed to return home from his office in the Ministry of Defence—and plenty of time for him to have reached Moscow, if that were indeed his destination. So far there had been no announcement from the Soviet capital that a most senior and important British Civil Servant had defected to the USSR, but it was still early for anything of that kind. It would almost certainly come, Cantel thought with resignation, sooner or later, public and jubilant or passed through discreet channels, depending on how the Soviet authorities in their present dubious state wanted to play the game.

The British media had already anticipated such a story. Cantel skimmed through the feature he was reading, threw it aside in disgust and poured himself yet another cup of coffee. Then his eye caught a name—Hank Christiansen—sprawled across a headline in one of the tabloids. An enterprising reporter had apparently interviewed, or claimed to have interviewed, all those who had been guests at the Laverys' dinner party—the party without a host, as he called it.

Most of the statements the journalist had collected had been noncommittal. Philip Glenbourne was reported to have commented that the whole business was a tragedy for the family. Joyce Sinder had said how sorry she was for poor Imogen. Cecil Green, who had been at Oxford with Neil, recalled that the missing man had once, probably because he was drunk, refused to stand for 'God Save the Queen'.

It was not a particularly edifying piece, and would have been of little interest if the people mentioned had not included Christiansen. Cantel knew that Munro Graffon had himself called on the American, and had promised to do his best to save Christiansen from any unfortunate publicity. This had clearly proved a hollow promise. Fortunately Hank Christiansen's job was not identified in the paper, but still the CIA would not be pleased.

Guy Cantel sighed. To him it was one of the minor mysteries of the affair that Neil Lavery should have invited the Christiansens to dinner if he had not intended to be present. Had he deliberately tried to compromise Hank Christiansen, or cause the Americans embarrassment and adverse publicity? Or hadn't Lavery known that he would not be present that evening?

As Cantel ruminated, the telephone trilled. Apart from the office, only his immediate family and a few close friends knew his unlisted home number, so he was surprised to find the duty officer on the line. But the message itself was surprising. Imogen Lavery wanted him to get in touch with her urgently.

And clearly she had been waiting for him to phone because she answered at the first ring. 'Guy.

Er—Mr Cantel. It's Verity, my daughter,' she exclaimed, her voice choked with emotion. 'She—she's disappeared too!'

Cantel wasted no time on sympathy. 'Have you any details?'

'According to Miss Crane, the headmistress, the school matron saw her about ten o'clock last night in the sanitorium. She was almost asleep then, because about half an hour before Matron had given her one of the mild tranquillizers the doctor had prescribed. This morning her bed was—was empty. They're searching the school premises and the grounds, but—Mr Cantel, I'm afraid.'

'Of course you are! First, give me a description—colouring, height, weight.' Guy Cantel made some quick notes. 'OK, Mrs Lavery. Now phone Mat's school and make certain he's all right. Then collect the latest photographs you have of Verity. I'll send a messenger round for them immediately. And wait for me. I'll be with you within half an hour, and I'll drive you down to Verity's school.'

'Should I tell the police?'

'No. Leave that to me. I'll set some inquiries in motion, but let's not give the media another sensation unless it's unavoidable. I suspect the school won't be anxious for publicity, either. So you'd better not tell anyone, except—' He paused and thought. 'Where might Verity have gone? Your sister, Rosalind, would have let you know if she'd turned up there, and anyway the Glenbournes live so close to you. Your father?'

'He'd have phoned me at once. But she might have gone to the cottage. I'll check with the housekeeper.'

'What about the Laverys, Neil's parents?'

'Yes,' said Imogen reluctantly. 'It's a possibility. She might have gone to them, but—'

'Don't worry.' Cantel understood the situation. 'I'll get Mary Derwent on to that angle. She's very good at asking tactful questions. If you'll cope with the rest, doing your best not to raise a storm—'

'Yes, indeed.' Imogen's voice shook. 'And thank you.'

The continuing police presence outside the Laverys' house and the passing hours had discouraged some of the media men and most of the merely curious, but there was still a whirr and click of cameras, some shouted questions and the odd abusive remark as Cantel hurried Imogen into his car. Faces pressed briefly at the windows while he fastened his seatbelt and started the engine. Conscious of Imogen beside him, stiff and upright, staring straight ahead of her, he accelerated fiercely down the street.

But he didn't fail to notice the white Ford that drew out from the kerb as he passed, or the motor-cycle that swung in front of it, successfully blocking the Ford's progress. The motor-cyclist, his job done for the moment, would join them later. The Ford, Cantel hoped, would have lost them. He had no desire to be followed to Verity's school, and so fuel the papers with more gossip.

'Do up your seatbelt,' he said gently. 'Or you'll get me fined.'

'Sorry!' Imogen did as she was told. 'I don't understand!' she went on in a sudden burst of emotion. 'The reporters, yes—the cameramen. They have a job to do. But that young woman back there—what right had she to call me a "traitor's whore"? She doesn't know me, or Neil. She doesn't know anything about us and yet—'

'There are always people like that about,' Cantel said soothingly. 'They're the kind who would enjoy a public hanging, Mrs Lavery.'

'Oh, for God's sake! Don't be so patronizing, *Mr* Cantel,' Imogen responded irritably, 'and stop calling me Mrs Lavery. My name, as you know perfectly well, is Imogen.'

'OK, Imogen. Mine as *you* know perfectly well—is Guy. Incidentally, did you do all the things I asked?'

'Yes. I found a whole collection of photos of Verity, and gave them to your messenger. I kept a couple in my bag for you to see. And I phoned the people you mentioned. Neither Rosalind nor my father has seen or heard from Verity, and she hasn't gone to our cottage.'

'You cautioned them about keeping quiet?'

'Yes.'

'And Matthew?'

'He's fine.' Imogen shook her head ruefully. 'He's no idea where she is, but he said that if she's gone after her father she's a fool. She'll never reach him, and even if she did, he wouldn't want her.'

'Do you think that's what she's done? Has she a passport?'

'A passport, yes—for school trips and holidays. As for going to her father—possibly. It seems a logical explanation. What else is there? That Neil arranged to have her kidnapped? If that's what's happened I'll never forgive him.' Imogen was bitter.

'Wait! We'll know more when we get to the school.' Cantel didn't add that Verity's name and description had already been circulated to all ports and airports. 'Incidentally, I heard from Mary Derwent. She's been in touch with Edgar and Nora Lavery. Verity hasn't gone to them.'

Imogen nodded her acceptance of this news. She wasn't sure whether to be glad or not. Edgar Lavery's smugness would have been difficult to take if Verity had fled to them. But she was ashamed that her feelings should be so mixed. All that was important was that Verity should be safe.

At this point Cantel spotted the motor-bike safely behind them again. The rider flashed his lights as a signal that all was well, and Cantel waved to him. There was no longer any sign of the white Ford.

After this they drove in silence for a while, but it was a companionable one. Imogen, gazing out of the window, appeared to have relaxed a little and Cantel wondered about Verity, and the kind of child she was.

He was surprised when Imogen suddenly said, 'Tell me about yourself, Guy. I know nothing about you and yet—you seem to be running my life.'

'That's something of an illusion. It'll soon pass.'

'Oh, sure. Life will go on, but not as it was—whatever happens.'

Cantel had not heard her sound so cynical before, and there was no comment he could usefully make. He knew that she was right. The last few days had irreparably changed her whole life. For distraction he began to talk about himself.

'I come from a medical family,' he said. 'My father and elder brother are both doctors, and my young sister will be qualifying shortly. But I wasn't that way inclined. All I really liked doing was playing cricket. I played for my school and my

94

university. I got my Blue. Then I drifted into my present job...'

Guy Cantel continued to talk. He didn't mention that his father was one of the country's leading ophthalmic surgeons, and his mother a best-selling novelist. He didn't say he had been at Eton and Oxford, or that he had taken a First Class Honours degree. Imogen was listening with obvious interest when she suddenly interrupted him.

'Here we are,' she said. 'This is the school. The big wrought-iron gates on the left.'

*   *   *

An anxious Miss Crane was waiting for them in her study. She foresaw unpleasant publicity for the school and for herself if, as now seemed certain, Verity Lavery had run away. She had to make an effort to greet warmly both Mrs Lavery and the young man with her. Imogen introduced Guy Cantel by name but, except to say that he had driven her down, gave no explanation for his presence. He immediately made it clear, however, that he was there to conduct an inquiry. Miss Crane began to bristle.

'Perhaps you would care to speak to Matron yourselves?' she said at length. 'I can assure you that she's highly qualified and most experienced. She's not the kind of person to mistake a pillow in the bed for a young girl's body.'

'Nevertheless—' said Cantel, unsmiling.

Miss Crane went to the door of her study and spoke to the secretary in the next room. On return she pointedly addressed herself to Imogen. 'I'm afraid Verity has never settled down here, Mrs

95

Lavery, and of course this—this tragedy would be devastating for any child. I can't believe she'll ever be happy here now.'

Before Imogen could reply Matron tapped on the door and was introduced. She was a young woman, in her early thirties, and was obviously very nervous. Cantel rephrased his earlier query about a pillow. She shook her head violently.

'No! I spoke to Verity and she answered me. I saw her face. She was there at ten last night. This morning, at seven-thirty, she'd gone.'

'And she's nowhere in the school,' said Miss Crane. 'Mistresses and senior girls have searched and double-searched the premises and the grounds. They've looked everywhere, in cupboards and storerooms and outbuildings.'

Cantel nodded. 'What about clothes, Matron?'

'Her nightdress was on the floor. She must have put on the clothes she was wearing when she came to the san. Grey skirt and white blouse. The school uniform.'

'No coat? It would have been cold early in the morning. And no money, or very little, I assume, if she left straight from the sanitorium.' Cantel seemed to be thinking aloud. 'Would you say that on the whole she was a sensible, practical child?'

'Yes,' Imogen said decisively, and Matron agreed, though Miss Crane looked dubious.

'So the chances are that someone helped her. Who are her close friends? We need to talk to them.'

'There's Lavin—' began Matron.

The headmistress overrode her. 'As I said, Verity hasn't really settled down here, and she had no one I would call a close friend.'

96

'Then we'll have to talk to this Lavin. Lavinia?'

'The Honourable Lavinia Broughton-Mills,' said Miss Crane. 'I hardly think—'

'Ah!' said Cantel. 'If she's as clever as her politician father I'm sure she'll be able to help us.'

To the headmistress's annoyance he was proved right. Lavinia, once her scruples about breaking her promises of silence had been overcome, was certainly helpful. She had been to see Verity in the sanitorium the previous day. She had tried, but failed, to dissuade Verity from an attempt to join her father, on the grounds that no one knew where he was and that it might be dangerous for her to travel alone. Eventually, however, she had succumbed to Verity's entreaties and had agreed to help. She had packed a bag with extra clothes, chocolate bars, toilet articles, all the money she could collect, a map of Europe and 'other bits and pieces that might be useful', and had hidden it, with a coat, near the school gates for Verity to pick up as she left.

However, Lavinia couldn't tell them what she didn't know. Verity had refused to disclose how she expected to reach her father.

★   ★   ★

Guy Cantel, maintaining that for the moment everything possible was being done to track down Verity, insisted that he and Imogen should stop for lunch on the way back to London. He knew of a small country hotel where it was unlikely they would be recognized or would meet anyone known to them, and had phoned ahead for a reservation. Imogen had protested, but was now glad to be sitting in the bar drinking a gin and tonic. Cantel had managed to inspire her with at least some confidence.

'Verity will be found within twenty-four hours,' he had predicted. 'You must be thankful that Neil and his—his supposed friends had nothing to do with it. Or—a possibility I haven't mentioned before—that because of the publicity you've had someone or some group might have kidnapped her on spec, as it were. That's happened before. But instead it seems to be fairly straightforward. A small, unhappy girl has run away to join her father—if she can. She won't get very far, Imogen.'

'I hope to God not.' Imogen finished her drink and sighed. 'I feel as if I've aged about ten years since Neil left,' she said, smiling ruefully.

Cantel returned her smile. 'Let's go and eat.' He offered her a hand and pulled her from her chair. 'You did say you weren't hungry, but—'

The food was excellent, perfectly cooked and pleasantly served. Cantel insisted that Imogen should have a half-bottle of wine, though he drank nothing but mineral water. He asked her about her childhood, and the years before she married, and, as they ate and drank and talked, the tension gradually seeped out of her. They might have been old friends, even lovers, enjoying each other's company.

Cantel was loath to spoil the atmosphere, but he had to ask her about Marta Stein's visit the previous evening, and he couldn't leave it until they were in the car. He wanted to watch her face when she spoke of Marta. A chance remark over coffee gave him his opportunity, but at once he felt her withdraw from him.

'Yes,' Imogen replied slowly. 'This woman came to see me. She said that she had been Neil's—mistress for two years, and she was desperately worried about his disappearance. It was as if—as if it was more important to her than it was to me. Then she was kind enough to say Neil would never have left me and the children for her. I could have hit her!' Imogen concluded with sudden passion.

'But did you believe her?' It was a vital question, but Cantel tried to make it sound casual.

'Yes. God knows I didn't want to,' Imogen said miserably. 'I'd told myself there could be an explanation for that letter your searchers found, that perhaps the woman was mad—you do read about people getting a crush on someone they've never even met—but Marta Stein is obviously sane. And it's shattering. I thought I knew Neil. I thought I could trust him. Now I have to accept both that he's been a traitor—a spy—for years, and that he's been cheating on me as well! Our life together was just one blasted lie!'

Her pain was so obvious that involuntarily Cantel said, 'My dear, it may not have been like that. This woman Marta could be exaggerating—'

'Why should she? They were lovers. She proved it. She knew things about Neil's body that only a wife or lover could possibly know. She—'

Abruptly Imogen pushed back her chair and fled to the cloakroom. Cantel paid the bill and waited for her in the lounge. When she rejoined him her eyes were red, but she was composed. And once again they were strangers.

CHAPTER NINE

Sunday was a day of mixed sentiments among those involved, professionally or emotionally, with the Laverys.

'It's infuriating!' Philip Glenbourne flung the heavy newspaper on to the kitchen floor. 'Who told them? How did they find out that Verity had gone?'

'Gone where, Da?'

'To Moscow, if you believe the reporters.'

'Philip!' Rosalind protested, frowning at him from behind Belle's chair.

Philip paid no attention to his wife's warning. 'This is going to add another whole dimension to Neil's defection,' he went on. 'It makes a wonderful sob-story. Nothing could be better for keeping the public's interest alive. Damn Verity!'

'No. Da! No. Not angry with Verity.'

Belle began to cry, and Rosalind glanced at her husband in exasperation. On Sundays the nurse who normally took care of the little girl liked to go to church, and the Glenbournes had got into the habit of making it a 'family' day, beginning with breakfast together. Philip, who was in fact extremely fond of his beautiful, retarded daughter, often said he didn't see enough of her, and usually made a big effort on these occasions. But today he was clearly in a disheartened and melancholy mood.

'She doesn't understand,' he said irritably.

'She often understands more than you'd think,' Rosalind retorted, taking Belle on to her lap and rocking her gently. 'It's all right, darling. Da isn't angry with Verity. He loves her. We all love her.'

100

'Where Verity?' Belle stuck to the point.

'She's at school, Belle.' Rosalind hated to lie to the child, but there seemed no alternative; explanations would be far too complex for Belle to comprehend. 'Come on, darling. Finish your breakfast.'

Philip reached across the table and poured himself another cup of coffee. His mind had been pursuing a different tack, unrelated to Belle. 'You know, Rosalind,' he said, 'we're not doing any good by pretending that nothing's happened. We've got to face the facts. Actually, I don't think I've got much choice about that, considering the way my colleagues at the Ministry have started to look askance at me.'

'But, Philip, that's absurd! You're not responsible for Neil. None of us are.'

'Maybe not. But, quite apart from the office, I bet you'll find our friends won't be phoning us so much and there'll be a dearth of invitations in the weeks to come. You'd better start getting used to the idea.'

'When and if I have to.' Rosalind was short. 'After all, Joyce Sinder phoned on Friday to ask us to dinner, and we had an invite to a drinks party yesterday.'

'Largely curiosity, I suspect. You wait and see.'

Philip pushed back his chair and stood up. He began to collect the Sunday papers scattered over the table and the floor. Rosalind watched him with annoyance. Belle, who sensed the tension in the room, was whimpering again.

'I'll be in my study,' Philip said curtly.

'All right,' said Rosalind, resigned to the fact that

101

the family was about to face a difficult and demanding day.

*   *   *

Guy Cantel's reaction to the Sunday papers was very similar to Philip Glenbourne's. He had hoped to keep Verity's unorthodox departure from her school out of the public domain, at least until she was found; the mere fact of her reappearance would cause the story to lose much of its news value. But he supposed that that had been almost impossible; word must have spread around the school, and schoolgirls and their mistresses talked.

What was even more disturbing was his knowledge that so far there were no indications that Verity had been seen by anyone, anywhere. She could have walked only a limited distance from the school before daybreak, when someone in the vicinity should have noticed her. The inquiries they had been able to make had been limited by the hope of avoiding publicity, but there was no evidence that she had taken a bus, or been seen at the local railway station. One obvious explanation was that she had been given a lift, but this was not a suggestion that relieved Cantel's concern. Children of twelve on their own were always at risk, and the possible consequences of Verity being picked up by a stranger were not pleasant to contemplate.

He thought of telephoning Imogen, but he had no news to impart, and to hear him on the line would only raise momentary false hopes. He spent a while considering the situation, and decided, with some reluctance, to trade on the fact that Verity Lavery's disappearance had now become public knowledge, and arrange for a full police search.

This would mean, as he knew well, that Imogen and all the family would suffer from yet more publicity and speculation about the absent Laverys, but that couldn't be helped. It was imperative that the child be found—alive if possible.

Guy Cantel was a sensible man. He was accustomed to analyzing the motives and behaviour of others, and he didn't spare himself. He knew that he was very attracted to Imogen Lavery, though he had known her only a few days, and he accepted that it was an absurd situation, and one he must not permit to get out of hand.

He shook his head, and wondered idly which of the girls he knew might be free to drive into the country that evening, and have supper at some pleasant pub.

*   *   *

Joy Aubyn didn't take a Sunday paper, and it was not until she was making herself brunch and switched on her radio that she learnt that Verity Lavery had seemingly run away from school, presumably to join her father. Joy was not surprised, or particularly interested. She was looking forward to her day. Stefan Cheski was coming to dinner with her.

She hadn't seen him since Friday, when Guy Cantel had interrupted their love-making, but in the hall, as he left, Stefan had whispered that he would be there on Sunday. She had spent the previous day shopping for a variety of luxuries for him and preparing the meal, though she still had a good deal to complete.

After she had cleared away her brunch Joy

decided to wash her hair. She was in the bathroom rinsing her head under the shower when she heard the snap of the letter-box flap. She lifted her face, promptly got some shampoo in her eye and swore. She would have to wait to discover what had come. There was no post on Sunday, of course, so whatever it was must have been delivered by an unofficial hand. It was either from one of her neighbours—perhaps an invitation—or someone had found a letter in the downstairs hall and had been kind enough to bring it up to her.

Joy towelled her hair dry, wound a towel turban-fashion round her head, and put on a robe. She was secretly proud of her red hair, and was happy that she would be looking her best for Stefan that evening. She went into the hall. There was a white envelope on the carpet, her name typed on the front.

No more than mildly curious, Joy went into the bedroom, sat at the dressing-table and slit the envelope with a nail file. The letter inside was brief. It read:

Dear Joy,
This is to say goodbye. It is unfortunately clear that you are at present an object of interest to your security authorities and, as I am sure you appreciate, this makes it impossible for our friendship to continue, totally innocent as it was.
With all best wishes for your future happiness.
Sincerely,
Stefan.

Joy Aubyn read the letter twice before she absorbed the meaning of the carefully drafted, stilted

104

phrases. Even then, absurdly, her first thought was that if only Stefan had let her know the day before she need not have wasted so much money on the expensive food and drink that he liked. As she realized what the letter meant, she knew she didn't want that food. It would choke her.

Suddenly she was filled with rage. She picked up the object nearest to her—it happened to be a shallow glass bowl that had belonged to her mother—and hurled it across the room. As it shattered against the bedhead with a satisfying crash, Joy burst into tears—tears of anger rather than grief.

She cursed aloud, calling Stefan all the names she could think of and swearing that she would make him pay for his hateful, insolent behaviour. After a while she grew somewhat calmer, and set her mind to working out a course of action. She thought of 'confessing' to Guy Cantel that Cheski used to meet Neil Lavery secretly at her flat, and that he too worked for Moscow. But what would that achieve, apart from casting more suspicion on herself than already existed?

Even if such an accusation was believed, and she was by no means certain that it would be, Cheski would have diplomatic immunity. He would merely be sent home to Poland, and would soon find some Polish tart as a lover. Whatever happened she would lose him. She *had* lost him—and after all she had done for him.

For a time grief and anger were intermingled. Then grief took over. She loved him, she told herself. In spite of his curt note, she must swallow her pride and make at least one appeal to him. If that failed . . .

Brigadier Faudin was yet another individual who was not enjoying his Sunday. He was paying his monthly visit to the nursing home where his wife was a permanent patient. Today, the matron had said, she was a little better, and for a fleeting moment he had thought she recognized him. Then she had called him Edward, the name of her dead brother, and he had known it was an illusion.

He sat beside his wife's bed and worried, not about her—that was a perpetual nagging distress—but about himself and the situation at the Ministry of Defence, which seemed to be deteriorating rapidly. He had been appalled to learn that Verity had run away, apparently to join her father. There was no way he could have foreseen it. He couldn't be blamed for it. But he couldn't rid himself of the thought that indirectly it was his fault. It wouldn't have happened if he had done his job properly. He should either have succeeded in putting his finger on the traitor, or appealed to Munro Graffon and his Service earlier.

Now it was too late. Neil Lavery had gone, leaving behind a confusion of suspicion and distrust in that peculiarly sensitive directorate of the Ministry. It was as if Lavery's defection, instead of clarifying what had been happening, had merely muddied all the issues. In his position as Director of Security at the MOD, and in spite of having called in the Security Service, he would have to take some action himself, or there would be more trouble.

'Tomorrow,' he said aloud.

'Yes, Edward,' murmured his wife, for once

responding to the sound of his voice.

John Faudin smiled sadly. Tomorrow, he promised himself. He would start with Robert Tyneman. Bob's drinking alone had become a security problem. The man would have to acknowledge the fact that his wife was never coming back to him. He should take sick leave and dry out. Then perhaps he would be able to do his job efficiently. At present he was a menace and he must certainly be shifted from his present position.

William Plimpton was a different matter. His case would be more embarrassing, but something had to be done about his ever-increasing debts. And now Guy Cantel had tactfully warned him that Joy Aubyn had a Polish boy-friend, and was seemingly deeply in love with him. She too had become a security threat.

Finally, the general morale in the directorate was a subject for concern. Philip Glenbourne, he gathered, was tense and bad-tempered—perhaps not surprisingly in view of his relationship to Lavery—and was behaving like a minor dictator. He had reduced two typists to tears in the last week, and had had a row with Joy Aubyn.

Faudin's thoughts returned to the Aubyn woman. The interview with her was the one to which he looked forward with the least pleasure. Perhaps he would see her first, rather than Tyneman, and get it over. He was not to know that his decision would be overtaken by her own determination.

★   ★   ★

Like Joy Aubyn, Imogen Lavery didn't bother to

read the Sunday papers. She had stayed up late the previous night, praying fruitlessly for the phone to ring with news of Verity. Eventually she had forced herself to go to bed, to toss and turn, becoming more and more exhausted. In the small hours she roused herself to take a pill, and fell into a deep slumber.

Her dreams were horrendous. She dreamt of a small girl, sometimes Verity, sometimes Belle. The child was with a strange man, who was pulling her into a clump of bushes. Imogen knew the child was about to be raped, strangled and buried on the spot. In her sleep she tried to cry out a warning, but could make only pathetic little sounds as she was forced to stand by and watch. Then the man unexpectedly turned and smiled at her triumphantly. And Imogen recognized her husband, Neil.

Her scream woke her. Her nightgown was damp with sweat, and she was icy cold. She began to shiver, and cowered under the bedclothes. When at last she lifted her head she saw that it was ten minutes to eleven. She had slept through much of the morning.

A little later the telephone rang, and she reached for it eagerly. Guy Cantel? Verity?

It was her father. He didn't care what she said. He was coming to fetch her in half an hour, and they would drive down to the cottage for the day. She couldn't stay at home, brooding; it would do her no good, and no good to anyone else. He would arrange for any messages to reach them.

But the day passed without messages.

CHAPTER TEN

'Has anyone seen Joy Aubyn this morning? Brigadier Faudin would like to speak to her.'

Robert Tyneman shook his head and immediately groaned aloud. His hangover was troubling him. 'Haven't seen her,' he muttered.

Faudin's secretary, Kate White, gave him a sharp glance. She was a woman in her early forties, and had a reputation for being something of a martinet. 'Would you know if you had?' she asked acidly.

William Plimpton, who had been trying for the last half-hour to persuade Tyneman to answer some simple questions, intervened. 'I don't think Joy's in today,' he said.

'Why not?' Tyneman demanded. 'If I can come in, sick as I am, why can't she?'

'You're not sick, you're still half drunk,' Plimpton said in disgust.

'I'm no such thing! Damn you, Bill Plimpton, you and your smug little wife!' Tyneman's voice had risen. He was angry and he didn't care who knew it. 'You haven't a clue how—'

'What the hell's going on in here?'

Kate White had left the door of Tyneman's office half open behind her when she had entered the room, and Philip Glenbourne, passing along the corridor, had heard the altercation. Now he came hurriedly into the room. There was a sudden silence.

'I'm looking for Joy Aubyn,' Kate said. 'Brigadier Faudin wants her.'

'She's not in the office, Kate. I've been trying to

find her myself. I badly need to check some data with her. I even phoned her home, but there was no reply.'

'You mean she's disappeared too?' Tyneman laughed. The idea seemed to improve his state of health. 'Maybe she's followed your dear brother-in-law to Moscow, Philip. I wonder who'll be next. Maybe the whole directorate will head east. And hasn't your niece gone as well?'

Glenbourne glared at Tyneman venomously. 'You drunken sot!' He couldn't contain his anger and moved fast, fist drawn back ready to strike, and would certainly have attacked Tyneman if Kate White hadn't seized him by the arm.

'For God's sake!' she said. 'You can't have a brawl in here.'

'No. No, of course not.' Philip Glenbourne was breathing hard, but his anger had subsided and he had himself under control. He smiled ruefully at Kate White. 'Thanks, Kate. I'm afraid we're all a bit fraught at the moment. Tell your Brigadier we've no idea where Joy Aubyn is, will you?'

'Yes,' said Kate White doubtfully, but Philip Glenbourne, ignoring his two colleagues, was already striding out of the office.

*　　*　　*

Had they but known, Joy Aubyn was in fact in central London, waiting for Stefan Cheski in Portland Place.

Overnight she had given a great deal of thought to the effort she was determined to make to persuade him to come back to her. The first thing was to talk to him, to assure him that Cantel was no

110

danger to him and that if he loved her, as she was sure he did—but if he refused...

Strangely, now she came to think of it, he had never given her an address or a private phone number; he had merely claimed to share an apartment close to the Polish Embassy with a couple of fellow diplomats. But she had no idea where this apartment was, so all she could do to meet him face-to-face was wait near his office, in the hope that he would appear.

Joy Aubyn was very pale and there were dark smudges under her eyes, but she was not tired. On the contrary, her determination to confront her lover made her adrenalin flow. But, if she were not to miss him in the crowded street, she could not afford distractions, and when a woman with a small child spoke to her she reacted angrily. 'What is it?' she snapped. 'What do you want?'

'I'm sorry, but I've got to find Harley Street. My boy has an appointment with a doctor and we're late already.'

Uninterested and uncaring, Joy Aubyn glanced at the child. She must get rid of this importunate mother and her brat as quickly as possible. She pointed across Portland Place.

'Down that road. Harley Street crosses at the first traffic lights.'

'Thank you very much,' said the woman a little dubiously.

Pulling the reluctant child by the hand, she had just managed to reach the corner when Joy saw Cheski. Without conscious thought, she had expected him to be alone, but he was with another man—probably a colleague, Joy guessed. They were talking animatedly and, with the scarf hiding

111

her conspicuous hair, she was able to cross the road and come to a halt in front of them before Cheski had a chance to recognize her and avoid her.

'St—' she began.

Joy Aubyn had given little thought to Cheski's possible reaction to such an unexpected meeting, but what did happen was the last thing she would have anticipated. Cheski glanced at her, apparently without seeing her, elbowed past her with a shrug to his companion and almost immediately mounted the embassy steps. In simple terms, he had merely cut her dead—passed her by without any awareness of her existence.

It was too much. For a moment Joy was tempted to run up those steps and pound on the doors of the embassy. Then her eyes filled with tears as she realized the utter hopelessness of her situation. She had been a fool. She had been used. He didn't love her. He had never loved her.

Blindly, with no notion of her direction, she moved, at first slowly and then more and more quickly, towards Harley Street and turned north towards the Marylebone Road, a broad and multi-lane thoroughfare, always thick with heavy traffic.

Perhaps at the back of her mind was the knowledge that there was a park somewhere near, where she could rest in peace and compose herself. Perhaps she was acting totally involuntarily. No one would ever know, for by the time she reached the Marylebone Road she was almost running and sobbing for breath. She paid no heed to the cars and lorries and buses.

At the inquest a traffic warden on duty at a nearby pedestrian crossing was to swear that she

112

saw a young woman dart between a car and a delivery van, straight into the path of an oncoming bus. The driver did his best—other witnesses exonerated him from all blame—but, though he jammed on his brakes, pitching his passengers forward, he was unable to stop in time and one large and heavy wheel passed over Joy Aubyn's pelvis.

★   ★   ★

By the next morning, thanks to a somewhat surprisingly rapid collaboration between the Met, the Special Branch and the Security Service, Guy Cantel had enough information to telephone Stefan Cheski at the Polish Embassy.

'Cantel,' he said shortly. 'Do you remember me? We met recently at Joy—'

Cheski responded at once, aware that, in spite of the recent reorganization of the secret police, their conversation on this line could readily be overheard, and might well be being recorded.

'Yes,' he said. 'What do you want?'

'We must meet again,' said Cantel shortly.

Cheski thought quickly. If he argued or prolonged the conversation, this British security officer might identify himself for what he was. He realized that he had no option but to acquiesce.

'Yes,' he said. 'Where?'

'Lunch today. Twelve-thirty.' Cantel named a restaurant in Soho.

'OK,' said Cheski, and rang off.

★   ★   ★

A few hours later Cantel and Cheski confronted each other across a secluded corner table in a dim room. They ordered a meal and spoke softly.

Cantel gave Cheski no opportunity to gain the initiative. He said, 'You may call yourself a Cultural Attaché, but you are in fact a member of the Polish intelligence service. You're a spy, and you suborned Joy Aubyn into joining you as one of your assets. You probably know, through Miss Aubyn, that as a result of Neil Lavery's disappearance there's a damage assessment exercise being conducted at the Ministry of Defence right now in the directorate in which both Lavery and Aubyn worked. We can now account for some of the queries, and lay them at the door of you and Miss Aubyn.'

'So what? I have diplomatic immunity. All you can do is declare me *persona non grata* and send me home for—what's the phrase?—activities incompatible with my status.'

'With all honour intact.' Cantel grinned. 'You underrate Joy Aubyn, Mr Cheski.'

'What do you mean? What's she been saying?'

'She hasn't said anything.' Cantel paused for a moment. 'You'll probably be glad to know she never regained consciousness after being hit by a bus in the Marylebone Road yesterday morning. She died last night on the operating table.'

'Oh God!'

Stefan Cheski began to cross himself, but realized at once that such a gesture would make him conspicuous. Sweat broke out on his brow and upper lip, and he wiped it away with his table napkin. His hand was shaking.

Cantel said, 'If you hadn't panicked when I found you in bed together, Cheski, and decided you

114

weren't getting enough from your relationship with her to warrant the risk of being investigated by the British security authorities, Joy Aubyn might not be dead. We've pieced together what happened yesterday. Morally, you're responsible for her death.'

'So? That may be true or it may not. In any case, it's my problem.' He paused. 'Or a problem between me and my Maker.' Suddenly aggressive, he went on. 'Not for you, Mr Cantel!'

'Oh, we're involved, Cheski. You underrate Miss Aubyn. She decided to cover all the angles. When she was knocked down she had a letter in her pocket. It was found at the hospital, already stamped and obviously ready to be mailed.'

'Addressed to me?'

'Oh no. Addressed to your ambassador, as a matter of fact. I've a photocopy here which you may read.'

Cheski almost snatched the piece of paper from Cantel's hand, and Cantel watched his face grow even paler as he read it. His expression became haunted.

'But it's not true,' he said at once. 'I love my country and never, never have I worked for the British.'

'Of course not.'

'Then you'd deny it? You'd explain it was a lie.'

'Oh, we'd deny it.' Cantel smiled. 'But would we be believed—in Warsaw, say? Even in these days?'

Cheski swore in Polish. From what Cantel could gather his curses were mainly directed at Joy Aubyn, who had so unexpectedly outsmarted him. But after a minute he grew calm. He knew he was trapped. His only hope was to make a bargain.

'So what do you want?' he asked grudgingly.

Guy Cantel told him. It was simple. Joy Aubyn's letter would be withheld; the British would make sure that a verdict of accidental death was accepted at the inquest, and Cheski's name would not be mentioned.

Cheski considered. 'Fair enough,' he said at last, and reluctantly. 'But that's not all?'

'Not quite all, Cheski. You will collaborate with us in an interrogation. You will explain in detail what information you obtained from Miss Aubyn, and you'll answer a series of other questions. In fact, in a sense, you'll do more or less what Aubyn's letter accuses you of. Don't worry. We'll make all the necessary administrative and undercover arrangements. And if your information proves sufficiently rewarding you'll be given the original of Joy Aubyn's letter before you leave the country. Then, as far as we're concerned the matter will be closed.'

There was a long silence, broken at length by Cantel. 'You agree, Cheski?'

Cheski nodded slowly.

*　　*　　*

Cantel returned to his office to report to Munro Graffon, but as soon as he entered Graffon's room he sensed that something had broken. John Faudin was there, and Mary Derwent, who gave him a wide, pleased smile.

'You've had good news?' he asked quickly.

Graffon answered. 'Mixed. But some definitely good. Verity Lavery's been found, alive and well. Mary has just collected her and returned her to the

116

bosom of her family.'

'Thank God for that! How and when?' asked Guy, hiding his annoyance that Graffon hadn't bothered to send a message to him.

'Mary was about to tell us when you arrived.'

'Verity's been staying at a cottage with a mentally handicapped woman, who lives alone, doesn't take a newspaper and has neither television nor radio. Luckily someone spotted her in the garden and told the police or she might still be there,' said Mary. 'It seems the child did set off to join her father, but she twisted her ankle crossing a field quite close to the school, and was found by this woman. The people in the nearby village call her "Mad Meg", as you might expect—'

'But she's been there for days,' John Faudin protested. 'Wasn't she frightened of this character?'

'On the contrary. Apparently they got on very well together. In fact, Verity wasn't at all sure she wanted to leave, certainly not if it meant returning to that school where—I quote—"they told me horrid lies about Daddy". But Mrs Lavery promised her she'd never have to go back there, so that difficulty was overcome.'

'I doubt if they'd take her back,' said Cantel, remembering Miss Crane's acid comments. 'She's at home then?'

'No. She's staying with her aunt, Mrs Glenbourne. Less publicity, and it's what she wanted.'

'It's a good arrangement,' Cantel agreed. 'The media can simply be told she was unhappy at school, went to stay with a friend and is now with relations. Let them make what they like of that.'

John Faudin was shaking his head. 'But I still

117

don't understand why the girl wasn't frightened of this woman. If she's mad—'

'She's not mad in any real sense, and she's certainly not dangerous,' Mary corrected him. 'She's just mentally retarded, like Belle Glenbourne, though not so severely. Verity's used to her cousin, and very attached to her. She liked the woman, and she intends to visit her again.'

'Well, that's fine,' said Munro Graffon. 'That's our good news.'

'And the bad?' said Cantel.

'From sources in Moscow we now know definitely that Neil Lavery has arrived there and is staying with some chums—doubtless being debriefed—in a *dacha* outside the capital. We can only wait and see which way the opposition want to play it—a grand announcement and a press conference, or silence for the time being. And we're keeping a strict eye on the wife.'

PART TWO

THE AGENT AT LARGE

CHAPTER ELEVEN

Neil Lavery knew that it was a dream. In the last week he had dreamt it more than once, though it had become no less ominous and frightening. Each time he had woken chilled and shivering, his pyjamas soaked with sweat. Yet in itself the dream was not really horrendous.

      *   *   *

The dream always commenced with the same scene. He was in his office in the Ministry of Defence. Joy Aubyn was with him, and he was giving her some last-minute instructions. He was in a hurry as he had promised Imogen to be home early because they were giving a dinner party; apart from showering and changing, there would be some minor chores to be done—coping with the wines, for instance—before the guests appeared.

Then Bill Plimpton came into the office. At first Lavery imagined that he had arrived to return the ten pounds he had borrowed earlier in the week. But no. Plimpton merely wanted to discuss some trivial matter that could easily have waited until the next day. Short of actual rudeness, it was difficult to get rid of the man—after all, he was a colleague—so Neil was even later than he had thought. And finally, when he was about to leave, Joy pointed out that it was raining.

Lavery swore to himself. This meant that his chances of getting a taxi would be slight. When rain was added to the evening rush hour in central

London, vacant taxis seemed to disappear in seconds. Resigned, he took the spare umbrella he always kept at the office, and went through the formality of signing out of the directorate's secure enclave. A few minutes later he waved his pass at the guard on duty in the main hall and ran down the steps at the north end of the building into Horseguards Avenue.

As he had expected there was no sign of a cab, and there was no point in waiting where he was. Whatever happened he was going to get wet; the rain was coming down more heavily now and the umbrella offered only inadequate protection. He turned left and crossed Whitehall. A couple of taxis swished past, both occupied. He decided to walk towards Trafalgar Square; at least there might be more chance there.

Then the unbelievable happened. He had almost reached the Whitehall Theatre when a taxi drew up in front of him and a man jumped out on to the pavement. Lavery felt a surge of triumph as, fighting to shut his umbrella, he ran forward and leapt into the cab. His pleasure at the achievement, however, was short-lived. To his surprise, the stranger, instead of paying his fare, climbed back into the taxi, which immediately accelerated away from the kerb.

He was a big man, dark-haired, brown-eyed, with a swarthy complexion. He wore a grey suit, a white shirt and what looked very much like an Old Etonian tie. He might have been a senior Civil Servant, like Lavery himself, or perhaps a politician or a company director. Whoever he was, he carried with him an air of authority, and smiled at Lavery, showing large, even teeth.

'Hope you don't mind sharing a cab with me, Lavery,' he said conversationally, 'but we're going in the same direction.'

'We are?' To his knowledge Lavery had never seen this man in his life. 'Should I know you?' he asked, taken aback.

'Indeed we are, my dear chap—going in the same direction, I mean—though of course I shan't be going with you all the way. As for knowing me, the answer's no. We haven't met.'

'Then how do—' For a moment Lavery searched for a suitable response. Finally, he said, 'You surprise me.'

It was always at this point that Lavery told himself he was merely dreaming, and had no need to be afraid. Yet, in his dream, he could feel that his heart was thumping and his mouth was dry.

He decided to take a facetious line. 'You're not coming to dinner with us, then?'

'Alas, no, Lavery.' His companion seemed not in the least nonplussed, as if he had already known of Lavery's plans for the rest of the night. 'I'm sorry. We seem to have picked an unfortunate evening, but you can't have everything in this life. It was never going to be totally convenient, was it? And really it hasn't been easy to make arrangements at such short notice.'

The taxi, Lavery suddenly realized, had reached Hyde Park Corner and turned into the Park, and was now travelling rapidly, directly away from his house in Knightsbridge. He leant forward and knocked hard on the glass partition that separated the passenger compartment from the driver. The driver paid no attention. Neither, Lavery found, could he open the panel. He swung round towards his unwelcome companion, who was smiling at him sadly.

'Where the hell are you taking me?' Lavery demanded.

'To Moscow—but by a somewhat devious route.'

'Moscow! To Moscow? But I don't want to go to Moscow!'

'Of course not. We know that. You've made it quite clear in the past that you've a poor opinion of the place. However, your journey's become necessary, and necessary very quickly. Your security people are closing in on you—fast—and, as you know, we always do our best to take care of our own.'

Suddenly the man pointed out of the taxi window on Lavery's side, as if he had caught sight of something of extreme interest. As Lavery involuntarily turned his head to see what it was, he felt a sharp prick on the side of his neck, followed by an agonizing pain. He cried out and clapped a hand over the area. There was only a small spot of blood, but—but...

Up to this point his dreams were always crystal clear. Sometimes the dialogue varied a little, but the sequence of events remained constant. From now on, however, he remembered little of what had happened. He had the impression of a long period of sleep, but also of being lifted, carried. And slowly, always with this sense of dread, he woke.

*　　*　　*

By now the room was familiar to him. It was a pleasant room, but impersonal, a room which gave the impression that a variety of individuals had

124

occupied it at different times. The furniture was what one would expect in a hotel—a bed, a desk, a comfortable chair. All was solid, the wood well-polished, the floor covered with oriental rugs; ignorant as he was of such things, Lavery surmised that they were valuable. The walls were painted a nondescript beige, and there was one picture; Lavery recognized it as a glamorized version of Red Square in winter with the Kremlin in the background, its towers capped with snow. In the few days he had lived with it, Lavery had grown to like it.

The room also had a window—a large window, from which he could gaze out across a vista of trees and shrubs and rough woodland, and forget that his dreams were based on reality and that he was effectively a prisoner.

At first he had protested to the only individual he had so far spoken to—one Igor Pavlovich Smerinov, or at least that was how he introduced himself. Lavery had claimed that he had been kidnapped, drugged, brought here against his will, but all his expostulations had been met with polite smiles and the single word, 'Soon—'

In the end Lavery had given up, and forced himself to accept his position. In fact, it was not so unpleasant. After the first two days he discovered that his bedroom door was no longer locked, and that he had the run of the main part of the house, though Smerinov had suggested politely that he should not attempt to penetrate the staff quarters.

Igor Pavlovich was his constant companion, helpful and affable—even congenial. His English was fluent though accented, and he acted as Russian tutor, informant—within limits—and, of course,

125

gaoler. After he had become accustomed to the man, Lavery realized that he couldn't bring himself to dislike him. They were much of an age and there was something appealing about Smerinov, with his dark curly hair and soulful brown eyes; he reminded Lavery of a spaniel, and he treated his prisoner like an honoured guest. The situation was artificial and ironic, Lavery appreciated, but he saw no reason not to take advantage of it.

There was a tap at the door and Neil Lavery pushed himself up in bed and arranged his pillows behind him in time to welcome his breakfast tray.

'Good morning, Neil. I hope you slept well.'

'Yes, thank you, Igor Pavlovich.'

It was becoming almost a ritual, Lavery thought, as he watched the Russian put the tray down on the bedside table.

'A fine English breakfast, yes?'

'Splendid!' Lavery agreed.

It was true. There was fresh orange juice, two eggs with crisp bacon, toast, butter and Cooper's Oxford marmalade, in addition to a pot of excellent coffee. Except in the school holidays when the children were home Lavery never ate a cooked breakfast.

But he had no wish to be reminded of those happy meals, which he suspected would never come again. He had to keep his mind away from Mat and Verity—and Imogen, especially Imogen. Smerinov had shown him an English newspaper the previous day. Admittedly it was from the lower end of the tabloid market, and not a paper likely to appear in his own house, but Imogen, if not the children, must by now have read of his public condemnation as a traitor and a spy. He couldn't bear to imagine

126

her feelings, and indeed he felt unprepared to face the full implications of the fact that he had been identified as a Soviet agent and a defector.

'You spoil me, Igor Pavlovich,' he said. 'If you continue to feed me so well I shall get fat.'

Smerinov laughed and patted his stomach. 'We Muscovites like to eat,' he said proudly.

'When you can find the food.'

Smerinov ignored the implied insult to the Soviet economic system. 'It's a lovely day,' he replied. 'Sun is shining. Sky is blue. Shall we forget our lesson and go for another walk in the woods? To salve our consciences we can speak only in Russian.'

'Whatever you wish.'

Lavery poured himself a second cup of coffee and buttered the last piece of toast. For some reason he couldn't have explained to himself, he was reluctant to make it too obvious to the Russians that he already knew a certain amount of their language, and was certainly not averse to adding to this knowledge. Besides, Smerinov was a good teacher and the lessons helped to fill the long days. But he saw no reason why he should be over-enthusiastic. After all, there was no getting away from the fact that he was here against his will.

'But you would like a walk,' Smerinov persisted.

'Yes, of course,' Lavery said. 'Our walks always give me a sense of freedom.'

'You mean you feel you could run away?' Smerinov laughed. 'My dear Neil, why do you think we take so few precautions? Where would you go?' he asked, as he picked up the breakfast tray and made for the door.

'Where, indeed?' replied Neil Lavery.

It was a pertinent question, he realized. Here he was, in a large opulent *dacha* outside Moscow, or so he had been told and he had no cause to disbelieve Igor Pavlovich. Where would he go? He had no friends in the Soviet Union. He had no roubles, no map, no place for which to aim—except home.

And even home was in a sense barred to him. He couldn't believe the British Embassy would accord him a champagne welcome, though they wouldn't be averse to collecting a reluctant defector. Of course, he could, and would, swear he was an innocent man who had been kidnapped. But who would believe him, especially as the British security authorities knew for certain that a Soviet agent had indeed been at work in his directorate of the Ministry?

But there was another reason why he couldn't attempt to bolt when he was out walking with Igor Pavlovich. It hadn't escaped his notice that their excursions were constantly under surveillance by at least two guards, armed and with dogs. He could choose to joke and chat with Igor, but he knew he had no hope of getting away.

*　　　*　　　*

Neil Lavery levered himself out of bed and went into the adjoining bathroom, which was surprisingly modern. He appreciated the large soft towels and the imported French soap. But these were impersonal objects which might have been provided for any VIP. The clothes in the bedroom were quite different. The shirts, slacks and underwear were not only of fine quality, but were all of his size and obviously carefully chosen for him personally. Even the shoes, though not made to his own last, were of soft leather and very comfortable.

There was no doubt that they had prepared for his arrival with great care and after considerable research. No time or trouble or expense could have been spared. Clearly the Soviet authorities were making extra efforts to ingratiate themselves with him. But why, exactly? Could it be that, apart from wringing out of him all the information they could, they intended to make him part of some propaganda coup, and for that needed his full support? He must make a resolute effort to get some answers from Igor.

Determined, Neil Lavery left his bedroom and went downstairs. He saw no one on the way. There never seemed to be any supervision inside the *dacha*. He found Smerinov in the living-room.

This was a spacious area, large enough to hold a grand piano and massive furniture. It had a polished wood floor, covered with more oriental rugs. Radiators upstairs and downstairs showed that the *dacha* was centrally heated but, in deference to Russian tradition, this main room had a huge tiled stove in one corner. Smerinov was sitting at the piano, playing an arrangement of part of Prokofiev's *Love for Three Oranges*. Lavery applauded as he finished.

'I've heard the piano before, but I didn't know it was you who played,' Lavery said. 'Congratulations.'

'Thank you. It is my hobby,' Smerinov answered modestly. He pushed back the piano-stool and stood up. 'Are you ready for our walk?'

'For a walk, yes.' Lavery paused, then went on, 'And I'm more than ready for a serious talk. First, I want to know when my interrogation will begin. This may be a pleasant life of a kind, but it can't go on for ever. I've already been here a week.'

Smerinov didn't answer until they were outside and striding over the rough grass towards a small wood. Then he said, 'You use the wrong word, Neil. There will be no interrogation. A debriefing, perhaps, yes. But that is not at all the same thing, as I'm sure you're aware.'

'Suppose that I refuse to be "debriefed"?'

'You won't refuse. Not when you are reconciled to your position. That is the reason for the delay—to give you time to think. My dear friend—' Smerinov stopped walking. 'We know you didn't want to come to Moscow. You'd rather be in London.'

'Yes. With my wife and children.'

'But in prison? Awaiting a trial for espionage?'

'That's absurd! There was no more proof against me than against a dozen others with access in the directorate.' He saw Igor Smerinov's mouth twist in a pitying smile, and added, 'But there is now?'

'You are here, Neil.'

'Yes, I realize that. I've defected—or appear to have defected—and that in itself has condemned me.'

Smerinov didn't reply directly. He said, 'You are here, Neil, and clearly it would be wise of you to make the best of it. After all, it's not that bad, is it? You'll be a very privileged person. You'll have a pleasant apartment in the centre of Moscow, a *dacha* in the country, holidays by the Black Sea, tickets for the Bolshoi, the right to use the *Beryozka* shops, access to the best medical facilities—in fact, every *blat* you could wish for.'

'What about my wife and family?'

'When you are settled Matthew and Verity can come for their holidays. So can your parents.'

'But I can't go to see them?'

'It would be unwise. If you did you would be arrested immediately.'

'Yes. For a moment I forgot,' Lavery said bitterly.

'As for your wife, it will be your task to persuade her to join you. She would be most welcome in the Soviet Union.'

'I'm sure she would.' Lavery thought of the great propaganda coup the Soviet authorities could gain from such a development—and of his father-in-law's predictable rage at the loss of his daughter.

They had started to walk again, and were now in the wood. Smerinov pointed under the trees. 'There are wonderful mushrooms here in the autumn,' he said. 'We Russians think mushroom-gathering is a great sport.'

'And you think that, as a good Russian-to-be, I should learn it?'

'Why not?' said Smerinov, but seeing his companion's expression, added, 'Cheer up, Neil. I can't promise, but I'll try to arrange for you to speak to your family on the telephone as soon as I can.'

CHAPTER TWELVE

'Progress is far too sluggish, Igor Pavlovich,' said the grating voice on the other end of the line.

'Yes, Comrade General.'

'We cannot wait forever for the next phase of this operation.'

'No, Comrade General.'

'So, your explanations—and suggestions, please?'

Smerinov drew a deep breath. In the past he had always found Vadim Belatov reasonably considerate as a superior officer, but the General did have a reputation for ruthlessness, and Smerinov's hand on the telephone receiver was damp with sweat.

'Well, have you nothing to say?' the voice demanded harshly as Smerinov remained silent.

'Neil Lavery is a difficult subject, Comrade General, full of contradictions. Sometimes he seems almost—almost happy, with all the luxuries we provide: the excellent food, the comfort of the *dacha*, for instance.' Smerinov hurried on. 'Then at other times he becomes moody and sarcastic, and is clearly very despondent—'

'And therefore unco-operative?' interrupted Belatov.

'I'm afraid so, Comrade General. Of course, his attitudes may be affected by the drugs he's getting—'

'Igor Pavlovich, as you well know it is your task to keep him euphoric rather than melancholy. That is the object of the exercise. We need his co-operation.'

'I understand that, Comrade General.'

'So?'

'Er—if I might make a suggestion—'

A great blast of air seemed to come over the line as Vadim Belatov heaved a sigh. 'That, Igor Pavlovich, is precisely what I asked for five minutes ago.'

'Indeed, Comrade General.' Smerinov steadied his voice. 'Comrade General, it seems obvious to me that Lavery's main worry is the well-being of his family, and I have been wondering if I could try to satisfy him by permitting him to speak to them for a few minutes on the telephone. I think he would be grateful—and might show his gratitude—'

There was a pause before Belatov agreed. 'Right,' he said finally. 'But the call must be short, and fully monitored. Make sure he understands the ground rules first, and cut him off immediately if he tries to send any seemingly private or coded message that gives anything away—especially the circumstances in which he arrived here. You understand me? You must use your judgement, and you will be held personally responsible, Igor Pavlovich. You realize this?'

'I understand, Comrade General,' Smerinov repeated slowly and obediently.

'Right. I think that in the circumstances you should attempt to arrange for him to speak to the children first, and then consult me again before he speaks to his wife. And make sure he grasps the fact that we are giving him a great concession and we expect some return. I shall assume that your next call will report a considerable improvement in his attitude.'

'Yes, Comrade General. I will do my best.'

Igor Smerinov wiped his sticky sweat off the receiver, and replaced it on its rest. He was pleased to have wrung approval for his suggested course of action from the General, but alarmed at the emphasis that had been laid on his responsibility for its success. He wondered if it might be a good idea to vary the dosage of drugs that Lavery was unwittingly receiving each day in his food or drink, but decided that he had better not tamper with the psychiatrist's instructions.

Smerinov would have been even less content had he heard the Comrade General discussing his progress, or rather lack of it, with his aide. Vadim Belatov was a short, thick-set man, given to bursts of irritation, but with a surprisingly subtle mind. He had risen rapidly through the ranks of the KGB, survived the recent and drastic changes and reorganizations, and was young for a general. If he had a fault it was impatience—a hatred of apparent inaction.

'"Yes, Comrade General. No, Comrade General."' He mimicked Igor Smerinov as he strutted up and down his office. 'But what does he *do*?'

'It can't be easy—' remarked his aide doubtfully.

'Of course it's not easy, but Smerinov's an experienced officer. He speaks excellent English. He knows London. He had a posting there for three years. And he's a sympathetic character. He and Lavery should get on well together.'

'That could be part of the trouble, Comrade General. He might have become too—too involved with the subject, or the subject's feelings.' The aide hesitated; he knew that Vadim Belatov had been a close friend of Smerinov's elder brother, who had been killed in Afghanistan. 'When you come to think of it, they do have quite a lot in common.'

It was a moment before the General responded, and his aide trembled. Then Belatov nodded. 'You may be right, Comrade. Certainly when this operation gets as far as Phase Four it may be wise to isolate Smerinov from it. Meanwhile we remain dependent on him, so we must hope he performs adequately.'

*   *   *

Although Maurice White had been warned by Cantel that Neil Lavery might try to contact his son, the telephone call supposedly from Russia on the private line to his study had shaken him. As he had been instructed he went immediately to the headmaster.

'I was thrown completely off balance, I'm afraid, Headmaster,' he admitted. 'I had no idea how to reply, so I told him to phone back in an hour.'

'You think he will?'

'Yes. I'm certain of it. He wasn't surprised by my request. He said, "OK. Have Matthew there or his father will be disappointed," and he rang off.'

'He sounds like a pretty cool customer.' The headmaster was thinking of Matthew Lavery, a clever and sensible boy, but only fifteen and already under great strain. 'You say he didn't give you a name?'

'No, Headmaster. He merely said, "You won't know me, but I'm a friend of Mr Neil Lavery. At present Neil's staying with me in the USSR, and I'm calling you to arrange for his son to speak to him on the phone." The chap spoke excellent English with only a slight accent.'

'You think that suggests he was genuine?'

'Genuine? Why, yes,' Maurice White said. 'I must admit that it did occur to me that it might be some sort of hoax or gag—or even a reporter's ploy. But it would be a cruel trick to play.'

'Fair enough, then. Let's assume it's not

135

someone's idea of a hoax, Maurice. I'll contact this man Cantel. If he agrees, we'll get hold of the boy, warn him to come to your study to take a possible phone call from his father, but warn him that it might be a sick joke. I think I shall come over and stand by during the call, if I may, Maurice.'

'Of course, Headmaster.'

Luckily Guy Cantel was in his office and readily available. He agreed at once with the headmaster's suggestions, and was excited at the prospect of making any contact, however remote, with Neil Lavery. But he kicked himself for having discarded as too complex the idea of arranging for taps on the school's phone lines. Now, as far as Matthew was concerned, there was no time to do more than ask the headmaster and housemaster to listen to the conversation and persuade the boy to repeat what was said while it was fresh in his mind. At the same time Cantel couldn't help but wonder how Imogen would react to this renewed link with her husband.

Matthew himself showed almost no emotion except a grim determination. Indeed, as he waited silently with Maurice White and the headmaster for the call to come through, the men appeared considerably more nervous than the boy.

The phone rang, exactly on time. White picked up the receiver and listened intently. It was the same, rather insolent voice, and he was convinced that this was no joke. He nodded encouragingly at Matthew.

'Yes, Matthew Lavery is here,' he said into the receiver, 'but let me speak to his father first. I must be sure that it really is Neil Lavery on the line.'

There was a laugh, then Neil Lavery spoke. 'Yes,

136

it's me all right, Maurice. How is Mat?' His voice was tight.

Maurice White fought with himself. There was so much he wanted to ask, so much he wanted to say. After all, he had been friendly with the Laverys for a fair period. He reminded himself that the call was primarily for the boy; in spite of his apparent calm this waiting must be traumatic.

'He's fine, Neil. A bit fraught, of course, but otherwise fine. Here he is. Just a moment.' He put his hand over the mouthpiece as he handed the instrument to Matthew. 'Now, remember, Mat,' he said. 'It's important you try to recall every word that's said. We have to ask you afterwards.'

Matthew nodded, and took the phone.

'Yes,' said Matthew tonelessly.

'Mat, dear old son. How are you? I've been so worried about you and Verity and—and your mother.' Neil Lavery seemed to choke for a moment.

'Perhaps you should have thought of that before you buggered off.' Matthew's reply was cool and immediate.

'Mat, I didn't—Please don't be like that. You don't understand.'

'I understand only too well, and if I didn't believe you were already on your way there, I'd wish you in hell. Goodbye.'

White and the headmaster stared at each other as Matthew Lavery banged down the phone. The boy gave the two men a horrified glance, then, as if surprised by his own words, put his head down on the housemaster's desk and burst into sudden tears.

★   ★   ★

'I'm sorry,' Igor Smerinov said. 'Truly, I'm sorry, Neil. If I'd known Mat would behave like that I'd never have suggested you talk to him.'

'It was cruel, cruel.' Lavery himself was close to tears.

Smerinov wasn't sure exactly what Lavery meant—had the boy been cruel or had Smerinov himself been cruel? But clearly Lavery was extremely disturbed and Smerinov had no need of a psychiatrist to persuade him that his plan to make the Englishman more amenable had failed dismally.

What was more, Smerinov told himself, there was no hope of concealing the fact. He knew perfectly well that every word of the conversation had been monitored and taped and was probably even now being translated for the General's benefit. Vadim Belatov would not be pleased.

Desperately he tried to save something from the débâcle. 'Neil,' he said, 'your daughter, Verity, doesn't feel like that. In fact, she ran away from school in an attempt to join you.'

'What! She what?' It was the first Lavery had heard of the episode. 'Oh God, poor Imogen! Is Verity all right?'

'Yes. She sprained her ankle crossing a field near her school, and was found almost immediately. She's fine now.'

'You're sure?'

'Positive. She's staying with the Glenbournes. She said she didn't want to go back to school and, as you can imagine, life's not too easy for your wife at the moment, so it seemed a good idea that her aunt should take care of her.'

By this time Neil Lavery had recovered from the immediate shock of his son's reaction, and he was looking curiously at the Russian. 'How do you know all this, Igor?'

Smerinov told himself to be careful. In his desire to be conciliatory to Lavery and undo the damage caused by Mat, he had not been watching his tongue. He had aroused Lavery's curiosity.

'Oh—just from the English newspapers,' he said, too quickly.

'And doubtless you have other sources—assets, as you'd call them, I believe.'

Smerinov ignored the comment. 'I did try to phone Mrs Rosalind Glenbourne,' he said, 'but there was no answer. Would you like me to try later, or would you rather speak to your wife, if it can be arranged?'

Neil Lavery swallowed hard. He yearned to talk to Verity, to be able to offer her some consolation, but Imogen was more important. Yet understandably he felt a certain reluctance, in case Imogen should treat him in the same wounding fashion as Matthew had done.

'Preferably my wife,' he said.

'I'll do my best,' Smerinov promised. 'As soon as possible—probably later tonight.'

It was a genuine promise. Smerinov knew that his own future could depend on the outcome of the call. General Belatov had a point. If Phase Two were to be successfully accomplished, and Neil Lavery's presence in the USSR was to have its full value—in propaganda terms and otherwise—not only must Lavery collaborate voluntarily, but he must do so soon. Too much time had already been wasted, and it was his—Igor Pavlovich Smerinov's—fault. He must make a greater effort. The General had ordered a consultation after the

139

calls to the children, and he must now persuade Belatov that the boy's reaction had been natural in the circumstances, and that the next move should be a call to Mrs Lavery. Maybe that would help.

* * *

The arrangements took some hours, and it was not until about eleven o'clock, Moscow time, that Smerinov came quickly into Neil Lavery's bedroom. Lavery was in bed, but he had been unable to sleep. This was unusual, and he wondered if for some reason he had been denied the nightly sedation that he suspected he was given. When Smerinov burst in he was not particularly surprised.

'Neil, come on downstairs. I've fixed for you to have a chat with your wife. You've got five minutes before the call comes through.'

Neil Lavery flung himself out of bed and seized his gown. He suddenly felt breathless. He couldn't really believe that he was about to hear Imogen's voice and his mind went blank. He had no idea what he should say to her.

Smerinov was almost equally nervous. He was afraid that Lavery's wife might be even more acerbic than her son, and that the call would achieve the opposite of what was intended. He was also afraid of Lavery's impulses, and impressed on him the care with which the conversation should be conducted.

'Keep it personal,' he had said. 'If she asks you leading questions, such as where you are exactly or how you got here, don't answer. Remember there'll almost certainly be a security officer sitting beside

140

her, listening to you and prompting her. And your whole conversation will be taped and played and replayed and analyzed. So please, Neil, for your sake—and for mine—don't give them any information you shouldn't.'

'Won't you be there to see that I don't?'

'Yes. I must. But I want this to be a happy time for you, Neil. I don't want to have to cut it short. Do be sensible.'

'I'll try.'

In spite of himself Neil Lavery was touched by the Russian's concern, which he had to believe was genuine. Minutes later, as he heard Imogen's doubtful, 'Hallo, Neil', he had forgotten Igor Smerinov and any faceless security man who might be listening at the other end.

'Imogen, darling,' he said. 'I—I'm sorry, desperately sorry. Are you all right? I've worried so much about you.'

'Perhaps you should have done that sooner, Neil.'

'Yes.'

There was silence. Then the conversation continued in staccato bursts. Neither of them knew how to handle the situation. Imogen reproached her husband for phoning Mat. He didn't ask if he had upset Mat. He enquired about Verity and got the impression that Imogen blamed him for the child's abortive attempt to join him.

'Neil, you must *not* try to contact the children again. It's not fair on them.'

'Very well.'

'Promise, Neil. For their sake, not for mine.'

'I promise.'

Although she had asked for his promise, Imogen

141

greeted it with some hostility. 'I suppose I have to trust you, though God knows why I should. When I think of all the times you must have lied to me and deceived me over the years it makes me sick.'

'Imogen—' Lavery was about to attempt some kind of explanation, but he realized at once that it would be impossible. He had never felt more frustrated.

'Darling, I love you,' he said at last, and hopelessly. 'I always have.'

There was a slight hesitation before Imogen, obviously close to tears, said, 'I love you too, Neil. Oh, why? Why did this have to happen? If only I understood.'

'Please, darling, please—just love me.'

'I will, Neil.' Imogen was crying openly now.

Neil Lavery glanced in exasperation at Igor Smerinov, who was tapping his watch. 'I shall have to go, Imogen. Look after yourself, darling.'

'You too, Neil.'

'You'll phone again,' Smerinov murmured.

Lavery nodded gratefully. 'I'll phone again, Imogen. Bless you, darling.' He put down the receiver. 'Thanks, Igor,' he said.

The Russian beamed at him. 'I'm pleased for you, Neil. As I've said before, we want you to be happy. Let's have a nightcap together, shall we?'

CHAPTER THIRTEEN

Neil Lavery lay sprawled in the armchair in the living-room of the *dacha*. He was tired and bored. His Russian grammar was lying open on the rug

142

beside him, but he had no inclination to study it. He had no wish to do anything. His head was aching and he would have preferred not to think at all. Nevertheless, he found that involuntarily in his mind he was recalling again and again the conversation he had had with Imogen the previous evening. By now he was no longer sure of the extent to which he could believe what she had said. For instance, she had claimed she still loved him, but . . .

Lavery sighed. At least one of his troubles, he thought, was lack of exercise. He was eating more than he usually did, certainly drinking more, and taking only gentle walks. What he needed was a good game of squash. He had been used to playing once or twice a week, and the bouts gave him the workout he needed. He wondered if squash was played in Moscow, and doubted it.

'Neil, I have a surprise for you.'

Lavery turned his head slowly. He hadn't heard Smerinov enter the room; the Russian invariably moved very quietly.

'Ah, your mysterious hints at breakfast are about to be explained,' Lavery said, obstinately refusing to show a great deal of interest.

'Neil, no! Don't respond like that,' Smerinov protested. 'You're going to be pleased.'

'OK. So what is it? I can hardly wait.'

'For you.' Smerinov dropped the parcel he was carrying into Lavery's lap. 'All the way from England. It came for you in our diplomatic bag.'

Neil Lavery sat up sharply. 'What on earth—'

He stared at the neat brown-paper parcel, so carefully wrapped. The typed address label merely said 'Neil Lavery, Esq., Moscow'. It was true that

143

the parcel had made the journey from London in the USSR's diplomatic bag, but even so the contents had been examined by General Vadim Belatov before being rewrapped and delivered to Smerinov, with certain instructions.

'Aren't you going to open it, then?' Igor Smerinov asked, simulating excitement, as if the parcel was a present and Lavery a small boy. 'Here's a pocket-knife. It will help.'

Slowly Lavery cut the string, undid the paper and opened the carton it enclosed. Each article inside was packed separately. His bewilderment grew as he identified the items. He found the green cashmere sweater of which he was so fond, one of his sports shirts, his old splendid walking-shoes, his College tie and the dreadful tie that Verity had given him for his last birthday. All these objects brought back vivid memories, though it was the final one that affected him most deeply.

This seemed to have been packaged with special care, and was the enlarged photograph of Imogen and the two children in its silver frame, which always sat on his desk at home. Immediately he recalled the occasion on which he had taken the snap: the holiday that the four of them had spent in Jersey. He studied the photograph wordlessly.

'You are pleased, Neil?'

'Yes. I'm pleased, all right. But I don't understand. How did you—your people—get hold of these things?'

Igor Smerinov grinned. 'If you must know, we stole them, or someone employed by us did.'

'Very clever,' said Lavery, and he was marvelling at the thoroughness with which the Soviet authorities had planned the affair. He found it difficult to believe that he was of such importance to them as to warrant this scale of attention to detail. 'It's a strange collection,' he added. 'Still, since it includes my favourite old shoes, shall we go for a brisk walk? I was thinking I could do with some real exercise.'

'Right.' Smerinov looked at his watch. 'A brisk walk, but not too far. We're lunching early today.'

'Why? Or is that another surprise?'

'We are having a visitor this afternoon. General Vadim Belatov wishes to meet you.'

'Is he your superior?'

Smerinov hesitated. Then he nodded. 'It was General Belatov who arranged for you to come to Moscow, Neil.'

Lavery gave the Russian a long cool glance. 'I hope,' he said, 'that your General Belatov doesn't expect me to be grateful. If he does, he's going to be very disappointed.'

'But you won't be difficult, will you, Neil? You'll be pleasant to him? You'll co-operate, for my sake?' Smerinov said quickly, his spaniel eyes anxious. He was clearly worried by Lavery's response. 'Please, Neil!'

'Otherwise you'll be thrown into the Lubyanka, Igor Pavlovich?'

'No, but—Don't tease me, Neil. My assignment is to keep you cheerful and happy, to help you adjust to life in the USSR, and if you insist on suggesting that I've failed—'

It was a form of emotional blackmail, Lavery thought, and there was no reason why he should fall for it. What was more, he couldn't help wondering about the sincerity of Igor Smerinov's plea, and the Russian's real feelings. However, considering the

145

circumstances, he and Igor were perfectly compatible, and he didn't want Igor replaced by someone else whom he might dislike on sight. He looked at the little pile of oddly assorted clothes, and at the photograph of Imogen and the children which he still held in his hands. He assumed that, taken together, they represented some kind of bribe.

'You'll have to trust me, Igor,' he said at last. 'Do you know what your General wants?'

'To meet you. To talk to you. I expect he intends to discuss your future.'

Lavery laughed. 'That's just what I'm waiting for—to talk to someone in authority here. I'll certainly tell him a thing or two.'

'Neil—my friend—General Belatov is not a patient man. It would be advisable for you, for your own sake, not to thwart him too—too much.'

'Is that a threat?' Lavery was a little startled by this first hint of hostility.

'A warning, that's all.' Smerinov spoke lightly.

But now Neil Lavery did not trust him. There had undoubtedly been a latent threat in Smerinov's words and Lavery felt his stomach muscles tightening in fear. He told himself that he must not forget that, however pleasantly he might be treated, he was still in Moscow and at the mercy of those who had brought him there.

*   *   *

After a brisk but silent walk and an equally silent lunch with Igor, Lavery retired to his room. This had become something of a habit. Usually he studied his Russian, managed to read with some help from a dictionary, a copy of *Izvestia* or *Pravda* a day or two old or merely lay on his bed and dozed. When he felt inclined he went downstairs to chat to Igor Smerinov, listen to taped music, or try to make sense of Soviet television.

Today was different. Smerinov had asked him to wait in his room until General Belatov arrived and expressed a wish to meet him. Lavery, assuming the General wanted to have some preliminary private words with Smerinov, had raised no objection. But he was too restless to concentrate on anything, and he found himself becoming increasingly nervous as the afternoon dragged on.

He spent some time gazing out of the window at the rough grass and shrubs and the woods in the distance. It was a view that normally gave him pleasure, but not at present. He would have preferred a room that looked out on to the front of the *dacha* so that he could have seen the approach of the General's limousine.

At last, when he was certain that Belatov must have arrived, Lavery could no longer restrain his impatience. He eased open his bedroom door and peered into the corridor. There was no one in sight. He walked quietly to the top of the stairs and listened. There were voices from below as if several people were arguing, and noises that sounded as if furniture was being moved around. Lavery couldn't imagine what was happening.

Then someone gave what seemed to be a curt command and there was silence. Lavery did not understand the words, but he guessed that the speaker had been General Belatov. Through the banisters he saw Igor Smerinov come into the hall below, and he hurried back to his room as quickly and quietly as he could. He was sitting in his armchair, reading, when Smerinov came in.

'We are ready for you, Neil,' Smerinov announced with some formality, his manner subtly changed.

'Right.'

Smerinov looked him up and down uneasily. 'You have put on your suit,' he said. It was the suit that Lavery had worn on his last day at the Ministry of Defence. 'It's too formal.'

'Surely not to meet a general—especially such an important general?'

Smerinov didn't comment on the sarcasm. Instead, he merely said, 'General Belatov is not in uniform. This is a casual visit.' Then he went to the chest of drawers and took out the cashmere sweater and one of the ties that had arrived from London. 'Quick, Neil, put these on. We must not keep the General waiting.'

'Not that tie,' Lavery objected. It was the hideous object that Verity had given him.

'Yes,' Smerinov insisted. 'And hurry, please, Neil.'

Neil Lavery shrugged mentally and did as he was asked. There seemed no point in making an issue of the matter. Besides, he was both curious and anxious to meet Belatov. But he did expostulate when Smerinov picked up the silver photograph frame with the obvious intention of taking it with them.

'What the hell are you doing with that?' he demanded.

'You'll understand, Neil. It *is* important.'

And Neil Lavery did understand, almost as soon as he entered the living-room. A short, square-set man strutted forwards, seized him by the hand and pumped it up and down, before clasping him, Russian fashion, in his arms. The first of a series of flashlights went off. Photographs. Before he could protest, even had he thought it worth while to do so, Lavery found himself sitting on the sofa beside General Belatov, with the silver-framed photograph of Imogen and the children on the table beside him. It made a charming, companionable scene.

There was no need for any introductions. They knew who Lavery was, the General's identity was obvious and his two aides remained nameless, as did the photographer. More pictures were taken as Belatov talked, and asked casual questions; Smerinov acted as interpreter. Lavery answered briefly. Everyone was very amiable but, apart from the photographs, whose propaganda value was apparent, the meeting seemed a waste of time.

'Ask the General when my interrogation is to begin,' Lavery said to Smerinov.

'Your debriefing,' Igor Smerinov corrected him immediately. But he put the question. 'The General says it will begin soon, but there is no hurry,' he said.

Lavery nodded. He was surprised that, though many of the words escaped him, he was able to understand the gist of much of what Belatov said. But, perversely, even when Smerinov urged him to try to speak a little Russian, he insisted on keeping to English.

Eventually General Belatov indicated that he had had enough. The photographer was dismissed, and the two aides departed, presumably to the servants' quarters. When they returned each carried a tray. One bore short glasses and three bottles of

Stolichnaya, that most prized of vodkas, moist from the refrigerator where they had been chilled, the other held the *zakuski*, a wonderful collection of hors d'oeuvres—marinated mushrooms, salted herring, caviare, brown bread, smoked salmon, salami, red beet, pickled cucumber.

It was four o'clock in the afternoon by this time, and Neil Lavery would have preferred a cup of tea and a plain Romary biscuit. Lunch, though early, had been fairly substantial, and he was not hungry. Nor had he been deprived of alcohol since his arrival in Russia. Georgian wines, Soviet brandy and champagne, even genuine Scotch whisky had been readily available, and Igor had taught him the vodka ritual—a toast, gulping the whole of a small glass of the liquor, followed by a bite of food. But they had both been reasonably abstemious; Igor had even once gone so far as to admit that alcoholism was one of the more serious social problems in the USSR.

This afternoon was a different matter. As toast succeeded toast—'*Za vashe zdorovye!*' (To your health!); '*Za Angliyu!*' (To England!)—Lavery felt himself obliged to make some response. He knew enough Russian to cry, '*Za CCCR!*' (To the USSR!) and was greeted by cheers and a shout from the General, '*Za vashu Korolevu!*' (To your Queen!), amid roars of laughter.

The levels in the vodka bottles dropped steadily, and Lavery forced himself to eat in an effort to offset the effects of the Stolichnaya, which he thought he could feel burning the lining of his stomach. As they continued to drink, the atmosphere changed. Belatov and Smerinov began to talk together rapidly, as if exchanging

150

heart-to-heart confidences, *dusha-dushe.*. The General's aides were holding a conversation of their own, but Lavery was compelled—or felt he was compelled—to continue to match them drink for drink, as glasses were suddenly raised and the toasts became increasingly outrageous.

He knew he was becoming drunk. He could hear his thickened speech as he proposed his toasts, and his stumbled words. He wondered fleetingly if he were being intoxicated on purpose. Suddenly, as is often the case with vodka, the full reaction hit him. His digestion revolted. He staggered to his feet.

'F—feeling sick, Igor, old son,' he said. 'Can't take any more. Tell General—must go to—to bed.'

He had the impression that there was a burst of laughter, and that glasses were raised to him. Then he was out of the living-room, and climbing the stairs on all fours, like an animal. At the top he managed to stand for a moment. He reached his bedroom and its adjacent bathroom, where he vomited violently into the lavatory pan.

After a while his condition began to improve. The stomach contractions had ceased. Though he was still dizzy, he was able to get off his knees and go to the wash-basin. Here he dowsed his face in cold water, gasping at the shock, and that helped too.

It is unusual for vodka to make one vomit in this way, but later Lavery was able to reflect that maybe his reaction had saved him from the worst of the after-effects—the numbness, almost paralysis—that usually follow an overdose of the stuff.

Now Lavery went into the bedroom, kicked off his shoes and threw his tie on the floor without thought of Verity. He loosened his collar and, still

151

in his clothes, dropped on to the bed. Within minutes he was snoring heavily.

CHAPTER FOURTEEN

Lavery woke suddenly, and lay absolutely still for several minutes. Then, slowly and carefully, he raised his arm and looked at his watch. He could have sworn that he had been asleep all night, and that the room was light because it was morning. In fact he had slept for little more than an hour.

When he came upstairs he had been in no condition to make sure that his bedroom door was fully shut, and he could hear from below the sound of voices, a bellow of drunken laughter, the crash of breaking glass—maybe it was this that had awakened him. So, he thought, Belatov and his merry men were still at it, drinking and eating. He was thankful not to be downstairs with them.

Cautiously Lavery moved his limbs. They felt heavy, as if they didn't belong to him. It was easier to lie, unmoving, cocooned in a comfortable stupor. But to his surprise he had no headache, and he was not nauseated. There was no sign of the hangover that he would have been suffering all day had he been drinking whisky or gin instead of vodka. He forced himself to sit up, after a pause, to slide his legs off the bed on to the floor, and stand. The room remained steady and his balance seemed unaffected. He walked slowly to the door.

His intention had been to shut it, but the noises from down below had changed character. The voices had become more subdued. The laughter had ceased. Lavery got the impression of movement and bustle, as if the visitors were about to leave. Suddenly curious, he made his way carefully along the passage to the top of the stairs.

There were people coming and going in the hall below and he stood well back, so that he had a good view of the scene but would not be noticed if one of the Russians happened to glance up. The front door was open. A man whom he guessed to be General Belatov's chauffeur emerged from the servants' quarters and went into the living-room. The sound of heavy objects being moved suggested that he had gone to assist Smerinov and one of the aides to replace the pieces of furniture in their accustomed positions. The other aide stood with the General at the foot of the stairs.

They were talking, their voices rising and falling, but Lavery could hear almost everything they said. Naturally they were speaking in Russian, but his knowledge of the language was sufficient for him to pick up their meaning. Suddenly he heard his own name.

They were speaking more quietly now, and he was able to catch only the occasional word. He thought he heard '*Faza Dva*', which must be a reference to 'Phase Two' of something; as far as Lavery could make out he would not enjoy this 'Phase Two' much. Then he caught the word *dopros*, which he knew meant 'interrogation'. There was nothing startling about this. Lavery was not expecting to enjoy his so-called debriefing. He had no pretensions to bravery, and he had read enough about some of the methods employed to realize that any attempt to resist would be absurd. He would have no alternative but to tell his interrogators anything they wanted to know; after all, it would be taken for granted during the damage assessment in London that, as a defector, he would do just that. His major fear was that he might be suspected of keeping back important information which he didn't possess, and steps might be taken to . . .

Abruptly Lavery's thoughts returned to the present. The aide had given a raucous laugh. And his words were clear: '*Dazhe menyshij nravitsya Lavery evo rokovoj neschastnyi stutsai.*'

'*Zamolchat, Gregor Gregorivich!*' snapped General Belatov. '*V Faza Chetyre, Smerinov nechigo ne znaet!*'

At that moment Igor Smerinov and the second aide came into the hall. The visitors were on the point of departure. Neil Lavery crept back to his room, shocked by what he thought he had understood.

Certainly they had been talking about him, and Belatov's sudden spurt of anger suggested that the aide had been indiscreet. Lavery was fairly certain of the meaning of the words '*rokovoj neschastnyi stutsai*'—a 'fatal accident'—which the rest of the aide's sentence suggested that he—Lavery—would enjoy less; less than he would enjoy 'Phase Two', presumably. The General had retorted, 'Shut up! Smerinov knows nothing of Phase Four.' As the full implication of all this hit Lavery, he swallowed the bile that rose in his throat.

It was obvious that there would be no 'accident' until after the interrogation, until after they had wrung from him everything he knew. That seemed to be Phase Two. His death was perhaps Phase Four. What was Phase Three? And did it matter? In any case, he reassured himself, the

154

interrogation would give him some time. But time for what? To make some plan to save himself? At the moment he couldn't conceive of any way he could prevent the Russians from killing him when and how they pleased. He would be better off standing trial for treason in the UK. Given a good barrister, who knew how light his sentence might be? Maybe, if he could reach the British Embassy . . .

But why am I assuming all this on the basis of some half-understood Russian? Lavery asked himself bitterly. It could be a complete fantasy. Why should the Russians want to kill me? When I've served my purpose why shouldn't they expect me to settle down in Moscow just as—as Philby and the others have done? God knows, it's not ideal, but that's no reason for allowing my imagination to run away with me.

Lavery pulled off his clothes, letting them drop on the floor, found his pyjamas and got into bed. It was still quite early, but he had no desire for food or company. He buried his face in his pillow and tried not to think. But reality kept stunning his brain. He knew that he had been deluding himself. He hadn't misheard or misunderstood. There was some complex plot under way, in which he was to play some unknown part. And when it was over, General Belatov intended that he should die.

Eventually, perhaps as a delayed effect of the vodka or because of mental exhaustion, Neil Lavery did fall asleep. He didn't hear the bedroom door open, and was unaware that Igor Smerinov had come to check on his charge and had taken the opportunity to replace on the bedside table the photograph of Imogen and the children that Lavery had left in the living-room.

*   *   *

It was early the next morning when Neil Lavery woke again and there was only the faintest line of light around the edges of the curtains at his window. He felt clear-headed in spite of the excess vodka he had drunk with Belatov and his aides. Or was it *because* of that party? It must be hard to tamper with food and drink that is to be communally shared, and he had not eaten or drunk anything else afterwards.

He was becoming more and more convinced that he was being kept under some form of sedation. It would account for the increasing lethargy of his mind and body, and especially for the sapping of his will, of which he was sometimes conscious. He resolved that whenever possible he would eat and drink only dishes and liquor that Smerinov was sharing. If this tactic became too obvious, he would keep his intake to a minimum.

He watched the light brighten, and thought about the events of the previous evening and what he had learnt from them. God and the Russians alone knew how he had got himself into this position, but he realized that his options were limited. On the one hand, he could put up no resistance, allow himself to be used, and hope that he had misunderstood General Belatov and would eventually be permitted to live as a privileged Muscovite. Or he could try to escape to the British Embassy, and take his chances with British justice. Either way the outlook was bleak.

But Lavery knew in his heart that these were not

156

realistic alternatives. In practice, the choice was between passively letting Belatov use him and then kill him, or making a fight of it. In the first case death would probably be quick and comparatively painless. In the second case, if he failed to make it to the embassy, he would still die, but, he suspected, in somewhat different circumstances. And wouldn't he rather be dead than face years in prison?

His eye caught the photograph of his family on the bedside table, and he picked it up. He had been thinking only of himself, he realized, when he should have been considering Imogen and Matthew and Verity—and his parents, not to mention Imogen's family. And oddly enough it was the thought of his father-in-law that finally decided him. He would do what he was certain the old boy would do in his place. He would plan and struggle and resist and, if necessary, fight. Even if he failed, perhaps one day the whole story would be known.

There was yet another dimension to the problem. He must make a decision now, before Smerinov brought him his 'English breakfast', for the party with General Belatov had provided the ideal excuse to justify a change of attitude, and demonstrate his intention to co-operate. He must create such an impression if he were to have any chance of getting away—whatever the risks. It was not an easy decision.

He had put down the photograph and was lying back on his pillows when Igor Smerinov brought in his breakfast. He made himself smile weakly.

'How can you look so healthy, Igor Pavlovich, after all that vodka yesterday?'

Smerinov laughed. 'My poor Neil! I warned you

157

that we Russians are hard drinkers and used to our vodka.'

'I hope my sudden departure didn't offend General Belatov?'

'Not a bit. He thought you did well. He said I was to tell you that he enjoyed meeting you and hopes to see you again soon.'

'Ah, good!' Lavery studied the breakfast tray that sat before him, and considered what might be reasonably safe to eat; eggs and bacon should be all right. But toast, made from home-baked bread? And coffee—especially coffee—would be easy to doctor.

Lavery looked up. 'You know, Igor,' he remarked casually, 'I've been thinking, and meeting the General like that decided me. You're right. It's perfectly true that I never wanted to come here, but here I am now, and it's stupid not to make the best of it. It's ridiculous to be unco-operative.'

'Of course it is, Neil. This is important news. I'm delighted.'

Lavery smiled with relief. He had been afraid that Smerinov might be suspicious of such a sudden reversal. He had risked the orange juice and had started on the bacon and eggs, and he ate with every sign of enjoyment.

'So we'll be able to get on to Phase Two,' he said cheerfully, his mouth full.

'Phase Two!'

'My debriefing. The General mentioned it.'

'But—but you wouldn't have understood.' Smerinov was clearly uncertain what line to take.

Lavery had counted on the probability that the Russian would not remember or even have heard all that Belatov had said while they were drinking together. 'Oh, I understand a fair amount now, Igor. It's much more difficult actually to speak your language than it is to understand it. Incidentally, I wasn't sure of the meaning of Phase Three.'

'Phase Three?'

'Don't be dumb, Igor. After all there's no reason why I shouldn't know something about it, is there? It does concern me, I'm sure of that.'

'Yes—yes. It's your—your resettlement. When your debriefing's complete, we shall have to find you an apartment, and you'll need a car, more clothes, lots of things. And you'll want to meet people and go to the ballet, perhaps even get yourself a job later on.' After a tentative start Smerinov had begun to sound fluent and enthusiastic, as if he were a salesman with a good product. 'I expect life in Moscow will seem strange at first, but you'll soon settle down.'

'I wouldn't expect it to take too long—for me to get used to the situation, I mean.' With some difficulty Neil Lavery kept the edge from his voice. 'And then—Phase Four, Igor?'

'What? Neil, you can joke about it. That's wonderful.' Igor Smerinov slapped his thigh. 'There is no Phase Four, my friend. I'm sure General Belatov said nothing of a Phase Four.'

'I thought he did. Perhaps I was mistaken.'

'You must have been.'

Lavery had been eating busily. 'OK. I'll settle for Three.'

He was not dissatisfied. He was prepared to believe that Smerinov's denial of Phase Four was genuine, and it confirmed that he hadn't misheard or misunderstood what General Belatov had said. Now, he thought, he needed to make a plan.

159

In the event, however, Lavery was given little time or opportunity. The Russians, who had previously appeared slow and sluggish, as if they were happy to await his convenience, seemed suddenly to have decided on action. Later that same morning Smerinov informed him that his interrogation—his debriefing, call it what you will—was to commence on Monday; events were moving too fast for him.

It was now Saturday. 'Monday? So soon?' Lavery's mouth was dry.

'Why not? Since you are ready to co-operate, as I've just told General Belatov, we should go ahead at once.'

So he had brought it on himself, with his promise to be a good boy, Lavery thought angrily. 'Will you be conducting the debriefing, Igor?' he asked at length.

'Oh no, no! I shall be here, of course, to help you in any way I can. But debriefing is a specialized job, as you must know. For a start, someone will come from Moscow, and later there may be others or a group. It all depends.' Smerinov grinned. 'It will be quite painless, I assure you, Neil. Think of it as consulting with a team of friendly psychiatrists. They can make you remember things you didn't even know you knew.'

'Yes, I understand,' Lavery said, resisting the temptation to add, 'only too bloody well.'

Less than forty-eight hours, he thought, and then the experts would be here and he would be spilling out his heart's blood. If he didn't they would know he had lied about co-operating, and the end result would be the same. But to attempt to escape from

160

the *dacha* into the open countryside would be suicidal.

Then, when he least expected it, Igor Smerinov provided a possible answer.

'Tonight,' he announced with some pride, 'General Belatov has invited us to have dinner with him.'

'Dinner? You mean he's coming here again?'

'No. We go into Moscow. The General is sending his limousine for us.' Smerinov was beaming. 'We shall have the honour of meeting his family—his wife and his daughter.'

'We'll be going to his apartment?'

'I doubt it. Probably a restaurant or a club.'

'That sounds—perfect,' said Lavery. Of course, it was not perfect, but it sounded as if it might be a God-given chance and the last one he would get.

CHAPTER FIFTEEN

An observer might have been forgiven for thinking that Neil Lavery was a young man preparing to take his favourite girlfriend to a party. He had showered, washed his hair and shaved meticulously. Now he was contemplating his clothes. The choice was not extensive.

He had only one suit—the suit he had arrived in—but, freshly pressed and with a white shirt and his College tie, it should be perfectly acceptable to General Belatov and his family. It might also serve to make a reasonably favourable impression on the duty officer at the British Embassy, should this official ever get a chance to see it. But, without some kind of coat, he would be conspicuous on the

161

streets of Moscow, in the evening, and if he had to walk any distance the black shoes that the suit required were too light. Nevertheless, they would have to do.

He wished he knew where the Russians were taking him. A day or two ago, browsing among the few books in the *dacha*, he had found tucked away in one of them a plan of the Moscow Metro, overprinted on an elementary street plan of the city. He had studied this at length, and tried to recall what little he could from his reading about Moscow. He knew, for example, that the Kremlin stood beside the Moskva River in the centre of the city, with Red Square, the Lenin Mausoleum and St Basil's Cathedral to one side of it.

More to the point, he also knew that the British Embassy had originally been the home of a Tsarist sugar tycoon, and stood on a bank of the Moskva River, immediately opposite the Kremlin. It had been a popular story in official circles in the West that Stalin was invariably angered when he looked out of his rooms in the Kremlin and couldn't avoid seeing the British flag flying from a building on the Embankment directly across the water. And it took Lavery only a few moments to find the embassy's probable location on the map. It must be on the Nabarezhnaya Morisa Toreza, presumably named after Maurice Thorez, for many years the secretary-general of the French Communist Party.

Lavery could not bear to consider the odds against his reaching the embassy. All he knew was that they were phenomenally high, and that the stakes for which he was playing were high, too. He could imagine what would happen to him if he were caught in an attempt to escape. He could be certain of only one thing: that, whatever the outcome of the night's events, it was unlikely that he would be returning to this *dacha*.

He glanced around the bedroom for what he believed would be the last time. It held nothing of any value to him. He had already taken the photograph of Imogen and the children from its silver frame, and had folded it into his inside pocket. The frame he had put in a drawer; he didn't care what became of that.

He went downstairs. Igor Smerinov was in the living-room, talking to one of the aides who had previously accompanied General Belatov to the *dacha*—the one who, Lavery reminded himself, was familiar with this so-called 'Phase Four'. The aide greeted Lavery warmly.

'Good,' he said. 'Now we go. It is rather a long drive.' He spoke in English, but with a strong accent which made him hard to understand.

'We're going to the General's home?' Lavery asked.

'Oh, no. No. To a club, very select, very splendid. You will like.'

Lavery doubted that, though it occurred to him that a club, however elitist, might be less heavily guarded than General Belatov's private residence. Certainly his escorts were taking no risks with him on the way. He was placed between Smerinov and the aide on the broad rear seat of the limousine. In front, beside the driver, was a square figure who watched the passengers in the back of the Zil in a special rear-view miror of his own. Undoubtedly he, at least, was armed.

The driveway leading to the *dacha* and the country roads were poor, and even the big car,

163

driven at some speed, bumped over the ruts. Conversation was difficult, and for long periods the three men sat in silence. Lavery gazed out of the window, though there was little to see; the countryside—such of it as could be glimpsed through the coniferous woods—was flat and uninteresting, and it was purposeless to ask questions about the area.

He hoped, however, that when they reached the suburbs of Moscow a basic, seemingly guileless, question or two might help to orient him. He was disappointed when, as the road improved and houses appeared, the aide, leaning forward, drew down blinds to cover the glass partition separating them from the driver and the windows on his side of the limousine, and motioned to Smerinov to do the same. The last thing Lavery saw was a couple of depressing tower blocks rising out of nowhere.

Some twenty minutes later the Zil drew to a standstill. The driver leapt out and opened the car door. The man who had sat beside him was already on the pavement. As Lavery, preceded by Smerinov and followed by the aide, emerged, he glimpsed a wide tree-lined boulevard, well-lit and busy with traffic and people out for the evening. Then he was being ushered through iron gates, along a broad pathway and through a door which seemed to open miraculously ahead of them.

Inside, the club was imposing. Everywhere the deep carpets and hangings were crimson, the walls and woodwork white and gold, all signifying the luxury that obviously pervaded the building. The walls of the hall were hung with huge paintings of scenes of battle, and a wide marble staircase led upwards from it. A man who appeared to be some

164

kind of major-domo came forward to greet them obsequiously. Lavery heard the mention of General Belatov's name, and the man became even more ingratiating.

Smerinov said, 'I've been in the Army and Navy Club in London, Neil, and in some of the other Service clubs. They're not nearly as fine as this, are they?'

'This is very—very impressive,' Lavery agreed.

Escorted by the major-domo they mounted the stairs. On his right Lavery caught sight of an elegant room, filled with groups of men in uniform. He heard the clink of glasses and the buzz of voices; evidently a party was in progress, possibly a service reunion of some kind. To his left was a large dining-room, so far only about a quarter occupied.

The major-domo led the way past the entrance to this dining-room, and threw open the doors to a small private room. Lavery's heart sank. Though he had only the glimmerings of a possible plan, it depended partly on the party being in a more public place. Now he saw his chances halved.

There were already six people in the room, clutching glasses of champagne—General Belatov and his wife, who was surprisingly young and attractive, another couple whose names Lavery never grasped, the second aide who had come to the *dacha*, and the Belatovs' daughter, Anna. All the women were expensively dressed, and Anna was a beauty. With Lavery, Igor Smerinov and the aide who had brought them, they were an unbalanced party of nine. The man who had sat beside the chauffeur in the Zil, and who had followed them into the club and up the staircase, didn't come into the room. Lavery guessed that he would remain on guard outside the door.

The General came forward at once to greet Lavery effusively, and introduced him to the others merely as '*Neil, nash Anglijskij drug*'—'our English friend'. Lavery responded suitably and accepted a glass of champagne, reminding himself that, frustrated as he was, he must play his part as an Englishman new to Moscow, but ready to admire all things Russian. He wondered how many of those present knew his history, or what was intended for him. He suspected that the men were aware of how and why he had come to the USSR, and that their women probably guessed some of the story, but had been taught long ago that it was unwise to ask awkward questions of their menfolk.

At this point the door of the private room opened and a man appeared carrying a flash camera—the same photographer who had been to the *dacha*. At a nod from the General, he took a series of candid shots as they stood drinking, and more after the party were seated at the table, and then disappeared as silently as he had come. Excellent material for propaganda if and when the need arises, Lavery thought, and almost certainly the reason for putting the entertainment before interrogation.

However, no one made this obvious. General Belatov and the other guests were friendly and convivial. It might have been a dinner party of any privileged Muscovites, happy to welcome a stranger to their city. When they took their places at the table Lavery, as the guest of honour, was seated on Belatov's right. Anna was placed on his other side, because she was studying languages at Moscow University and spoke some English. In addition, Igor Smerinov was nearby, ready to continue to

166

interpret when necessary.

At first attention was centred on the guest of honour, and Lavery listened attentively, hiding his cynicism, as plans were made for him to visit the wonders of the Kremlin, the Bolshoi, Moscow's museums and art galleries. He doubted whether he would ever have the chance. But, as the meal progressed the conversation became less general and, to his relief, Lavery ceased to be the centre of attraction. Anna, eager to practise her English, monopolized him, asking questions about London, and he had to believe that she at least was harmless. He ate and drank automatically, failing to appreciate the excellent food and the fine Russian wines.

As the dinner approached its end, Lavery reflected on the trace of a plan that had been in his mind. Obviously, one way to leave the room was to ask to do just that—to use the lavatory. Of course, the man he should ask was Smerinov, who would immediately leap to his feet and accompany him; possibly some of the other men would also take the opportunity.

He contemplated the beautiful Anna, and wondered how he might use the daughter of General Vadim Belatov. He sensed that she was attracted to—or at least intrigued by—him; out of ignorance she might be able to help, if he could think of an angle—But he was aware of Smerinov watching and listening.

When Anna's chatter ceased for a moment, he said quietly, 'Tell me, in the Soviet Union is it the custom for the ladies to retire at the end of a meal, and leave the gentlemen to themselves to drink their port—or vodka?'

167

Anna threw back her head and laughed. She was well aware of how attractive she was. 'Oh, Comrade,' she said, emphasizing the form of address, 'You must know we don't have *ladies* and *gentlemen* here, even nowadays.'

Lavery grinned at her. 'That wasn't quite the point of my question,' he murmured. 'What I meant was, when do the—er—the female comrades go to powder their noses? That's a polite English idiom for going to the cloakroom.'

She giggled. 'I must remember that. The answer's when it suits them. What about you men?'

'It's not always so simple. Protocol and the workings of one's insides don't always agree.'

Anna frowned, and Lavery realized that his English had been too colloquial. Though she wouldn't admit it, she hadn't understood what he had said. If he were to take advantage of this situation he must speak more simply.

He lowered his voice still further. 'At this moment I really do desperately need to go to the cloakroom, but I can't be the first. It's so embarrassing.'

'You have no need to be embarrassed.' Anna was amused.

'But I am. In a new country, and in these circumstances—' He looked at her appealingly, thinking that he had nothing to lose. 'I suppose you wouldn't lead the way for me? Please.'

She scarcely hesitated. 'Of course.'

She said something to her father in Russian, which Lavery didn't understand. Then she was on her feet and crossing the room, almost before Lavery realized she had left his side. He pushed back his chair. Here was his chance and he had to take it.

'Toilet,' he said to Smerinov. 'Must go. Urgent.'

Conversation had ceased, but the company were slow to act. Taken by surprise and unsure how to interpret these movements, no one knew quite what to do. Lavery had reached the door and shut it behind him before General Belatov barked an order and the two aides went after him, followed by an anxious Igor Smerinov.

Anna Belatova had waited in the corridor. Lavery seized her by the arm and propelled her past the startled guard, who would certainly have stopped him had he been alone, and along to the top of the staircase. The large party he had glimpsed on his arrival was over, but there was still a lot of activity in the club. There were groups of people standing in the hall, talking, while others were intent on their own business. Lavery knew they could be both a help and a hindrance to him.

He was counting on Belatov and his men being anxious to avoid a public spectacle, especially as long as Anna was involved. But when he began to urge her down the stairs, she protested.

'There are cloakrooms on this floor. What are you doing? Where are you taking me?' She spoke sharply, trying to wrest her arm from his grasp.

'It's all right. Don't worry.'

They were half-way down the stairs by now, and their momentum would carry them forward a few steps, but Lavery knew that Anna would stop dead as soon as she could—and would possibly scream for help. He would never make it across the hall to the main doors. The major-domo, who had been talking to a member, had spotted the General's daughter and was starting towards her, and a couple

169

of men in uniform were closer. Lavery thought quickly.

'Anna, is there a back way out of this club?'

She replied without thinking, 'Yes. Of course.' But her voice was troubled. She was no longer sure of herself.

Lavery paid no attention to her changing attitude. 'Show me!' he ordered fiercely, his fingers digging into the soft part of her upper arm, bruising her.

'You're hurting me,' said Anna, but she seemed too frightened or astonished to cry for help. At the bottom of the stairs she swerved to the left. For a moment Lavery thought she was trying to free herself, but she pushed through a door so well hidden in the white and gold panelling that there was no indication of its presence. It brought them into a complex of passages.

This was clearly a service area. There was no carpeting, and the walls were merely painted a dull grey. They passed a couple of waiters who stared at them in surprise, and Lavery knocked against a bus-boy carrying a tray of dirty glasses, which made a resounding crash as they hit the floor.

However, no one tried to stop them, but when they reached a cross passage Anna hesitated.

'I—I don't know which way,' she whimpered.

There was a shout from behind, and the sound of running footsteps. Lavery had no time to argue. Anyway the girl had served her purpose. He opened the nearest door, and thrust her inside what appeared to be a linen cupboard.

'Keep quiet!' he said viciously, and shut her in.

There was no key, and he wouldn't have bothered with one. It would have meant wasting precious seconds. He ran. He had chosen the passage at random, and found himself in what was obviously a laundry room. At first he thought he had come to a dead end and almost gave up hope. But there was a door, presumably leading to the outside—and, as was to be expected, a window.

Breathing heavily, he hurried across the room. The door was locked. He peered out of the window. It was a clear night, bright with stars, and he could see into a small yard surrounded by a wall, with double doors in its centre. Beyond was a tall building, and in between, he could only hope, a lane or alleyway. He fumbled with the window latch. This was his final, his only chance. The Russians were searching for him now and he couldn't retreat.

At last and with a fearful screech the sash window opened and Lavery clambered over the sill. He made straight for the door in the wall but without great expectation. It too was locked, offering him no hope. The wall was ten feet high, but he had to get over it or be cornered.

Desperately he looked around for anything that would help to give him a leg-up, but the yard was empty except for a small pile of coal, which was in the wrong place and anyway quite useless. As the lights went on in the laundry room he had just left he took a running jump at the wall.

One arm reached over the top, but the other slipped. He felt himself falling and scrabbled for a foothold. Mercifully the toe of his shoe found a crack and this slight support enabled him to get his other arm over the wall. He hung there. For the moment he had insufficient strength to pull himself further up.

There were shouts behind him. 'Neil, come back! Neil!' He recognized Igor Smerinov's voice. Then someone was climbing out of the window. His legs would be seized and he would be hauled down. He had to make a supreme effort. Gritting his teeth—the pain in his arms was becoming intense—he tried to heave himself upwards.

Three things happened simultaneously. There was a cry of *'Niet! Niet!'* from Smerinov, the sound of a shot—and a bullet hit the wall beside his shoulder, sending splinters of brick about his head. If Lavery had needed any incentive, this was it. He never heard the second shot. He was up and over the wall, lying in a heap in the alley beyond.

CHAPTER SIXTEEN

Neil Lavery had hit the paved floor of the alley hard, but he forced himself to his feet in a matter of seconds and started to run between the walls which bordered the path, without conscious choice of direction. It was not until he had gone some fifty metres that he started to stumble and realized that all was not well with him. His left thigh was hurting, and when, still moving forward, he slid his hand down the inside of his trousers and felt a warm, sticky area, he knew he had been hit by a bullet. He certainly hadn't expected his pursuers to be gentle if they had caught up with him while he was hanging on the wall; he had known he would be pulled roughly to the ground, and probably kicked and beaten. But that in present circumstances the Soviet authorities were prepared to act so dramatically—to fire at him, if only to wound rather than kill, and not as a warning—was an additional chilling shock.

He continued his rapid but stumbling progress. He had no choice but to put as much distance as possible between General Belatov's thugs and himself, though he had no idea where he was or where he was heading. As far as he was concerned the British Embassy could be a thousand miles away. And steadily he saw his chances of outdistancing his hunters diminishing. His thigh was becoming increasingly painful and his pace was slowing. His best hope was some kind of ruse. But what?

He glanced back over his shoulder and saw quite clearly the outline of a figure on top of the wall, by now more than a hundred metres away. The Russians had been slow. If he weren't seen now, they wouldn't know whether he had turned right or left, and at least that might confuse them. And, what was more, there was what looked like a door on his left a few metres ahead. He could scarcely believe his luck when the handle turned easily and he found himself in a yard at the rear of a large building.

There was a lock on the door, but no key. Instead, there was a stout piece of wood that could be swung down into a socket, effectively preventing entrance. At best, finding the door secure, any pursuers might pass it by; at worst they would be delayed. For a moment Lavery leant back against the door revelling in a momentary sense of security that he knew was false. But he was beyond caring. By now he was acting largely on instinct, like a wounded and trapped animal looking for a place to

173

hide or die.

The building was dark, though a few glimmers showed through some curtains, and in the half-light he limped towards it. He stumbled over a bucket, which rolled away with a fearful clanking noise, and he fell. As his injured thigh hit the hard earth he had to bite his lip to swallow the pain and prevent himself from crying out.

Almost immediately a voice called softly, '*Eto ty, Dimitri?*'

It was the voice of an old man, hoarse but not lacking in authority. A window opened ahead of Lavery, but the question was not repeated.

Lavery lay where he had fallen, in a dark shadow thrown by the wall of some outhouse. He prayed that the owner of the voice would conclude that the noise he had heard had been caused by a dog or a cat, and that he wouldn't emerge to investigate or to search for the missing Dimitri. And, indeed, after a minute the window was shut again.

Lavery expelled his breath gently. He was sweating, and he didn't dare to move, for outside in the alley there was the sound of running footsteps and subdued voices. Someone tried the door in the wall, and Lavery was grateful for the wooden bar that secured it. He waited for his would-be captors to begin to pound on the door, demanding entrance, but the footsteps and the voices retreated. For the moment he was safe.

But he couldn't stay here for ever. He must move, and quickly. Quite apart from his pursuers, the unknown Dimitri might appear at any moment, and the old man come out to open the door for him. Presumably Dimitri's obviously expected arrival was the reason the door had been left open in the first place. Before anything of that kind happened he must find somewhere to hide, somewhere to examine his thigh, perhaps bind it up, and take general stock of his situation.

All this was clearly sensible, but in the circumstances the difference between the sensible and the practical was vast. It came home to Lavery bleakly that he hadn't given nearly enough serious thought to the details of his plan of escape. Perhaps naïvely, he had imagined himself causing some kind of fracas (which he supposed he had accomplished) and bursting out of house or club or restaurant into a well-lit public thoroughfare where he could elude those pursuing him. He had hoped that he would eventually manage to find a taxi to take him to the embassy; he had no money, but his watch would have been more than adequate payment.

He had not imagined that this would be simple. On the contrary, he had been acutely pessimistic. He had accepted the possibility, or rather the probability, that he would be caught. What he had not foreseen was anything like his present predicament. Admittedly he was free for the moment, but he was bruised from the two falls and his hands were bleeding as a result of his frantic climb over the wall at the club where, seemingly aeons ago, the General had been so glad to entertain him. He was exhausted, his appearance disreputable, suit torn and shoes scuffed—a figure that would be alarmingly conspicuous on the streets of Moscow at any time of day or night. More importantly, he had been shot and he had no idea of the seriousness of his wound or how much blood he had lost. And, to cap it all, he was lying, hardly able to move, in the back yard of what he could

175

only think was a large block of flats; he could be anywhere in Moscow, perhaps far from his goal, the embassy.

Move somewhere, however, he must, unless he was to give up and lie there until he was discovered and handed over to the authorities. But when he tried to rise he found that the enforced rest, however welcome, had caused his wounded leg to stiffen. Slowly, supporting himself against the wall of the outhouse against which he had been lying, Lavery managed to stand. But when he put any weight on his left leg it buckled under him and he fell again.

Nevertheless, in the brief moment he had been upright, he had caught a glimpse of a possible hiding-place—a collection of large garbage cans. If he could reach them, they would afford some minimal protection that would be better than nothing. There was no way he could walk to this shelter, so he steeled himself and crawled, like the animal he had become.

His effort was rewarded, and rewarded beyond his expectations. He found that one of the garbage cans was empty and lying on its side, with its lid nearby. The interior of the can smelt loathsome, but he didn't care. Like a large dog in too small a kennel he backed into his hideaway and drew the lid towards him. Then he lost consciousness.

★   ★   ★

Igor Smerinov had never before beheld General Belatov so enraged. His face was purple, and the veins on his neck were so prominent they threatened to burst. Smerinov, quailing before him, hoped they would.

It was six o'clock the next morning and they were in the Kremlin, where Belatov maintained an office, in addition to a suite in his headquarters. Neither man had had any sleep, but the General had the advantage of having washed and shaved and changed his shirt. Nominally they were reviewing the state of the search for Lavery, but in fact the General was taking the opportunity to vent some of his frustration.

Belatov banged his fist down on the desk and Smerinov, standing opposite him—he had not been invited to sit—jumped nervously.

'Lavery tricked you!' Belatov repeated explosively. 'What we wanted, needed above all else at this moment, was his collaboration. But he had no intention of collaborating with us, in public or otherwise. It was a pretence to give himself a chance to get away—and you never saw through it. You were completely ensnared by the Englishman, Comrade Major Smerinov!'

'Yes, Comrade General.' Smerinov had no difficulty in refraining from pointing out that Belatov had also been decieved. He trembled. 'I—I can't tell you how distressed I am. It was an appalling misjudgement on my part.'

'It will be more than that if Lavery reaches the British Embassy!'

'But he can't, Comrade General! We've established a strict guard on the place, and on the block where most of the embassy officials live, and put a cordon round the whole area. Anyway—'

'You had a guard outside the dining-room door at the club. What good did that do? He just let the wretched Englishman go past.'

177

'Lavery was with your daughter, Comrade General. The guard was reluctant to intervene—'

'He's paid to think as well as use his blasted weapon. It should have been obvious to any moron that my daughter was being forced along by the Englishman. The poor girl is dreadfully upset by the affair. She was in fear for her life. He could have strangled her. And I hold you—you—responsible, Comrade Major.'

Smerinov said nothing. He knew it would be useless to argue that Anna Belatova must have waited for Lavery in the corridor and, at first, have gone with him willingly. Smerinov had to blame himself. He should have been more suspicious when he saw Lavery whispering so earnestly to the General's daughter.

'You chose that guard yourself,' Belatov went on. 'You said you'd worked with him before and he was the best. But he can't even shoot straight. As I understand it there was the Englishman hanging from the top of the wall by his fingertips. A perfect target, and he missed him—not once but twice! How do you explain that, Major Smerinov?'

'Comrade General—' Smerinov was sweating. He had hoped that question would not be asked. But the point had been raised and he would have to answer it truthfully because there had been witnesses. He couldn't lay the blame on the guard. 'I shouted at him to make the first shot a warning,' Smerinov said. 'I hoped—I expected that Lavery would be scared by it and—'

'You fool! You inefficient fool! What the hell have you been doing since Lavery was brought to the *dacha*?' Belatov thumped his desk again. 'Your orders were to get to know the man, really know

178

him, gain his confidence. But what happens? *He* gets to know *you*, and you—you get so attached to him you actually help him to escape.'

'No, Comrade General, no. It wasn't like that—' Smerinov protested weakly.

'All right. I accept that a warning shot was not unreasonable, but as for the second round—'

He knows, Smerinov thought, and he's waiting for me to lie. 'I accept responsibility for that too, Comrade General,' he said at length. 'I purposefully diverted the shot by distracting the guard. Otherwise Neil Lavery would now be dead, and we have not yet commenced the interrogation.'

'Brilliant, Igor Pavlovich! A brilliant excuse. I wish I could believe it. You thought of the interrogation, and therefore saved his life—but you did it *so that he could get away*!' Belatov's voice rose to a shout. 'So what about the interrogation now? Answer me that!'

'Lavery will be found, Comrade General, and before the day is out. He has no money, nowhere to go. His understanding of our language is limited. He has no idea where he is, or how to find his way round Moscow.'

'You say he has nowhere to go. I say he'll do his best to get to the British Embassy, and then home to England.'

'But, Comrade General, he wouldn't be able to return to his old life. He would be arrested immediately he arrived in England; in fact the British would have to send him back under guard, and there is no way we could prevent them without a major scandal. In England he would be tried for espionage and sent to prison for years. The British are not lenient with those who betray them. And if

179

the main reason he didn't want to come to Moscow in the first place was concern for his family—well, his return now wouldn't change the situation. He would see very little more of them than if he were here, and the publicity of the trial would make things worse for his wife and children. Lavery's not a stupid man. He must understand all this.'

It was the longest statement that Smerinov had made since he had arrived in the General's Kremlin office, and it was met with silence. Smerinov wondered at his temerity in addressing the Comrade General in this fashion. He could feel the sweat on his upper lip, and wiped it away with the back of his hand in a quick, nervous gesture, like a small boy wiping his nose.

At last General Belatov spoke, clearly choosing his words with care. 'Comrade Major, because we always do our best to look after those who have served us well, it was imperative for Neil Lavery to be brought to Moscow. For the same reason—so that our assets in foreign countries should continue to know that we intend to continue to make every effort to protect them—it's equally imperative that Lavery should not be allowed to return. So he must be captured, preferably alive, but if that proves impossible he must be killed. Afterwards, and if necessary, we can claim an accidental death. You had better understand this, Comrade Major, for your own future depends on it. Do you understand?'

'Yes, Comrade General,' said Igor Smerinov, his mouth so dry that he could hardly speak.

*   *   *

180

It was daylight before Neil Lavery regained full consciousness. He had spent the latter part of the night in a troubled half-sleep, beset by hideous dreams from which he woke, terrified, only to drowse and dream again. Now he was not immediately certain if he were awake or not.

Then, suddenly, he became aware that the lid of the garbage can which had protected him from view had been thrown aside, and that a face was within inches of his own. It was a strange face, long and narrow, with a straggling grey beard and bright brown eyes that reminded him of a squirrel. There was a flood of Russian which he failed to understand, though its import was self-evident.

'What are you doing in there?'

Even if Lavery had spoken the language fluently, it would have been hard to explain, so he merely shut his eyes and groaned. He knew that most Soviet apartment blocks had a warden—an *upravdom*—but this character hardly looked as if he bore such a responsibility. It was almost certainly the old man who had heard him last night, and thought he was someone called Dimitri. But, though he might not be a representative of the authorities, undoubtedly he would send for them.

Nevertheless, Lavery lacked the strength to resist when he felt surprisingly strong hands reach under his armpits to pull him from his refuge. He cried out as his wounded thigh hit the ground, and fainted. He was unaware that his cry and the smothered oath that accompanied it had been in his native tongue, or that the old man had stared at him in amazement for some minutes.

When he recovered consciousness again Lavery found himself alone, and his first thought was that

181

the old man hadn't wasted much time in going to fetch the Militia. He was wrong. Moments later the man returned. He knelt beside Lavery and, gently supporting him, held a mug of water to his lips. Lavery drank thirstily and thanked him.

'*Spasibo.*'

The old man smiled. His teeth were brown and broken. He wore a round woollen cap, a kind of smock, and trousers held up with string. But he was very clean. The unpleasant smell that hung around them came, Lavery realized, not from the old man but from himself. He stank after the hours he had spent in the garbage can.

'You can't stay here,' the old man said. 'D'you think you could walk if I helped you?'

It was Lavery's turn to stare. The old man had spoken in fluent, idiomatic English that was scarcely accented. Lavery's hopes soared. Perhaps, since there was no language barrier, he could plead with this Russian, who was obviously kind. He was also clearly poor, so that he might be open to the promise of reward from the British Embassy.

'I'll try,' said Lavery, 'but I've hurt my leg.'

'That I can see,' said the old man. 'Come. Try to get up.'

It required a major effort for Lavery to rise to his feet and, as soon as he put weight on his left leg, he nearly fell once again. But this time the old man was there to support him, and help him move towards the building, careful step by careful step. Even with this assistance it was a slow, laborious progress. Though light of frame, Lavery was tall, and the old man was short and bent, but apparently not in the least frail.

At last they reached a door leading to a narrow

passage, with a short flight of stairs ahead. Another door on the right led to what was clearly the old man's domain. This was one all-purpose room, and the strangest that Neil Lavery had ever seen. Even in his present weary state, he wondered at it. About ten metres by twelve, it had in one corner a large sink, next to which was a stove, providing washing and cooking facilities. The furniture consisted of a table, two chairs and a bed. There was shelving for a few clothes, and a packing case in which the old man kept his food. The only window was barred, and large pipes ran around the walls. The floor was bare cement.

The old man smiled grimly as he saw Lavery looking about him. 'The lavatory is at the top of the stairs,' he said. 'Otherwise I have every convenience here—and I'm lucky to have the place. But we'll talk later, Englishman. First we must clean you up, and attend to your wound.'

CHAPTER SEVENTEEN

An hour later Neil Lavery was considerably more comfortable. He was lying in his shirt and underpants on the old man's bed. His gun-shot wound had been examined, carefully cleaned and dressed with such supplies as were available. Lavery had been lucky. Although he had lost a fair amount of blood, the bullet had passed through the fleshy part of his upper thigh and had apparently done no serious damage to muscle or bone; both the entry and exit holes were small and neat. The only possible trouble was infection, the old man assured him. What he must do was rest for a few days, and then, all being well, he would be vastly improved.

Lavery doubted it. In spite of a thorough wash, he could still smell the lingering odour of the garbage can in which he had spent the night. It was, he supposed, the least of his troubles, but he found it hard to believe that he would ever get it out of his nostrils. More importantly, whatever he smelt like, he certainly did not have a few days in which to recover. Belatov's men, if not the Militia, would be searching for him even at this moment, and God alone knew what his fate would be if (or more likely when) he was caught. So much depended on this baffling old character.

'Breakfast, Englishman, and then we must talk. I'm afraid it's not the bacon and eggs to which you're accustomed.'

Lavery thought fleetingly of Igor Smerinov and the *dacha*. 'I'm very grateful for anything,' he said, and indeed he had no wish to exchange the milkless tea and the sweet-tasting Russian bread for the 'English breakfast' provided by Smerinov—not that he would get any more 'English breakfasts' were he recaptured. 'You've been more than kind to me,' he added.

'In the past certain people have been kind to me, or I wouldn't be here. So, if God gives me the chance, I repay my debts to them by helping others. To be honest, I don't often get such opportunities these days.' The old man smiled, again displaying his neglected teeth.

Lavery stared at him, and then around the room. 'I don't understand,' he said at length. 'For one thing, you speak such good English—'

The old man grinned. 'You mean, what is a man
184

like me doing in a place like this? You flatter me, Englishman.'

Lavery hesitated for a moment, and then said, 'My name's Neil Lavery.' The name brought no reaction from the old man. Clearly the story of the defection—or the escape—had not been released in Moscow.

'And mine's Josef Spaslov,' the old man replied. He poured more tea for Lavery, and then for himself. 'You are curious about me? My story is simple. I was a teacher of English, a professor at Moscow University, but I fell into bad company—or at least the authorities regarded it as bad company. It was in the time of Stalin, and I am a Jew.' For a moment he was silent, as if reminiscing to himself, lines cut deep in his elderly face.

He sighed, and continued. 'I was sent to a *Gulag* camp—a labour camp—in the north. My wife died and my son was taken away. I had nothing. Fortunately the camp was not one of the worst, but even so life was barely tolerable. Strangely enough I clung to it, and eventually I was allowed to return to Moscow. So here I am, an ex-professor, now a cleaner in this apartment block. Times are changing—have changed—of course, but too late for me.'

Lavery could think of nothing to say. Though he knew this kind of story was by no means unique in the Soviet Union he was appalled. But it was impossible to offer sympathy, and he was ashamed that he couldn't help wondering how the old man might be able to be of service.

'Now tell me about yourself, Mr Neil Lavery,' Josef Spaslov said.

Lavery didn't want to lie, but he was afraid that if he told the exact truth his new host might be reluctant to help him. And help he had to have, if there were to be any hope of evading those who had shown themselves prepared to kill him.

'I'm an English Civil Servant,' he said. 'I work in the Ministry of Defence in London. I was here in Moscow merely as a tourist, but I've been accused of being a spy. This is totally untrue. I've never been a British agent—or any kind of agent, for that matter—or had any wish to be such a thing.'

'How did it happen that you were arrested? Were you taking photographs?' Spaslov sounded dubious.

'No. I didn't even have a camera with me. Yesterday evening I was standing in Red Square admiring the skyline, the wonderful domes and spires, when two men came up to me and seized me. Of course I protested, but I was hurried towards a car and driven somewhere. I can't even begin to describe our route or our destination, because the car had blinds on the windows. I was scared stiff, naturally.'

'Naturally,' repeated Spaslov. 'Then what?' he prompted.

'The car stopped and we got out. After my first protests, I'd become quite docile, and they'd become careless. By now it was dark and I seized my chance. I hit one and fled. The other one shot me, but I managed to get away. When my leg began to fail I looked for a place to hide. The door to your back yard was open and—you know the rest.'

'I opened it for one Dimitri, a young friend of mine who goes secretly to visit his sweetheart. He had to climb the wall when he returned this morning.'

186

'I'm sorry,' Lavery said untruthfully, knowing that the barred door had saved him from his pursuers. He wondered to what extent the old man believed the story he had been told; it was, he realized, pretty thin. The Militia wouldn't have let him out of the car until they were safe inside some prison or police post. But he went on. 'They took my wallet with my money and my passport. I've nothing except my watch. I can't imagine why they didn't take that too.'

Josef Spaslov looked at the watch that Lavery was holding out to him. He turned it in his hand as if admiring it and finally slipped it into his trouser pocket. Unreasonably, since he had offered it to the old man, Lavery felt disappointed at Spaslov's reaction.

Then Spaslov said, 'I know someone who will buy this, and not cheat me—or at least not much. A watch like this will bring good money in Moscow, for food, some antiseptic and proper bandages for your thigh—and you'll want some clothes. The suit you were wearing is ruined.'

Immediately Lavery was ashamed. He realized that he had been expecting a reluctant acceptance of the watch and profuse thanks, but in fact Josef Spaslov had never thought of it as a gift. He had thought only of his guest.

'There's something I need even more, my friend,' Lavery said. 'And that is for you to telephone the British Embassy. Give them my name and say—' He paused, thinking. 'Is there somewhere not far from here where I could be picked up at a given time?'

'Not today. You couldn't walk ten yards. Or tomorrow. Perhaps the next day.'

187

'But—but that's impossible.' He couldn't stay there for days, taking the old man's bed. In any case, it was too close to the club he had escaped from. If Belatov hadn't already mobilized his resources to mount a really thorough search, taking the club as its centre point, they soon would.

'I'm afraid you have no choice.' Spaslov was washing up the remains of their meagre breakfast and tidying the already tidy room. 'I have to go now,' he said. 'I mustn't neglect my regular duties or it will cause comment, but you'll be all right here. The water in the sink is potable. No one will come. And I'll do what I can to buy things for you.'

'Thank you very much indeed. But it's equally important to phone my embassy. If they brought a car to the lane after dark possibly you could help me get as far as that. Please! I know it's asking a lot, but—'

'Do you know anyone at your embassy to whom I should speak? It would be helpful if I could ask for someone personally.'

'No. I'm sorry. I don't.' Lavery thought suddenly of Kevin Sinder who had once had a Moscow posting, but he was back in London—and London was in a different world.

'Anyway, I'll do my best,' said Spaslov finally. 'Trust me. Even an old Jew can be a good Samaritan on occasion.'

*   *   *

It was several hours before Josef Spaslov returned. For Lavery, who had no means of telling the time, the waiting was interminable. In his whole life he had never been so glad to see anyone as he was

188

when the old man at last opened the door. He swore to himself that if he ever got out of his present mess he would do anything he could to repay him for his kindness and trust.

'Not bad, not bad at all,' said Spaslov. 'I got a fair price for your watch. Not its true worth, of course, in a hard currency, but we want roubles and, as I said, in Moscow a watch like that is valuable on the black market. I've managed to buy you trousers and a pseudo-leather jacket, a woollen cap and some shoes. I only hope they fit. They'll make you look like a genuine Muscovite.'

'What can I say, except thank you? I'm so very grateful.' Lavery yearned to ask about the British Embassy, but knew he must be patient. 'That will have cost you a lot.'

'Unfortunately, yes. A wicked price for shoddy goods, but that's the way it is here for people like me. Still, there was enough left over for medicines and bandages and some food—and a bottle of vodka.'

The old man busied himself with arranging his purchases on the table, and Lavery could bear the suspense no longer. 'And the embassy?' he asked. 'Did you get through?'

'Yes. I did.'

'And—'

Spaslov considered his guest curiously. 'Well, they weren't exactly helpful,' he commented at last.

'What do you mean?'

'I'm sorry. It could have been my accent—'

'But your English—'

'Oh, I know it's perfectly fluent, but telephones sometimes accentuate accents, if you see what I mean. Anyway, for whatever reason, I couldn't persuade anyone to take what I had to say about you seriously. I spoke to two different men, one obviously more senior than the other. They seemed to know your name, but they were more interested in me. They kept asking questions and—and frankly I didn't trust them.'

'Oh God!'

This was a problem Lavery had not foreseen. Of course the officials at the embassy would have recognized his name; they would have been informed of his defection and of the possibility that he would appear in Moscow. For this very reason he had expected them to be eager to reclaim him, as they would see it, so that he might pay the price for his treachery. That they should have failed to believe Josef Spaslov, and thought of his phone call as some kind of hoax—or possibly, Lavery reflected, some kind of provocation—had simply not occurred to him.

'When you are stronger you will be able to telephone them yourself, and convince them who you are and that you need their help,' the old man said consolingly, seeing Lavery's distress. 'I'll get you a stick to support your leg and make walking easier.'

Neil Lavery blinked the tears from his eyes. He was touched by the old man's continuing kindness to a stranger and a foreigner—and possibly a dangerous stranger and foreigner; the embassy's reaction to his call must have given Josef Spaslov pause for thought. But, as Lavery strove to find words to express his gratitude, there was a loud knock on the door, and he could think only of himself. There was no time and, as far as he could see, no place to hide.

190

'It's all right,' Spaslov murmured. 'The authorities in this city wouldn't bother to knock on my door before breaking it down.' But he put a finger to his lips, urging silence, and Lavery lay, sweating in spite of this reassurance. Then there was a second knock, and the old man went to the door and opened it a few inches.

'Dimitri!' he said loudly, as a cue for Lavery.

There was a low, hurried conversation in Russian, and Spaslov shut the door. 'Quick!' he said to Lavery. 'That was a warning. The Militia are searching all the buildings along this street, especially the rear premises. The chances are they're looking for you; you couldn't have gone far with that leg, so it was probably somewhere nearby that they lost you.'

'They mustn't find me here. I must go. Better they find me in a garbage can than with you.'

'They're not going to find you!'

While they were speaking the old man had brought up a chair and helped Lavery to hoist himself on to it. Then he pulled the bed away from the wall. There were more pipes behind the bed, but the old man pulled them apart with seemingly practised ease, and was then able to push aside a small wooden sliding panel to reveal a narrow crawl space. He threw in an old rug from the bed and struggled to help Lavery get in after it. They managed the movement with some difficulty, but eventually succeeded. Then Spaslov arranged round Lavery the clothes he had just bought and the bag of food. As an afterthought he added the bottle of vodka.

'The devils would steal it,' he said by way of explanation. 'You hang on to it. We'll open it when

191

they've gone.'

'What about air?' Lavery asked anxiously as Spaslov began to slide the partition back into place.

'There's plenty.' The old man paused, then added cautiously, 'You're not the first to hide in here, you know.'

The next minute Neil Lavery was in darkness. Something brushed gently across his face, and before he realized it was merely a spider's web he nearly cried out. He bit his lower lip hard. He could hear Josef Spaslov fitting together the obviously unused or fake pipes and pushing the bed back into place. Then silence, and the thought occurred to Lavery that if the old man were to be taken away, no one would know of his presence.

Earlier he had thought the slowly passing hours while he waited for Spaslov's return intolerable. But, in comparison with his present position, he had then been at the height of comfort. Here he couldn't see. He couldn't stretch his limbs. He dared not cough or sneeze. And the chances that he would escape capture seemed to him to be minimal. All he could do was contemplate anxiously the fate of those others whom Spaslov said had been concealed here. He comforted himself with the thought that if they had been found, Josef Spaslov himself would no longer be in residence.

It seemed like days, but in reality it was merely thirty minutes before Lavery heard the Militia arrive. They certainly did not knock, but suddenly burst into the room with no warning. He thought there were three of them. They had harsh, strident voices, but their words were muffled by the partition, the pipes and the bed itself. Then the bed must have been pulled back from the wall because the voices became clearer. He heard the old man say *'Niet'*, over and over again in a high whine that ended in a shriek, as if he had been struck. Then there was a thump that might have been a body falling to the floor.

Lavery braced himself. Any moment now he expected to be discovered, to be dragged triumphantly from his hiding-place. But what he feared didn't happen. There was a raucous laugh as if someone had suddenly seen a joke, and the door slammed. Slowly Lavery released his breath.

Minutes passed. Lavery could hear nothing, and now he was beset by different fears. Where was Josef Spaslov? Why didn't he release him? Was he lying out there unconscious? And, if so . . .

He was enormously relieved when, on the other side of the wooden panel, quite close to him, he heard Spaslov say softly, 'Be patient. Sometimes they bluff—they pretend to go away, but come rushing back. It's a trick they like to play.'

'OK,' Lavery muttered in return. 'I'm all right.'

This time the wait seemed relatively short. Nevertheless, Lavery was glad when the pipes were dismantled, the panel opened and, with Spaslov's assistance, he was able to crawl out. But it was not until Spaslov had helped him up on to the bed that he took in the appearance of the little room—and of Josef Spaslov himself.

One chair lay on its side; the other had escaped attention. The packing case in which the old man kept his food had been kicked over, and the few items in it trampled. His extra clothes, scarcely more than a change, had been added to the heap and trampled too. And Spaslov had a split lip—there was blood on his beard—and a bruise

193

beginning to spread across one cheek.

'They hit you,' exclaimed Lavery, 'and they made all this damned mess. But why? They could search without that. Or did they think you knew where I was?'

'No, of course not.' Spaslov was quite definite. 'If they'd thought that I'd be in a much worse condition, and I'd have told them. They don't allow anyone to become a hero or a martyr, Neil Lavery. No, it's just that I'm old and I'm Jewish, and therefore I'm fair game.'

Spaslov began to tidy the room. 'Let's be thankful for both our sakes that they didn't find you,' he said. He gave Lavery a lop-sided smile as he went on. 'Or the vodka. We both need it. We can drink to your return to England.'

CHAPTER EIGHTEEN

For three days Neil Lavery lived with Josef Spaslov in his small and primitive room. In spite of Lavery's protests, the old man insisted that he sleep in the bed, which was hard and uncomfortable, but certainly preferable to the space on the cement floor which Spaslov took for himself. Lavery ate the old man's food and drank the old man's vodka, both supplemented by Josef's daily forays.

Lavery urinated in the sink, and twice was reduced to using a bucket, which the old man had no alternative but to carry up the stairs and empty in the lavatory. Lavery detested such arrangements, and the general squalor of the place, and in spite of himself and his genuine gratitude, he came to dislike the almost constant presence of the old man. Most of all, though, he began to despise himself, as he felt his will—his self-discipline, his persistence—being sapped by the conditions.

Sometimes he even found himself wishing he had been killed as he was escaping over the wall. But, when Josef Spaslov brought him a walking-stick, and he was able to hobble up and down the room and sometimes the passage outside, hope returned, together with a renewed determination to return to the UK. By this time, of course, he knew where he was in Moscow, and the way to the British Embassy, but even if he had been able to hobble there he could hardly limp up to the main door of the embassy, past the Soviet Militia who would undoubtedly be on duty at the gates—and extra-watchful. The only alternative was a phone call, in spite of the likelihood that it would be monitored. That was a risk he must take; after all, there had been no repercussions from Spaslov's effort. He told Josef that he could wait no longer.

'All right,' said the old man with some reluctance. 'What with your limp and those clothes and your unshaven face you should fade into the Moscow background. Luckily there's a public phone kiosk not too far from here.' He gave Lavery meticulous directions. 'You turn left along the lane at the rear of this building, and continue till you come to a main thoroughfare. Then turn left again. Cross this street when you see what looks like a church on the opposite side—actually it's a museum now. It's not far, only a matter of a few hundred metres. By the steps are a couple of post-boxes, a blue one and, for mail within Moscow, a red one. Next to them is a public telephone.'

Lavery repeated the instructions. 'I shouldn't have any difficulty in finding it,' he said. 'There'll be a directory?'

Spaslov was amused. 'It's highly unlikely. Telephone directories are still worth their weight in gold in the USSR,' he replied. 'But I made a mental note of the number of your embassy. I'll write it down for you.' He found a scrap of brown wrapping paper and the stub of a pencil. 'Here you are. And here are two kopecks, which is what the call will cost. You must put in the money *before* you pick up the receiver. If you can't get through it'll be returned. These are the only kopecks I've got, but you'd better have some other money just in case—'

He reached into the depths of one of his pockets and produced a rouble coin. Lavery hesitated before taking it.

Then he said, 'Right. And very many thanks, Josef.'

'If you'd prefer, I'll try again myself.'

'No. I think I may be able to cope with the authorities more easily.'

The old man nodded. 'Good luck, then. I'd come with you, but I'm well known around here and we might meet someone who would want to stop and chat and wonder who you were—'

'I understand,' said Lavery.

Spaslov helped Lavery up the few steps and watched him cross the yard before he shut the door. In the lane Lavery turned left and began to limp fast, although he was soon obliged to slow his pace. Not only did his leg hurt as each step jarred it, but after being shut up in that claustrophobic room for days he felt strangely uncertain in the open air. He was reminded of the moment when, as a child, he had been allowed out to play for the first time after a long illness. His surroundings had seemed unreal. Now, on this occasion, they *were*, at least figuratively, unreal.

It was worse when he reached the main street, which seemed to consist of second-class shops and neglected offices. But it was busy with people, who either bumped against him as if he were not there or, so he imagined, stared at him with undue interest. But he hobbled along until he saw a gilded dome on the other side. Here he made the mistake of joining a queue of individuals he assumed were waiting for some traffic lights to change, only to realize at length that they were waiting for a trolley car. Eventually, however, he managed to cross the street. There, next to the red and blue mail-boxes, was a phone kiosk, just as Josef Spaslov had promised, and Lavery tasted a sense of triumph. He fumbled in his pocket for the essential two kopecks and, carelessly, let one slip between his fingers. He watched helplessly as it skidded along the pavement towards a drain. Then a small boy pulled free of his mother and chased after the coin. He reached it just as it got to the drain, picked it up and stared at it with pleasure.

Lavery felt the bile rise in his throat. He shook with senseless rage. True, he had the rouble the old man had given him, but if he lost one of his two vital kopecks, how could he seek change without running the risk or arousing suspicion because of his limited Russian? For a second he could have killed the boy for the money he held in his small hand, but then the child was running towards him, palm outstretched, offering his prize. Lavery took it.

'Thank you,' he said. 'Thank you.'

It was only when the boy stared at him, wide-eyed, that Lavery realized that he had spoken in English. He cursed his stupidity. The boy was running back to his mother, pulling at her skirt, jabbering at her, pointing back to the strange man who had spoken such a funny language.

But luckily the boy's mother was in a hurry, or perhaps had no wish to become involved. Maybe she thought Lavery was a Russian from some remote republic, or a Pole, or from some other East European country; he certainly didn't look like a Western tourist. At any rate, she merely glanced at him, took the excited child by the hand and pulled him across the road. Lavery breathed hard, but the incident had an odd effect on him.

Though it had shaken his nerve, it had strengthened his resolve, and when he finally got through to the British Embassy, he spoke with purpose and authority. To the operator who answered he said, very clearly, 'My name is Neil Lavery. If you don't know the name, I'm sure your ambassador does. Connect me with a senior officer, please, at once—and waste no time about it. This is urgent.'

Lavery was unaware that Josef Spaslov's abortive call to the embassy had been reported, and caused a flow of ciphered telegrams between Moscow and London, which resulted in orders being issued to the embassy staff that anyone even mentioning the name 'Lavery' was to be put through immediately to Colin Dreyton, the embassy's Security Officer. Thus he was gratified by the speed with which a strange voice came on the line.

'Mr Lavery, I'm Colin Dreyton. I rank as a

Counsellor at the embassy here. What can I do for you?'

It was a drawling voice which Lavery disliked at once, but he knew that he had to impress this man with his need for help. 'I'm in bad trouble,' he said, 'and I want to come home—to the UK. I've been shot in the thigh. It's healing, but it's not easy for me to walk. I've no money, no valuables, no passport. You know who I am?' he added, almost as an afterthought.

'Oh yes. We have—heard of you, Mr Lavery. And remember this line is almost certainly tapped. May I say we scarcely expected you to want to return to the land of your birth so soon?'

'I never wanted to leave it!'

'Really?' The scepticism was obvious, but Lavery ignored it. Instead, he became both more imperious and more appealing. 'For God's sake, Dreyton,' he said, 'you *must* help me. If you don't, they'll kill me, and you'll be responsible.'

Colin Dreyton made up his mind. He was an experienced intelligence officer, and Lavery's urgency had come across to him with conviction. He loathed and despised traitors, but he accepted that it was his duty to save Lavery if he could, not so much for Lavery's own sake, as for the information he could undoubtedly provide.

'OK. We'd better be pretty quick about it. I'll pick you up in half an hour. I'll be driving a blue Rover with CD plates. Where will you be?'

Lavery gave him rapid instructions. He couldn't stay where he was for half an hour, and anyway he had promised old Josef that if possible he would return and reassure him about what was happening. Briefly he explained his circumstances and arranged

199

to meet Dreyton in the lane behind Spaslov's apartment block. He knew the old man wouldn't mind acting as a lookout for him; that would merely be one more kindness that he must persuade Dreyton to repay on his behalf.

'In half an hour,' said Lavery.

But he had no more kopecks and the line had gone dead. Still, he had achieved all that was needed. Full of hope, Lavery left the telephone kiosk.

As he began his slow limping walk back to Josef Spaslov he thought of the British Embassy, where at least for the moment he would be safe from the attentions of General Belatov and his thugs. It would be the first step towards home, Imogen and his family. Whatever the future might hold, however dark it might become, it must be an improvement on the present.

He had sensed Dreyton's dislike of him, and he didn't blame the diplomat, but he felt certain that the man would do as he had promised. He would be at the rendezvous at the appointed time, and tonight . . .

Lavery found himself thinking of a hot bath, a decent dinner, and a comfortable bed—simple pleasures that he would once have taken for granted.

★　　★　　★

General Belatov fingered the watch that lay on the desk before him. It was an expensive Swiss watch and had probably been a present. On the back were engraved the initials 'NSL'—Neil Simpson Lavery. It would have been too great a coincidence for the watch to have belonged to anyone else.

'You questioned the shopkeeper yourself, Comrade Major?' he said to Igor Smerinov.

'Yes, Comrade General. He knew he should never have bought the watch, that it was either stolen or black market goods, and he was happy to be of assistance to us.'

'I'm sure he was,' Belatov said absently, unaware of any irony. 'You say he actually named the man who sold it to him?'

'Yes. An old Jew called Josef Spaslov. He's tolerated as a cleaner in an apartment block. It's not far from your club, and they both back on to the same alley.'

'*Akh!*' It was an expression of satisfaction. The General saw the connection immediately. 'So either this Spaslov stole it from Lavery, or Lavery gave it to him for—shall we say "services rendered"? Hiding him, perhaps?'

'Spaslov lives in one small room. There's nowhere to hide anyone, and the whole block was searched thoroughly, Comrade General, though not, I admit, that same night.'

'And the position at present, Comrade Major, is that Lavery is still at large, in spite of all your efforts.'

'Yes, Comrade General, but not for long now, I hope. Josef Spaslov is being taken into custody at this very moment. We've got a file on him. He's been in trouble before, though there's no suggestion he's ever been a thief. Almost certainly he helped Lavery and will lead us to him. In any case, I'm confident it won't be long before he's told us all we want to know.'

'I trust your confidence is not misplaced yet

again, Comrade Major.' Belatov was acerbic. 'You can't afford another balls-up. It's quite absurd that the Englishman should have escaped in the first place, but that he has managed to remain free for so many days is an insult to our Service—and our country.'

'Yes, Comrade General.' Smerinov was somewhat aggrieved that he had received no word of praise for remembering that Lavery had still been in possession of his watch when he made his run, and for ordering intensive inquiries to be made about the watch in the immediate district. It was thanks to this effort—inspired and directed by him—that the watch had been found, and Josef Spaslov traced. 'Is that all, Comrade General?' he asked, almost curtly.

'One more point! Once you've found Lavery—if you do—he's to be shot dead rather than allowed to escape again. Don't take risks and, above all, do not become sentimental. He is a dangerous man. Do you understand?'

'Yes, Comrade General,' said Smerinov, suppressing a sigh. He hoped it wouldn't fall to him to be forced to kill Neil Lavery. And the General's words had confirmed his suspicion that there was more to this affair than he had been told.

*　　*　　*

Only ten or fifteen minutes now, Lavery was thinking. Without his watch he couldn't judge the time accurately, but it must have taken him at least a quarter of an hour to limp at his slow pace from the telephone kiosk to the end of the lane. Soon he would be in the company of Colin Dreyton, who might despise him, but nevertheless would escort him safely to the sanctuary of the British Embassy. After that it would be up to them to get him out of the USSR.

Lavery's hopes were high as he rounded a curve in the lane, and came within sight of the door leading to the yard behind the pathetic home Josef Spaslov had shared with him. Then he stopped, cowering back against the wall. There was a large black Zil in the lane with a uniformed driver leaning negligently against it.

As Lavery watched the driver jumped to attention, and four men came through the door. One was obviously in charge, and between two of the others hung Josef Spaslov, his head on his chest, his legs dragging along the ground. Lavery, his own plight forgotten for the moment, stared in horror as the old man was flung into the back of the car, and his abductors climbed in, using him as a kind of footstool.

Afterwards Lavery was to tell himself that if he had had the slightest chance of helping the old man he would have taken it, and he almost believed this to be true. In fact, as he realized that the Zil was facing in his direction and would drive past him if he remained where he was, he turned and fled, his painful leg almost forgotten.

He was hurrying blindly. He had turned right at the end of the lane, so that this was new territory for him, and soon he had no idea of his location. When he came to a small, dusty park he turned in and gratefully found a bench where he could sit in the pale sunshine and rest his wound.

He was still fearful, but his immediate panic had given way to anger. Bitterly he cursed Colin Dreyton, the ambassador and the entire staff of the

British Embassy. He knew nothing of his watch being found and subsequently traced to Spaslov. He assumed that Dreyton, for reasons of his own and with or without the connivance of his colleagues, had betrayed him to the Russians.

This meant that all his hopes—which had been centred on the embassy—were barren. Where could he go now? To whom could he appeal? He was in a foreign country, with no money, no friends, scant knowledge of the language, and even the clothes he wore and the stick he carried were no longer a disguise. Josef had warned him that the authorities had no patience with heroes or martyrs; soon they would have extracted from the old man everything he knew.

*   *   *

Colin Dreyton arrived in the alley precisely on time—ten minutes after the Zil had left. He drove down the lane as Neil Lavery had instructed him, and parked some metres short of the door from which he expected Lavery to emerge. He was surprised to find that the door was wide open, but he waited.

When fifteen minutes had passed and there was no sign of Lavery he debated with himself whether to leave, or to explore further. He was by nature a cautious man, but a scrambled call to London before he set off for the rendezvous had emphasized the vital importance of collecting Lavery if it were at all possible. Slowly he got out of his car.

Then, unexpectedly, a head poked itself out of the doorway, stared at him and seemed about to retreat. Dreyton shouted and sprinted forward. He spoke good Russian, and had no difficulty in making himself understood.

'*Ho!*' he cried. 'I'm looking for an old man by the name of Spaslov. Do you know him?' he asked.

The youth—Dreyton guessed he was in his late teens—regarded him suspiciously. 'Yes, I know him,' he said. 'He worked here.'

'Worked?' Dreyton caught the boy by the arm and drew him into the lane. 'Please tell me. I'm a friend. Where is he? I need to speak to him.'

'He was my friend too. He used to open this door for me, so that I could visit my girl at night.' Suddenly the young man was voluble. 'They took him, just a few minutes ago—and two of them are still here, waiting.'

'Who took him? The Militia?'

'Yes. They beat him up. Then they dragged him away.'

'Why?'

'They don't need a reason, but it was something to do with a watch, an expensive watch. They wanted to know how he'd got it. I was listening, but I only heard when they shouted. And—and this time they found the hiding-place.'

'Tell me,' Dreyton said gently.

'A day or two ago they were searching the whole district. There was a rumour that someone had got away from them and was being hidden. It may not be true. Anyway, today they pulled Josef's room to pieces, and they found the panel behind the pipes, and the space big enough for a man to hide in. But no one was there, and that was what made them extra savage.' Dimitri shook his head. 'Poor, poor Josef,' he added.

'Yes, poor Josef,' Dreyton agreed, though he was

thinking of Neil Lavery. He found a twenty-rouble note in his pocket, and thrust it into the young man's hand. 'Buy a present for your girl,' he said, 'and forget you met me.'

He turned and went to his car. In his mind he was already drafting the long telegram to London.

CHAPTER NINETEEN

For a long time Neil Lavery sat gloomily on the hard wooden bench in the dusty park. He wondered if Colin Dreyton had actually driven to the rendezvous in his blue Rover with its blasted diplomatic plates, to wait with the men who would surely have been left behind after Josef Spaslov had been arrested, or if he were sitting smugly in the embassy, proud of his day's work.

What would they do when their quarry didn't appear? Probably they would become more and more incensed. The Russians might suspect that Dreyton had played a trick on them, but eventually, having learnt all that Spaslov could tell them, they would recommence and intensify their search for the man who had eluded them.

Lavery smiled grimly. He knew that he should get out of the district, but how? Even the inadequate little map he had found at the *dacha* had been inadvertently thrown away by Spaslov, together with the photograph of Imogen and the children. Not that he could have kept them, smelling as they did of that squalid garbage can. So now he had what he stood up in, plus one rouble and a walking-stick—and, so far, his life.

The last, he decided, was worth fighting for, if only in memory of old Josef Spaslov. And his first need was money, money to buy means of transport—and food; until now he hadn't noticed his hunger, but he realized that he had eaten nothing since a meagre breakfast.

Then there was the question of finding some kind of shelter for the night. And it would also be more than a good idea, if it proved at all possible, to change his appearance, for Spaslov would surely have described his clothes in detail—though perhaps not with total accuracy.

Thankful that his wits were working again, and he was recovering from the shock of Dreyton's betrayal, Lavery tried to consider his plight and his options rationally and realistically. To borrow would be impossible; to beg might prove dangerous; clearly, he had no choice but to steal.

Almost immediately he was given a chance to put the thought into practice. An elderly woman, clutching a bulging string bag in one hand and a small boy by the other, sat herself at the far end of Lavery's bench. He guessed she was on her way home from shopping, and had stopped for a rest. The small boy, however, had a different idea; they were in a park, and for him parks meant only one thing—an opportunity to play. His *babushka*—if indeed she was his grandmother—couldn't refuse him. She produced a rubber ball from her bag, and the small boy ran off.

A minute later he had fallen on the gravel path and, though he had probably done no more than graze a knee, he lay and screamed. The *babushka* rushed to him, completely forgetful of her bag of shopping. Lavery didn't hesitate. He seized it and limped off in the opposite direction.

He was lucky. He expected to hear angry cries behind him, but none came, and he reached the shelter of some bushes where he hurriedly inspected the contents of the string bag. There was a little knitted jacket, obviously bought for the child, and momentarily his conscience pricked him as he remembered Mat and Verity. But any regrets were quickly supressed when he saw the other purchases that the *babushka* had made.

She had had a most successful expedition. There was bread—Russian black bread—two kinds of sausage, some smoked fish that Lavery couldn't identify, and a bottle of vodka of unknown brand but luckily with a screw cap. Lavery took a large bite of the bread and sausage and in his eagerness nearly choked on them. By now he felt no guilt, only elation. He forced himself to move, carefully but as rapidly as he could, to the other side of the park, and then found another secluded spot in which to sit down and eat slowly and take two swigs of the vodka.

His hunger satisfied for the moment, he began to walk. He emerged from the park and wandered the streets. He saw a large 'M' and knew it marked a Metro station. The steady stream of people going in drew him towards it, but he hesitated over the twin problems of money and procedure. He couldn't spare his single rouble, and was dubious about appearing lost or helpless. He was idly wondering if it might be possible to cheat the system when he saw a grey-uniformed figure patrolling up and down carrying a white truncheon. The man was clearly some kind of policeman, and looked as if he meant business. Lavery, unsure how widely his description might have been circulated by now, turned away.

He limped on. The sky had become overcast and a few drops of rain fell. He sheltered in the doorway of a shop, but evening was approaching and the problem of where to spend the night would soon become pressing. He ate a little more bread and sausage, and drank some vodka. His leg had begun to trouble him, and he was worried that he might not be able to continue his seemingly purposeless ramble for much longer.

He moved again, vaguely searching for somewhere that might provide protection from the weather, which was becoming increasingly cold and wet, and more importantly, where he stood a chance of being free from any possible official interest. But he could find nothing better than a shop doorway, though these had become more imposing as he reached a wider and apparently more affluent thoroughfare.

Finally he settled on an entrance that seemed deeper and darker than most, and he huddled himself into the farthest corner. Here, by now too tired to care much what happened to him, he slept fitfully—but undisturbed—till dawn. He was not to know that he was not alone; many Muscovites slept rough, even in the worst weather, and the authorities often enough turned a blind eye to the pathetic bundles of humanity scattered around the city.

*　　*　　*

Lavery woke, stiff and chilled, and resolved not to spend another night in that fashion. But during his broken dozing a plan had formed in his head. Somehow, he had decided, he must reach a railway station and do his best to get on to a train. He remembered reading that the Soviet rail system was efficient, and it certainly offered more hope than trying to catch a flight or hitch a lift.

He breakfasted on smoked fish and bread, washed down with vodka. The fish was salt, but he dared not drink too much. He yearned for something hot, but that was impossible.

He would have liked to move at once, but thought he would be conspicuous on the almost empty streets where, apart from the occasional workers going on an early shift and the women street-cleaners, there was no one about and no traffic. He forced himself to wait, testing his bad leg and doing simple exercises to ease his aching limbs and restore his circulation.

It was then that he had what was perhaps his first real stroke of luck.

A drunk came weaving his unsteady way along the pavement, and Lavery, having no wish to invite any trouble, drew back into his corner. But either the drunk spotted him and was curious, or he tripped sideways as he reached the entrance, because without warning, he suddenly spread-eagled himself in the deep doorway at Lavery's feet. There he remained, breathing hard. No one else—neither the odd passer-by nor the street-cleaners—seemed to have noticed.

For a moment Lavery stared at his unexpected visitor, his first inclination being to step over the man and get away as quickly as he could. Then reason asserted itself. In spite of the fact that the man was dead drunk, he was obviously no down-and-out. He was well-dressed, in a suit with a short topcoat over it. His shoes were good leather and he was wearing an expensive watch. So the chances were that he would be carrying money.

Carefully Lavery inserted his hand inside the man's jacket and eventually found his wallet. It was disappointingly thin, but in the circumstances five ten-rouble notes represented a small fortune. The drunk remained dead to the world, and Lavery continued to pillage. He slid the watch off the man's wrist, took his hat—felt and wide-brimmed—and looked enviously at his coat.

He wondered if it were worth the risk. The shoes were useless—the man had surprisingly small feet—so there was only the coat. The temptation was irresistible, and the theft was nearly accomplished without provoking any objection from the man. Indeed, at first he seemed inclined to help, as if he were happy to be free of the garment. But, as Lavery was about to ease off the last sleeve, he suddenly recovered from his drunken stupor and began a violent resistance.

By chance he hit Lavery on his wounded thigh, so that Lavery cried out with the pain. But it was too late to stop now. Lavery had no alternative but to punch the drunk hard on the jaw. Then he wrenched the coat away, struggled into it and forced himself to make off as fast as his leg would allow. His victim was either knocked out, or too drunk to follow, and when Lavery considered that he was a safe distance away he slowed to a walk. It was at this point that he realized that though he had acquired some money and a coat and a hat, he had left behind his walking-stick and the string bag with the remains of the food and the vodka. His gains

211

were great, but the loss of the stick was serious.

How serious he soon began to appreciate as his leg became more and more painful. Then he saw a car draw up a short way ahead of him. A woman got out, handed the driver some money and went into a building.

A taxi? A green light went on in the top right-hand corner of the windscreen. Lavery waved. When he got level with the car he knew he had been right; there was a large 'T' in a check design on the door. He began to climb in, and the driver turned round and said something that Lavery failed to understand.

Instead, he fumbled inside the topcoat and took a ten-rouble note from the wallet he had stolen. He waved this at the driver, while he dredged his memory for the words necessary to ask to be taken to a railway station. *'Vokzal,'* he said finally.

Immediately the driver replied, *'Kokoi?'*

And Lavery cursed himself for being so bloody stupid. Of course there were innumerable railway stations in Moscow, and he knew the names of none. *'Zapad,'* he said—'West'.

The driver stared at him curiously, but apparently was satisfied, for he nodded, switched off his green light and startred his meter. After all, his passenger had money and looked respectable enough. It wasn't his fault he was some kind of foreigner.

In spite of his precarious position, Neil Lavery enjoyed his taxi ride. In fact, the seating in the cab was not particularly comfortable as the springing was hard, but the car gave him a sense of security that he hadn't felt for many hours. He thought nostalgically of London taxis, and wondered if he would ever again travel in one. He was sorry when the journey came to an end and he was forced to face Moscow again. He knew that his chances of getting on a train were slight and that this—probably his last—hope was slender. But it was the only hope he had.

Reluctantly he got out of the cab as the driver said something incomprehensible. He gave the man the ten-rouble note, receiving some coins in exchange. He hesitated about tipping, and in the end returned a couple. The driver answered, 'Spasibo', looked pleased and drove off happily, so all seemed well.

Lavery stood and read the Cyrillic lettering across the front of the building. *BELORUSSKIY VOKZAL*, it said. Of course! White Russia—the republic on the USSR's western frontier—the frontier with Poland, for example. Squaring his shoulders and trying to hide his limp he went through the entrance and into the concourse.

He did not fail to notice the official-looking characters—some in uniform and some in plain clothes—who were carefully regarding everyone entering the station, and he blessed the drunk's hat and coat that had changed his appearance. He passed the initial scrutiny and, once inside, did his best to move about confidently. But the place was incredibly confusing. There seemed to be an alarming number of different ticket offices, each with a long queue. And, for so early in the day, the station seemed extraordinarily busy. Everywhere was bustle. People were greeting those who had arrived. Others were being bidden sorrowful goodbyes. The Russians, Lavery thought, were an emotional lot.

213

In some ways the confusion was in his favour. He was able to lean against a pillar, waiting like so many others, and watch the scene around him—especially behaviour at the booking offices. He saw almost at once that, as he had feared, buying a ticket to anywhere would be impossible without documentation of some kind, and he suspected that an attempt to buy a ticket to a destination outside the USSR would present totally insuperable difficulties. Then his attention was distracted.

He noticed the other man primarily because he was supporting himself with a stick as he limped forward, but also because he seemed suddenly to become a focus of attention. Two men in plain clothes were making towards him, pushing people aside in their haste. To Lavery it looked as if the man became aware of them and made an attempt to hide himself behind a tall, thin woman who appeared to argue with him. Then suddenly, without warning, the man turned and ran, clearing a path with his stick. The woman began to follow him. It was at this very moment that Lavery realized how similar to himself the other man was. They were of the same height and build. There was the obvious limp, the dark beard, the clothes—a round woollen hat and a pseudo-leather jacket. No one who knew them would have mistaken one for the other, but if a search was on for someone of that description—a description that would have fitted Lavery before his encounter with the drunk—this man was an obvious suspect. And now, by fleeing, he had condemned himself.

As Lavery watched, horrified, the two plain-clothes men drew their pistols. They fired simultaneously and without hesitation. The man staggered and fell. The tall thin woman screamed and continued to scream, before she threw herself on the body. Otherwise a momentary hush descended on the station.

The silence was broken almost at once. There were angry shouts, a babble of voices, orders issued, and people started going about their business again, glad, Lavery felt, not to be involved. The authorities acted with efficiency and despatch. The tall thin woman was prised from the body, and was led away. A stretcher was produced and the remains of the man removed in a plastic body bag. Two cleaners in brown overalls began to mop up blood.

Meanwhile, more faceless officials—some in uniform and some in plain clothes—had appeared, and were checking papers very thoroughly and systematically, while guards were being posted at all the exits to prevent anyone from leaving the station. Why, wondered Lavery? If they thought they'd got their man, one would have expected vigilance to be relaxed. If by now they knew they hadn't, why concentrate on this railway station merely because a look-alike had been shot here? Perhaps they thought he had somehow changed clothes with the man they had killed, and so was somewhere near. In any case, there was little doubt that the search was for him, and he began to sweat. A stolen hat and coat and a few roubles weren't going to help him now.

Unaware that he had moved Lavery found himself standing with his back against a wall, next to a door marked in bold lettering, *VEZDA NET*. Below was the red horizontal bar in a circle—the

215

international symbol for 'No Entrance'.
Involuntarily Lavery reached behind him and tried
the handle. To his surprise it turned and the door
began to open. Anything, he thought, was better
than idly waiting for inevitable capture. He pushed
the door open a little more and sidled gently
through the gap.

CHAPTER TWENTY

A long, shabby corridor, badly in need of a coat of
paint, stretched directly ahead of Lavery, leaving
him no choice. Grimly he set off along it. His leg
was giving him a lot of trouble and pain, and he
cursed the drunk for hitting it, however
unintentionally. He knew that he wouldn't be able
to limp far and that, if he were compelled to run,
the leg would almost certainly betray him.

There were doors on either side of the corridor.
One was half-open, and revealed a man sitting at a
computer terminal. Lavery edged past silently. He
heard voices from behind another door, the sound
of a telephone, the flush of a toilet and, finally,
approaching footsteps. He acted instinctively. He
opened the door beside him and went in.

He was resigned about what he might find
beyond the door, with no hopes or expectations. If
he were fortunate it would be a storeroom or even a
cupboard in which he could hide; if not, he would
be confronted by curious faces and the alarm would
be raised immediately. But, even as these thoughts
flashed through his mind, he realized that luck was
with him.

216

He found himself in what appeared to be a workmen's locker-room. There were rows of metal lockers, presumably containing personal possessions. Vastly more useful, there were rows of pegs, mostly empty, but some holding brown uniform overalls and caps.

The possibilities were obvious. Lavery chose the set of overalls that looked the largest, and with some difficulty managed to get his legs into them, and button them over his coat. They created a startling change in appearance, making him look much fatter than he was. The corresponding cap was too large for him, so he promptly picked one off a different peg. Then he noticed a brown canvas bag on the ground beneath it. He wasted a moment investigating the contents, but was delighted to find, along with some tools, a vacuum flask, a chunk of black bread and a small bottle of colourless liquid. The whole bag was well worth taking, and he slung it over his shoulder by its twin straps.

There was a second door to the locker-room. Lavery opened it carefully, hoping it led to something other than baths or showers. In fact, he found himself in a short passage which brought him out on to a long raised platform overlooking what seemed to be the station's freight yard. Here there was a great deal of activity. Engines shunted, first in one direction, then in another. Men shouted, metal clanged, whistles blew. But clearly there was order in this apparent confusion.

Lavery regarded the scene with apprehension. He knew that he was committed. He couldn't go back, and he couldn't just stand where he was for very long. But he was unsure of his next move. At last, he went forward in a businesslike manner, trying to look as if he were going about his duties, but praying that no one would shout an incomprehensible order at him so that, by failing to obey, he would draw attention to himself.

His most immediate need was to find somewhere to rest his leg. He jumped down from the platform, as he had seen another man do some fifty metres away, but it was more of a drop than he had expected and he landed awkwardly, knocking his thigh yet again. For a split second he blacked out. Moments later, as somehow he managed to keep himself upright, he remembered old Josef Spaslov's warning that if he didn't take care of the wound it might well become infected, and he felt physically sick.

Then someone did shout. Lavery had no idea if the cry were intended for him, but he promptly started off in the opposite direction. And there before him, across some tracks, he saw a line of covered freight cars of the kind once used for transporting troops to the front—or victims to concentration camps. The rearmost of the row, and the nearest to him, had the sliding door on its side partly open.

Lavery made for the van and peered in. It was no more than a third full, but at the far end were some crates covered by a tarpaulin. They offered at least a temporary shelter. If he had been fit, to haul himself up into the van would have been no problem. As it was, hampered by his injured leg and the bag he had stolen from the locker-room, Lavery found that it required a considerable effort; he was so exhausted that he was forced to crawl on hands and knees towards the crates, dragging his

218

bag behind him.

There was just room to squeeze between the crates, and enough space behind to sit and stretch out his legs. It was a cramped position and far from secure. Anyone searching seriously could not fail to discover him at once, but by adjusting the tarpaulin he was able to construct a kind of tent which he hoped would protect him from a casual inspection.

His first action, after having established this lair, was to undo the overalls and his trousers and feel the wound that Josef had dressed the previous day. It felt hot and damp, which was less than encouraging, but when he withdrew his hand there was no blood on his fingers. He had no idea if this was a good sign or a bad one, but he suspected that the dampness must be pus—probably some form of suppuration from an infection. It was just another problem, he thought resignedly, but there was nothing he could do about it. He had no means of washing and dressing the wound, and worrying about gangrene wouldn't help.

He decided to explore the stolen bag. He unpacked it carefully, putting the few tools on the wooden floor beside him. He had already seen the bread, but to his enormous satisfaction the flask held, not tea as he had expected, but hot soup. He could have drunk it all, but he rationed himself and ate a little bread. Then he sniffed at the bottle of colourless liquid and tentatively tasted it. This time his expectations were realized. He grinned at the thought that a Soviet citizen would be carrying anything other than vodka. He took a deep swallow, choked on it and had to eat more bread.

*   *   *

As time passed, Lavery slept—fitfully but heavily—partly because of the disturbed night he had spent in the shop doorway and partly from physical and mental exhaustion. But towards the late afternoon he was shocked awake by the sound of voices, a violent thud as the door of his sanctuary was slid wide open, and jolts and bangs as further goods were loaded into it. The whole wagon seemed to be shaking with a frenzy of activity.

Lavery's first reaction had been that the Militia, having realized they had shot the wrong man, had renewed their search for him. But this was quickly replaced, as he interpreted the various noises, by a fear that the crates hiding him from sight might be pushed against the wooden wall of the van to make more room for whatever else was being loaded. Then either he would have to cry out and reveal himself, or he could be crushed and injured further.

So Lavery lay, every muscle tensed, listening hard. At one point a crate was pushed a couple of inches nearer to him, and his mouth went dry, but there was a shout and, minutes later, after more thuds, the door of the freight van was banged shut, and he heard the clear sounds of the door being padlocked shut.

Lavery breathed again. He had no objection to being locked in the van, for he had no intention of attempting to leave it. Indeed, the padlock gave him an added feeling of security. He realized, nevertheless, that though any immediate danger had passed, this might be only a temporary respite; the men could return at any time, or supervisors might come to check the load. He had to make a movement of some kind; he couldn't remain where he was for much longer because he had painful cramp in what he now thought of as his good leg. Slowly and carefully he started to crawl out from behind the crates.

It had grown darker while Lavery was in his hiding-place and, with the door of the wagon shut, it wasn't much lighter beyond the tarpaulin. But, as he pulled himself upright, he could see there was little floor space left, except immediately inside the door. Large wicker hampers were packed close, and it was hard to believe that any more goods were intended for this truck. Soon perhaps the train would move off, he thought hopefully, and he would be going with it—out of Moscow, and presumably towards the West.

There was lettering painted on the hampers, in both Cyrillic and Roman characters, but because of the uneven wicker surface, the age of the paint and the semi-darkness, it was difficult to read. Lavery traced it with a finger as if he had been blind, and finally realized that one word said 'BOLSHOI'.

Neil Lavery had been to Covent Garden more than once with his wife and the Glenbournes to see the Bolshoi Ballet. He had no knowledge of theatrical procedures, but he had a vague recollection that on tour drama or ballet or opera companies traditionally carried their costumes, tights, shoes and properties in large wicker hampers such as these. The vital question, of course, was where this particular company was to perform next, for that would obviously be the destination of both this van and himself—if there were no search and he were not discovered before the journey commenced.

Because there was so little space between the

221

hampers Lavery had difficulty in reaching a label that he might be able to decipher, but finally he found one he could pull off. It read WARSZAWA. His spirits soared. It didn't need much imagination to work out that—in either Russian or Polish—the word meant 'Warsaw'. There was little doubt that the train was going to Poland, and if only he could stay with it . . .

★   ★   ★

It was several hours before Lavery began to be assailed by serious doubts. He had crawled back behind the crates to the area he considered safe from a casual inspection. He had finished the soup, most of the bread and drunk some vodka. And still the wretched train had not moved. There had been one violent clash of metal on metal, and the wagon had shuddered. For a moment Lavery had thought of an engine being attached. But that was all.

He was bitterly disappointed. He hadn't got cramp again, but his wound throbbed and he yearned for the train to start. He tried not to wonder what he would do if it stayed in the freight yard overnight, and perhaps even the whole of the next day, but he couldn't completely drive that possibility from his mind.

Eventually he must have slept again, because suddenly he became aware that the train was moving, slowly but steadily. Then it stopped. Lavery strained to hear what might be happening outside but, though there seemed to be plenty of activity, the sounds were muted and indeterminate. At one point he heard the sound of a key in the padlock of his van, and he cowered back in his

222

hiding-place as the door was slid open. However, the inspection, if such it was, was cursory, a mere formality, and the door was quickly slammed shut and padlocked once more.

Minutes later Lavery's waiting came to an end. The train shuddered to a start. Soon it had gathered speed and by its steady rhythm Lavery was assured that he was at last on his way out of Moscow. His relief was enormous, but tempered with caution. He had been extraordinarily lucky so far in his attempt to evade his pursuers, but he was under no illusions; it had indeed been luck, rather than brilliant planning or astute enterprise on his part, that had preserved him—and the luck might not continue. He was still in the USSR. To reach Poland meant crossing a frontier. And at that frontier, especially in view of the alert that must be in effect on his account, without doubt the train would be thoroughly searched.

But to be captured at such a moment would be ridiculous—absurd. It would render pointless so much effort and stress and pain—the escape from Belatov's party, the bullet through his thigh, Josef's incredible kindness that had led to the old man's arrest, and possibly death or God knew what other suffering. Then there were the thefts he had committed, and which might have had unknown but disastrous consequences.

All this effort—on his own part and particularly that of Josef—would prove to have been a total waste if he were to be caught at the border and taken back to Moscow. He would have done better to have waited meekly for the 'unfortunate accident' that was promised in Belatov's 'Phase Four'. At least it would have been quick and probably

223

painless, and he would have betrayed no more MOD secrets than he would do if caught now. In a very real sense he owed it to Josef Spaslov's memory not to get caught. But the future was not in his hands.

Lavery shivered and yet felt hot. He was tempted to stay in his present hiding-place and pray that the border search wouldn't discover him, but he knew that would give him almost no chance, and his pride forbade such passivity. He had to find somewhere better, so as to get into Poland—and, from Poland, home.

★　　★　　★

Neil Lavery was right. The security checks at the border between the USSR and Poland had always been conducted thoroughly and, in spite of many changes in relations between the two countries, this rigour had continued. Moreover, as Lavery had suspected, because of the state of alert on his behalf, extra precautions were being taken at all potential border crossing-points.

On this particular main railway line between the USSR and Poland and the West, the number of men on duty at the frontier station, where the change of gauge took place, had been doubled; some had been recalled from leave, which demonstrated the importance the authorities attached to the present operation. All the border guards had been briefed on Neil Lavery's appearance, warned that he might have changed it, might be carrying false documentation, told that he was a clever, resourceful, dangerous man, a foreigner—not one of them—and that if he showed

224

any resistance they were to shoot to kill.

They had not, however, been given his real name, or his nationality. They had not been given any information on what he had done or why he was wanted. There was nothing especially unusual about this kind of briefing, but it did hamper the men, inasmuch as it made the elimination of potential suspects more difficult and therefore more time-consuming.

At the Soviet frontier station every exit from the train was secured, while inside it the border guards worked meticulously, checking and rechecking passports and papers, peering into individuals' faces and searching every space where a man—or indeed sometimes only a child—might be hidden. Conscientious efficiency was more important than the passage of time, but as the train became later and later, tempers got shorter. There was a certain amount of grumbling. One passenger was arrested for obstructing the border guards, and a youth was threatened for making a snide remark. Another youth was caught trying to climb out of the window of a locked lavatory, and was found to have no papers. All these complications increased the delay, which was added to by the fact that the train was longer than usual, with more freight cars, due to the Bolshoi Ballet's tour.

This also meant that Neil Lavery had a long and tormented wait. It was quite obvious what was happening outside, but all he could do was wait—and hope, and pray. And eventually the searchers reached the freight cars at the rear of the train. In some ways they were easier to search than the passenger coaches. Freight was always securely packed and little space was allowed between bags and boxes, crates and hampers.

Lavery had hidden in the very last van, and by this time even these searchers' enthusiasm had begun to flag. The last van was examined with somewhat less care than the others. A young and active border guard climbed over the Bolshoi's hampers, glanced at the crates which were nailed down and tore away the tarpaulin under which Lavery had sheltered.

He was no longer there.

PART THREE

THE AGENT IN QUESTION

CHAPTER TWENTY-ONE

'Is there really nothing we can do for him?'

As John Faudin asked the question he caught the glance that passed between Munro Graffon and Guy Cantel, and he added, 'OK. I realize that Neil Lavery is a traitor and a defector, but neither of you knew him as I did. I liked him. I respected him. Your feelings towards someone don't change overnight, whatever the circumstances,' he finished despairingly.

He was met with silence. Cantel was thinking that Imogen had used much the same words of her husband. Graffon, in whose office the three men were sitting, mentally dismissed Faudin's plea as sentimental, even maudlin. John Faudin was a nice guy, he thought, but not sufficiently hard-headed for his present job.

Cantel said, 'Well, what would you suggest we did about Lavery, John?'

'I'm not sure, but I can't help feeling—'

'We've got absolutely no idea where he is, or what game he's playing,' Cantel broke in as Faudin hesitated.

'We know he's on the run in Moscow and that he wants to return to the UK.'

'Do we? He seems to have become disillusioned with his Soviet chums very fast,' Cantel said gently. 'Why do you suppose he went in the first place if he's so eager to come home now?'

'You're sure you do want him back?' It was a more perceptive question than the two Security Service officers would have expected from Faudin.

'Oh yes,' Graffon said easily. 'He's done all the damage to us he can. They'll have cleaned him out. He won't have a scrap of classified data left. He'll have a certain propaganda value for them, but that's about all. Nevertheless, it would be a tremendous blow to their pride if he returned, and we might learn a hell of a lot from him. On the other hand, we might not. Remember, you never know who's on whose side in such cases. It's an interesting situation.'

'If it's the true situation,' Cantel said, watching Faudin's discomfort at what he evidently considered Munro Graffon's inhumanity. 'We can't be sure of anything. As Munro was implying, Lavery's sudden change of heart may not be genuine. It could be part of some devious ploy.'

'You told me Colin Dreyton believed Lavery was telling the truth,' Faudin protested.

'Sure, he convinced Dreyton, and Dreyton's an experienced intelligence officer. But the two of them never met. They merely had one phone conversation, and that had to be brief,' said Graffon. 'The supporting evidence, the increased activity before and after this call, and the arrest of this old man Josef Spaslov could all be part of an operation.'

'You think that Lavery would agree to be a party to something like that?' Faudin remained doubtful.

Graffon shrugged. 'Maybe not willingly. Who can tell? If it is a game of some kind—and, remember, we're only speculating that it might be—we haven't the faintest idea of its purpose. On the surface, it would seem senseless so far. The Russians aren't so stupid as to think we'd accept Lavery back into the fold and let them run him as

230

an agent again.'

'And it would be totally out of character for them to carry out an operation without a purpose,' Cantel added. He glanced enquiringly at his superior, and Graffon nodded. 'There's one factor we've not told you about yet, John, and it argues against it being a plot. We had another telegram from Colin Dreyton this morning, just before you arrived here.'

'They've caught Neil!' It was an involuntary exclamation.

Cantel shook his head. 'No, it seems not. But you know the Byelorussian Railway Station in Moscow—the terminus for lines to and from the West. Well, officers on duty there yesterday apparently sighted someone who might have been Lavery from a description. The man panicked and ran. It was enough for them to shoot him.'

'Dear God!' John Faudin said. 'I suppose it could be a coincidence, but—'

'They don't usually shoot in public places these days,' Graffon said, 'and Dreyton claims there's a rumour going around that the chap was killed in mistake for someone else. It's amazing how the grapevine works, even in Moscow.'

Cantel said, 'And we don't believe that they would go so far as to kill a man like that, in order to support the story that Lavery's on the run from them.'

Faudin nodded. 'I see. So, if you had to bet?'

'Evens.' Graffon laughed. 'Perhaps I'd come down a shade in favour of an operation of some kind. From what I know of Lavery I wouldn't have thought he was the type to take the bit between his teeth for any reason in his present circumstances.'

'I wouldn't have thought him a traitorous type

231

either,' retorted Faudin bitterly, and once more a remark of his produced a heavy silence.

At last Graffon said, 'What about the MOD? How's Lavery's directorate faring at the moment?'

'Just as you'd imagine, Munro—it's purgatory, if not hell, for everyone. You can feel the tension; you know—you always can when there's a damage assessment in progress. Tyneman's drinking even more than before. I'm told his wife has definitely refused to return from Canada. Plimpton's so worried about his wretched sons that his temper is absolutely foul; personally I think it would do those kids good to go to a tough comprehensive for a change. And Glenbourne—well, he's as tense as anyone, and who can blame him? After all, Lavery's his brother-in-law.'

'At least you know of no more leaks?'

'No; that's true. I'm hoping the general situation will improve after tomorrow.' Faudin didn't sound particularly hopeful.

'Tomorrow?'

'Joy Aubyn's funeral. You're going?'

'Guy's going,' Graffon replied. 'As usual, I shall mind the store.'

'Perhaps I could give you a lift, John?'

'Thanks, Guy. I'd like that. Moral support, you know.' Faudin sighed. 'And there's still nothing we can do for Neil Lavery?'

'No!' Graffon was definite. 'All we can do is wait—for developments or information.'

⋆　　⋆　　⋆

'The one thing we can't afford to do is sit on our arses and wait.' General Belatov spoke with surprising tolerance.

Igor Smerinov was not deceived. He knew from experience that the Comrade General's outbursts of temper, however alarming they might appear, were not as dangerous as the periods of false amiability that sometimes followed them. He stood rigidly to attention in front of Belatov's desk in the Kremlin office. This wasn't the time to appear relaxed in any way. He had been forced to admit failure once again; Neil Lavery was still at large.

When the General remained silent, seemingly more interested in studying his well-manicured nails than addressing himself to the problem, Smerinov ventured to say, 'Comrade General, I don't understand how Lavery has managed to remain free for so long, but I assure you that every precaution is being taken. There is no possibility that he can leave the USSR.'

'My dear Comrade, you give me constant assurances about the wretched Lavery.' Belatov spoke pityingly. 'Unfortunately they have all proved to be without substance.' His tone changed. 'Stop standing there like a tailor's dummy. Sit down, man, and start using your brains. Lavery's got to be found, and damned quickly. What's more, anyone, other than our people, who knows that he's been running around Moscow on the loose must be eliminated.'

'The British Embassy officer—Dreyton?' Smerinov was startled.

'No, of course not, you fool. That was just a phone call. As long as Lavery doesn't get to them in person it doesn't matter. With any luck they'll decide the call wasn't genuine; they might even think we made it. No, I mean the old Jew, Josef—'

'Josef Spaslov, Comrade General. That has already been attended to. He died during interrogation. His heart gave out.'

'Good. Now, what about the shopkeeper who bought Lavery's watch?'

'He knows nothing of Lavery, Comrade General. Spaslov just sold him the watch without explaining how he came by it.'

Belatov nodded. 'Right. Listen. Obviously the search for Lavery must continue, but I want you to keep it low-key, Comrade Major. We don't want any more stupid incidents like that shooting at Belorusskiy Vokzal. It's bad publicity, if nothing else. You understand?'

'Yes, Comrade General.'

'I hope so, Comrade Major. I sincerely hope so.' Belatov heaved a theatrically false sigh. 'But, to judge from your past efforts, I'm not unduly optimistic. And, as I said, we can't afford to sit and wait.'

'What have you in mind, Comrade General?'

'If we can't find Neil Lavery, Comrade Major, with all our resources, we must persuade him to find us—to return to us of his own accord.'

'But—but how, Comrade General?' Smerinov couldn't hide his surprise. 'He knows we were prepared to shoot him —'

'And thanks to another bit of crass stupidity on someone's part, we failed,' interrupted Belatov. It was quite clear to whom he was referring.

'Yes, Comrade General,' answered Smerinov. He paused, and continued, 'But, knowing that, Lavery's not going to come back and give himself up to interrogation and—as he'll see it—probable death. He can't believe that after he's spurned all

234

we were offering him before, he can return as if nothing had happened and expect us to welcome him.'

'Maybe not. So we offer him something else—a bait—a bait he can't refuse.' Belatov smiled his self-satisfaction. 'In other words, Comrade Major, we bring his wife to Moscow.'

'How? She'd never agree.'

'Why not? She's said to love her husband. An appeal from him, perhaps saying he's ill or he's been involved in an accident, should fetch her—and ultimately him.'

'And if it doesn't, Comrade General? She has her children to consider.'

'I think she'll come, if it's put to her that it's only a visit for a limited period. If not, we might consider spiriting her away as we did her husband. That, however, could lead to complications when it came to her return to the UK. But—'

General Belatov paused to give weight to his words. 'As I said, Comrade Major, we cannot afford to sit on our arses and wait. We act now.'

★   ★   ★

'It's this waiting that's so dreadful,' Imogen Lavery said despondently. 'Waiting and wondering, not knowing what's happening to Neil. I hoped he'd phone me again, but he hasn't. Perhaps it's my fault. I should have been nicer to him when he called the last time—the only time.'

'You must try not to worry about him.' Guy Cantel was matter of fact.

'How can I help it? Of course I worry about him.

235

For God's sake, he's still my husband, whatever he's done.'

'And you still love him?'

Imogen didn't answer. She had no idea what the answer was. And there was a certain irony in the question—in this whole conversation—as both she and Guy realized. If she did still love Neil, miss him, want him, what was she doing in bed with Guy Cantel?

They had been lovers for three days. Physically attracted to each other, and thrown together in the most tense and dramatic circumstances, they had drifted into a relationship that had been almost inevitable from the time of their first meeting. In their short acquaintance she had found Guy kind, considerate, reliable—and there. She had come to depend on him. A good-night kiss, which could have been casual, and—

She had never before been unfaithful to Neil, but she didn't regret it, she told herself. She had to admit that she enjoyed making love with Guy, but there was no way she could avoid a sense of guilt; she wasn't even sure she wanted to.

Brushing aside these thoughts, she said once again, 'I can't understand why Moscow hasn't announced that Neil's gone over. After all, it's a triumph for them.'

'They often take a while, and it hasn't been so long since Neil made his run.'

'It seems like a lifetime.'

Guy accepted the bald statement. He knew that Imogen's feelings towards him were ambivalent, and he distrusted his own. He had considered asking Munro Graffon to take him off the Lavery case, but realized that this wasn't possible; he was committed far too deeply. And he had kept faith

236

with Graffon, putting his job first. He hadn't told Imogen that Lavery might, just conceivably, have changed his mind and want to come home. She would, he reflected, have worried even more about her husband, had she feared he was the object of a man-hunt.

'How are the children?' he asked suddenly. Just like any husband, he thought.

'Matthew is fine—I hope,' Imogen said slowly, surprised by the change of subject. 'He's working hard and playing a lot of cricket. I've phoned him a couple of times. His housemaster told me he's immersing himself in games and other school activities and it's best I shouldn't appear to fuss over him at the moment, though he put it more tactfully than that.'

Guy grinned. 'And Verity?'

'More of a problem. According to Rosalind she's happy playing with Belle, but she's living in a dream world. She's decided that Neil's gone to Moscow on some secret mission, and he'll be a hero when he returns. I think she has visions of going to Buckingham Palace with him when he receives his decoration.'

Imogen had sounded slightly exasperated and Guy said, 'She's living very close by. You must see a lot of her.'

'She doesn't particularly want to see me.' Imogen couldn't keep the bitterness from her voice. Guy reached for her, but she moved away, slid out of bed and put on a robe. 'It's because I won't play her stupid pretend game about Neil. Rosalind believes this day-dreaming, if you can call it that, doesn't do her any harm, but I agree with Philip. Verity should accept what Neil has done and what he is.'

'She's very young.'

'Yes, but if this refusal to face reality continues I'll have to think about taking her to a psychiatrist.'

Imogen went across the bedroom and opened the curtains. It was seven o'clock in the evening, still light outside, and she knew that anyone walking around the square and looking up would see her in the window. They'd guess I'd just had a bath and was dressing for dinner, she thought. They'd speculate that I was a lucky woman with a beautiful home, no money problems, a loving husband and fine children—and less than a month ago that would all have been true. But now—

She caught sight of the police officer on the pavement below. He wasn't really needed any more. The media and therefore the public had lost interest in the Laverys, at least for the time being. Another scandal had taken the place of Neil's defection. But there would undoubtedly be renewed interest when Moscow announced his presence there, and Neil appeared on Soviet television.

Imogen turned away from the window. 'I do wish Neil would declare himself,' she said yet again. 'If he was seen around Moscow, in restaurants or public places, at least I'd know he was leading a normal life, one he had chosen. But this silence—I can't help worrying, whatever you say, Guy. It's—it's as if I were waiting for something—some event—some dreadful event. I want to get it all over. The waiting's the worst part.'

'So let's hope you'll hear from Neil soon.'

'Guy, you haven't any news, have you—really? You would tell me?' The questions were tentative.

Guy Cantel had to meet them with direct lies. 'Yes, I would tell you, but I haven't any news. The

238

last I heard of him he was staying in a *dacha* outside Moscow.' Then he added truthfully, 'We're all waiting for information—just like you. There's nothing else we can do. Darling, come back to bed and forget for a while.' He held out his arms and this time she didn't refuse him.

* * *

'Surely it can wait till tomorrow,' Pavel Kaski said irritably. 'My son is far from well. The doctor's worried about him, and so is my wife. That's why I came dowm to Kent this afternoon, as you know, Nina. Now I'm expected to drive back to London almost as soon as I get here.'

'I'm sorry, Mr Cascon, but it *is* important. The patient insists on seeing you. He's in great pain. It's a wisdom tooth that's become inflamed. There could be an abscess underneath.'

Kaski sighed heavily. He would have to go. It must be an emergency. Nina rarely called him at home, and she had been extrmemely emphatic, using the voice code they used on such occasions. But he couldn't imagine what had happened. Since Neil Lavery had arrived safely in the USSR, life had been relatively tranquil. None of his red-starred 'patients' were operational at the moment. Yet now, suddenly, it seemed to be panic stations.

'OK, Nina,' he said. 'I'm on my way.'

'Thank you, Mr Cascon,' she said primly.

Kaski put down the receiver. His boy didn't really need him; the doctor was competent. As for his wife, he'd just tell her that his patient was a VIP, a minor royal perhaps, and that would keep her quiet.

Fifteen minutes later he drove out of the garage and headed for London. The emergency, he had decided, must be somehow connected with Neil Lavery, and that was bad news, very bad news indeed. He was glad that he hadn't delayed. If action were required, it should probably be taken as soon as possible.

CHAPTER TWENTY-TWO

The following morning Guy Cantel picked up Brigadier Faudin at the latter's flat. Joy Aubyn's funeral was due to take place at noon at the church of St Anne in the village of Bluebury in Berkshire. It was here that her elder sister still lived in their childhood home. The sister, a Mrs Harrison, had not been particularly close to Joy, but she had been shocked by her sudden and violent death, and was determined that after a dignified church service Joy should be buried next to her grandparents in what the Harrisons chose to consider as the family grave.

Notices of the funeral were placed in the quality newspapers, cards were sent to friends and relatives—with most of whom Joy had had no contact for many years—and neighbours of the Harrisons received personal invitations, even appeals, to swell the congregation. As a result, when Cantel and Faudin arrived on the scene, the church was more than three-quarters full.

Cantel, who had expected the mourners to be sparse, was surprised. 'The family seem to be making a great occasion of this,' he murmured as he and Faudin seated themselves in an empty pew towards the rear, and began to study the printed orders of service that had been placed in readiness along the cushioned pews.

'They certainly have.' In spite of the sombre atmosphere, Faudin grinned. He gestured to the bows of purple ribbon attached to the ends of alternate pews, and the purple and white flowers on the altar. The coffin, too, was covered with a purple pall, though this was obscured by three large wreaths. Under cover of the solemn organ music the two men continued to talk quietly.

'Did you send a wreath?' Cantel asked.

'I contributed to one. "From Joy's colleagues in the MOD",' Faudin replied, 'and Philip Glenbourne sent a letter of condolence. Of course, it should have come from Lavery, as he was Joy's immediate boss, but in his absence, Philip thought he should write. However, he decided that it wasn't necessary for him to come to the funeral, and pressure of work made a good excuse. No one else in the directorate seemed awfully anxious to attend, either—'

'So you're representing the MOD, John?'

'In the circumstances, it seemed appropriate.'

Guy Cantel appreciated the cynicism but before he could comment the organist ceased playing, the church bell began a mournful toll, and the vicar, a purple stole around his shoulders, appeared from the vestry and approached the altar rail. Before intoning the traditional opening prayers of the funeral service, he pronounced a few words of welcome to the congregation and announced a hymn. The organist started to play again and a choir, previously unnoticed in the gallery at the rear of the church, declared their presence. With a shuffle of feet, everyone rose.

The Brigadier, who had a fine tenor voice and rather enjoyed hymns, opened his mouth to sing, and no sound issued. He squeezed Cantel's arm. 'Look,' he hissed. 'Over there. A dozen rows in front of us and to our left.'

'Well, well!' In fact, Cantel was less surprised than Faudin. 'Our friend from the Foreign Office, Kevin Sinder.'

'What's he doing here?' Faudin demanded suspiciously.

'Paying his last respects, just like us,' said Cantel mildly. 'Joy did tell me she'd had a brief affair with him, but I wasn't sure I believed her. His presence suggests I was wrong.'

The service proceeded—prayers, another hymn, and a eulogy which caused Cantel and Faudin to exchange glances. The two men were sharing the same thoughts: if only the clergyman had been aware that Joy Aubyn had betrayed her country for the sake of her lover—a lover who had subsequently betrayed *her*—he might have chosen more appropriate words. Neither of the two men paid any attention as the church door creaked open, and a late mourner slipped into the rearmost pew.

Though he had been brought up as a Roman Catholic, Stefan Cheski, Polish diplomat and the lover in question, was no longer a religious man, and the church was alien to him. Nevertheless, memories made him cross himself and kneel. He didn't pray for Joy; he didn't even think of her. Instead, he thought of Guy Cantel. He had seen the notice of Joy's funeral in *The Times* and had come on a hunch that Cantel might also attend. He was flying home to Warsaw the next day and, realizing

242

how much he owed Cantel, he was anxious to meet him and pay a last instalment on his debt.

When he rose from his knees his eyes searched among the congregation. Once he was sure Cantel was there, in a pew a few rows nearer the altar, Cheski sat through the eulogy without listening to it and stood for the final hymn. He watched Cantel's back as the coffin was carried down the aisle, followed by the priest and the chief mourners, and then the straggle of the rest. He intercepted Cantel, who had spotted him a moment earlier, as Cantel came out of the church with Faudin.

'A word with you, Mr Cantel,' he said.

Cantel nodded immediately. 'Excuse me a moment, John,' he said to Faudin.

'Of course. I'll meet you by the car,' Faudin replied, inspecting Cheski curiously. He had agreed with Cantel that they should not go to the graveside for the interment.

'You must be surprised to see me here,' said Stefan Cheski, as he and Cantel walked off together among the tombstones. 'First, I want to thank you. You've kept your side of our bargain.'

'Did you think I wouldn't?'

Cheski shrugged. 'Neither of us is in the trusting business,' he said. 'But I have received the original of Joy Aubyn's letter with all those lies about me. I go home tomorrow, my reputation intact. Indeed, I'm informed I'm due for a promotion.'

'Congratulations!'

Cheski ignored the slight derision with which Cantel had spoken. 'For my part, I co-operated with your colleagues when they interrogated me about Joy Aubyn as part of your damage assessment.'

'Yes. They weren't displeased,' Cantel admitted warily. He wondered where this conversation was leading. He found it hard to believe that Cheski had come to Joy's funeral merely on the off-chance of finding an opportunity to thank him. 'So—?' he said.

'Well, there's some information I didn't give them, because I didn't have it myself at the time, Mr Cantel—information you might consider important.'

'And what do you want in return for it?'

'You are being too cynical, Mr Cantel.' Cheski gave every sign of amusement. 'As far as I'm concerned this is an extra effort to retain your goodwill—an extra piece of insurance that the photocopies of Joy's letter that I'm sure you've taken won't be used against me in the future.'

'OK, I think I understand, Mr Cheski. What is this mysterious information?'

'First of all, it can do no harm of any kind to my country. If it could, I wouldn't be telling you when I have no need to. What I did for you previously, I did because you gave me little choice—and I did it with regret, though it was mostly retailing to you your own information—the information I had gained from the Aubyn woman.'

Guy Cantel gave the Pole a searching glance, but made no direct comment. It was true that, thanks to Joy Aubyn, he had been subjected to blackmail because of a crime he had not committed. It was, Cantel thought, a dirty game—certainly not a 'trusting business'. He looked deliberately at his watch. 'Suppose you get to the point,' he said.

'All right. This information concerns Marta Stein. In brief, Mr Cantel, I gather she's a plant—an agent. She's actually an East German. She wasn't born in the Federal Republic, as she professes. And she's been operating here for the Soviet Union over a number of years.'

'How do you know this? Who told you?' Cantel couldn't hide his surprise.

'I'm not prepared to answer that, except that it was a colleague. But I will say that we were apparently asked to help get her out of Britain if any problem arose suddenly.'

'And has one arisen?' Cantel needed to give himself time to think.

'I've no idea. My colleague—he's a personal friend—shouldn't have told me what he did, but he wasn't especially keen to work with the Soviets over what seemed to be a sensitive matter, and he needed to confide in someone. You understand, surely?'

'I understand, I think. Now tell me just why you imagine that I'm interested in Marta Stein?'

The Pole smiled. 'I'm afraid you showed your interest when I mentioned her name just now, but anyway I knew you'd be concerned about her. She was supposed to have been Neil Lavery's mistress, wasn't she? So of course British Security would be interested in her.'

'You said "supposed". Isn't it true?'

'I've no idea,' Cheski said again. 'My colleague was told by the Russians that it was so, but the fact that this piece of information was volunteered unnecessarily made him somewhat suspicious of it.' Stefan Cheski threw up his hands in a helpless gesture. 'It's possible the Soviet officer was just being indiscreet. Maybe he thought it didn't matter telling a Pole who was going to collaborate with him. Or perhaps he let it slip on purpose to show

how important Stein was.'

'Complicated, isn't it?' remarked Cantel. 'And is that all, Mr Cheski?'

'Yes.' Cheski grinned. 'My little extra bit of insurance.'

Cantel nodded. 'I won't forget. Thanks. Have a good flight home tomorrow. And don't worry.'

He turned and walked away, conscious that the Pole was watching him, and conscious also that in spite of his reassuring farewell he had ignored Cheski's outstretched hand. He wasn't certain what to make of Cheski's story. He didn't trust the man, but he was inclined to believe what he had said. He reckoned that if Cheski had wanted to invent a story he wouldn't have admitted to so much ignorance, throwing doubt on its reliability, and giving grounds for a dozen different interpretations. Neither would he have been prepared to state quite so openly that, as far as he was concerned, the whole thing was hearsay.

Cantel found John Faudin sitting on a wall beside their car and apologized for keeping him waiting, but offered no explanation. They drove back to London, for the most part in companionable silence.

*　　*　　*

When he had dropped the Brigadier at the Ministry of Defence Guy Cantel set off at once for the block of mansion flats near Westminster Cathedral where Marta Stein lived. There was a Harrods delivery van outside, and the front doors of the building were standing wide open. Cantel went into the hall.

The door of the ground-floor flat where he had

visited Marta Stein was also open. A young woman was standing inside it, instructing some Harrods' men where they should put a large bookcase they were delivering. She was in slacks and a shirt, her hair dishevelled, and she looked tired and slightly fraught. She gave Cantel a vague smile as he stood to one side while she thanked and tipped the men.

'Can I help you?' she asked.

'I came to see Miss Marta Stein,' said Cantel.

'Oh, I'm afraid she's not here any more.'

Cantel had known what to expect before the woman spoke, but he pretended to be surprised. He peered over her head. 'Miss Stein has sold you the flat, Mrs—er—?'

'Mrs Duncan, Moira Duncan. What remains of the lease, yes. Actually we don't really own it until the first of next month, but as it was going to be empty she said we could move in when we liked.' The woman frowned suddenly. 'There's nothing wrong, is there?'

'Oh no, Mrs Duncan.' Cantel gave her his most reassuring smile. In the circumstances, he saw no reason to assume an alias. 'My name's Guy Cantel. It's not long since I saw Miss Stein—I'm a business acquaintance—and she gave no hint she was thinking of moving from here.'

'It was very sudden, Mr Cantel. Her mother was taken ill—a stroke, I think—and Miss Stein had to go home to nurse her. She left two days ago.'

'Home?'

'To Bonn, West Germany. That's where her mother lives, apparently. Miss Stein said she didn't expect many letters—her lawyer's dealing with all her affairs—but she left me the address just in case. Come in and I'll find it for you.'

'Thank you very much.'

Cantel followed the woman into the sitting-room which was much as he remembered it. The grand piano was still there and the chairs were the same, the lamps, even the pictures. The only difference he could see was the new bookcase propped against a wall, some cardboard cartons overflowing with books, and the absence of Neil Lavery's photograph.

Mrs Duncan was rummaging in a desk. 'It's here somewhere,' she said, 'but everything's in such a mess. Do sit down, Mr Cantel. I'll find it in a minute.'

Guy Cantel took the chair he had sat in when he had first met Marta Stein. 'You've got Miss Stein's furniture,' he remarked conversationally.

'Yes. It came with the flat. We'll have to get rid of a lot of it, especially the grand piano. Neither of us plays.'

'Have you known Miss Stein long?'

'We don't know her at all. We met her just the once when we came to look at this place—we heard of it through an agent—and we said we'd take it there and then. The price was quite reasonable and we were thrilled to get it. My husband's a professor at the London School of Economics, and it's far more convenient than Richmond where we lived before.' Mrs Duncan's flow of words ceased for a moment. 'Ah, here it is,' she said.

She handed Cantel a piece of stiff cream paper, the letterhead of a well-known firm of house agents. In the centre of the sheet, in bold handwriting, was an address in Bonn. He made a note of it, though he had little faith that it would help. Then he thanked Mrs Duncan and returned to his car. He

248

was grateful that she had been so unsuspicious, and seemed to have told him everything he needed to know without hesitation. But it would all have to be checked.

*   *   *

By that evening the details of Mrs Duncan's statements about herself and her husband and their purchase of the flat's lease from Marta Stein had been confirmed. However, there was no direct evidence that Stein had left the UK; certainly she hadn't gone openly by any recognized air or sea route. And the address in Bonn she had provided was, according to the German authorities, the headquarters of the police there. Marta Stein, Cantel thought, clearly had a sense of humour. But that didn't necessarily make her a Soviet agent.

Nevertheless, it seemed likely that that was her role. Stefan Cheski's information, though it could not be verified, was at least supported. The question remained as to why Stein should have fled at this particular moment. The British had nothing against her, except that she had been Neil Lavery's lover—or so she claimed. Apart from the letter found in Lavery's study, which could have been planted by the bogus telephone men who had visited the house, there was only Stein's own word to give the story any credence. But she *had* convinced Imogen Lavery.

Reluctantly Cantel decided that he would have to talk to Imogen about her meeting with Stein again. She had been upset and bitter the last time he had broached the subject, and he hadn't pressed her for details. He admitted to himself that, in spite of his feelings, he should have done. It would be even more difficult now with their present relationship, but the sooner he tackled it the better.

Cantel was still at the office. He tapped out Imogen's phone number. It was his elder brother's birthday and he had promised to go to a party for him, but that was not until later in the evening. He had time to have a drink with Imogen and talk to her first. While he waited to hear her voice, he thought of Marta Stein and came to the conclusion that it was a fair assumption she had been warned to leave the UK, because if Lavery did reach the British he might betray her.

There was no answer from Imogen. Cantel tried the Glenbournes' number and Belle's nurse said that Mrs Lavery was not there. The Glenbournes were on their way to dinner with Mr and Mrs Sinder, but she was sure Mrs Lavery wasn't intending to accompany them. Cantel thanked her and replaced the receiver. His talk to Imogen would have to wait till the next morning.

It was lucky for his peace of mind that he didn't know where Imogen Lavery was at the moment, or what she was doing.

CHAPTER TWENTY-THREE

The day of Joy Aubyn's funeral had begun badly for Imogen Lavery. Her first waking thought was that she would have to do her stint at the Oxfam shop that morning, and she yearned to forget about the commitment, ignore the alarm clock, turn over and sleep again. Since the scandal of Neil's disappearance and assumed defection had broken, she had been to the shop only once. And she had hated it.

She had been in constant fear that one of the customers would recognize her from the many photographs of the Laverys that had appeared in the newspapers and on television, and she had resented the other helpers, who had been so compassionate, too compassionate. She had silently objected to being treated like an invalid or someone with a physical disability. In the past, attendance at the shop during the day while Neil was away from home working at the office had been a pleasant duty. Now it had become an ordeal.

But there was no escaping it. She had promised she would go. One of the regular helpers was ill and another had a sick child, and she was needed. She couldn't bring herself to make an excuse. Wearily she got out of bed.

For some unknown reason every taxi she tried to hail was already occupied, and when finally she caught a bus it was crowded and she had to stand. She arrived at the shop late and in a bad temper.

The greeting from the other woman on duty that morning did nothing to improve her mood. 'My dear, I'm so glad you've come at last. I was afraid I was going to be all by myself, and there's so much work to do. Lady Gee's chauffeur has delivered a huge box of goodies for us.'

Imogen drew a sharp breath to stifle the retort she wanted to make. There were no customers in the shop, and she wondered why this large, fat woman, at one time a second-rate actress but now the wife of a peer, was sitting behind the counter doing nothing when she might have started to

251

unpack Lady Gee's box of 'goodies'.

'I promised to come,' Imogen said shortly, 'and come I have. I'll deal with Lady Gee's box.'

She went into the room at the back of the shop, took off the jacket of her suit and put on an overall. She expected little from the box, so she was not disappointed. Lady Gee was clearing out her mother's house, and anything that was valueless she dumped on Oxfam. Today there were clothes, all unfashionable and some none too clean, a few knick-knacks and a little costume jewellery. At least the jewellery might sell.

Imogen found her task of unpacking, sorting these articles and pricing some of them distasteful, and she completed it as quickly as she could. She tidied the room and glanced into the shop. A girl was buying a pretty party dress for a child. A man and a woman were deliberating about a china lamp. As she turned back into the room, having decided that it was time for mid-morning coffee, she noticed a woman with a headscarf staring through the display window. When Imogen returned to the shop with the coffee for herself and her companion, the woman had gone, but ten or fifteen minutes later she returned.

This in itself was not unusual. People often saw an article in the window that attracted their attention but hesitated to enter the shop, either because they didn't like to buy second-hand goods, or were perhaps a trifle embarrassed at the thought of being seen buying them. Often such potential customers retreated, but returned, having regained their confidence; such situations could be amusing. But somehow this woman was different, or so it seemed to Imogen, who felt that she herself was the

252

attraction—the focus of attention—rather than any of the objects on sale.

Imogen sat behind the counter and drank her coffee. Then the door-bell pinged and the woman with the headscarf came in. The girl who had bought the child's party dress was inspecting some rompers and the other couple had finally decided to buy the china lamp, so that Imogen's co-worker was busy. The young woman went straight to a tray of superior costume jewellery, picked up an ivory necklace seemingly at random, and brought it to Imogen.

'I'll have this,' she said.

Imogen glanced at the price tag. 'It's five pounds,' she said.

'So I saw.'

The eyes behind the spectacles were hard, the voice peremptory, but Imogen got the impression that the woman was nervous. She was fumbling in her bag for the money with a hand that seemed to be shaking. Imogen picked up the necklace, and wrapped it in tissue paper before putting it in a small Oxfam bag.

'Here you are,' she said, trying to sound both businesslike and pleasant. 'Thank you from Oxfam.'

The young woman took the bag. 'You are Mrs Neil Lavery, aren't you?' she asked abruptly.

Oh, God! Imogen thought, but, 'Yes,' she answered, her mouth suddenly dry.

The young woman nodded as if satisfied, thrust a five-pound note into Imogen's hand and walked quickly out of the shop. As Imogen watched her leave with some relief she realized that she was holding more than just a banknote. She opened her fingers and found a piece of paper folded into a small square. Automatically her fingers unfolded it.

If you want N to live be in the Brompton Oratory on right of main aisle in second pew from rear tonight at seven. ALONE.

Crumpling the paper, Imogen walked blindly into the back room. She went into the lavatory and sat on the toilet seat. She felt faint. She forced herself to breathe slowly and she put her head down between her legs. After a minute the faintness passed. She smoothed out the piece of paper and reread the message.

There was a knock at the door. 'Imogen, are you all right, my dear?'

'Yes, I'm fine,' Imogen lied. 'Be with you in a moment.'

She continued to sit where she was. She thought about the person who had delivered the message. The headscarf had covered her hair. Her spectacles had been slightly tinted. The baggy jacket and the long skirt had disguised her figure. In different clothes and without spectacles, she wouldn't know the woman again.

Imogen flushed the toilet, tried to cope with her appearance and emerged from the lavatory. In spite of her efforts, she was pale and there was a line of sweat on her upper lip, but she did her best to smile. She told herself that it was absurd to be so upset by this mysterous woman and her message. It was a black joke, she decided, played by someone sick, like the many whom she knew had vomited their abuse down the telephone line when Neil had first disappeared. Of course she had no intention of

254

going anywhere near the Oratory. She would tell Guy and—

'My dear you look ghastly. You must be ill.'

'A tummy upset. I must have eaten something that disagreed with me.'

'You were all right when you arrived this morning.'

The look that accompanied this last remark was shrewd, and Imogen could imagine what the wretched woman was thinking. She made an effort to control her temper. 'Please don't make a fuss,' she said. 'I'm fine now. And there's the bell. A customer.'

For the rest of the morning Imogen busied herself about the shop, talking to customers, dusting, rearranging, keeping herself occupied so that she had no time to think. Luckily the helper who was to replace her arrived early, so that she was able to leave sooner than she had expected. She was lucky, and caught a taxi directly outside the shop.

By the time she reached home she knew, with no need to give the matter any further consideration, that without doubt she would keep the appointment that evening, alone—and that she would not tell Guy Cantel or anyone else about it.

*   *   *

'I don't like this, Pavel. Not one bit.'

'Neither do I, Nina, but we've got no choice. There simply was no time to find someone reliable to organize these contacts with Mrs Lavery. There was no alternative but to carry out the operation ourselves. Remember, the emphasis was on *immediate* action. We'd be contravening orders and

255

neglecting our duty if we were responsible for any delays.'

Pavel Kaski spoke sharply. He had spent a trying morning. Until Nina had returned to report that she had successfully delivered the message to Imogen Lavery he had been tense and anxious, and during the afternoon, while he explored a succession of mouths for cavities, scaled teeth and made polite conversation with his patients, he had become increasingly aware of the risks that were attached to the part he would have to play that evening.

'But what happens if you're caught, Pavel?' The last patient had departed and he and Nina were in the bedroom attached to the surgery. She was working on Kaski's appearance.

'There's no question of being "caught", Nina.' He was speaking as much to reassure himself as to quell her fears. 'All I'm doing is meeting a lady in a public place and relaying some information to her.'

'You know that's not the whole of it,' she objected sharply. 'If Mrs Lavery doesn't come alone, if she has security people with her and they question you, your cover could be blown. They may not be able to take any action, but it could well mean the end of your—our—work here.'

'My dear girl, you exaggerate. You know perfectly well we've always been prepared for contingencies, in case we had to get out quickly. Anyway, it would only be my secondary cover—the one you're fixing now—that might get blown. With luck, there'll be no trouble. If there is, I should be able to talk my way out of it easily enough. Remember, no one's going to connect John Brownier, carrying documents to prove his identity,

256

with Paul Cascon, the well-known dentist. Oh, I know quite well they'll try to keep me—or at least keep me under surveillance—while they check everything, but the cover will stand up to a quick investigation, and I'll make sure I don't lead any of them here. Don't worry. By morning, I'll be the respectable Mr Cascon once again.'

'I hope you're right, Pavel.'

'I am.' Kaski spoke with more confidence than he felt. 'Nina, have you finished with me? We'll have to leave soon.'

'Yes. You can look at yourself now.' She swung him round to face the dressing-table mirror, and laughed at his expression.

'Good heavens! What a difference! My mother wouldn't know me. Is that really what the Brownier passport photograph looks like? I can't remember. Anyway, I won't be carrying a passport. It's wonderful, Nina.'

Indeed, Kaski was pleased. Nina had darkened his hair and his eyebrows with colour that would readily wash out. She had, with a minimum of cosmetics, hollowed his cheeks and given him a sallow complexion. Spectacles—not plain glass, but with very weak lenses—completed the disguise.

'Wonderful, Nina!' he repeated. 'Let's go, then. You drive, so that I don't have to worry about a place to park. The traffic may be heavy, and we must get there well before Mrs Lavery. I want to be able to watch her arrive, and try to ascertain if she's followed instructions, or if she's—accompanied.'

'What if she is—accompanied?'

'We'll abort.'

'And what if she just doesn't turn up?'

'We'll face that problem if it arises—but,

somehow, I don't think it will.' Suddenly Kaski grinned; the excitement of the operation was beginning to grip him and override any fears. 'If she doesn't come, at least I'll be in the right place to pray—for myself and for you.'

It was about eight minutes past seven that evening. Imogen Lavery sat in the second pew from the rear to the right of the main aisle of Brompton Oratory. It was not a church she knew well, though she had been there once or twice for the weddings of Catholic friends, and she looked about her with nervous interest, constantly glancing at her watch. She wondered if the individual she was to meet had already arrived, and was thankful that there were at least a dozen people, including a priest, in the church so that she wasn't really alone or isolated.

Clearly a service had been concluded only a short time ago. The air was heavy with incense. Two ladies were collecting hymn books. The priest went into a confessional box, and a man seated not far from her rose as if at a signal. She expected him to follow the priest into the confessional, but instead he came towards her and slid into the pew beside her as she automatically moved along it.

He spoke quietly. 'Mrs Lavery?'

'Yes.' Imogen was suddenly cold. Instinctively she began to turn her head towards him.

'No!' Kaski said, putting up a hand to shield his face. 'Keep looking straight ahead, Mrs Lavery.' But before she could obey he shone a pencil torch into her eyes, momentarily blinding her. 'That's fine. Relax now, but keep looking straight ahead.'

'What do you want of me?' Imogen heard herself say, turning away from him.

'First, I must apologize on two counts. One, for

258

shining that light on you a second ago, but it's very dim in here and I had to make sure of your identity—that you were in fact Imogen Lavery, and not some police substitute. Secondly, I'm sorry for the somewhat melodramatic invitation to this meeting. We were merely trying to do our utmost to ensure that you would come to the rendezvous—and come alone.'

Imogen didn't quite know what to make of this preamble, but she summoned her self-control. 'Well, here I am,' she said. 'I'm alone, and I've told no one about your message.'

'That's good.'

'I repeat, what do you want of me?'

'Mrs Lavery, do you love your husband?'

It was the question Imogen least expected, and she was wary. 'Yes' she answered at length.

'Then I'm afraid I have bad news for you. He was involved in a car accident shortly after he arrived in Moscow and was seriously hurt. Indeed, for a while they despaired of saving his life. However, fortunately for him, Soviet medicine is extremely good and he has excellent care. There is now hope that he will live, though it remains a slim hope.'

'Thank you,' Imogen said, and thought how stupid was gratitude in these extraordinary circumstances. 'Why—why are you telling me this?' she demanded after a pause.

'Because, Mrs Lavery, your husband keeps asking for you, and the doctors are convinced that your presence would make an enormous difference, perhaps all the difference. The slim hope could become a real chance, if you could be beside him.'

'But that's impossible!' Imogen's immediate reaction was emphatic.

'Is it, Mrs Lavery? Think. I appreciate that you don't approve of what your husband has done, but he has been acting from the best of motives—'

'Betraying his country? Abandoning his wife and children?'

Kaski laughed gently. 'I don't think you can consider yourself abandoned, Mrs Lavery. You have a supportive family and friends, and you're a rich woman. As for betraying his country, which I suppose is a fair accusation, your husband didn't act for financial gain or personal advantage. He did what he did because of strongly held beliefs. Give him credit for that.'

Imogen shook her head; she was not prepared for a speculative discussion of the reasons for Neil's behaviour. 'I'm sorry he's had an accident,' she said slowly. 'I hope he gets well soon and makes a complete recovery, but I can't—' Involuntarily she turned towards the man beside her.

His hand came up at once. 'Straight ahead, Mrs Lavery. Keep looking straight ahead. It's better that you shouldn't be able to recognize me again.'

Imogen obeyed him quickly, and he went on, 'Mrs Lavery, I don't think I made it clear how ill your husband is, and how much he needs to see you. Is it really asking too much of you to give up three or four days to visit him?'

'Three or four days?'

'A week at most. No one expects you to stay permanently, Mrs Lavery. To tell you the truth, I don't believe anyone would have suggested even a short visit at this time, if there weren't great anxiety for your husband's life.'

Imogen was silent. She thought of Neil, dying, needing her—and she was filled with love for him.

The last thing she wanted was to go to Moscow. She was sure that the Russians would make propaganda capital out of such a trip. Nevertheless—She swallowed her tears.

'Mrs Lavery, I'm sorry, but you must make up your mind. Your husband will have to be told. It's not fair to let him hope if there's no hope, is it?'

'No, but—'

Kaski, seeing that she was silently crying, decided to exert extra pressure on her emotions. 'If you don't go and your husband dies, you'll regret it, Mrs Lavery. But of course it's your decision.'

Imogen was thinking of Guy Cantel, who she knew would be horrified at the idea of her going to the USSR and would prevent her if he could. But it was not Guy who was important to her at this moment. It was Neil.

'All right,' she said, 'but you'll have to make the arrangements. When?'

'Of course, Mrs Lavery. As for timing, it's tomorrow. There's not a moment to be wasted.' Kaski patted her on the arm. 'And don't worry. You won't regret it.'

CHAPTER TWENTY-FOUR

'Yes, it *is* a sudden decision, as you say, Mrs Price, but one I felt I had to make. The strain of the past couple of weeks—surely you understand?' Imogen wished she were a better liar.

Mrs Price regarded with dismay the duster she had been wielding. 'Of course I understand that you want to get away by yourself for a few days,

Mrs Lavery. What I don't understand is why you're making such a secret of it, not wanting me to tell anyone else, not your sister, or your father, or—or—' she hesitated for a moment '—or Mr Cantel, until tomorrow.' She shook her head, mystified. 'Are you sure you should be doing this, Mrs Lavery? It would be different if you were staying in England, but abroad—Paris—well—'

'Quite sure.' Imogen lied again; she could scarcely have been less certain of herself and her feelings. The man she had met last night had given her specific instructions. She was to be at Terminal 2 at Heathrow Airport at ten o'clock in the morning prepared to catch a flight. She must take hand baggage only. She would be met at the airport with tickets and further instructions. She was to tell no one where she was going, especially that she was going abroad. That was vital, he had said; the British authorities would be sure to try to prevent her leaving the UK. But to forestall any panic on her behalf she could say she was going to stay with a friend in the country.

Imogen had agreed, but later, during the night, reservations had begun to creep into her thoughts. She realized that if she were to help save Neil's life, she must avoid British intervention and get to Moscow. On the other hand, for her own peace of mind—if only as some slight 'insurance' for herself and her safety—she needed to leave some clue to her whereabouts behind. She dared not mention Moscow, but Paris, she thought, should be enough to set alarm bells ringing.

'There's no secret, as you call it, Mrs Price,' she said, 'but if my family and friends knew in advance that I was going to Paris they'd try to dissuade me.'

262

Guy, she thought, wouldn't be content with an attempt at mere dissuasion; he would damn well prevent her from leaving the country. 'So please don't mention Paris till tomorrow. Just stall. Then, tomorrow, if anyone phones or comes to the house, you can say I've gone there, only for a short visit, but you don't know when I'll be back. You understand?'

'I understand, Mrs Lavery.' It was clear that Mrs Price was not relishing the situation. 'And that will be the truth, won't it? I'm not to know when you'll be back—or where you'll be staying.'

'It's none of your business, Mrs Price.' Imogen regretted the remark as soon as she had made it.

'No, madam,' said Mrs Price, who never called Imogen 'madam'. She resumed her dusting, adding over her shoulder, 'I'll follow your instructions, of course.'

'Thank you.' Imogen had a sudden desire to hug Betty Price, and say that she had changed her mind and wasn't going anywhere. Instead, she picked up her overnight bag and said goodbye. 'I'll be back in a few days,' she repeated unnecessarily.

'Yes, Mrs Lavery,' said Mrs Price, but when she heard the front door slam behind Imogen she added, 'I hope so, my dear. I do hope so.' She was not an imaginative woman and she couldn't define her fears, but Imogen's nervous irritation had affected her and convinced her that something was amiss—and inevitably she connected whatever was wrong with Neil Lavery.

Continuing her housework, Mrs Price worried. It was, she conceded, none of her business if Mrs Lavery decided on the spur of the moment to go to

263

Paris without the knowledge of her family, but still—

A few minutes later, when Rosalind Glenbourne phoned, Mrs Price was tempted to tell her the truth. But Rosalind had been in a hurry—she had to take Belle to the doctor—and Mrs Price let the opportunity slip.

Ten minutes after Rosalind's call Guy Cantel rang the doorbell. The previous evening's celebration of his brother's birthday had lasted into the small hours. It had been a good party, but when he eventually reached home Guy had forgotten to set the alarm and had consequently overslept. As a result, this morning, bleary-eyed and hungover, he was later than he had intended and not in the best of tempers.

'I'm sorry, Mr Cantel,' said Mrs Price, 'but Mrs Lavery isn't here.'

'Damn!'

'Is it important?'

'Comparatively. I need to see her about something. Tell me where she's gone, Mrs Price? She's not at her sister's, is she?'

'No. She's not there.'

Guy Cantel usually got on very well with Mrs Price, and had always found her helpful. Something about the brevity of this reply and the emphasis that Mrs Price had placed on these four words caught Guy's attention. He gave her an enquiring stare. 'Is anything wrong?' he asked.

'No. No, I hope not, Mr Cantel.'

'And just what do you mean by that—you *hope* not?' By now all Guy's instincts were alert. 'Let me come in, Mrs Price. We can't talk on the doorstep.' He pushed her gently back into the hall and shut the front door behind them. 'Tell me,' he said,

264

'where is Mrs Lavery?'

Guy Cantel spoke quietly, but Mrs Price sensed his urgency—even his concern.

'She's gone away for a few days, Mr Cantel. She said she wanted to be alone for a while. It was a sudden decision and she's not told anyone because—because she was afraid they'd try to stop her.' Mrs Price paused, but something in Cantel's expression made her hurry on. 'I don't know what to do, Mr Cantel. I shouldn't be telling you—Mrs Lavery made me promise not to tell anyone till tomorrow—but I'm sure it's not right. At this very moment she's on her way to Heathrow. She's going to Paris.'

★ ★ ★

Imogen Lavery followed her instructions exactly. Her overnight bag was not heavy and she walked to Harrods. She went in by the main door, mingled with the customers in the food halls on the ground floor for a while, and then left by the back door leading to Basil Street. Here she caught a taxi to Hammersmith Broadway, where she hailed a second cab which took her to Terminal 2. Terminal 2 at Heathrow, she reflected, served both Air France flights to Paris and elsewhere, and Aeroflot flights direct to Moscow.

She accepted that these precautions were necessary, though irritating, as she hadn't been able to assure the man at the Oratory that she no longer had a minder—a bodyguard. In fact, the plain-clothes man who had been shadowing her, ostensibly for her own protection but also to observe her contacts, had, to Guy Cantel's annoyance, been withdrawn a couple of days before in view of a sudden shortage of available staff. So she was not being followed, but she had to resist a persistent temptation to look about her.

What had not occurred to her was that she might meet anyone she knew at the airport, and she was startled to hear a familiar voice behind her call her name as she was entering the Departures Hall. She swung round.

'Hallo, Kevin,' she said weakly.

Kevin Sinder kissed her affectionately on the cheek. 'Hallo, my dear. How are you? What are you doing here?'

'I—I'm waiting for a friend,' Imogen said.

'Waiting for a—But this is the departures area.'

'I know! I've come to say goodbye to her. She's in the cloakroom at the moment,' Imogen improvised quickly. 'What about you, Kevin? Where are you off to?'

'To the most delightful city in the world. In other words, to Paris. Unfortunately it's to attend a tedious meeting.' Sinder gave a shrug of disgust. 'But I must go. The flight's been called. Look, I'll be back next week. Then you simply must have dinner with us, Imogen, even if it's only *en famille*.'

'That would be—' Imogen began, but Kevin Sinder was already striding away, a hand waving in farewell.

Imogen watched him leave with relief. She was fond of Kevin, if not of his wife, but in her present situation she could do without company. Whoever was to meet her wouldn't approach unless she was alone. She was wondering what she should do, when over the loudspeakers came the announcement, 'Will Mrs Lavery please come to

266

the Airport Information Desk in this terminal. Mrs Lavery to the Information Desk, please.'

As Imogen hastened to obey the summons she wondered if Kevin Sinder had heard it and, if so, what he would make of it after the lies she had told him. She consoled herself with the thought that it didn't matter. He wouldn't risk missing his flight to Paris in order to investigate what she was doing.

She found the Information Desk, and gave her name to one of the attractive uniformed girls behind it. As she did so a man in a navy blue suit stepped forward, looking a little like an airline or airport official. He smiled pleasantly, but he spoke with an air of authority.

'Would you come with me, please, Mrs Lavery?'

Imogen nodded. The Soviet agent who had given her instructions in the Brompton Oratory had said she would be met at Terminal 2 but he hadn't explained how the meeting would be arranged. She had been expecting some semi-clandestine arrangement; she certainly hadn't anticipated such a normal and public greeting.

'Let me carry your bag for you, Mrs Lavery,' he said in perfect English. 'And if you'd follow me, please.'

He led her through a door marked 'PRIVATE' and along several corridors. He was tall, with a long stride, and Imogen had to hurry to keep up with him. If he was aware of this he gave no sign. She thought that perhaps he was taking her straight to one of Aeroflot's Ilyushins without going through any boarding formalities, but he stopped in front of another door.

'Here we are,' he said in a businesslike tone. 'Sorry to have made you walk so far, Mrs Lavery.'

He returned her bag, opened the door and waved her into the room, which was furnished as a small VIP lounge with leather chairs, a rack of magazines and newpapers, and a well-stocked bar at one side. Her escort closed the door behind her, and Imogen found herself alone.

She waited some ten minutes, pacing up and down the room, and finally tried the door. To her surprise, she discovered that it was locked. She was a prisoner. Apprehensively she sat down in one of the chairs and attempted to review the situation. The she heard a key in the door, which opened. She jumped to her feet, to find herself confronting Guy Cantel.

The mere mention of Paris had been enough to induce Cantel to take action. Calls to Passport Control and the Special Branch at Heathrow had been enough to set the machinery in motion. If only—he thought, as he drove as rapidly as he could along the M4 towards Heathrow—if only she can be intercepted before—before what? He was pretty sure he could guess.

'Guy!' she said. 'Guy!'

'Sit down, Imogen.' Cantel pointed to an armchair. He didn't smile. 'I think you've got some explaining to do,' he said. He spoke coldly, though what he wanted to do was take her in his arms and hold her. He was overwhelmed with relief that she was safe.

Imogen glanced past him at the door, but she knew that an attempt to flee would be hopeless. Her only chance was to appeal to him. She did as she'd been told, and sat down. 'Guy,' she said. 'Please let me go. Neil's had an accident in Moscow. He's been badly hurt. He's probably going to die and

268

he's asking for me. I must go.'

'How do you know this?'

She told him about the woman who had brought the message to the Oxfam shop, and the man in the Brompton Oratory. He listened without interruption.

'It's just for a few days, Guy,' she concluded, 'and it might make all the difference. It might save his life. Look at my overnight bag. You can see I'm not planning to defect or anything like that.'

'There's no point in your planning to do anything, Imogen, except go home and stay there. Incidentally, may I have your passport, please.'

'No! You've no right to treat me like a—a criminal.'

'I've every right to treat you like a criminal—a criminal fool!' Suddenly Guy Cantel gave his anger full rein. His relief at Imogen having been caught before she was met by a Soviet agent and taken on board an aircraft was so enormous that he had to have some release for his emotions—and anger was the safest. He berated her for a full minute.

'—to believe the good, kind Russians are going to fly you, free, to Moscow, so that you can be at the bedside of your dying husband. It's—it's absurd, fatuous. You must have been out of your mind to accept such a ludicrous story.'

'It could be true,' Imogen protested feebly.

'If Neil's dying, it's because the Russians have done their best to kill him.'

'What do you mean? Why should they want to kill him?'

Guy Cantel realized that he had gone too far. Now he would have to tell Imogen the whole story, as he understood it—or almost the whole story. 'I don't know the answer to that question,' he began slowly, 'but the last the British authorities heard of Neil was when he phoned our embassy in Moscow a few days ago. He had been shot in the leg trying to escape and was on the run. Our chap there arranged to pick him up, but Neil never arrived at the rendezvous they made. Of course, he may have been caught by now,' Cantel added brutally, 'and he may be asking for you on his death-bed. But I can't imagine why they would bother with you, even if he were. And in any case such information as we have suggests that he's still loose.'

'Oh God!' Imogen said piteously. 'Why did he ever go to Moscow? And, as you say, why should they want *me* there? Why—why—' She buried her face in her hands and began to cry convulsively.

Cantel got up, went to the bar and poured a stiff brandy. He knelt beside her and made her sip it. 'I'm sorry,' he said, though he didn't know why he was apologizing. 'Darling, I'm sorry.' He gave her a handkerchief and she wiped her eyes and blew her nose while he gently stroked her hair. She tried to smile her thanks and he could have wept for her. It was by such a narrow margin that she'd been saved from a flight to Moscow.

Recalling Mrs Price, and how he had come to learn of Imogen's intentions, Cantel remembered why he had gone to the Laverys' house that morning. But this was scarcely the right moment to question her about Marta Stein, and he knew it would have to wait.

'Would you like to go home now?' he asked gently.

'Yes, please,' Imogen said. She was exhausted and confused. 'Nothing makes any sense,' she

270

added in exasperation as Guy helped her to her feet.

Cantel nodded his agreement. But the trouble, he thought, was not that *nothing* made sense; it was that they couldn't make sense of the little they knew.

*   *   *

If Imogen Lavery was suffering from frustration, her sensations were trivial compared with the feelings of General Vadim Belatov. His plan to use her to provoke the elusive Lavery into giving himself up had failed. The wretched woman had clearly disobeyed her instructions and told someone of her intended departure, so of course the British had restrained her. The British Security Service weren't all fools.

It was true that, even had it succeeded, the plan had had imperfections. Lavery might not have surrendered himself, even if he learnt of his wife's presence in the city—and there was no guarantee that this news could be conveyed to him. He could conceivably be already dead or, as his wife had been told, dying. Or, if it came to a choice, he might put his own safety before that of his wife, devoted though he was to her—and they had only Comrade Major Smerinov's word for that devotion.

What was more, if the ploy had worked, and Lavery had voluntarily returned to their protection, there would have remained the problem of the wife. They couldn't hold her indefinitely in Moscow against her will, and it was unlikely that she would want to stay. He had hoped that Lavery could be made to put pressure on her to support some reasonably credible story but, in any case, such

271

thoughts were no longer relevant.

The General heaved a sigh. What to do now? Igor Smerinov's suggestion that they should kidnap Mrs Lavery was absurd; after today's abortive attempt to leave the UK, she would be well guarded. No, they could forget Imogen Lavery. They would just have to count on Lavery's reappearance, alive or dead. Vadim Belatov was not optimistic.

CHAPTER TWENTY-FIVE

It was ironic that, at the same time as Pavel Kaski was deceiving Imogen Lavery with the disinformation that her husband was lying in a Moscow hospital on the point of death and Imogen was grieving for him, the hoax was perilously close to the truth—and the grief justified. But Kaski was wrong on two counts. First, the hospital was in Poland, not the Soviet Union; secondly by the fourth day after his arrival there, Lavery's health was improving.

He still had a fever, but his temperature was coming down. His throat was no longer parched, his skin no longer burning to the touch. What was more, he could at last lift his head from his pillow without the cubicle in which he lay turning such cartwheels that he was forced to grip the edges of the mattress to avoid falling sideways to the floor. He knew now that he was in a hospital and was very ill, but that was all. He had no idea where the hospital was, how he had got there or how long he had been a patient.

And he remained fearful, though less anxious

than when he had first regained consciousness. Then he had thought for one heart-stopping moment that he couldn't feel his leg, and he was convinced that it had been cut off. When eventually he was able to pull up the rough hospital gown he was wearing, touch his heavily bandaged thigh and probe the skin below the bandage, his relief had been enormous.

This morning, however, he felt considerably better, but he still refused to respond to the nurses who came to wash him and dress his wound. He knew he was in Poland; though he couldn't speak the language he could recognize it, and he was able to recall shivering among costumes belonging to the Bolshoi Ballet Company in the freight van of a Soviet train bound for Warsaw. He knew that when he had felt the search coming closer, he had managed to break open the padlock of one of the rearmost hampers with a tool from the bag he had stolen, and struggled inside. He could only assume that the broken lock hadn't been noticed, and he could only guess that he had been found unconscious when the hamper was finally unpacked; presumably someone had taken pity on him and arranged for his admission to this hospital.

But that was no guarantee that he wouldn't be handed back, if the Soviets produced a valid-sounding story. He dozed for a few moments, and visualized Igor Smerinov pulling aside the curtains of his cubicle, standing over his bed and calmly shooting him, or General Belatov storming in with a couple of his thugs and pulling him out of bed. He knew he needed to be much stronger before he could make any attempt to cope with his situation, if indeed any 'coping' was possible. He argued to himself that as long as he was seriously ill he would be cared for, but once he appeared to be out of danger he would be pestered with questions and probably transferred to a prison hospital of some kind. From such a place it could be but a short journey back to Moscow and God alone knew what.

In the event the subterfuge—simple malingering for as long as possible—that he was vaguely planning proved both useless and pointless. It was mid-morning when the doctor came on his rounds. He inspected Lavery's wound, checked the charts that hung on the foot of the bed and had a quiet word with the nurse who accompanied him. Then he pulled up a chair and sat down beside his patient.

Lavery, who had been watching these procedings through his lashes, closed his eyes and breathed evenly and steadily. He expected the man to depart, but there was no scrape of the chair legs, no rustle of the cubicle curtains. He tried a gentle snore, but the doctor merely laughed.

'Whoever you are, you're not a very good actor, Mr Englishman,' he said in good if accented English. 'Come now. Stop pretending. I know you're conscious.'

Lavery opened his eyes and regarded the doctor. It was the first time he had studied the man at all closely, and he was surprised to see that he was young—about thirty—and extremely good-looking. The doctor was grinning at him amiably.

'I'm Dr Mandreski,' he said. 'What is your name?'

Lavery ignored the question, but he shook the hand that the Pole was offering him. 'What made

274

you think I'm English?' he asked.

'It's very simple. When you were first admitted you were delirious at intervals—and you were delirious in English. I am happy that you are, if not yet well, much improved, and there is no longer any danger that we shall have to amputate your leg, an operation which once I feared would be necessary.'

'Thank you.'

'Don't thank me. You were lucky we had a supply of some useful antibiotics.'

There was a pause in their conversation, and Lavery said tentatively, 'I gather I'm in Poland, and almost certainly in Warsaw. Have you told anyone I'm here?'

'If you mean the authorities, it was the police who brought you here. The Russian wardrobe mistress found you in one of the Bolshoi's costume hampers and called them. It was assumed that you were a Soviet criminal of some kind who was trying to escape. At that point you hadn't yet started to babble in English.'

'But when I did?'

'You were my patient. In my view that relationship takes priority over everything. I saw no reason to phone the police or the Soviet Embassy, at least not until I'd spoken to you. You weren't going to run anywhere for a while.'

'What about inquiries?'

'The Bolshoi people are too busy staging their ballets to bother over you. The wardrobe mistress did her duty by calling the police. I gather she was more worried about any damage you might have done to her precious costumes than about your identity. As for our police, even nowadays they do not feel a great sympathy for the Soviet Union.'

'You mean they won't take any action against me?'

'No, not exactly. But they won't hurry themselves to intervene, and perhaps I can help you in the meantime.'

'Why should you, Doctor?' Lavery was suspicious.

'Well, you're an interesting case. I don't have many patients emerging from theatrical hampers, suffering from septic bullet wounds. Besides, I've always been pro-British. I have a favourite aunt who's English. My uncle met her when he was in Britain during the war, married her and later brought her back here.'

Neil Lavery nodded. He needed help, as much as he had done when old Josef Spaslov had found him in the garbage can. He had no option but to trust this doctor, just as he had trusted Spaslov.

'My name is Lavery, Neil Lavery,' he said slowly. He watched the other man's face as he spoke but saw no reaction, no sign of recognition. Clearly Dr Mandreski had never heard of Neil Lavery. 'And, as you deduced, I am English. I was a tourist in Moscow and, unluckily for me, I got mixed up in some kind of protest march that was broken up by the police. I ran away, but I was shot. I lost consciousness and when I came to I realized that I'd lost everything—passport, money, the lot—and I had only a few words of Russian—certainly not enough to ask the way to anywhere. My one desire was to get out of the country. I was going round in circles looking for the British Embassy and I found myself near a railway station, with *Belorusskiy* in large letters over it. Byelorussia, I thought—White Russia—and I

276

guessed that trains from this station went to the West. So I stowed away in one. That's all I remember.' Lavery hesitated. 'I know it makes me sound stupid, but remember I was shocked, what with the wound and fainting and—'

'I understand, *Pan* Lavery. You're a lucky man, lucky to be here and lucky to be alive.'

'I am indeed,' Lavery agreed heartily, and wondered how much of his somewhat bizarre story the doctor believed. 'And I'm extremely grateful, both to you personally and to the staff here for all the care you've given me. But now more than anything, I want to get home. When will I be well enough to travel?'

'It depends on your mode of transport, doesn't it?' Mandreski grinned again. 'Costume hampers are not advised, and of course there are complications—no papers, no money, no proof of identity.'

'The embassy—' Lavery hesitated before continuing, remembering the fate he believed he had suffered at the hands of the British Embassy in Moscow. But he saw no alternative. He could hardly travel rough all the way across Europe in his present condition. He decided to take the risk.

'My embassy will look after that sort of thing,' he went on. 'Can you get in touch with them for me?'

'Of course,' said the doctor. He pushed back his chair and stood up. 'You must rest now,' he said. 'You're getting over-excited and overtired.'

Lavery protested, but Dr Mandreski was already leaving the cubicle and signalling to a nurse. She came at once. She was young, pretty and full of chatter which she knew Lavery didn't understand. But her meaning was clear; he was to take the two pills she was offering him, lie quietly and sleep well. She made appropriate gestures and rearranged his pillows. Lavery could have resisted if it would have achieved anything, but he knew it was useless. Obediently he resigned himself to her ministrations, took the pills, lay down and within minutes was asleep.

⋆ ⋆ ⋆

When Neil Lavery woke there was a stranger sitting beside his bed in place of Dr Mandreski. Lavery studied him through half-closed eyes. The man was about forty years old. He had red hair—what was left of it—protruding ears, a thin nose and gold-rimmed spectacles. His shirt looked expensive, his suit was tailor-made and he wore an old Harrovian tie. He jumped when Lavery spoke.

'Who are you?'

'The question is who are *you*,' the man replied. 'You claim to be Neil Lavery, I gather.'

Lavery stared at him. 'I *am* Neil Lavery,' he said.

'Last heard of in Moscow. How did you get here?'

'Didn't Dr Mandreski tell you?'

'No. He merely said that he had an English patient who had been very ill but was now recovering, that you had given him your name as Neil Lavery, but you had no identification, and you had asked him to contact the British Embassy. We queried him about the police, and he was decent enough to remark that, as you were his patient, their inquiries were no concern of his.'

The stranger's clothes and his effortless English with its Oxbridge accent had gone some way

278

towards reassuring Lavery. He didn't take to the man and he didn't appreciate his approach, but he didn't doubt that he was an embassy officer, and he was grateful to the doctor for having telephoned on his behalf—and apparently with such tact.

When Lavery spoke next there was less aggression in his manner. 'The doctor and everyone here have been very kind to me,' he said, 'but I want to get back to England.'

'Why—if you're Lavery? To face the music? You'll get a stiff sentence, you know.'

'Probably, but I'll be a damned sight safer in a UK prison than on the run in the USSR.'

'You will? Are you telling me you've already had an altercation with your Soviet chums?'

'Please, Mr—?'

'Neville Bridges-Stott. And now perhaps you'd make some effort to convince me who *you* are.'

You would have a double-barrelled name, you bastard, Lavery thought, but he kept his temper. 'And how do you expect me to do that?' he asked mildly.

'Answer a few questions.'

'Such as?'

Bridges-Stott referred to a notebook he had taken from his pocket. 'What's the name of your son's housemaster?'

'Maurice White,' replied Lavery immediately.

There were several more questions of a similar nature, and finally Lavery shook his head in incredulity. 'Dear God!' he exclaimed. 'Here I am, a presumed traitor and defector, wanting to give himself up and go home, and all Her Majesty's representative can do is ask me fatuous questions. Are you crazy?'

279

'Not as fatuous as you think, Lavery.' Bridges-Stott was suddenly decisive. 'The Office is going to look pretty bloody foolish if they take any action on the basis that Neil Lavery's in a Warsaw hospital, and then he suddenly appears on Moscow television.'

Lavery nodded. 'Yes. That's a point of view all right, Bridges-Stott. But think of the other side of the coin. If I'm taken back to the USSR, and appear on Moscow television, I swear to you I'll say that it's all due to the kindness and understanding of a British diplomat called Neville Bridges-Stott, acting under instructions from the Foreign Office. And how do you think that's going to look in the London papers, chummie?'

Bridges-Stott laughed, but it was a nervous laugh. 'All right,' he said. 'You've convinced me. You are Lavery. I still want to know how you got here.'

'I stowed away on a train, and I was lucky. I wasn't caught. But—it's a long story. You must move me to the embassy—I should be safe enough there—and contact Brigadier John Faudin of the Ministry of Defence. Tell him—'

'Lavery, you're in no position to give orders,' Bridges-Stott interrupted. 'I've got my own. No one expected you to turn up in Warsaw, but when I reported that someone who claimed to be you had done just that, I was told to establish your identity without doubt and, if you were Lavery, to send a priority signal to a certain officer in a certain department.'

'Who?'

'That,' said the Foreign Office man with satisfaction, 'is confidential information. Goodbye for now, Lavery. You'll be hearing from me.'

Bridges-Stott was gone before Lavery could argue, and he closed his eyes. He felt exhausted. The future, he knew, was now out of his hands. He was too weak to fight any more but, after what he considered had been a betrayal in Moscow, he no longer trusted his British compatriots, and he had little faith in Bridges-Stott. He contented himself with the reflection that the ultimatum he had delivered should be enough to make them think twice.

★   ★   ★

As Lavery had misjudged Colin Dreyton, so he was misjudging Neville Bridges-Stott. Bridges-Stott obeyed his instructions meticulously. He sent Munro Graffon a long telegram reporting his meeting with Lavery accurately, and added his own comment that he was convinced of the patient's identity, though Lavery appeared to be in a very nervous and suspicious state.

It was this last remark, and Colin Dreyton's failure to make the planned contact with Lavery in Moscow, that had decided Graffon to ask John Faudin to accompany Cantel to Warsaw. According to Bridges-Stott, Lavery was physically incapable of leaving the hospital at the moment but, Graffon told himself, one never knew. Who would have thought that Lavery could have got out of the USSR and into Poland, when an alert had apparently been ordered and every train was being systematically searched? They must act quickly. He didn't want Lavery disappearing again, as he had done in Moscow.

281

Though it was late in the evening by now, Munro Graffon paced up and down the length of his office. There was plenty of paperwork to be done, but he couldn't settle to it. His mind was too occupied with thoughts of Neil Lavery. When his secure phone rang he snatched up the receiver, but it was too soon to be Cantel calling from Warsaw. In fact, it was a summons to Number 10, which was the last visit he wanted to make. He had taken enough shit from the Government over this affair, and he was unpleasantly aware that the Prime Minister would not be pleased, now that most of the publicity had died down, to learn that Lavery might be returning to the country he had betrayed. The waves that his return would create would be breakers.

CHAPTER TWENTY-SIX

'John! Oh John! How—how wonderful to see you! Thank God.'

To Faudin's surprise—and acute embarrassment—Neil Lavery began to weep. He tried to control himself, but he failed. Tears poured down his cheeks and he shook with sobs. Faudin moved quickly, as his own feelings began to overcome him. In a couple of strides he was across the little cubicle, sitting on the bed and gripping Lavery's arms tightly.

'It's all right, old chap. You're all right now, and we'll soon have you home.' Faudin spoke as if to a child.

Cantel watched this emotional reunion with some

disapproval, until Dr Mandreski drew him out of the curtained cubicle. 'It's weakness,' the doctor said. 'Apart from the wound in his thigh, which is healing nicely, *Pan* Lavery's been through a bad time. He nearly lost a leg, you know, but we managed to avoid that calamity. He's improving now, but he's weak, as I say, and any stress is hard for him to bear. You understand?'

'Oh yes, I understand. Now tell me, what's his official position here?'

'Official position? What do you mean? He's my patient.'

'I mean, in relation to your authorities? Have the Polish police interviewed him, as far as you know?'

'No, as I told your embassy, he was found unconscious in a Bolshoi Ballet costume hamper on a train from Moscow, and the police brought him here. I've not thought it my business to inform them that my patient is English, or anything else about him.'

'I see, Doctor,' said Cantel slowly. He paused, and decided to go further. 'Look, Doctor, it's not for me to tell you what to do, but I'd be grateful if you'd leave it at that for a few days, until we've had a chance to sort things out. When will he be fit enough to be moved to the British Embassy, or to travel home?'

The doctor regarded Cantel with some interest. 'Very mysterious,' he remarked. 'Who is this Lavery—a British agent or something? I mean, the bullet wound and—'

'No, Doctor! You've been seeing too many films. That's the last thing your patient is, or ever has been.' Cantel's expression was wry. He contemplated Dr Mandreski for a moment and

283

suddenly changed the subject. 'Now, is there anything we can do for you or for your hospital? Are you short of anything—particular drugs, or some equipment, perhaps?'

Cantel had misjudged this man. The doctor spoke sharply. 'I don't need a bribe. I know how to keep my mouth shut.'

'I'm not offering you a bribe, Doctor. Just a gift to thank you for your care of Mr Lavery.'

The Pole laughed. 'We're short of a lot of things, as I'm sure you know. I'll give you a list, and you must do what you think is appropriate.'

'Fine. Now, about Lavery's condition—'

So far Dr Mandreski had been accommodating, but now he became adamant. His patient had had an exhausting day; the emotional strain would have affected him physically and he could not be moved from the hospital—not even the short distance to the British Embassy. As for travelling to England, it would depend on the means of transport, but perhaps not before the beginning of the following week.

Eventually, however, a compromise was reached. The patient would be moved at once to a separate room, where an extra bed would be available for John Faudin. Faudin would remain in the hospital with Lavery until an air ambulance with a doctor and a nurse arrived from England to collect them. On hearing this, Dr Mandreski became less pessimistic. 'In those circumstances,' he said, 'there's no medical reason why Lavery shouldn't be moved in a day or two.'

Cantel gave a sigh of relief, and thought about his own tasks. With the aid of Bridges-Stott, and possibly the intervention of the ambassador, he had to cope with the Polish Foreign Office and its formalities and bureaucracy, in an attempt to arrange for someone who had never officially entered Poland to leave it in a somewhat unusual manner.

'You're impressive,' said Mandreski as he saw Cantel out of the hospital. 'I wish I could achieve everything I want with such seeming ease. Air ambulances are scarce over here.'

'It may not all be as simple as that,' Cantel replied. 'I'd only hope your authorities will be as amenable as you have been.'

'I should think you'll be lucky. The Government is pretty pro-West at the moment. It's not likely to go out on a limb to annoy the British.'

'Let's hope you're right.'

In fact, Cantel was less pessimistic than he sounded. He knew that, if it became necessary, pressure could be exerted on the Poles. He certainly wasn't going to waste any sleep over this particular problem. He had something else on his mind.

★   ★   ★

Cantel's problem was personal, though it concerned Neil Lavery. He thought that he had had a fairly clear picture of Imogen's husband, both as to his appearance and his character. He knew now that he had been wrong. The pathetic figure in the hospital bed with its gaunt, bearded face and eyes dim with tears was completely unlike the Lavery he had imagined.

It wasn't possible to hate him, or even to dislike him—merely to feel jealous of him. Knowing Imogen, Cantel was convinced that whatever harm

Lavery had done to his country or to his family, she would never desert him in his present state. And that meant it was a bleak future as far as he himself was concerned.

Guy Cantel lay on his back in the big double bed that had hurriedly been made up for him in Neville Bridges-Stott's apartment. Bridges-Stott had been extremely helpful. He had met Cantel and Faudin at Okęcie Airport, driven them to the hospital, waited while they were inside and finally taken Cantel to the embassy, where it was possible for him to talk to Munro Graffon on a secure line. What was more, he had insisted on putting Cantel up, as the Residence was overflowing with a visiting minister and his entourage and it was thought inadvisable to try for a hotel so late at night. Mrs Bridges-Stott had at first been less than pleased to receive an unexpected guest at such short notice, but she had done her best to make Cantel feel welcome.

It was not their fault that sleep evaded him, Cantel reflected. The bed was comfortable. He had been served soup, sandwiches and a night-cap. But he couldn't rid his mind of the vision of Neil Lavery as he was trundled into a private room, eyes again filling with tears after his request that his wife be informed that he was alive and safe had been refused.

Lavery hadn't argued. He had not even begun to protest. He had merely made an attempt to smile through his tears. And to Cantel it seemed like the smile of a child who thinks he is being punished by uncomprehending grown-ups for something he hasn't done, though he is too tired to object. But that was a sham, Cantel reminded himself. Neil

286

Lavery was no innocent, and others would suffer from his crimes, not least Imogen and her children.

Cantel turned on his side and willed himself to sleep. There would be much to do in the morning, and he couldn't afford to be less than mentally alert. He began to plan his day and, planning, fell asleep.

*   *   *

It was the next evening before Guy Cantel was free to return to the hospital. He found Lavery sitting up in bed, and looking considerably improved. John Faudin was staring gloomily out of the window. The pair appeared to have run out of conversation, which didn't surprise Cantel, who before leaving them together had given Faudin two warnings. In the first place, Lavery must not be treated as a friend or colleague, but as an alleged traitor. And further, Faudin must make no attempt at even a preliminary interrogation; all that must be left until they got home—and, Cantel added to himself, in Faudin's absence.

'Good news,' Cantel greeted them. 'A special ambulance aircraft, complete with doctor and nurse, will fly us to the UK tomorrow. In the end the Polish authorities raised no real difficulties. It took a lot of hard talking to convince them, but eventually they were persuaded it would be best for everyone if they accepted the scenario that Lavery's a tourist who's been taken ill while he's here, and is now under the protection of the British Embassy.'

'Well done,' said Faudin. 'That's a relief.'

'What happens when I do get home?' Lavery asked. 'A prison hospital until you consider I'm fit enough for a cell?'

'Good heavens, no.' Cantel sounded amused. 'Nothing like that. You, plus your doctor and nurse, will be met at the airport and driven directly to a safe house outside London, where you'll have every attention.'

'English breakfasts?'

'What?'

'You make your safe house sound like the *dacha* near Moscow where I spent a little time recently. They gave me excellent breakfasts.' Lavery thought of Igor Smerinov, and wondered if the Russian had paid a price for failing to trace him.

Cantel said coldly, 'When your doctor says you're fit enough, your interrogation will begin.'

'Ah yes. Phase Two, or was it Phase Three?'

Cantel didn't pause to ask what he meant. Detailed explanations would come later. He couldn't resist one comment, however. 'You were eager to return to England,' he said. 'Have you changed your mind again?'

'No!' Lavery sighed. 'I didn't mean to sound hostile. It's just—just that my first relief at being in your hands has begun to wear off a little, and it's difficult to accept that the hands aren't friendly.'

'What did you expect?'

'I know,' Lavery said sombrely.

'Guy, the man's ill,' Faudin protested. 'You said that all this should be left till we got home.'

'Yes, of course.' Cantel was irritated by Faudin's attitude. If it hadn't been for the Brigadier's trust in types like Neil Lavery, he thought, the present situation would never have arisen; Lavery would have been caught months, if not years, ago. He addressed himself to the man in bed. 'You'll be arriving in the country incognito so as to avoid any publicity,' he said.

Lavery's eyes widened; this was a possibility that had not occurred to him. 'Then—' he said slowly, 'then no one will know I'm back. What about Imogen—my wife—and my family? When can I see them, and my parents? They must all be desperately worried.'

'I'm afraid you should have thought of that a very long time ago.'

'I would have, damn it, if it had been possible.' Lavery spoke through clenched teeth. Suddenly he felt overwhelmed by fatigue. All he wanted to do was sleep. His hand groped for the bell that would summon the nurse.

Faudin found it for him and looked anxiously at Cantel. 'He must rest, Guy, or he won't be able to travel tomorrow.'

Cantel nodded. 'Yes, you're right. At best it'll be a tiring journey. I'll be off now. I'll have a word with Dr Mandreski before I go, tell him that everything's under control and break it to him that we'll be removing the patient from his tender care at noon tomorrow.' He smiled at the nurse who had just come in. 'Goodnight to you.'

The nurse returned his smile, and Faudin said, 'Goodnight, Guy. See you in the morning.'

Neil Lavery said nothing. He was thinking how glad and thankful he had been when John Faudin and Guy Cantel had appeared on the scene yesterday. He was still thankful. But Guy Cantel's obvious lack of sympathy was a warning of what to expect once he was back in England. He had no means of knowing that Cantel's attitude was inevitably tinged by his love for Imogen.

289

Twenty-four hours later, Neil Lavery, classified as a traitor and an erstwhile defector, was once more in the land of his birth. He had been under sedation for most of the journey and was to remember little of it, except that at one point there had been a fair amount of turbulence. In fact, they had been routed around the edges of a thunderstorm.

They landed at an RAF station, where an ambulance and a car were waiting for them. The car took Guy Cantel and Brigadier Faudin straight to London, where Faudin was grateful to be dropped at his flat, while Cantel went to report to Munro Graffon. Lavery, accompanied by his doctor and nurse, was taken by ambulance to the safe house.

This particular safe house, situated in a rambling old mansion on the border that separated Kent from East Sussex, was unusual. It was one wing of a nursing home which offered a small number of elderly patients who could afford its exorbitant fees the chance to spend their last days in great comfort. The medical attention was excellent; the nursing care couldn't be bettered and the general amenities rivalled those of a luxury hotel.

The occasional occupants of the special wing were able to share most of these advantages. They remained, however, quite separate from the main part of the building, and they had their own private garden. It was understood by patients and nursing-home staff alike that these were individuals who, while certainly not insane, were mentally disturbed. In the years since the house had served its dual purpose there had never been any trouble.

Neil Lavery had returned to England to become

an occupant of this wing on a Friday, and Munro Graffon decided that he should be allowed to recuperate in peace and quiet over the weekend. Then on Monday, subject to medical clearance, the debriefing would begin. The days ahead would be full of stress for Lavery, and an interruption in the proceedings caused by his collapse could affect their success.

Lavery himself had no cause for complaint. Because of the greater resources that were available, the care he received was superior to that provided by Dr Mandreski and the Polish nurses. The food, for example, was a great improvement. Moreover, perhaps surprisingly the select number of the staff whom he met treated him with kindness and respect, though the English doctor—the same one who had travelled from Warsaw with him—was an oldish man and seemed somewhat severe and impersonal. But there was no suggestion that he was any kind of prisoner, ignominious or otherwise, though this comfortable and well-furnished room lacked certain amenities that normally would be taken for granted. There was no telephone, for instance, or a radio or television set, and he knew it would be useless to ask for them.

His tentative request for a newspaper or a magazine, something to read, was met by half a dozen of the latest books, three novels and three non-fiction, all brand new. He didn't mention newspapers again but, when he wasn't dozing, contented himself with one of the novels. He had no wish to contemplate the weeks ahead, or to think of Imogen and how she would greet him when at last he was permitted to see her. On the whole he was glad of the respite offered by the weekend.

The reverse was true of Guy Cantel. Returning to his flat late on the Friday he had found a message from Imogen asking him to phone her. He had ignored it, but she had caught him at lunchtime on the Saturday.

'I've missed you,' she said.

'I had to go away for a couple of days.'

'Away? Do you mean abroad?' Her voice was suddenly sharp. 'Guy, was it because of Neil? Is there any news of him?'

'No,' he lied and, resenting the fact that her thoughts had immediately turned to her husband, elaborated his story. 'My mother's not too well. I'm going to take leave next week so as to be with her.' And that would give him cover to be at the safe house with Lavery, he thought, appreciating the irony.

'Next week? Then—' There was a pause before Imogen continued. 'I've promised to spend tomorrow with the Glenbournes, not that Verity would mind if I didn't. It's just that I think Philip's getting a little tired of her, and I might help to lighten the atmosphere. I'm free tonight, Guy.'

There was nothing he wanted more than to say he would be with her, but he knew that if he went, Imogen would expect them to make love, and now Neil Lavery was too real—too near—for that. He made an excuse, heard the disappointment in her voice as she replied, and said goodbye.

He spent a miserable weekend and was glad when Monday came.

CHAPTER TWENTY-SEVEN

Monday morning was fair and bright, and the nurse who brought Neil Lavery his breakfast carried with her an air of anticipation. The doctor came next. He too seemed full of purpose, and today, for the first time, after he had concluded his examination he drew up a chair beside the bed as if for a personal discussion. Lavery waited expectantly though with some apprehension.

'Physically you're in fairly good shape, Mr Lavery,' the doctor began, his manner pleasant but dispassionate. 'Your thigh is healing nicely. You must rest, but you must also start to exercise—to walk a little each day, so that your muscles don't become flabby. You'll tire quickly at first, of course, but—'

Since he seemed loath to continue Lavery said, 'How long before I'm more or less normal?'

'A week or two. We're talking about your physical condition, you understand?'

'Yes. There's nothing wrong with me mentally.'

'Good! You reassure me. You must realize that as your physician I'm responsible for you. We all know you've been under considerable stress, but clearly there are certain matters which can't be delayed indefinitely and—'

'You mean the authorities don't want a clever barrister to be able to plead that a confession was forced from me when I was in no fit state? Don't worry, Doctor.'

'I shan't, Mr Lavery.' The doctor pushed back his chair and stood up. 'It's quite clear there's no need. A nurse will come for you in a few minutes and take you downstairs. There you'll find two officers waiting to interview you. All right?'

'Yes. Oddly enough I'm looking forward to a chance to tell my story.'

The doctor's face remained impassive except for a tightening of the lips. He nodded and left the room. Almost at once the nurse appeared, pushing a wheelchair, and five minutes later she took Lavery, in pyjamas, dressing-gown and slippers, along a corridor to a lift and down to the ground floor, where she knocked at a closed door. It was opened instantly, and Lavery recognized Guy Cantel.

'Ah, thank you, nurse,' Cantel said. 'I'll take him now.'

He pushed the chair into a pleasant, high-ceilinged room that could have been the sitting-room of a private house. The furniture was modern but comfortable. A bowl of flowers stood on a side table, a bookcase full of well-read books was against one wall, and there was a good print of Van Gogh's 'Sunflowers' over the mantel. French windows gave on to a small walled garden.

There was absolutely nothing to suggest that the room was other than it appeared. In fact, it was a highly efficient interrogation centre. The equipment to record every word that was spoken and video every move that Lavery made was neatly concealed.

After his first glance around Lavery ignored the general background, and focused his attention on the short, dark man who had turned away from the window and now wished him a curt good-morning. Lavery didn't respond to the greeting. He had guessed immediately that this individual, in spite of

294

his unprepossessing appearance, was Guy Cantel's superior, and someone to be reckoned with. Further, he was becoming increasingly aware that his invalid's attire and his position in a wheelchair would place him at a psychological disadvantage in the forthcoming encounter. He felt certain it had been planned.

'Mr Munro Graffon,' Cantel said.

Lavery bowed his head in acknowledgement. He had heard of Graffon, though he had never met him, and he knew he had a formidable reputation. This, he was aware, was the man he had to convince.

'Mr Lavery.' Graffon didn't offer his hand, but went and sat down immediately opposite Lavery's chair. He said, 'Perhaps I should commence, Mr Lavery, by making it clear that this is merely a preliminary question-and-answer session. You'll be seeing Mr Cantel and me again, of course, but others will be taking a leading role in your debriefing. As I'm sure you appreciate, yours is an unusual case. It's not unheard of for a defector to wish to return to his mother country, but never as quickly as you, and certainly not in such a dramatic fashion—and never to my knowledge without assistance, as I gather you claim to have done.'

'How—? Ah, I see. Reports from the embassies in Moscow and Warsaw?'

'Of course.'

'You used the word "dramatic". My return was no more dramatic than my departure, Mr Graffon, but—'

'All right, tell us about your departure.'

'First, I wish to make a statement.'

'A confession?'

295

'A confession? On the contrary. Quite the reverse. I wish to state unequivocally—and I'll repeat this on oath wherever and whenever you like—that at no time have I served as a Soviet agent, at no time have I betrayed my country. I have never passed any information to any foreign power, not even inadvertently. And my so-called defection was *not* voluntary—I was kidnapped.'

'Well, that's interesting,' said Munro Graffon after a moment's pause. 'Very interesting indeed.'

'It's more than interesting. It's true. But you don't believe me?'

'Mr Lavery, if it's true, why didn't you protest your innocence as soon as you could—when you first saw Brigadier Faudin and Mr Cantel in Warsaw, for example—or even before that, to Bridges-Stott?'

'I tried!' said Lavery. 'I tried to tell John Faudin everything that had happened to me, because at last here was someone I knew I could trust, but he cut me off. He wouldn't listen. All he did was tell me to wait till I got back to the UK. I tried, I tell you, as well as I could! I was wounded and ill, you remember?'

'All right, Mr Lavery, calm yourself. These are early days. To go back to your question—I wouldn't be prepared to offer an opinion as to whether or not I would tend to believe you. However, we do take note of your statement.'

'Thanks.' The reply was no more than he had expected, but Lavery failed to keep the bitterness from his voice.

'Perhaps for the moment we should begin at the beginning. Now, we understand that one evening a few weeks ago—I've got the date here somewhere, but it doesn't matter—you left your office in the Ministry of Defence a little earlier than usual because you and your wife were giving a dinner party, and you had naturally promised to get home as soon as you could. Is that right?'

'Yes. It was an important party because the new CIA Head of Station London and his wife were going to be among the guests, and my wife had never met them.'

'Why did you ask Mr Christiansen to join a party composed of relations and old friends?'

Lavery opened his mouth and shut it again. He didn't fully understand the purpose of the question, but suspected the reason for it. 'Why not?' he replied at last.

'You could have wanted him and our cousins to get some unwelcome publicity through an association with you.'

'Only if I'd known I wasn't going to turn up at the party myself, which I did *not* know.'

'Is that so? You claim that your Soviet friends took you by surprise?'

'Mr Graffon, it would be best for all of us if I told you what really happened, as far as I know it. The Americans are irrelevant in this context. But to answer your query first, yes, I was taken by surprise. I had no desire to defect, then or ever. I had no *need* to defect. I repeat, I was kidnapped.'

Graffon and Cantel listened without comment while Lavery described in such detail as he could remember his departure from his office in the Ministry of Defence and his subsequent awakening in bed in a *dacha* outside Moscow. He did his best to be factual and to avoid mentioning his emotions and suspicions, except to say that until he had been

297

rendered unconscious he had protested vehemently to the man whose taxi he was sharing.

'How were your protests received?' Graffon asked.

'It seemed as if they weren't unexpected,' said Lavery after a moment's reflection.

'Then you don't think it possible that you were mistaken for someone else, someone who *was* wanting to go—or needed to go—to the USSR?'

Lavery was aware of the careful wording of Graffon's question. 'When I was at school and doing elementary Latin,' he said slowly, 'that would have been a question that demanded the answer *num*. And the answer is definitely in the negative. The chap in the taxi called me by name.'

'Really?'

'I know it sounds damning, but—'

'So it would seem that there's no doubt it *was* you they intended to take. Why you, Lavery?'

'I've no idea. Perhaps I was—suitable?'

'Suitable? That's a strange word to use.' Graffon shook his head, and glanced at Cantel, who took up the questioning. Lavery turned to him in some surprise.

'Mr Lavery,' said Cantel, 'you're aware that there have been serious leakages of classified information to the Soviet Union from your MOD directorate?'

'You know perfectly well I'm aware of it,' Lavery replied irritably, and chided himself inwardly for becoming rattled. 'Everyone knew. How could it be otherwise with John Faudin constantly ferreting around us?'

'And now you're seriously suggesting that the Russians were busy seeking yet another source in the same directorate—one who could provide them with whatever data they hadn't already received?'

Lavery lost some of his cool. 'How the hell should I know what they were after?' he demanded. 'All I can tell you is what happened to me.'

'But, as a member of that directorate, you were under possible suspicion as the original source.'

'Of course I was, damn it! But no more than anyone else with access.'

'Who did you yourself suspect?'

Lavery stared from Cantel to Graffon and back again. 'What the hell does that matter?' he demanded.

'We'd be interested,' Cantel said.

'I didn't suspect anyone in particular.'

'Mr Lavery, that's hardly credible. I think you're lying,' Graffon said quietly.

Lavery drew a deep breath. 'Look,' he said, 'Plimpton has money troubles. Tyneman's become a drunk since his wife left him. Joy Aubyn has a foreign boy-friend. And there are others. Take your pick. All I know is that it wasn't me.'

There was a pause before Cantel said flatly, 'Joy Aubyn is dead. She fell under a bus.'

'Dear God!' Lavery was clearly shaken.

'Her boy-friend was a diplomat, and he's gone home. How did you know about them?'

'I met them once—in the Zoo, of all places. I'd taken my daughter there. It was pure chance—the meeting, I mean. I saw them—they were holding hands—and I heard them talking. He spoke good English with an accent, Czech or Polish, I'd guess. Joy didn't introduce him. Poor Joy!' Lavery was silent.

'You didn't think of following regulations and reporting the incident?' intervened Graffon.

'I did think of mentioning it to John Faudin, but—'

'It might have taken the heat off you, Lavery.'

'There was no heat on me, Mr Graffon—no more than on anyone else!'

'You might have guessed that the boy-friend was using Joy as a source of classified information.'

Reluctantly Lavery nodded. 'Yes, I suppose I might have done, but—'

'Perhaps you were sympathetic?' Cantel suggested.

'To Joy, yes! To leaking secrets, no!'

Suddenly Graffon said, 'Tell us about your time in the *dacha*, Lavery.'

Neil Lavery looked from one of his inquisitors to the other. He was tiring. His mind felt torpid, unable to cope with the constant changes of subject. He knew that these were intentional and part of the technique of interrogation, intended to confuse the subject, but that knowledge didn't help. He began to describe the *dacha*, Igor Smerinov and General Belatov's visit.

'Those damned toasts! I had to keep up with the Russians, but I wasn't used to vodka—not in those quantities. In the end I couldn't take any more and I bolted—to the Russians' amusement. They thought it a great caper.' His voice cracked. His throat was dry and he didn't feel he could continue. 'Could I have some—some water?'

'Of course.'

Cantel got up at once, went to a side table and poured Lavery a glass of mineral water. Lavery's hand shook as he sipped it, and Graffon signalled to Cantel, who rang the bell for the nurse.

'Lunch,' Graffon said, 'and a rest for you, Mr Lavery. Then we'll start again.'

* * *

The meal served to Munro Graffon and Guy Cantel was excellent: asparagus soup, Scotch salmon with cucumber salad, cheese, fruit, coffee. To drink there was a Petit Chablis. Graffon, who enjoyed his food, made the most of it, but Cantel had no appetite and pushed his salmon idly around his plate.

'What did you think of Lavery, Munro? First impressions?' he asked.

'He's a clever man. His record shows that. And he'll be difficult to intimidate. We mustn't underrate him. It was a good ploy on his part to make that opening statement. He'll have known we're recording everything. It'll sound pretty sincere when we play it back.'

'But you didn't believe it?'

'I'll keep an open mind. Lavery's had plenty of time to work up a story.' Graffon helped himself to some more cheese. 'So far he's offered no reason for his alleged kidnapping. If the Soviets had wanted to take a hostage, why pick on him?'

'Alternatively, why not? They might have considered him—suitable, as he said—for exchange purposes, perhaps, but not have had time to start negotiations.'

'It's possible, I suppose,' said Graffon.

Cantel said, 'Personally I can't see what the Soviets had to gain by returning him to us—if they did. What use can he be to them? As we agreed before, they must know we'd never trust him again, unless he could prove that he really was kidnapped

301

and made that bizarre escape. On the other hand, as far as the escape's concerned, it seems incredible that one man with so much against him should be able to accomplish what other trained agents have tried and failed to do.' Cantel poured more coffee. 'There's also the fact that he was shot, and he damned near didn't make it back at all.'

'Someone could have been standing by to make sure he did, Guy. It could have been arranged—even if he did finish up unconscious in a costume hamper in Poland.' Graffon cut off yet another sliver of cheddar and nibbled at it ruminatively.

'But in that case why didn't they allow him to get to the embassy in Moscow? It would have been a great deal simpler. And it wouldn't have involved the Poles.'

'Perhaps too simple. If General Belatov is controlling this operation, as Lavery implies, the whole affair will be subtle and dodgy. That man's got a devious mind.' Graffon glanced at his watch. 'There's a long way to go yet, Guy. We've only heard a fraction of Lavery's account of his adventures.'

'Indeed,' Cantel said, and thought of Imogen, still convinced her husband was in Russia. But he knew better than to ask Graffon when Lavery's family might be told that he was back in England. 'Time to return?' he asked.

'In a few minutes. We must let Lavery have his rest. Tell me, Guy,' Graffon belched gently. 'You actually talked to Joy Aubyn, and as the girl's dead we have to depend on your impressions. Do you believe, considering what Lavery admitted this morning, that there was no connivance between the two of them?'

'I certainly do,' Cantel spoke with conviction. 'Lavery had already admitted he knew about Stefan Cheski before he learnt anything about Joy's death, which clearly was a hell of a shock to him. He need not have told us and thus involved her. Besides, Soviet agents don't normally work like that, do they?'

'No, that's true. It's rare for two of them to act as a team, though it's been known.' Graffon rose to his feet.

'As far as Lavery's concerned I'm more interested in Marta Stein,' said Cantel. 'If we believe Cheski, and there would seem no reason to doubt him, she was heavily involved with Moscow. Whether or not she was Lavery's mistress, she might well have been his controller.'

'It's possible,' Graffon agreed. 'We'll ask about her during the afternoon session. His reactions should be interesting.'

*   *   *

But once again Neil Lavery pre-empted them. He had been offered the same food for lunch as others, but had eaten even less then Cantel, just some soup and fruit. Then he had rested. He had slept and he had had one of those vivid dreams that remain clear and immediate when the sleeper awakes. He had dreamt of General Belatov. In the dream, the General was talking to his aide about the unfortunate accident that was to befall the Englishman.

'We can't afford to let Lavery live,' Belatov had said. 'We could never trust him. He'd be dangerous. He might deny us at any time. As soon as possible we must put Phase Four into operation.'

So real was the dream that it absorbed Lavery's thoughts, and scarcely had the nurse left the room where Graffon and Cantel were waiting to continue the interrogation when he burst out: 'The Russians intended to kill me, you know. When I'd served my purpose—whatever that was—I was to have what they called an "unfortunate accident". That's why I had to try to escape, however hopeless it seemed.'

Graffon and Cantel exchanged glances. 'But you did succeed.' Graffon's tone was dry.

'Yes. Thanks to luck, and the kindness of people like old Josef and Dr Mandreski.' Lavery looked at Cantel. 'You've met Mandreski. And I take it you've heard of Josef Spaslov?'

'We know the story bits. We'll have to go into it in more detail later. In the meantime, why should they want to kill you after they'd gone to such trouble to get you to Moscow?' Cantel made no attempt to hide his scepticism.

Lavery opened his mouth to say he had no idea, but Graffon interrupted. 'Let's keep things in order. You were telling us about the party at the *dacha* when our morning session ended. Perhaps to start with you'd elaborate on that.'

'Yes. It was when the party was breaking up that I discovered they planned to kill me...'

Lavery went on with his story and the questions continued. Tea came and went. Lavery grew tired, but Graffon was relentless, desisting only when it was obvious that Lavery could no longer concentrate.

'Maybe that's enough for today,' he said, and nodded to Cantel to ring for the nurse.

'Just one more thing,' Cantel said. 'What was your relationship with Marta Stein, Mr Lavery?'

'Marta Stein? Who's she? I don't know any Marta Stein.'

'Marta Stein is—or was—a Soviet agent, who claims to have been your mistress.'

'What! I've never had a mistress!'

Without speaking, Cantel produced a photocopy of the letter found in Lavery's study and showed it to him.

'I've never seen that before!' Lavery was becoming agitated. 'What is all this? When can I see this bloody woman?'

'As I said, Mr Lavery, Marta Stein claims that you and she were lovers. She had an autographed photograph of you in her flat—and she managed to convince your wife. As for confronting her—'

But Lavery was listening no longer. 'My wife? She told Imogen, and Imogen—No! I don't believe you. It's some rotten, filthy lie you've invented for some goddamn purpose of your own. How could you? It's not true! I've never looked at another woman since I married Imogen.'

In his agitation Neil Lavery got up from his wheelchair and staggered towards Cantel, but his leg gave way and he would have fallen if Cantel had not caught him.

'Dear God!' Lavery said as Cantel returned him to the chair and rang for the nurse. 'I'm in enough trouble already without you ruining what's left of my marriage.' He paused. Then he exploded. 'What the bloody hell do you think kept me going, with a festering bullet wound in my leg and half of Moscow after me, if it wasn't the hope of seeing my wife again?'

305

CHAPTER TWENTY-EIGHT

Guy Cantel telephoned Imogen from the safe house and arranged to visit her later that evening. By saying that he would keep her only half an hour he hoped he had shown that he had no intention of staying the night. He had been appalled by Lavery's outburst, and the idea of making love to Lavery's wife had become unthinkable. Imogen had come to him willingly. In no sense had he seduced her, so he had felt no guilt—until he actually met Neil Lavery. Now things were different. After today, Guy told himself, whatever Lavery might or might not have done, his own relationship with Imogen had come to an end. Yet he loved her desperately and wondered how he could face the prospect of never possessing her again.

He was relieved, if a little surprised, when she opened the front door and, without kissing him or showing him any sign of affection, led him up to the drawing-room. For a moment he feared that this was because her sister, Rosalind, or some friend might be with her, but in fact she was alone.

'A drink, Guy?' She was distant, he thought.

'Please, a long whisky. I need it. I've just driven up from the country.'

'Ah yes. And how is your mother?'

'My mother?' He was slow to remember his lie. 'She's much better. Thanks.'

'She must be. A quick recovery, wasn't it? She was signing her latest book in Hatchards this morning.'

'Damn!' Cantel swore softly. He had completely

forgotten the date. He grinned ruefully. 'Sorry about that. I'm afraid I used her as an excuse—'

'An excuse to avoid seeing me?' Imogen cut in as she handed Guy his whisky.

'Er—no. For being out of London. I didn't want to tell you because I thought you'd assume my trip was connected with your husband.' Cantel hadn't meant to say that; he knew at once that it was a mistake.

'And was it?' Imogen demanded immediately.

Cantel's hesitation was only momentary. 'Yes.'

Imogen had grown pale. 'Guy, are you saying that Neil's here in England, somewhere in the country?'

'Imogen, even if he were, you know I couldn't tell you.' He wondered what was the matter with him; his usual fluency had deserted him and he was making a mess of this conversation, a conversation that could be of crucial importance—to Imogen, to Lavery, to everyone. 'Look,' he went on. 'I've got a job to do. It's not always pleasant, and it sometimes interferes with my personal relations. Surely you can understand that?'

'Yes, but—' She realized that whatever had happened Guy was not going to tell her.

Cantel hastened to change the subject. 'Imogen, I have to ask you this. It's about Marta Stein.'

'Marta Stein? I've told you all I know about her.'

'You said there was no doubt that she and Neil had been lovers, but you never said how she managed to convince you.'

'No.' For a lengthening minute Imogen seemed unable to reply. Then at last, her voice cold, she said, 'There was the letter, of course, and—'

'And?'

307

'If you must know, Neil has a small brown mole high up in his crotch. That woman knew about it.'

'Surely someone could have told her.'

'Who? His mother? Can you imagine old Mrs Lavery talking about something like that? She'd think it improper. And I certainly didn't.'

'Who else would know? A hospital nurse? A doctor?'

'Neil's not been in hospital since he was very ill once as a child, and he disliked going to doctors.'

'What about swimming? Or showers after games, for instance?'

'It would have been concealed by bathing-trunks—and not too obvious even in a shower.' She paused. 'You would really only notice it if you got up very close.'

'I see,' said Cantel slowly. 'So—'

Imogen interrupted him. 'What is all this? Is that why you came to see me? Is that what you wanted to know? Why? Why on earth should anyone tell Marta Stein about the mole, even if they knew?' Imogen shook her head in exasperation and puzzlement.

'Yes, that was all I wanted,' said Cantel bluntly as he finished his whisky and put down the glass. He hesitated. 'I can't explain, but the possibility—I stress the word possibility—has arisen that Stein was lying, that she was never Neil's mistress.'

'Well, now you know. You can be sure she was,' Imogen said bitterly.

'Yes,' repeated Cantel, though doubt showed in his voice.

Imogen looked at him enquiringly, but he was silent for a couple of minutes. He was reflecting that Stefan Cheski, Joy Aubyn's boy-friend, had cast doubt on Stein's integrity, and Cheski's story had been supported by Stein's disappearance. Moreover, Lavery's blank denial that he had ever heard of Marta Stein had seemed convincing at the time, and Cantel would have sworn that the man's anger when he learnt that Imogen had been told of Stein's claim had not been feigned. Yet, if Stein hadn't been Lavery's lover, why had she come forward to expose herself at all. The only answer seemed to be that she was acting under instructions, perhaps playing a part in setting up Neil Lavery, trying to shake his wife's faith in him and show that he was not the honest, open man he pretended to be.

Imogen was still staring at him in silence when at last he said, tentatively, 'Imogen, Marta Stein's tale was a shock to you at first, I know, but now you're used to the idea—'

'I'm not,' she retorted sharply. 'I can't get used to it, whatever that means. The idea still hurts, hurts like hell. I guess it always will. All those years I lived with Neil I believed we had a close, happy marriage. I never suspected him of having another woman—but then I didn't suspect him of being a traitor. He was good at keeping secrets, wasn't he?'

'It would seem so,' Cantel said non-committally as he stood up. 'Imogen, I must go.'

She didn't suggest that he should stay, and he was grateful because he wouldn't have had the strength of will to refuse her. But in the hall she put a hand on his arm.

'Guy, if it hadn't been for you, I'd have gone to Moscow. You weren't lying then, were you, when you denied that Neil was desperately ill and asking for me—that it was just a trick to get me to Russia?'

309

'No. I wasn't lying. It was a trick,' Cantel said, and realized that now Imogen had caught him out in one lie she didn't trust him any more than she trusted her husband.

'So Neil is—all right? He's not dead, is he? Is he, Guy?' Imogen persisted.

'No. He's alive and well. He has been ill but he's recovering.' Cantel knew he shouldn't be telling her this, but he had been unable to resist the fear and urgency in her questions. 'And he's safe,' he added softly.

'How do you—?' Imogen began and stopped. 'He *is* home,' she said, almost to herself.

Cantel didn't contradict her. He kissed her lightly on the lips, murmured a goodbye and fled. Another minute, he thought, and he would have seized her in his arms, his good resolution not to make love to her again forgotten.

*   *   *

Guy Cantel drove through the night back to the safe house where Neil Lavery was sleeping after a mild tranquillizer, and Munro Graffon was listening to the tapes and watching the video of the day's proceedings. He greeted Cantel with a wide yawn.

'I was just on my way to bed,' he said. 'Any joy in London?'

'According to his wife, Lavery has a small brown mole high up in his crotch—so high that it would have been hidden under bathing-trunks and apparently hardly noticeable in a shower, say. But Marta Stein knew about it. That was what convinced Mrs Lavery that she and Lavery had been lovers.' Cantel outlined the rest of his

310

interview with Imogen.

'Why the hell didn't you discover all that earlier?' Graffon was feeling liverish, and not in the best of tempers.

'Sorry. I suppose because I could see how—how painful she found it.' If Cantel had considered admitting he had given Imogen Lavery the slightest hint that her husband might be in England, this was clearly the wrong moment.

Graffon grunted. 'Never heard of Marta Stein! My God! What a lie! If we were his Russian chums we'd drag the bugger out of bed this very minute, get him down here and wring a confession out of him, sick man or no sick man.'

'Lucky for him we're not,' replied Cantel sardonically.

'You'd better tell *him* that!' said Graffon as he stomped up the stairs, leaving Cantel to put out the lights.

But after some sleep and a good breakfast Graffon's mood had improved, and he was prepared to agree that Lavery should be given the chance to expand on his denial of Marta Stein. He also agreed that they should approach the subject subtly to avoid putting him on his guard before they confronted him with their new knowledge.

'We'll start with what you told us about these four so-called "phases" you say the Soviets had planned for you, Mr Lavery,' Graffon said when the three of them had settled down for the morning's session.

'All right.'

Lavery was tired in spite of his night's sleep, but he was calm. He regretted his outburst over Marta Stein the previous day, and had promised himself

311

that whatever the questions and whatever the provocation he would keep control of his temper today.

'Stop me if I'm mistaken,' went on Graffon, 'but, as I understand it, Phase One was to be your adjustment to the Soviet way of life, Phase Two was to be your debriefing, Phase Three your settlement in Moscow as a Soviet citizen, and Phase Four your death—your murder. Am I correct?'

'Yes, but you over-simplify. They knew—or thought they knew—that I had no choice, but they still wanted me to accept the situation so that I would co-operate *willingly*. I think—I'm sure, because of the photographs they took—they intended to use me primarily for propaganda purposes. Then, of course, they would drain me of information. After more propaganda, perhaps, I would be more or less worthless to them.'

'That applies to almost any agent who defects, Mr Lavery, but they don't all have "unfortunate accidents".'

Lavery gave a weary smile. 'Mr Graffon, I was not an agent, or a defector. I never worked for the Soviet Union. The only hold they would have had over me was fear—not an inconsiderable hold, I admit—but in the long run they couldn't trust me as they might trust a real defector. So, once I'd served my purpose, why not get rid of me? At least, that's how I saw the position.'

'It has a kind of logic, I suppose,' said Graffon.

And Cantel took up the questioning smoothly, as if what he had to say followed with equal logic. 'When you regained consciousness in the bedroom of the *dacha* you were wearing pyjamas?'

Lavery stared at him. 'Yes. I said so yesterday.

312

They'd gone to immense trouble to provide everything I was accustomed to—from brands of underwear to toothpaste. And all the clothes were the right sizes.'

'You didn't mention toothpaste yesterday,' Cantel said.

'Is it important?'

Cantel didn't answer. 'To return to your pyjamas. Did it occur to you that you'd been stripped, and possibly given some kind of physical examination without your knowledge?'

'Mr Cantel, I never thought about it.'

'Do you ever swim in the nude—skinny-dip, as they say in America?'

Lavery looked hopelessly from Cantel to Graffon. 'Is he crazy, or am I? Of all the stupid, irrelevant—'

Graffon said, 'Please answer the question, Lavery.'

'The answer's yes, occasionally, when we're at our country cottage. It's my father-in-law's house but he scarcely ever goes there. We share it with the Glenbournes.'

'And you swim in the nude there, in the pool? With friends?'

'We don't have wild parties, if that's what you're suggesting. It's no Cliveden in the sixties, Mr Cantel.' Lavery couldn't hide his irritation. 'In fact, come to think of it, I may be a bit of a prude, but I wouldn't think of stripping off in front of my sister-in-law, or the children. As for friends, we almost entirely reserve the cottage for family.'

'Never anyone from London? Colleagues, for instance?'

'We don't ask them, as I said. We like—' Lavery stopped abruptly. 'I suppose I should be putting all

313

this in the past tense. We *liked* to be alone, to get away from everyone. We were always so busy in London.'

'So, no colleagues?'

'No—unless you count Kevin Sinder. He came fairly frequently, but he's an old schoolfriend of Philip's. The Glenbournes and the Sinders go around together a fair amount.'

'But you, personally, are not so close to the Sinders?'

'No. I have, as you know, a very different background. But that hasn't made me bitter or envious, so don't start thinking along those lines.' In spite of himself Lavery was becoming exasperated by what he considered a series of pointless, time-wasting questions. He heaved a sigh. 'What next?' he asked resignedly.

'We start again from the beginning,' said Graffon. 'You and your wife were giving a dinner party, but you never...'

*   *   *

It was very late that evening. Lavery was already in bed, exhausted but sleeping restlessly. Graffon and Cantel were having a night-cap together. They had spent the last few hours listening to the day's tapes, and they were worried.

'It's not conceivable that Lavery's story could be true,' said Graffon, 'and yet—'

'You're having doubts?'

'Yes, I'm afraid so. He's horribly convincing. I know in these situations one swears to keep an open mind, but really that's a joke. It's impossible not to have some prejudices, and I must admit I've been

314

against Lavery from the start. What about you, Guy?'

'Well, in the first place, all the circumstantial evidence is against him. There's no doubt that one of the dozen or so people who had access was a traitor. Then Lavery disappears and turns up in Moscow. And it emerges very conveniently that this open, non-secretive man had at least one secret—a mistress, who was probably a Soviet agent. And as for his fantastic escape to Warsaw, it defies belief. Yet—as you say.'

'You've got doubts, too.' Graffon shook his shaggy head. 'If his story *is* a tissue of lies, he must be one of the world's great actors.'

'There's more to it than that, Munro. There's another angle. If Lavery's story is *not* a tissue of lies, then we haven't found our man—or woman. In effect, the Soviets have substituted Neil Lavery for him or her, leaving their true agent free to run. We could have had the wool pulled over our eyes good and proper.'

'I think,' said Graffon reluctantly, 'that we'd better go through those damned tapes again, assuming for the moment that Lavery is telling the truth, and see if we can catch him out at any point.'

'We might also see if we can get any clues as to who could be the real agent, if Lavery isn't. For instance, it should be someone who knows what sort of toothpaste and other accessories he uses—and that he's got this mole. Glenbourne and Sinder are among the obvious—'

'Don't let's jump to conclusions, Guy. If we've made one mistake we don't want to compound it with a second. And, remember, we're far from

315

certain it was a mistake. Let's go and listen to those tapes.'

'Yes,' said Cantel, and thought that it was going to be a long, hard night.

CHAPTER TWENTY-NINE

Vadim Belatov was deep in thought, reconsidering the events of the past months and—especially—weeks. It was a cardinal rule to attempt to extract valuable assets if they were in danger. In this case they had tried—they had tried bloody hard—when it was believed that their London man was under suspicion, but he had proved reluctant, so reluctant that they had been forced to accept the fall-back operation that he suggested.

At first this had seemed unfortunate, but they had quickly come to realize that it might have advantages. If they could provide the British with a traitor convicted by his own actions, it would relieve the pressure on the real agent in place. And what was this but a simple kidnap job? Further, if they chose a suitable subject, one whom they could persuade to play the part of voluntary defector, later he could be interrogated at length. Still later, to ensure the man didn't regret what he had done, he could be eliminated.

The trouble was, their chosen subject had proved too smart for them and the whole operation was in danger of falling to bits. Once Lavery reached England, he would protest his innocence and the British authorities would be compelled to reopen their investigations, this time even more thoroughly. Of course, Belatov mused, the outcome

316

could be favourable. Lavery might be convicted, so that the other could remain and eventually resume his activities. But the risks were great. On balance, there was now no alternative but to cut their losses.

At last Belatov made up his mind and spoke aloud. 'Damn him! There would have been no need for any of this nonsense if he had behaved sensibly. Others, even arrogant Englishmen, have learnt to enjoy life in Moscow. Why couldn't he try?'

Igor Smerinov made no attempt to respond directly. Instead, 'Comrade General,' he began tentatively, 'are we certain that Lavery is back in England?'

'Not a hundred per cent, no, Comrade Major, but we must assume he is or soon will be.'

Smerinov shook his head. 'It's difficult to conceive how he—'

'There are holes in the finest of nets,' Belatov interrupted him. 'The English have a saying—a proverb—about not crying over spilt milk, and our milk is spread across the kitchen floor.' The General rose to his feet. 'No, let us be practical. We must ensure there are no further repercussions. We've had to sacrifice Marta Stein, but she's safely out of the country and will certainly be of future use to us. But we can't lose anyone else—especially Pavel Kaski.'

'So what can we do?'

'There is only one option—a tragic accident.'

'There, in England?'

'Even the English aren't immunized against accidents.'

'But, Comrade General, surely in his position Lavery will be so well guarded that—'

'Comrade Major!' Belatov's temper was growing

short. 'What the hell would be the point of eliminating Lavery at this juncture?'

'I—er—I can't think of any reason, Comrade General, not now. We can be sure he'll have seized his first opportunity to tell his compatriots all they want to know.'

'And this elimination would tend to prove his story, wouldn't it?'

'Would it?' Smerinov was doubtful.

'Of course!'

'Yes, Comrade General,' said Smerinov.

The General glared at Smerinov. He said, 'The little accident that must be arranged, Comrade Major, will not be for Neil Lavery. It will be for our own man—our asset—who by his determination to stay in London rather than come to Moscow set this whole stream of nonsense in motion. True, the idea of providing another defector to satisfy the British had something to be said for it—'

'Exactly, Comrade General,' interrupted Smerinov. 'So—'

'So what?'

'There is an alternative, Comrade General.' Smerinov spoke doubtfully. 'If I might suggest...'

★   ★   ★

By the end of the week Neil Lavery had told his story so often that he could have repeated it in his sleep. Again and again he had reiterated his innocence, sworn that he had never heard of Marta Stein, denied that he had gone willingly to Moscow. At his own request he had undergone a polygraph examination, which according to the operator had shown up no anomalies. If doubt about his

318

innocence remained, which indeed it did, it was because of the extravagant—almost fantastical—nature of the tale his interrogators were expected to believe.

He had seen neither Graffon nor Cantel since the second day of his interrogation. Of the others who had come to question him, one had been aggressively disbelieving, a second bored, a third apparently sympathetic. Lavery distrusted them all.

His general health had improved. He was able to walk with a stick, and no longer needed the wheelchair. But he found the battery of questions and the constant attempts to catch him out wearying, so that by the end of each day he was exhausted and wanted only to sleep. Though he had asked repeatedly, he had still not been permitted a visit from his wife, or even a conversation with her on the telephone, and this depressed him. He wondered if the first time he would see his family again would be from the dock at the Old Bailey.

So far there had been no talk of a trial. Lavery knew that the evidence against him was all circumstantial, and that he had at least shaken the Security Service's faith in his guilt but, as the days passed, his hope of finally convincing them of his complete innocence waned. He thought a lot about Imogen and the children, and a little about his parents. Whatever happened to him he realized that his life could never be the same as it was before this—this incident—and it seemed bitterly unfair. Sometimes he felt tempted to confess to what he had not done, merely to put an end to the insane questioning and retreat into peace.

On Saturday morning Munro Graffon and Guy Cantel returned. They had not been idle in the meantime. They had held repeat interviews with all who had had access to the leaked material. Because of its source and significance access had been tightly restricted, so their task was simpler than it might appear. But they got no joy from their investigations, or from the bulky files which they had read and re-read.

As Munro Graffon said, Neil Lavery was as likely as any of the other potential suspects to have been the agent, and after all it was Lavery who had gone to Moscow.

'It would have been easier if the wretched man had stayed there,' he added to Cantel in a moment of acute exasperation. 'The damage has been assessed, and the worse of the scandal's over. He would have had propaganda value for the Soviets, but that's about all. As it is, he represents a colossal problem. We can't keep him incommunicado for ever, and think what a bloody stink there'll be when he reappears and starts proclaiming his innocence.'

'It's a pity we can't follow Belatov's suggestion and arrange a tragic accident,' Cantel agreed bleakly.

Graffon grunted; in the circumstances he was not in the mood for black humour. And, in the event, by Saturday the dimensions of the problem had changed. His hand was being forced. A rumour was spreading in the MOD that Lavery was back in England.

As soon as he heard it Brigadier Faudin had gone to Graffon, denying responsibility. He maintained that he had no idea how the gossip had started. William Plimpton had approached him about it, and Tyneman, half-drunk as usual, had said he had heard it in a bar. True or not, it suggested that the story was in the public domain, and it could not be long before the media was in hot pursuit of what they would consider a newsworthy sequel to the Lavery saga.

Guy Cantel had his own ideas about a possible source of the rumour. He suspected that his stupidity in admitting to Imogen in a weak moment that Lavery was safe had led her to tell Rosalind, who had told her husband, who had told his friend Sinder—who—And the story had spread, as was only to be expected. But Cantel had no intention of confiding this to Graffon. Never before had he let a woman get to him as Imogen Lavery had done and, though that part of the tale was over now, he was left with a residual feeling that he owed Lavery something.

Because of this sense of obligation he had persuaded Graffon that no harm could be done, in the face of the rumour, if Lavery were permitted to speak to his wife on the phone. He himself had called Imogen from the office, addressing her as 'Mrs Lavery', and made it clear that the conversation would have to be monitored. She had overwhelmed him with gratitude.

For his part, Lavery expressed no such gratitude. By Saturday the fatigue brought about by the strain of the long, daily interrogations had reduced him to a state of stupor from which he had to make a mighty effort to free himself, even when he was told he might speak to his wife. Cynically he thought of the telephone calls the Soviets had allowed him from the *dacha*. They had been less than successful and, though he yearned to hear Imogen's voice, he feared her response. No one had told him that she had been prepared to go to Moscow when she believed that he was desperately ill and needed her.

Before the call was made Munro Graffon briefed him about the ground rules under which the conversation must be held. There was to be no mention of his precise location, not even that he was in the hands of the Security Service. There were to be no protestations of innocence, no reference to his claim to have been kidnapped. All the exchanges must be personal. Lavery agreed to these terms.

When Cantel had dialled the number and Imogen had answered, he said curtly, 'Your wife, Mr Lavery,' and handed over the instrument before he and Graffon left to listen in the monitoring room.

Lavery had to steel himself before he spoke.

'Darling,' he began. 'This is Neil. I'm home.'

It was a tongue-tied conversation, full of half-finished sentences and punctuated by sudden silences, embarrassing for both the Laverys and for those forced to listen. For Guy Cantel it was almost intolerable. He could only hope that Graffon wasn't aware of his feelings.

Questions about each other's health brought meaningless answers. Then Neil asked after the children, and even here there were pitfalls—why was Verity staying with the Glenbournes, for instance? And Imogen did not really know how Neil's parents were; she supposed she had neglected them, but she had had other problems to face.

She heard herself growing irritable, and in an effort to avoid showing it she said, suddenly and with feeling, 'Oh Neil, I've been so worried about you.'

'Yes, of course, dearest, I know. I'm sorry. Oh God, I'm sorry! If I could have avoided causing you all this distress and anxiety I would have done. You do believe that, don't you?' And when Imogen didn't reply immediately he added tentatively, 'You do still love me?'

There was the merest hint of hesitation before Imogen said, 'Darling, you know I love you. I've never stopped loving you, in spite of everything.'

She choked over the last words, and began to cry. Cantel forced himself to unclench his teeth. He glanced at Graffon to gauge his reaction, but his superior was impassive.

'Darling!' Lavery said, almost in tears himself. 'Darling, don't! Please don't! Imogen, I'm not a traitor. I didn't defect. I was kid—'

Graffon cut the connection and swore. True, Lavery could hardly be blamed. Clearly he had been overwhelmed by the emotion his wife had shown. He hadn't deliberately broken his word. Nevertheless, the damage was done.

Graffon looked at Cantel. 'Can we trust her not to repeat that,' he demanded, 'if we impress on her the importance of secrecy?'

Cantel thought of the rumour that Lavery was in the UK, and its probable source. 'No,' he said decisively. 'I wouldn't bet on it. She'll probably tell her sister, Rosalind Glenbourne—and after that, who knows? We might well have another rumour.'

'OK, we'll let it go. We might even spread the glad news ourselves. It could put a squib under someone else, and help to prove what I guess we're both beginning to believe—that Lavery's telling the truth. Though, if there is another agent in place, he seems to be keeping his cool pretty well at the moment.'

'And Lavery—if we decide to fly this kite?'

'We'll have to keep him here at present. We've

no wish to charge him—I'm not sure we could—and we can't let him loose. If nothing happens in the next few days we'll think again.'

*   *   *

Mrs Cascon, the unsuspecting wife of the dentist, Pavel Kaski, couldn't understand why her husband was so anxious. Pleading an incipient cold he refused to leave the house throughout the weekend, and every time the telephone rang he jumped to answer it, though he always appeared disappointed with the calls.

On Sunday evening he spent much longer then usual saying good night to the children, and he was kind and unhurried when he made love to her later. As was his habit, since he always left the house early on a Monday he retired to sleep in his dressing-room, but unexpectedly he came into the bedroom again in the morning before he went to London and kissed her on the brow. She had shut her eyes and pretended to be asleep. Somehow she was glad when she heard his car drive away.

Pavel Kaski, too, was relieved. He had loathed the uncertainty of the last few days, while he was waiting for instructions. He had hoped they would arrive during the weekend. Now he was sure the crunch would come during the coming week, and it was easier to wait away from his children and the observant eyes of his wife. Nina was able to share his feelings, his doubts and his fears, just as she would join him in his departure from the United Kingdom—if it came to that.

His car-phone trilled as he reached the outskirts of London. At last, he thought. After the waiting, it

324

had come. A decision had been made. His mouth was dry as he answered.

'Paul Cascon speaking,' he said.

'Good morning and good news, Paul.' The voice was businesslike. 'The message I have for you is this. The Board has reached its conclusion. The difficulty will be eliminated, but your assistance is not required. There should be no need for you to worry further.'

'Thank you. Thank you,' said Kaski, but the air was already dead.

Seeing a parking place at the side of the road, Kaski drew into it. He was shaking with relief. Considering the kind of instructions the message might have contained, Pavel Kaski decided that he and Nina indeed had a reason to celebrate.

CHAPTER THIRTY

The days that followed seemed endless and tried the nerves of all those concerned with Neil Lavery. It was as if there were a kind of hiatus in the stream of events—a period during which expectations were high, but with no result.

Since the abrupt termination of her telephone conversation with her husband, Imogen Lavery had been consumed by worries and doubts. An unknown voice had informed her that the time available for the call had ended, but she knew instinctively that this was not the real reason why the connection had been cut so suddenly. She guessed that it was because of what Neil had said, or perhaps was about to say. The stress of the

325

moment had made it difficult for her to recall his exact words, but she was certain he had denied any treachery or intention to defect to Russia.

Rosalind suggested that she must have misheard. Imogen was certain that she hadn't. Yet it made no sense. She debated whether or not to ask Guy Cantel for an explanation, aware that not so long ago she would have done this without a second thought. Now, knowing instinctively that their affair was over and she would be embarrassing him, she couldn't bring herself to act. She hoped that he might call her, if only officially, but he didn't.

Friday came. The weather had changed. It was a bleak, rain-sodden day, when earth and sky seemed to merge in a cloud of grey mist. Mrs Price arrived at the Laverys' house, her umbrella soaked, her raincoat dripping, her stockings spattered with mud. She was taking off her wet coat when the telephone rang.

'I'll take it,' said Imogen. 'You make some tea to warm yourself up. The chores can wait.'

She answered the phone, and was less then pleased to find that the caller was Joyce Sinder. Joyce, never a close friend, had kept her distance since Neil had disappeared, and she didn't bother to hide the reason for her present call.

'My dear, I've just heard the news!' she exclaimed without preamble. 'You must be excited.'

'What news?' Imogen's hand clenched around the receiver. Fearful of what Joyce might be about to say, she managed to keep her voice steady. 'Why should I be excited?'

'But, my dear, isn't it right that Neil's back in the UK and declaring his innocence?'

326

'I don't know where Neil is, Joyce.'

'You don't?'

'No, I don't,' repeated Imogen, truthfully.

'Really?' Joyce was obviously credulous, but she didn't press the point. 'Kevin says that if Neil's acquitted he'll be able to sue the newspapers for a mint of money. But of course there's a lot of difference between declaring one's innocence and proving it in court, isn't there?'

'Presumably.' Imogen was becoming angry. 'You'll have to consult Kevin, Joyce. He's clearly much better informed about Neil than I am.'

'Don't be horrid, Imogen dear.' Joyce was reproachful. 'We've all felt deeply for you in the last few weeks, but you can't expect people to go on showing you affection if you don't . . .'

Joyce Sinder continued, but Imogen was no longer listening. She had been distracted by the sound of the front-door bell and the sight of Mrs Price letting in a wet, bedraggled Verity who was struggling with a large suitcase. Mrs Price immediately took the little girl into the kitchen, but moments later poked her head round the door.

'Please come, Mrs Lavery,' she whispered urgently. 'Miss Verity's very distressed.'

'Coming,' Imogen said, and to Joyce, 'Sorry to interrupt you, but I've got to go. Verity's here and needs me.'

'But I thought Verity was staying with the—'

'Goodbye,' said Imogen, slamming down the receiver.

She found her daughter sitting on a kitchen chair with Mrs Price kneeling in front of her. Mrs Price had taken off Verity's coat and shoes and socks, and was drying her feet with a towel. She had given her another towel, but the child was making no effort to dry her hair or her face, which was streaked with grime.

Imogen knelt beside her. 'Darling, what is it?' she asked. 'What's happened?'

'That horrid man!' Verity said, and Imogen saw that her cheeks were wet with tears as well as rain. 'I hate him! I won't stay in his house. I'll go to see Belle when he's at his office but I'll never speak to him again.'

'You're talking about your Uncle Philip?' Imogen was surprised.

'I disown him!' cried Verity, with a sweeping theatrical gesture of her arms.

'Unfortunately it's not so easy to disown relatives, not just like that,' Imogen answered briefly. She suspected that Verity, safely at home, was half-enjoying the small drama she was creating. 'You can't choose them either.'

'You should have heard what Uncle Philip said. He said Daddy's back in England, but it would have been better if he'd stayed in Moscow. He'll only bring more disgrace on the family with a big trial and lots more publicity. He said they'll put Daddy in prison for years. But I love Daddy. Unlike Matthew I've never believed he was a spy, and now he's back in England he's going to show everyone he's innocent.'

Imogen gathered her daughter into her arms, though she could think of no words of comfort.

'Is Mr Lavery back in England?' Mrs Price couldn't contain her curiosity.

'I don't know where he is,' Imogen said sharply, for the third time that morning. Then, realizing how frayed her own nerves were, she found she had some sympathy with her brother-in-law.

*   *   *

Philip Glenbourne was not in the habit of losing his temper, least of all at breakfast with his wife and niece, and he wasn't proud of his comments on Neil.

He was thankful to get out of the house, though it was a disgusting morning. There was no question of finding an empty taxi, so he had to queue for a bus and then was forced to stand among steaming raincoats and wet umbrellas for the whole journey. He was late getting to the Ministry and found William Plimpton waiting for him.

'I was beginning to think you weren't coming in either,' was how Plimpton greeted him.

'What do you mean by "either"?' Glenbourne demanded.

'Tyneman's not in, and there's no answer to his phone. I want to speak with him. He's meant to be preparing some figures for me. I need them. I needed them last week. He's holding me up.'

'He's probably on his way. Traffic's hell today.'

Plimpton hesitated. 'As you weren't here I took the liberty of phoning Brigadier Faudin's office.'

'Why on earth—'

'Because—' Plimpton was taken aback by Glenbourne's reaction. 'Because—I suppose it was because I was worried. I thought of Joy Aubyn and—'

'What the hell's Joy Aubyn got to do with it?' Glenbourne demanded, and drew a deep breath. 'I'm sorry, William,' he apologized. 'I must have got out of bed the wrong side this morning.'

329

'That's all right. Anyway, Faudin's not in. His secretary said he phoned to say he wouldn't be in today, but he didn't give any reason.'

'I see.' Glenbourne paused. 'OK, William. I'll deal with it. And I'm afraid you'll have to wait for your figures.'

Once in his office Glenbourne dialled the number Guy Cantel had given him, and explained the situation. 'I'm sorry to bother you about this,' he concluded. 'It's probably stupid of me, and normally I'd certainly have gone to John Faudin. Unfortunately he's not in either this morning.'

'Do you know where *he* is?'

'No. There's no reason why I should. I gather he just phoned to say he wouldn't be coming into the Ministry today.'

'You do seem to have a crop of missing persons over there.'

'Yes.' Glenbourne was beginning to wish he hadn't called Cantel.

'Well, let me know if Tyneman turns up. Meanwhile I'll make some enquiries.'

'Thanks.'

'That's okay. We like to keep track of all you chaps at the moment.'

Glenbourne yearned to ask why, though he believed he knew the answer. Lavery *was* back in England, and claiming he was not the agent. Security were looking for someone else. Their seemingly renewed interest in the directorate wasn't merely a matter of tidying up loose ends after Joy Aubyn's death and Lavery's defection. The distressing business was not all over.

Glenbourne's reflections were interrupted by his secretary, who brought him a cup of coffee and reminded him that he would have to leave in half an hour to accompany Kevin Sinder to a meeting at one of the Ministry's other offices near Baker Street. He asked her to get him a staff car, but she had already tried and failed. So this blasted day, Glenbourne thought, was to continue as badly as it had begun.

★   ★   ★

Guy Cantel was more fortunate. He had no trouble locating John Faudin. When there was no answer from Faudin's flat he tried the nursing home where the brigadier's wife was a patient. He was told that, yes, Brigadier Faudin was there, but he was resting; his wife had died during the night.

'Good!' said Graffon unfeelingly when Cantel gave him the news.

'Good?'

'Yes. Now Faudin has every excuse to retire gracefully, instead of being sacked—which he deserves for the ineptitude he's shown over this job. The MOD can replace him and he can go and live in Canada with that married daughter of his. A happy solution for everyone.'

Cantel laughed. 'You're being pretty heartless—and cynical,' he said.

'Not a bit. I'm a pragmatist, that's all.' The external phone rang and Graffon lifted the receiver. He listened, said, 'Thanks for letting us know,' and replaced it. 'That was really for you, Guy. I gather you asked to be told if Robert Tyneman turned up.'

'Has he?'

'No, but there's been a message from him. That was William Plimpton on the line. Glenbourne's not

331

in the office. According to Plimpton, Tyneman collapsed last night. He's said to be suffering from chronic alcoholism, and on medical advice he's taking a long sick leave to be dried out.'

'More good news, you could say.'

'Sure. But all this isn't getting us very far, is it? I've never considered Tyneman a serious suspect. I suspect it's someone much closer to Lavery.' Graffon sighed. 'Anyway, we must make a decision about the man soon. I'd be interested to hear what you think of his general health and mental outlook when you see him today, Guy.'

'Yes. I'm off right now, if that's OK with you. I'll be down there by lunch and I'll stay overnight.'

'Fine. Give me a call this evening.'

'Will do,' Cantel agreed. But, in the event, his plans were changed for him.

He was still in central London when his car-phone trilled. A delivery van was just moving out of a parking space and he shot in. It was Munro Graffon. He said sharply, 'Forget Lavery.' Cantel listened to Graffon with mounting excitement, and asked one question.

'What about security?'

'We're all right, I think. I couldn't ask much on the phone, but he says he's spoken to no one but me. I've told him to keep quiet till you get there. I'll fix things with the authorities.'

Cantel drove fast to the hospital, cutting between other traffic and racing the lights. He parked in a 'Doctors Only' slot and went into the Casualty Department. Graffon had been as good as his word, and he was expected. At once he was shown into a small office, where Kevin Sinder sat alone, his elbows on a table and his face in his hands. But he

332

seemed reasonably composed when he raised his head as Cantel came in.

'Philip's dead, as I told Graffon,' he began. 'Though it's ghastly, and I can't believe it. It wasn't an accident, you know. He did it on purpose. I'm certain, and I was there. I was just feet away on the platform as the train came through the tunnel. There was that rush of hot air you get on the tube. It makes people automatically move back, and Philip didn't. Deliberately he moved forward. If he'd been a bit quicker he'd have gone under the train and been killed on the spot. As it was, the edge of the driver's cab just struck him and he was thrown back on the platform. Not that it makes any difference now.'

'What were you and Glenbourne doing on the underground?'

'We were going to Baker Street. The MOD has some offices there, and we were going to a meeting. We tried to get a staff car without success, and on a day like this a taxi's impossible. Time was running out, so we decided to take the tube. God, I wish we hadn't—though he'd probably have found some other way of ending it.'

'Why should he want to end it?'

'Ah, you don't know the rest. The ambulancemen were first on the scene and I went with them—and Philip. He wasn't quite dead, they said. The police hadn't arrived yet, so they didn't get a chance to question me.'

Sinder stopped and stared at Cantel. 'You know, I've known Philip practically all my life, from prep school days. We stayed with each other's family on holiday. I'm George's godfather, and Philip's my son's godfather. I—I can't believe what I've got to tell you. All those years I thought we were friends.'

'You told Munro Graffon that Glenbourne spoke to you before he died,' Cantel said.

'This is the part I don't want to tell you, but I must. Philip said I must. Yes, he did speak. It was when we got to the hospital. We were left alone for a minute. I had my face close to his, and he knocked away the oxygen mask they'd put on him. He could only whisper. No one else heard, and of course I've not told anyone.'

'And he said?'

'He said he knew he was dying. He said to tell you that Neil Lavery was never a Soviet agent. He said they thought you were closing in, and Lavery was kidnapped to take the heat off the real spy. That was Philip. He was the guilty man. I—I never particularly liked Lavery, but—but this—I found it shocking.'

'Why do you think Glenbourne told you?'

'Why?' Sinder laughed mirthlessly. 'Why? As I said, the bastard knew he was dying, and he wanted the part he'd played to be known. He was proud of it. He—he boasted, almost exultantly. I think that was when he died.'

EPILOGUE

In Moscow, Belatov and Smerinov were studying the latest reports, and for once Belatov was grinning.

'Well, Comrade Major,' he said, 'we've retrieved something—probably a great deal—from what looked likely to be a débâcle. The wretched Lavery's no longer a threat to us, all our assets—with the exception of the Stein woman—are still in place, and as far as we can tell, the British authorities seem satisfied to let the matter rest. The heat is off.'

The General paused, and then he went on, 'And it's thanks to you, I must admit, Igor Pavlovich. Your suggestion that we should get our agent to arrange a fatal accident for Glenbourne was a stroke of genius—and his bungling of the attack, which could have been catastrophic for us, turned out to be a stroke of luck. All we expected Sinder to do was make Glenbourne's death appear to be suicide—and leave the British to assume the rest. As it was, since Glenbourne was still alive when they reached the hospital, Sinder could claim to have heard his confession. Congratulations to all of us are in order, I think.'

General Belatov went to his cabinet and produced the vodka bottle and short glasses. The two men drank.

*   *   *

In London, Munro Graffon burst into Cantel's

office after an exhausting day and a half of meetings in Whitehall. 'The decision's been made,' he said. 'And it's been agreed at the highest level. There's going to be a cover-up—a complete cover-up—'

'But what about Lavery—surely we owe him the truth?' interrupted Cantel. 'And his wife.'

'Let me finish,' said Graffon irritably. The tension of the last few days was beginning to tell on him. 'Of course Lavery's got to be told the truth, but he's bright enough to appreciate that none of it was our fault. The blame lies with the Soviets and General Belatov's little plan. Anyway, our instructions are to see Lavery immediately and put a proposition to him. I'll explain on the way.'

It was four days since Philip Glenbourne's death, and Lavery was still living in the safe house, though the interrogations had ended abruptly, and he had been allowed television, radio and newspapers, so that he knew of his brother-in-law's death.

The news had grieved him, though more for Rosalind's sake than because of any personal feeling for Philip, to whom he had never felt close. And though he had not yet been told of Philip's death-bed confession, he had been momentarily alarmed by the phrase 'tragic accident' used by some television newscaster. However, a few second's reflection had persuaded him that this was a common expression with no hidden meaning.

In fact, there had been no suggestion in the media that Philip's death had been other than an accident. Kevin Sinder seemed to have been the only witness to what had happened, and he had been readily persuaded to support this story. What was more, even the tabloids had not stressed the fact that the dead man had been Neil Lavery's brother-in-law, and his superior in the Ministry of Defence. Indeed, the press had been kind to Philip Glenbourne. *The Times* had given him a flattering obituary, and unofficially the Minister of Defence had commented that he was a great loss to the department and the country.

Nevertheless, subconsciously Glenbourne's death worried Lavery, and the first question he asked when Graffon and Cantel came into the sitting-room was, 'How did it happen—exactly?'

Graffon told him, holding nothing back. To Cantel it said much for Lavery that his immediate reaction was incredulity about the confession and concern for Rosalind. It was only after some minutes that he seemed to realize what it all meant to him personally.

'So I'm in the clear,' he said at last. 'You know I've not been lying, that I've never been a Soviet agent, that—'

'Yes. We know, Lavery—Neil—'

Lavery looked up abruptly. Attitudes were changing rapidly, it seemed. But he refrained from comment.

'Neil,' Graffon went on. 'We know you were unwittingly involved in a plot designed to protect your brother-in-law. All we can say is that we're sorry for our suspicions, though I know you'll agree that in the circumstances—'

'Of course. Of course. But what the hell's going to happen to me now?'

'My dear fellow, there's no reason to be resentful. Your future's been given a great deal of thought—and at the highest levels. We know we owe you a great deal, and we've a proposition to put to you, which we hope you'll accept for the sake of your country and your family. You can probably guess the first priority—'

Lavery thought for a moment. Then, 'Yes,' he said. 'My silence.'

'You're right. But let me explain, Neil. First of all, Glenbourne's part—and the Soviet's part—will be covered up. As far as you're concerned a statement will be made in the House in answer to a planted question that you have never been a traitor, that all the rumours about you were completely ill-founded and that you were never even under serious suspicion. What happened was that you were mugged on your way home from the office and as a result suffered from amnesia, from which you have only just recovered. That's the broad outline; we'll go into the details later. And everything will be arranged so that the story's fully supported.'

'And you think that's going to be believed?'

'Why not? You can threaten to sue if any part of the media shows signs of doubting it. We'll help you with that. And you'll be reinstated in your old directorate in the MOD; in fact, they plan to promote you to take Glenbourne's place. That should surely be evidence that you're to be trusted.'

'And my wife? And the Stein woman's lies?'

'Of course we realize that your wife must be told the whole story, including the fact that Marta Stein was merely part of the plot, but there is one point—Mrs Lavery will have to sign the Official Secrets Act, so that there's no question of her passing on the truth—even to her sister, or to your children when they're older. Do you think she'd agree to that?'

'I'm sure she would,' replied Lavery. 'When can I see her?'

'Just as soon as you—and she—have agreed to this plan.'

'I guess I've no alternative.'

'Do you want one? We know the episode has been unfortunate and unpleasant—and at times dangerous—but it's over now, and there's no reason why you can't eventually get back to your—your normal life. After a long leave for recuperation, of course. We'll provide you with another safe house where you can live with your wife—and your kids, if you like—until the worst publicity has blown over.'

Lavery nodded in acquiescence, and Graffon and Cantel exchanged glances of relief. Guy Cantel was glad for Lavery, but it was asking too much of human nature for him not to think of Imogen. If Lavery had been the agent, and therefore Belatov's target, Imogen might now be a widow. And later he and she might have found a future together. But that was not to be, and he accepted the fact.

* * *

It was on the way to London in their car that Cantel voiced his doubt. 'You know—' he began.

'Don't say it,' said Graffon. 'The same thought's been on my mind. This whole outcome's been a little too convenient for the Russians. We'd reduced our most likely suspects to two, and suddenly one of them decides to kill himself. Just suppose—just suppose—'

'—that Kevin Sinder's story is a fabrication—that he—'

'This case isn't over yet,' said Munro Graffon. 'We must keep digging, Guy, and from now on we

339

must make sure that every movement Sinder makes, practically every breath he draws, is monitored. Perhaps we'll be third time lucky.'